THE LIGHT ARISES

Ed —
thanks for continuing to
follow Raynu's journey
I hope it blesses you —
C.S. Wa...
Ps 103:8-12

C. S. WACHTER

Shadowfall Publishing

The Light Arises
The Seven Words Book 2

Copyright © 2018 by C. S. Wachter
www.cswachter.com

Published by Shadowfall Publishing

Printed in the United States of America

Wachter, C. S.
    The light arises / C. S. Wachter
    The seven words; book one
    ISBN: 978-0-9998861-2-0 (paperback)
    ISBN: 978-0-9998861-3-7 (e-book)

Lyrics from: What God Ordains Is Always Good; Samuel Rodigast, 1649-1708

Cover Design by: Mountainview Books, LLC
Maps by: Nexgenstudio
Print formatting by: Mountainview Books, LLC

For my Lord. You continue to bless me with your guidance and steadfast love.

For Ben, Tom, and James.
Having you in my life is a joy and a blessing.
Love you guys.

ACKNOWLEDGMENTS

Thanks to those who encouraged me to begin this journey: Jan, who followed me all the way, Mac, and Peggy. Thanks to all those readers whose input and comments helped make this book what it is today. Kelly, Janae, Bryan, Marcia, Thom, Carla, Mary, Sharon, Alice, Dan, Jamie, Alissa, Matt, Becky, and the Lancaster Christian Writers.

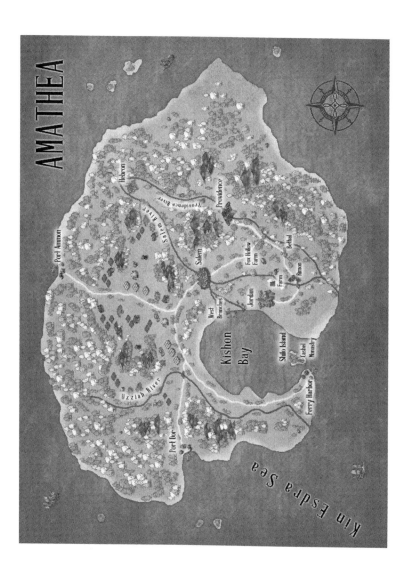

AMATHEA

Hebron

Providence River

Salem River

Providence

Port Ammon

Salem

Fort Hollow Farm

Bethel

Illk Farm

Hanan

Jordan

West Branches

Kishon Bay

Shilo Island

Lashel Monastry

Uzziah River

Ferry Harbor

Port Dor

Kin Esdra Sea

ARISIMA

Oasis

Oasis

Zaraya
Oasis

Oasis

Oasis

Monastry

Monastry
Monastry

Oasis

Oasis

Aleppo
Monastry

Oasis

Oasis

Monastry

Monastry

Oasis

Monastry

where the desert
drinks itself

Oasis

Great Desert

Oasis

Jadeth Sea

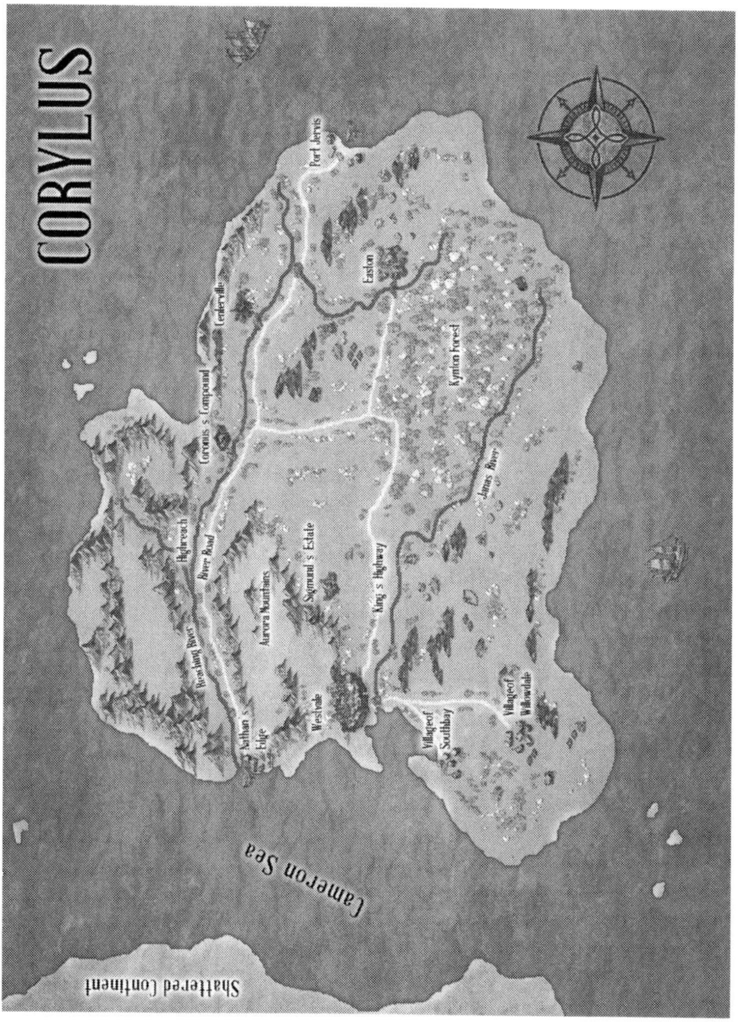

CORYLUS

Fort Jervis

Easton

Kynton Forest

Corvinus Compound

Corlorville

Highreach

River Road

Boneslang River

Aurora Mountains

Sigmund's Estate

King's Highway

Arthan Edge

Westvale

Village of Southbay

Village of Willowdale

Jane River

Cameron Sea

Shattered Continent

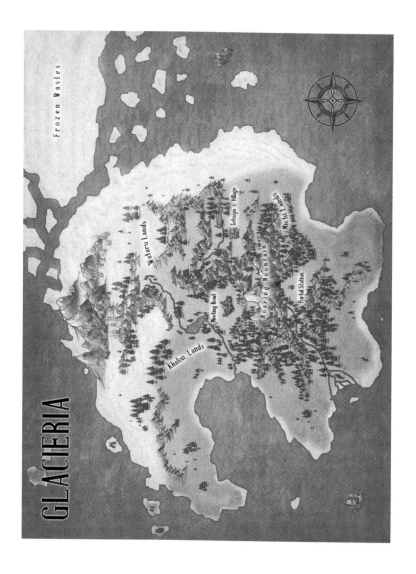

GLACIERIA

Frozen Wastes

Wataru Lands

Tetsuya's Village

Michi Lands

Roaring Mountain

Kneeling Road

Portal Station

Khalon Lands

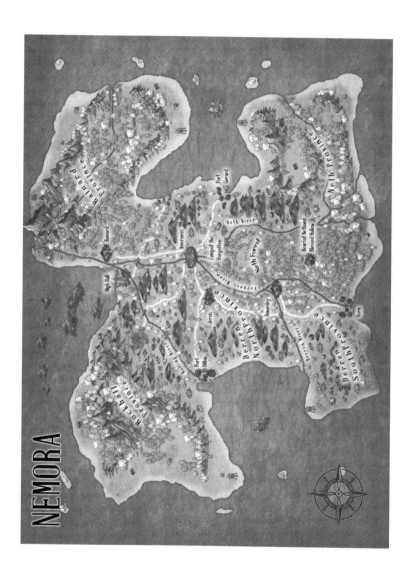

NEMORA

15

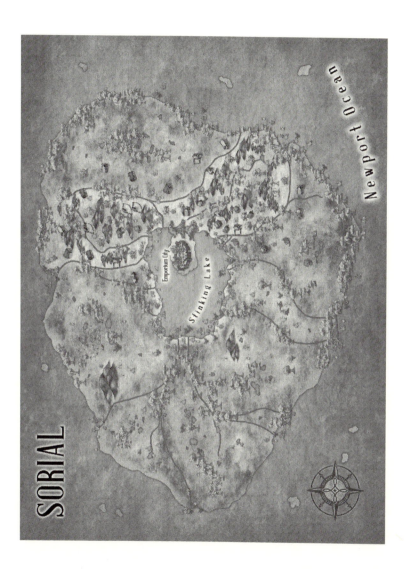

SORIAL

NewPort Ocean

Emporium City

Stinking Lake

VERES

Mount Caarwyn — Headwaters of Caarwyn Hill

Wistal

Iron River

Andersen Mine

Andersen Gunning Complex

Talisein Mountains

Ilory

Griffon Mine

Sharrox River

Sharox River

Naameth Sea

LIST OF CHARACTERS
BY ORDER OF APPEARANCE

BOOK ONE

MRS. WORDON—Travis Illk's housekeeper

TRAVIS ILLK—resident of Amathea; hired by Sigmund to kidnap Rayne

MARCUS PONCE—Sigmund's Second; a rubiate

RAYNE KIERKENGAARD—Crown Prince Rayne Nathan Samuel Kierkengaard of Corylus and the Ochen system; son of Theodor and Rowena; kidnapped by Sigmund and given the name Wren

ROWENA KRAFTSMUNN KIERKENGAARD—Queen of Corylus and the Ochen system; originally from Nemora; mother of Rayne

MARTHA—Rayne's nurse

REGINALD CLOUSON—master manipulator; places wire in kidnapped Rayne

SIGMUND OF BAINARD—ancient evil being; Wren's owner

THEODOR KIERKENGAARD—King of Corylus and the Ochen system; enemy of Sigmund; father of Rayne

MORROW—daughter and only child of Sigmund; executed by Theodor for murdering King Samuel, Theodor's father

VAN CORONUS—leader of a group of highly-skilled assassins; owner of the compound where Wren grows up

ANNE PARSONS—Coronus's slave and healer; originally from Veres; friend of Wren/Rayne

THORVIN KRAFTSMUNN—Coronus's trainer; master swordsman

WARREN—tutor to nobility; kidnapped and enslaved by Coronus

BRIAN, DONALD, MARCIE—people Wren meets on the way to Coronus's compound

LEN FERNHARDT—ferryman

ALAN (AL)—Coronus's cook

RUFUS, CAINE, LOGAN—assassins-in-training at Coronus's compound

WALTER—A guard at Coronus's Compound

MITCHEL—Coronus's Stable Master

LORD WILLIAM ANDERSEN—powerful Sorial merchant; head of Merchants Guild

JASON ANDERSEN—Lord William's son

BISHOP JONATHAN HEDRICK—head of the church of Corylus; Bishop of Westvale

SHAW RADINAJAN—monk from Arisima; friend to Light Bringer

ELSIE—church cook; friend of Theodor and Rowena

YORMUND—Glacierian fighter/warrior hired by Sigmund

SIR HECTOR—target of Wren's first contract

Cole Wright, Tyson Wright—brothers; residents of Highreach

SION—Cole's and Tyson's dog

ROGER—a guard at Coronus's compound

SAYER—the slave who takes over Wren's duties

LADY LILITH—best friend of Morrow; friend of Sigmund

ROLAND, DENNY—friends of Lady Lilith

CAPTAIN ELLIS—young captain of palace guard

STEVIE KASPER—twin to Sashi Kasper; friend of Rayne

SASHI KASPER—twin to Stevie; friend of Rayne

KORI & MACE KASPER—parents of Stevie and Sashi

CAPTAIN ANTON FONTAINE—captain of palace guard

PRIVATE RICHARD MATHESON—palace guard

SERGEANT PETERSON—palace guard cook

LIAM, ABBY WRIGHT—parents of Cole and Tyson

BOONE (LIGHTNING BOONE)—Rayne's dog

ANDREW—Rayne's page

NOAH REESE—palace guard; friend of Rayne

BOOK TWO:

LORD BRAYDEN WOODFIELD—Rayne's cousin; son of Duke Miles and Duchess Cailyn (Rowena's sister)

LADY ELAINE—member of court; friend of Brayden

LANDON WESTON—son of Duke Weston; friend of Brayden

WESLEY HARTSON—son of Sidney Hartson, Earl of Sidmore; friend of Brayden

SIR TYLER OF BAINARD—friend of Brayden

SHALIMAR—Rayne's horse

RUTHIE—kitchen maid

LOUVAIN ANDERSEN—Lord William's nephew

SHIN—Guard at the Andersen Family's Eleri Gaming Complex

YURI—Takes care of slaves at the Andersen Family's Eleri Gaming Complex

BRAN & ALICK—village boys taken to fight at the Eleri Complex

LADY ALEXIANNDRA ERLAND (LEXI)—Daughter of Duke Justus Erland, leader of rebels

SILAS—Rebel leader, friend and mentor of Lexi

ETHAN—Rebel leader, friend and mentor of Lexi

CAI—Rebel

SEREN—Rebel healer

DUKE JUSTUS ERLAND—Lexi's father, friend of King Theodor, noble ruler of Veres

LUCIUS—Duke Erland's caregiver

TAL—Keeper of horses for rebels

ZACHARY—Theo's son and assistant

ALEC & KEMP—Rebel spies at the Andersen Family Mining Complex

EMMA—Stevie's friend from the mine
JIRO—Shin's twin brother, Caarwyn Rill elder
TEGAN—First Eldest, Caarwyn Rill
OWAIN—Caarwyn Rill elder
AFON—Caarwyn Rill elder
ARI—Ancient guardian of Veres
MILO—Sigmund's assistant, Ponce's replacement

SEVEN WORLDS OF THE OCHEN SYSTEM

AMATHEA:
Farming world; magic deficit

ARISIMA:
Desert world; magic saturated

CORYLUS:
Royal world; home of Kierkengaard family line; magic saturated

GALCIERIA:
Ice world; magic saturated

NEMORA:
Woodland world; home of Kraftsmunn family line; healing sun, two moons: Rem and Ledia; most magic saturated planet

SORIAL:
Merchant world; two suns: Xanthe and Ortrun; magic deficit

VERES:
Mining world; source of veredium; magic deficit

1

In the fullness of time the Light Bringer will arise. The lost will be found and he will bring to light my seven words hidden on the seven worlds and I will guide his steps. Sing for joy my people, the broken will be restored; the lost will be found. When the broken is restored and the lost is reclaimed, he will bind the living darkness. Know my people, the fullness of time has arrived; the time is now. Arise my Light Bringer.

Rayne gulped in a breath of sun-warmed air. His fingers tingled and twitched. The words of the One echoed within his spirit.

Trust, my beloved Light Bringer and be courageous, for I am always with you.

He had been cutting across the park-like area that separated the palace grounds from the barracks, distracted, his mind jumbled by what he and Thorvin just discussed. Was his decision to reveal the truth about himself to the people of Corylus—his past and his calling to be the Light Bringer—really the best course? Or should he wait a bit longer to see if the rumors would just fade away as time passed? Tell? Don't tell? Submit to the call? Deny it? To accept this calling of the One would impact his life so completely. Once he shouldered the mantle of Light Bringer, he would not be able to let it drop and he wasn't sure he was ready to face that kind of responsibility. *By the seven, I'm only sixteen.*

One moment he was moving forward, pros and cons circling each other in his mind like combatants in a ring, the next he was pulled up short in his tracks as intense bitter cold infiltrated his spirit and a murky fog of threatening evil engulfed him. The shadowy remnants of darkness planted within him roused in response, dredging up ghosting memories of the horrors he had lived through as Sigmund's slave. Rayne shuddered.

Am I losing myself? The darkness waxed thicker around him like the drippings of a melting candle mounding at its base.

The dark haze thrummed. *Prince of Ochen, slave of the living darkness, you feel it, don't you? Embrace the truth; you are no bringer of light, it is death you bring. You have always brought death; it is what you are. The prophecy is a lie. You still nurture evil at your core.*

Boone barked, intense and demanding, piercing the cocoon of darkness that enveloped Rayne. She jumped up and planted her paws on Rayne's thighs, whimpering and nudging his hand with her nose. With an effort of will, he shook off the memories and the aura of penetrating cold that seeped into his very bones, but the premonition of coming darkness had wormed into his spirit, shaking him to the core. Boone looked up at him, her eyes speaking unconditional love and trust. He steeled himself against the strong external influence pressuring him to just give up and admit he was too corrupted to be the One's chosen Light Bringer.

Then the words of the One cut through the lies, exposed them, and shredded them into harmless bits of dark venom.

Trust, my beloved Light Bringer and be courageous, for I am always with you.

Rayne bent down, spoke words of comfort to Boone, quieting her while he scanned the area. *Sigmund? Doesn't matter.* This attack wasn't enough to make him back down. It was like the lies Sigmund forced into him when he was a child. But he wasn't a child anymore and he would never bow down to Sigmund again. The One had strengthened him and now Rayne was certain of his path. He would move forward in that strength, embrace his dual identity as both the Crown Prince of Corylus and all Ochen, son of King Theodor and Queen Rowena, and as the One's chosen Light Bringer. He would not feed the dark remnant that still dwelt deep within him. Whatever the darkness just tried, it failed. Instead of discouraging Rayne, it ignited his inner spark. He would fight this just as he had always fought Sigmund.

Rayne, still shaken when he reached the palace, sought out his parents. He hoped to approach them with the plan he discussed with Thorvin. Both were occupied; his father in a meeting with representatives from the Interplanetary Council regarding complaints about his investigation into the activities of certain Sorial merchants, and his mother down at the docks with the healers treating several people wounded in an accident.

Mumbling and taking the steps two at a time, Rayne climbed to the second level and returned to his suite, where he found Andrew, his page, straightening the bedroom and setting out formal clothing. Boone hopped up on Andrew, who did his best to keep the newly pressed clothing away from the dog's paws.

"Boone, stop that," Andrew ordered. "Go sit."

With a look of shame, the dog walked to her sleeping mat and, after circling twice, sat down, staring at Andrew. Rayne chuckled; it seemed Andrew and Boone were building quite a bond.

"If you're not too busy," Rayne asked, "would you mind watching Boone for the rest of the afternoon?"

"Certainly, Your Highness. I'd be happy to watch her. Can I take her out to play?"

"I think she would like that."

Andrew finished laying out the clothes he had been holding. "Your Highness ... I mean, Rayne. I'm supposed to let you know that there will be noble guests in attendance for dinner followed by dancing this evening. That's why I laid out different clothing for tonight. Her Majesty said to tell you the meal will start *promptly* at eight in the formal dining room and you are to be on time. So, I'll watch Boone later too, if you want."

"Thanks. Hey, Andrew, want to join me for the midday meal?"

"I'm sorry, I already ate. I'd have waited for you if I'd known you would be eating so late."

"No problem." Rayne washed his hands and face, changed his sweaty tunic, and headed back down to the dining hall.

Eating later than everyone else meant Rayne had the large hall to himself. Though he would have enjoyed Andrew's company, having this time alone allowed him the quiet he needed as he mulled over what happened on the way to the palace earlier. Staring at nothing, he relived those moments in his mind. What brought on the attack, if it truly was an attack? Sigmund? They'd had no word of him for months. Now, sitting in the quiet normalcy of the dining hall, Rayne questioned if he had just imagined the whole thing. Was it nothing more than a trick of his own mind? But, try as he would, he couldn't completely shake the cold and the premonition of danger.

A well-dressed young man Rayne didn't recognize sat down next to him, breaking his concentration. Other than Rayne and his parents, nobody sat at the table on the raised dais unless invited. It was reserved for the royal family and their guests. Still half immersed in his thoughts, Rayne stared bleary-eyed at the stranger, stunned by his audacity. Had this young man gotten permission to sit here? Just who was he?

The visitor looked to be several years older than Rayne, perhaps twenty-four or twenty-five years old, and he was a few inches taller with broad, muscular shoulders. He wore a well-tailored, stylish green and gold brocade doublet. His neatly trimmed, shoulder length, chestnut brown hair framed a hand-some, aristocratic face. When the stranger turned in his direction, a contemptuous grin curling his lips, Rayne's jaw dropped. Lavender-blue eyes close in color to his own pierced him, sending a shiver up his spine.

Before he could ask the stranger who he was, the man spoke, his voice dripping disdain. "Well, well, well, the prodigal prince has finally decided to grace us with his presence, I see.

Or should I call you *Light Bringer?* I've heard some rumors, but that is a joke, isn't it?" He grinned again, though the expression didn't reach his cold eyes, and let out a deep sigh. "I suppose, like it or not, you were bound to return, although I had hoped that would have played out differently. Everything was falling into place so perfectly. Your return at this moment is quite ... untimely.

"But then, I assume I must welcome you back home, *Your Highness.*" He looked Rayne up and down, his mouth pursed, his eyes calculating, reminding Rayne of Sigmund's inspections. "After the stories I've heard, I did expect you to have grown into something more remarkable. What a disappointment. You're still really rather puny, not very impressive at all, especially for someone alleged to be a master assassin. You do have your mother's coloring though, just as I remember. I guess some might consider you physically attractive."

Rayne opened his mouth to respond to the rude stranger as a multitude of half-formed questions clouded his mind. Being pulled unexpectedly from his deep thoughts and then shocked to the core by the man's hateful words and attitude, left him speechless. And, somewhere deep in his fragmented memory, an alarming feeling of deja vu hovered.

Feeling rather foolish sitting with his mouth hanging open, Rayne said the first thing that came into his mind, "Where did you get those eyes?"

It was stupid. Rayne knew that the moment it came out of his mouth.

The critical young man stared for a moment and then laughed. "Oh my, you haven't changed. You're still rather dim-witted, aren't you?"

That's it. Rayne bristled. He'd had enough of this incredibly offensive idiot. *Does he realize who he's talking to?*

Rayne began to rise from his seat, ready to show this callous noble just how impressive he could be, when his mother stepped past him and up to the man. Putting her hands on his shoulders, she kissed his cheek fondly. "Welcome back, dear, dear Brayden. You have been gone for far too long. It's wonderful to see you again. I'm sorry I was unable to greet you sooner. How are your mother and father? I can't remember the last time I saw my sister and Miles."

Rayne's mouth dropped open again as a sick feeling settled in his stomach. The stranger, Brayden, grinned at him, exposing unusually sharp canines in a wolfish look of predatory superiority.

Rising, Brayden turned to Rowena and kissed her on both cheeks. With a broad, innocent smile he said in a smooth as honey voice, "Auntie Rowena, it is so good to see you as well. Why, I believe you grow more lovely every time I see you. Mother and Father are quite well and send their love. Mother asks that you come visit her soon. She says you're always far too busy and you should take some time for a vacation in Inverness. She and Father insist you bring little Raynie as well. They are most interested in meeting this person face to face. Mother is quite concerned that you and Uncle Theodor have been duped by some imposter."

He smiled down at Rowena with a look of total innocence and Rayne bit back a comment about the two-faced nature of this *cousin* who called his mother 'Auntie'.

My Cousin? This obnoxious jerk is Mother's nephew? He's my cousin? No! No way!

"No impostor," Rowena said with a strange little laugh. "I know you don't believe that. But you'll see. Just spend some time with him, and you will know he's the same Rayne we all loved as a child."

Rowena turned back to Rayne. "I'm so glad you two have found each other. You do remember your cousin Brayden, don't you Rayne? You used to play together as children. You were quite close back then. You followed Brayden around like a little puppy and he was always so protective of you."

Really? Rayne's stomach twisted and he began to regret eating as much as he had.

Then, turning to Brayden, Rowena rested her hand on his broad chest. "We haven't seen you here in Westvale since before Rayne returned and I am so glad you are finally back. I need you to help our dear Rayne reacclimate. He's far too serious and withdrawn, not socializing at all with the other young people here at the palace. He spends too much time with commoners or with his nose stuck in that scroll he brought back. I'm afraid the other nobles are beginning to avoid him. You must introduce him to your friends and help him develop relationships with his peers. You know how important that is."

Rowena focused once again on Rayne. "My dear, tonight's formal dinner is in honor of Brayden's return and we have invited a number of his friends. Don't think I haven't been aware of how you have gone out of your way to avoid the nobles here at court these last few months. Please take this opportunity to get acquainted with people of rank. You must overcome this shyness. You will need these people to support you when you become king. I'm sure Brayden can explain how important it is to develop strong political alliances with powerful families.

"Oh, and Rayne, you must let Brayden show you the gift Cailyn and Miles sent with him for you from Nemora."

Rowena paused, catching her breath before continuing. "Oh, yes. That's right. The reason I was searching for you, Rayne. I understand you were asking for me. That you wanted to talk?"

Rayne stumbled over his words not wanting to discuss his plan in front of his cousin. "Later … can we talk later?"

"Of course, my dear." Rowena leaned over and gave him a motherly peck on the cheek.

She turned back to Brayden and gave him a fond kiss. "My dear Brayden, seeing you again fills me with delight. I always feel more secure when you are near. Please take care of our lovely boy. Now that you're here to watch over him, I'll tell the guards that they can leave his protection to you. It'll be just like when you were children. You always took such responsibility for him then. I know you'll keep him safe; as always, you have my complete trust."

"Certainly, Auntie Rowena." Brayden stepped in behind Rayne and placed his hands on Rayne's shoulders in an affectionate gesture, while flashing his disarming smile at Rowena once again. "You know I'd do anything for you and Uncle Theodor. Just like before, I'll be sure to take good care of our dear little Raynie."

Once Rowena was out of sight, Brayden drew back his hands as Rayne shrugged them off his shoulders. The smile was once again replaced by the toothy wolfish grin and Rayne barely caught the words his cousin mumbled, "Just like before, huh? Sure, Auntie Rowena, just like before."

2

"So, *Little Raynie*," Brayden said. "Walk with me. We need to talk. Besides, I am under obligation to deliver the gift my parents sent."

Without waiting for Rayne's response, Brayden turned, descended the steps from the raised platform, and strode purposefully toward the far exit. Rayne scowled as he watched Brayden stalk away. It stirred memories of Coronus and the way he would lead Rayne around with a collar and chain. Rayne's stomach churned again. He may not remember this cousin, but something about him set Rayne on edge. That he was two-faced and not to be trusted was obvious, but there was something more, something deeper that called up a latent anxiety.

Despite Brayden's claim to want to talk, he exited the palace and cut across the lawn toward the stable without a backward glance. As Rayne plodded along behind, kicking at pavers, his face screwed up into a frown, the afternoon sun warmed his back. A mix of dark and light clouds moved across the sky, periodically blocking the comforting rays. In those moments when shade blanketed him, the soft breeze coming off the Cameron Sea soothed Rayne's spirit while chilling his body. The afternoon air was brisk with the promise of a beautiful autumn.

As they advanced up one of the stone walkways that crisscrossed the manicured lawns, a young lady rushed up the path to Brayden. "Oh, Lord Woodfield! How delightful! You've been away from court far too long. I've missed your wit sorely. Westvale is so dull without you. Please tell me King Theodor isn't sending you away again and that you plan to stay for a long visit this time."

She pressed her body against Brayden, leaned in, and licked her lips before curving them up into an inviting smile. Rayne look away. Obviously the two knew each other very well.

"Why Lady Elaine, you're making my little cousin blush." Brayden smirked, showing his perfect white teeth, with the elongated canines that reminded Rayne of a wolf. "Unfortunately, due to certain unforeseen changes, I doubt Uncle Theodor will be sending me anywhere … now."

Lady Elaine leaned back and cooed. "How marvelous."

Brayden's eyes roamed her curves and his smirk morphed into a full-fledged disarming smile. "As I will be in Westvale for an indeterminate length of time, I hope we can renew our *intimate* acquaintance."

He breathed out heavily and sighed as if he had just performed a strenuous task. "My dear Lady Elaine, you know I detest leaving the capital. It was only at Uncle Theodor's behest that I have been away from Westvale. Though it was my duty and I was most eager to serve my king, these last several, tiresome months spent world skipping, strengthening Uncle Theodor's political networks, have drained me beyond belief. And now I find it was all for naught."

He skewered Rayne with a frigid look before returning his attention to Lady Elaine. "I am quite elated at finally returning to Westvale. It is such a relief to spend time with people of my own class and resume warm relationships."

Rayne looked across the lawn and hunched his shoulders as the two conversed. Though she ignored him, he knew Lady Elaine. Months ago, when he first returned, she approached him on several occasions, offering sexual favors, fawning over him. But after spending a brief time with her, he realized she was only interested in his title, not him as a person. She had gone so far as to use an unsuspecting servant to lure Rayne to her bedchamber. He walked in to find her lying across the bed, dressed in nothing more than a ribbon tied in a bow at her throat. After a moment of frozen shock, he stormed out of her room with his face flaming.

It wasn't that he didn't find her physically attractive, she was. But he wanted more out of a relationship than just satisfying physical appetites. Warren had taught him how the One called his people to a standard of faithfulness to a marriage covenant. He knew others did not take that commitment seriously, but he did. He would not dishonor all the One had done for him by allowing pure physical appetite to control his life. He saw up close what that had done to destroy men like Ponce and Coronus. And there were so many other areas where he had been forced to act against the will of the One, that he needed to remain true in this.

In the days following the bedroom incident, Lady Elaine spread rumors about him among the nobles at court. He never learned exactly what she said, but after that, many of the ladies gave him disgusted looks and avoided him altogether. Though he hated the idea of lies being spread about him, Rayne hadn't confronted Lady Elaine. He kept quiet, hoping the whole thing would settle in time. He hadn't even tried to stop her rumors from spreading, it didn't seem worth the effort. He was content to leave things that way. But deep down he knew his parents were right to be concerned; good relations with those in power were necessary to keep the crown strong.

After several uncomfortable incidents in the first weeks after his return, followed by Lady Elaine's spiteful talk, most of the nobles his age thought he was strange and uncouth, unacceptable as an equal despite his lineage. Rayne knew they gathered in the anterooms of the court, partying and socializing into the early morning hours, but he avoided those areas when his nightmares drove him to roam the halls and sleep eluded him. His nerves set him to stuttering when he was with them;

he didn't understand the games they played and never knew what to say. He considered using the hidden passages Andrew had shown him to avoid awkward situations, but after trying once and coming out with his stomach in knots and his body trembling, he decided to keep to the back hallways instead. Many days he shunned the palace altogether and spent time with Shaw and Anne, or the twins, Stevie and Sashi, and their parents. He talked easily with men of the palace guard, like Noah, and even Thorvin.

When Brayden and Lady Elaine continued whispering and laughing together, Rayne withdrew behind his shields. He refused to allow them to make him feel small or unacceptable.

While Brayden and Elaine were talking, three well-dressed young men came up the stone walkway and greeted the two warmly. After some mocking comments about one of the court ladies, which caused Lady Elaine to laugh and blush, they moved on to discuss their level of boredom.

"I know," Brayden said. "Let's go for a ride. I haven't had much chance to ride lately and would enjoy the exercise. In fact, Lady Elaine, if you would care to join us, I'm sure I could offer you some *exercise* as well."

"Excellent idea, Lord Woodfield," one of the other men said. "I'm sure we would all enjoy Lady Elaine's *exercise.*"

The men laughed, but Lady Elaine aimed a scornful look at the young man who had spoken. "Wesley, I'm quite surprised you would even mention it. The last time we *exercised* you proved to be quite deficient."

Wesley went red in the face as the others snickered. Lady Elaine fluttered her eyelashes at Brayden. "But you, my Lord Woodfield have never proven lacking in any way. But much as I would enjoy your company, I refuse to accommodate your friends. Besides, I deplore riding; it's uncomfortable and taxing. Pledge you'll join me later, though, and I can promise you will not be disappointed."

"My most delectable lady." Brayden winked. "I promise to give you my complete and undivided attention later, after the party."

Once again, she molded her body into Brayden. Her blue

eyes flashing, she pulled his head down and whispered in his ear. After releasing him, she took a step back, sent a final scowl in Rayne's direction, and sauntered away, her low-cut pink and white multi-tiered gown swinging as she rolled her hips.

"Fun playmate, that one," one of the men said and they all laughed.

"Quite so, Landon," Brayden said. "But tonight, we owe it to ourselves to hunt more tender game. I think you know who I mean."

They all nodded, smirking. Then Brayden turned to Rayne and opened his eyes wide as if surprised. "Oh. You're still here little Raynie? And, by the seven, he's blushing." Brayden looked at his friends and rolled his eyes. "I guess with his upbringing our little princeling must still be a virgin." He turned to his friends, palms up, hands spread to either side. "I must apologize gentlemen, Auntie Rowena asked me to watch over my virginal little cousin. It seems he needs babysitting. And I did promise to deliver the gift my parents sent." He turned his focus back to Rayne. "Oh dear. I hope you know how to ride. Of course, if you don't, the gift my parents sent will be totally wasted."

The four young men snickered at Brayden's cruel comments.

Rayne fisted his hands and the muscles in his back clenched. "I can ride just fine."

Brayden stared at Rayne a bit longer and the wolfish smirk once again returned. "Of course. But with your substandard background I couldn't be sure." He and his friends snorted again, as if sharing an inside joke. "But I suppose, *if* your riding abilities are at least mediocre, I am compelled by the constraints of civility, to invite you to join us this afternoon, *Your Royal Highness*. I promise we'll ride slowly for your benefit, even walk the horses if we must."

Rayne wasn't certain what game Brayden was playing, but he was willing to let it run its course and see where it led. It couldn't possibly be worse than what he had gone through with the assassins-in-training back at Coronus's compound. "I think my skills will suffice for more than just a walk, and I would enjoy the exercise."

"Exercise!" Brayden barked out a laugh as his friends all hooted. "That's a good one. Yes, I suppose riding is another form of *exercise.*"

Rayne ignored Brayden's crass joke and chose instead to focus on the other young men. He didn't recognize his cousin's three friends, so he was certain they must have come from Nemora with him. Although claiming to adhere to the constraints of common courtesy, Brayden hadn't even been civil enough to introduce his friends. Instead, he turned his back on Rayne and began to converse with the others, ignoring his cousin.

Rayne needed to decide. *Walk away or ask for an introduction?* His hackles rose at the idea of asking to be formally introduced to three more nobles he couldn't care less about. But his mother's voice came back to him. *You must overcome this shyness. You will need these people to support you when you become king.*

Though it flew in the face of accepted protocol, he stepped forward and pressed for the introductions Brayden had neglected. "Would you be so kind as to do me the honor of introducing your friends?"

After flinging an annoyed glare at Rayne, Brayden glanced at the others. His shocked expression flowed into a smirk and they all chuckled again.

If that's the worst you guys can dish out, trying to make me feel small because I don't know your inside jokes, well bring it on. This I can handle.

With another exaggerated roll of his eyes, Brayden introduced his friends as Landon Weston, son of Duke Weston; Wesley Hartson, son of Sydney Hartson, Earl of Sidmore; and Sir Tyler of Bainard.

The last man introduced looked to be several years older than the others, but what caught Rayne's attention was his designation of origin being Bainard, Sigmund's home district on Nemora.

"Sir Tyler," Rayne said. "Where is Bainard? That is the Bainard where Sigmund of Bainard's holdings are, right?"

"It's a beautiful hill country north of Rockhall Province. And yes, Lord Sigmund still has family holdings in Bainard, though he does not stay there very often. From what I hear, he is a well-respected and thoughtful host and quite cultured. I've never met the man myself, but several of my friends who know him personally, speak highly of him. Do you know him?

"Oh wait. That's right. Didn't you claim he kidnapped and enslaved you? And if I remember correctly, your father accused him of being involved in the Hundred Years War and then causing some ill-fated rebellion more than twenty years ago. It all sounds so outlandish. Many of our mutual friends on Nemora believe the accusations against Sigmund are nothing more than fabrications dreamed up by your family because your father fears Sigmund's power. And the idea that he has lived many lifetimes is just laughable. But from what you've claimed, you would know more about that than I. He was your supposed master, no?"

Can people really be so naïve? "Tell those friends of yours they're wrong. My father didn't fabricate anything. The stories about Sigmund are true. He was behind my abduction and he kept me as a slave. Sigmund is evil. Before they, in their ignorance, seek to defend him, they should search out the truth of the man. I know what he did to me, the evil he's capable of, and I know all the accusations aimed at him are manifestly true. I was forced to spend the last ten years as an assassin and a slave because of Sigmund, so don't try to defend him to me."

Tyler gave Rayne a noncommittal look and shrugged. "It's just your word against his."

Rayne choked back an oath and reached for the sword at his side. The one he wasn't wearing. Brayden quickly stepped in and, after giving Tyler a warning look, grabbed Rayne's arm and propelled him toward the stables, while changing the subject.

"Come now, little cousin, it's time I presented you with the gift my parents sent. We need to lighten this mood; it's gotten too dark." Brayden propelled Rayne into the stable. They entered the gloomy interior, feeling the temperature drop as they left the light and heat of the sun behind.

3

Delight bubbled up in Rayne when he saw the gift his aunt and uncle had sent, even if it had come by way of Brayden. The mare was magnificent, a beautiful ebony black that seemed to reflect Rayne's own raven hair. Although not as large as many of the other horses in the stable, the proud lines and finely formed head with large, luminous eyes declared her descent from the fabled bloodlines of the horses of the desert planet of Arisima. Rayne had never seen one of these horses before, but he knew without a doubt this was of Arisimanian stock. Their son may be a self-centered, arrogant fool, but Aunt Cailyn and Uncle Miles sure knew how to give a gift.

Rayne approached the mare cautiously making soft comforting sounds in his throat, holding his palm flat for the horse to check. The mare lowered her nose and as Rayne felt the velvet smoothness, tickling whiskers, and warm breath, he wished he had a treat to give to the animal. Without looking back, he asked, "What's her name?"

"Her name is Shalimar. She should be mine," Brayden said, rancor sharpening his voice. "My parents were supposed to give her to me when I returned to Inverness after all the time

I spent traveling for Uncle Theodor. But then, hearing of your unexpected return, they chose to give her to you instead. Mother told me it was because of all you supposedly suffered. I personally don't understand it, but that was their decision, so for now, like it or not, I am forced to abide by it.

"You know, little Raynie, before now, my parents had never denied me anything! Not once! When I questioned them why they were giving you *my* horse, do you know what they had the audacity to tell me? They said I should take joy in this opportunity to share some of my privilege with you. *Me* share privilege with *you*? What a joke. *You're* the one born to higher privilege, the one who will be king of Ochen. From the moment you were born, you were always the perfect little heir. Everybody loved and fawned over you. It was disgusting. I will never take joy in sharing anything with you. So know this, *Little Raynie*, I will not forget that you have taken Shalimar from me. I would take her back from you right now if it wouldn't embarrass Uncle Theodor and Auntie Rowena. Maybe someday I will." His voice dropped to a quiet whisper. "Just like I took the pony you got for your fifth birthday."

Rayne tried to ignore Brayden's ranting, but something about the words caused him to shiver. Talking softly to the mare and stroking her muscular neck helped to calm him. While the others waited as the grooms readied their horses, Rayne spent time getting to know Shalimar by performing the task himself. He took pleasure in how she watched him with an intelligent expression and he couldn't wait to ride her. As two stable boys walked the other horses out into the yard, Rayne followed with Shalimar. Brayden and his friends made no effort to hide their amusement at him doing such a menial task, but Rayne ignored their comments.

Shalimar was a joy to ride, with a smooth, even gait and a soft, responsive mouth. Rayne would have preferred to take her for a good run on the beach, but he followed Brayden and his friends as they left the palace grounds and entered the King's Park. Owned by Rayne's parents, the King's Park was a large tract of rolling land with two lakes and numerous small groves of trees scattered throughout. Though it was a private park, King Theodor often gave permission for locals to hunt or ride there.

The air, now warmed by the autumn sun, was ideal for riding and the few remaining clouds cast moving shadows across the yellow-green of the fields. If not for the incessant chatter of Brayden and his friends, Rayne would have found the ride pleasurable. Their conversation drifting back, grated on his senses and destroyed any chance of enjoyment. He had decided to turn back and cut across to the Cameron Sea, when he caught sight of another rider approaching.

Sitting ramrod straight, his chin jutting forward in an aggressive manner, Brayden called a halt and waited for the rider to come abreast of them before challenging him. "By whose authority do you ride here?"

Recognizing the other rider, Rayne spoke up before he could respond. "This man is a King's Guard and as such has the right to ride or hunt here whenever he wants, as do all the guards. And he is a personal friend."

Rayne shifted to pull alongside Noah and smiled. "I thought you would still be with Sashi, Noah. Why are you here instead?"

Noah blushed as a grin lifted his mouth, lighting his eyes. "They had to get to work, Sire. But I did enjoy my time with Sashi and her family very much. Her mother invited me to come by any time. Thank you again for giving me leave to go with her and Stevie earlier."

Brayden mumbled a comment to the other nobles about not lowering themselves to associate with common soldiers before addressing Rayne. "Looks like you've found a friend on your level, little cousin. We shall leave you to it." He lashed his horse into a gallop, his friends following his example. They moved quickly across the hill toward a wooded copse beyond.

Rayne snorted, glad to be rid of the insufferable snobs. He had put up with their arrogance long enough and would much rather spend time with Noah.

"Are you heading back to the stable?" he asked Noah, after Brayden and his cronies vanished over the crest of the hill.

"Yes, I must get back. I have some things I should do

before supper. My horse needed exercise though, and as I had some time, I decided to take her out for a quick ride. Are you heading back or following your friends?"

"Those brainless idiots aren't my friends. One of them, Brayden, is my cousin." Rayne scanned the distance with a sour look. "I don't fit in with them." He sighed his frustration. "I really don't fit in with any of the nobles. Unfortunately, I must dine with them this evening. But for now, yes, I think I'll head back to the stable. Ride with me."

As the two walked their horses toward the palace grounds, Noah filled Rayne in on the details of his time with Sashi's family. "Kori and Mace were so friendly. They made me feel like I was family and not an outsider. After lunch Kori showed me around the workroom and explained what it takes to make a quality blade. It gave me a whole new appreciation for their craft."

"They are such kind people," Rayne said. "Kori promised she would help me make a sword someday. I think it would be incredible to use a sword I made myself."

Noah chuckled. "You do know their family has been crafting swords for generations, don't you? I'm not sure if you would want to actually use the first blade you make. Not to be disrespectful or anything, Your Highness, but it probably won't be very good."

"You're right; it'll probably be pretty terrible." Rayne laughed. "But I'll do my best to make it look good, then hang it in my room."

When they got back to the stable, Rayne and Noah took care of their own horses rather than handing them off to a groom. They returned their saddles to the rack and replaced the bridles with halters, then wiped their horses down and brushed them. The conversation flowed easily as they worked, and a comfortable calm replaced the tension Rayne had been harboring since meeting Brayden. He enjoyed sharing the easy conversation and simple tasks with a like-minded friend. It was so different from the time spent with Brayden.

After a bit, though, Rayne got quiet. It suddenly hit him. As the Light Bringer, he needed to bring the One's message to nobles as well as commoners. *I'll have to talk to nobles? Well now's as good a time to start as any.* Rayne decided that tonight he would please his mother and make an effort to blend in with the nobles. He huffed out a deep sigh. He still hadn't talked to his parents about his earlier conversation with Thorvin.

When Rayne got back to his rooms, Andrew and Boone were waiting for him. Warmth rose in him at being greeted by a loving canine who just wanted to lick his face, and a caring friend who tried to help him act more like a prince, or at least dress like one. Rayne would be lost with the clothing if Andrew didn't help him. Though young, the page had a knack for knowing what Rayne should wear in different social settings. Andrew had the tub already set and sent servants for hot water.

"You're good at this," Rayne said after the tub was filled and the servants had left. "Perhaps you can help me with something else. You're of noble blood and you've lived your whole life around nobles. You seem to fit in easily and understand them better than I ever will. Answer me this, if you can. Why are they always so nasty and arrogant? I know you're only nine, but you see and hear things. What can you tell me?"

While Andrew thought about the question, Rayne slipped into the tub and started washing his hair. After lathering, he dunked his head and then popped up and looked to see if Andrew had an answer for him.

"Your Highness." Andrew's face was a mask of serious consideration. "I don't know why some nobles act the way they do. It's not like we take classes in how to be snooty. And not all nobles are like that."

Rayne grimaced at Andrew and flung some water across the side of the tub at him.

"There's your problem." Andrew huffed, wiping at the water spattered across his shirt. "You act more like a little kid than I do, I guess because you never got to be one when you were younger."

Andrew sighed. "You smile and let your feelings show. You care about people, even commoners and servants, something a lot of nobles don't do and can't understand. To them anyone of a lower station is not worthy of notice or care.

They're only there to serve. You're different and they don't like different. They look down on anybody who isn't like them because it makes them feel superior."

Rayne nodded as Andrew's words struck a chord within him. But Andrew wasn't finished yet.

"Everything has to be a huge bore because revealing emotion is weakness. The strongest and meanest always control the others, who follow like mindless sheep. They enjoy abusing everyone, even other nobles. They treat the servants like they aren't even people. You're not like them. As long as you care about other people, especially commoners and servants, they'll never accept you as an equal."

Andrew paused as if considering what he had just said. "But don't change for them. Everybody else at the palace, we all like you just the way you are. You make all of us feel as though we have worth. Please don't change. You're not their equal, you're better than them."

Andrew backed against the wall and kicked at the carpet, his face turning beet red. Boone, as if sensing his discomfort rose from where she had been lying, walked up to the boy, licked his hand, and sat down next to him.

"Thanks," Rayne said quietly. "How about you help me get into this outfit you laid out for me? Growing up wearing leggings and sleeveless tunics did not prepare me for this kind of formal clothing."

Once Rayne was dressed and his hair was combed, Andrew pulled its length back into a loose tail and tied it with a purple silk ribbon that matched his shirt. Just as following Brayden from the dining hall earlier had brought back memories of Coronus, being dressed in formal clothing reminded Rayne of the times the assassin master would dress him to blend in at noble functions. He shivered as a cold tendril of disquiet wormed through him.

He shook the feeling off. He hadn't thought of Coronus for months. But since meeting Brayden, images of the man and his past had risen to haunt him three times in just a few hours. At least back then when he was required to attend a formal function, Rayne didn't have to talk to anyone, didn't have to pretend he was interested in the small talk of self-centered, spoiled sons and daughters of the noble class. Now he was expected to fit in, and even though he was royalty, he found it hard to relate to any of the people he would be dining with tonight. At least Thorvin and his parents would be there.

He chuckled. *Who would have ever thought I'd be happy to have Thorvin around?* But whether Rayne felt the part or not, he looked the part. And when it came to impressing the nobles, Rayne had learned at least one important lesson. Appearances mattered.

4

Rayne slipped into the room, his fingers twitching and his palms sweaty. This was Brayden's party, and if not for Rowena's request that Rayne attend, he would avoid the noxious affair.

Two long tables covered with blue tablecloths trimmed in silver embroidery stood lengthwise on the main floor of the formal dining hall. A raised dais running perpendicular to the long tables supported a smaller table at the front of the room. A storm-cloud gray tablecloth with a silver lace overlay announced the table was reserved for the royal family and their special guests. Silver and white candles filled numerous wall sconces, their flickering light casting shadows on the blue and silver washed silk walls. Five-arm candelabra marched in perfect lines down the center of the tables.

Nearly fifty nobles were in attendance. Most were younger friends of Brayden's and all were formally dressed in the latest fashions.

Rayne was grateful for Andrew's restrained sense of style. Some of the younger men were wearing more flounces than the ladies present. Rayne was elegantly dressed in fitted black trousers, black doe-skin boots, and a simple deep purple silk shirt with slightly billowed sleeves. Over the shirt he wore a snug, form-fitting, waist length jacket of deep gray with black trim. It was a simple outfit but well-tailored and it accentuated Rayne's athletic build. He was amazed that Andrew had such talent for picking clothing he would not only feel comfortable wearing but would also be appropriate for the occasion.

Theodor sat at the center of the small table on the dais, looking out over the room. Rayne sat to his father's left with his mother to his father's right and Brayden next to her. Rayne glanced surreptitiously at Brayden as his father prayed a blessing, then grimaced and rolled his shoulders in an attempt to ease the tension building across his back.

Dinner was served in several courses starting with a creamy pumpkin soup and ending with a variety of desserts. After eating lightly of each serving, Rayne picked an apple tart, wishing it was blueberry, still his favorite, for dessert. But after the first bite, he put his fork down, his stomach souring, when he glanced over and noticed Brayden putting his arm around Rowena. As Rayne watched, Brayden moved in close enough to kiss her and whispered something that made her laugh. Rayne choked at the intimacy and forced himself to look away. His mother seemed to accept the attention and proximity as normal, laughing and putting her hand on Brayden's chest while he smiled down at her.

Thorvin, who Rayne learned was some kind of distant cousin to Rowena, sat to Rayne's left until, half way through the meal, he moved between Rayne and Theodor. After that, the two men spent the rest of the meal engaged in conversation, laughing about something that had happened when they were young men on Nemora. Rayne mentally thanked his mother for freeing him from having to carry on small talk, especially with some girl who would be more interested in his status than him. But the situation prevented him from keeping his commitment to connect with some of the younger nobles.

Perhaps after the meal, when the dancing and mingling started, he would try to be more sociable.

The seating arrangement did give Rayne the opportunity to watch the interactions going on at the two lower tables and he took advantage of the situation during the meal. Lady Elaine's annoyance was palpable as she stared up at Brayden who was not only inaccessible, but more interested in talking to Rowena than looking at her. At the other table, Brayden's friends focused their attention on one young noble. Rayne could tell by the pinched expression on his face, that the others were badgering him. Though his build reminded Rayne of Brayden, the young man had sandy blonde hair and dark blue eyes. Rayne made a mental note to find out who he was and try to talk to him later, if he could.

Moving his gaze back to his own table, Rayne's eyes caught Brayden's. Brayden flashed him one of his arrogant, wolfish smirks and, holding Rayne's eyes, purposefully adjusted his hand on Rowena's shoulder in a possessive manner. His smirk morphed into the full-fledged wolf grin, triggering a vision from Rayne's distant past.

The memory came to him full-blown, vivid, and complete. He was sitting in the Queen's Garden with his nurse, Martha. Someone called to her and she left him alone on the bench. He couldn't have been more than four or five at the time and Brayden must have been about thirteen. It was before he had been taken. Rayne experienced anew his anxiety when Brayden came up behind him. With stealthy movements, he placed a small, stiff branch with long sharp thorns sticking out in all directions, on the bench next to Rayne, in the exact spot where the nurse had been sitting. Rayne recognized it the moment he saw the wicked thing. Brayden had once whipped his arm with a similar branch. Not only were the thorns sharp and painful, they left a residual sap that caused a stinging and burning rash for days after contact. It was from a bush that grew in the woods around Inverness and Brayden must have brought it with him from home.

Giving Rayne that wolf-like grin, Brayden promised that if he said anything he would be sorry. And even at that age,

Rayne feared Brayden. He had been terrified. And so, Rayne had remained obediently silent, cringing as Martha returned and sat on the nasty branch.

Immediately, she felt the thorns. The poor woman leaped up and twisted to grab the offending branch. But with her full skirt she couldn't reach the bough which stuck fast through the fabric and into the skin beneath. She began sobbing at the pain as she swung first one way and then another trying to dislodge the firmly stuck spikes. Soon, blood began to seep through her skirt and dribble onto the ground beneath her.

Rayne heard malicious laughter bubble up behind him but before he could say anything, Rowena, who was nearby cutting flowers, noticed the nurse's behavior and hurried up the path.

Once Rowena got close, Brayden sprang from behind the bench and with down-cast eyes said in a very sorrowful voice, "I'm sorry Auntie Rowena. I tried to stop Raynie. I told him not to put that branch on the bench. I told him it was a mean thing to do and Martha might get hurt. But he did it anyway. He said it would be fun. I did try to stop him Auntie Rowena, but you know how he is."

He looked up at her with wide eyes and an innocent smile. When she turned to the nurse to help her gently pull the thorns from her skin and back through the torn fabric, Brayden faced Rayne with a triumphant look of superiority and mouthed, *you're in trouble again.*

Rayne remembered. It was not the first time that his mother believed Brayden's lies. And there was something else, something dark that he couldn't quite grab hold of, a memory that brought back feelings of terror even before Sigmund had taken him. Rayne must have stuffed these memories so deep that only now, after seeing that insufferable grin on Brayden's face, did he remember them.

Looking back to Brayden, Rayne made a vow; his cousin would not get away with that kind of behavior now. Things had changed, and Rayne was no longer an innocent child. Needing to move, his breath coming hard, he rose and stalked into the adjoining ballroom.

Myriad white candles set in sconces and four immense

chandeliers filled the room with flickering light that reflected off the polished wood floor and the wall of French doors leading out to a terrace. Rayne continued through the room and out one of the glass doors, all of which had been left open to catch the evening breeze. As he slipped through the open doors, he heard a quartet of musicians behind him warming up and the eager chatter of the guests as they sauntered into the ballroom and began claiming partners.

The cool air soothed his rising heat as Rayne moved into the nighttime darkness and stepped into a shadowed alcove that was sheltered by several bushes of varying heights. He needed to be alone with his thoughts, to wrestle with the freshly resurrected memories. Then he heard a young girl's voice coming from the other side of the bushes. He recognized it. Ruthie. The pretty little teenager with large brown eyes and wheat blonde hair had only been working at the palace for a few months and was serving at dinner tonight. She must have been using the path that ran along the terrace as a shortcut between the party and the kitchens. But she wasn't alone.

"Please, please stop!" she pleaded. "Please, let me go. Don't do that! No, please!"

The crack of a hard slap and a cry followed. Without thought, Rayne vaulted the railing that ran around the veranda and landed soundlessly next to one of the bushes. Years of training kicked in as he moved forward with cat-like grace to find Brayden's three friends surrounding Ruthie.

Stepping out from the bushes, Rayne spoke, his voice hard and cold as veredium. "What's going on here?"

The three turned to him and Wesley said, "Oh, it's just you, Prince Rayne. Nothing's going on here except a little fun, you know, a friendly tumble with a serving girl. You know how these servant girls lead on young noble gentlemen like us. They pretend to shrink away and say no, but they really mean yes. You're probably not aware of this yet, but every serving girl dreams of a tumble with a noble. It's a well-known fact, right?" He leered at Ruthie, but she shrank back in fear, tears leaking from her wide eyes. "We're just doing what's expected of us."

The three men nodded and laughed as the heavy odor of alcohol permeated the evening air.

"Brayden showed us that little garden shed just the other side of the path the last time we were here," Tyler said. "It's quite handy. We put it to good use a couple times on that trip. He'll be here soon and, of course, you're certainly welcome to join us, Your Highness. I'm sure this tender little piece would enjoy bragging to her friends how she lifted her skirt for the Crown Prince of Ochen. We'll even let you go first, then she can say that she lost her virginity to royalty, if she really is still a virgin. With these commoners, one can never tell."

Wesley turned back to grab Ruthie, who shrank from him, her large eyes growing even larger in her pixie face.

Growling, Rayne shifted position and grasped Wesley's right arm in an unyielding grip. With a huff, he twisted the arm up behind Wesley's back. The man gasped and moaned.

"What are you doing?" Tyler asked, his voice rising an octave.

Rayne snorted, disgust with the three young men souring his stomach. "I don't know how things are done on Nemora, but here in Westvale we don't force servants for our own pleasure."

Wesley moaned. "You're hurting me."

"You're lucky I'm not doing worse." Rayne gave Wesley's arm another slight jerk and then he turned to Ruthie.

The terrified girl stood trembling as tears ran down her cheeks. An outline of fingers traced in red showed clearly on her pale skin.

"Ruthie." He spoke in a soothing whisper. "Ruthie. Go back to the kitchens. Tell the head cook I said you need to stay there for the rest of the evening. You are not to come out to serve again tonight. Do you understand?"

Blinking back tears, she nodded.

"Then go. Now!"

After Ruthie ran off toward the kitchens, Rayne released Wesley's arm and shoved him toward his two friends. "I know you've heard stories about me and my background. Well, they're true. I am more than capable of killing the three of you here and now without even breaking a sweat. If I catch you abusing any of the servants again, I won't be as understanding as I am now. Go back to Brayden and tell him I won't let him get away with whatever it is he thinks he's going to do here. I'm not five anymore and I'm not afraid of him. Do you understand?"

Rayne glared at the three, expecting some kind of response. In the hush, he heard footsteps approaching from behind. Turning at an angle so he could keep a watch on the three while observing who was coming, he waited.

When Brayden materialized out of the darkness, Rayne wasn't surprised. "Come to join your friends in a little *fun?*" He fought to keep his voice restrained despite the fury bubbling through his veins.

Sheer loathing flashed across Brayden's face before he gained control. But then, with a look of wide-eyed innocence, he said, "What are you talking about, cousin?"

Rayne huffed an aborted laugh. "You don't expect me to believe you're innocent in all this, do you? Like I told your friends, if you harm anyone here, you'll answer to me. I won't allow you to abuse anybody in Westvale."

He glared at Brayden, palpable tension sparking the air between them. His voice strained and rough, Rayne said, "And stay away from my mother. I know she thinks she knows you, but if you don't leave her alone, I'll tell her what a two-faced piece of slime you really are. Stay away from her. And my father."

With one last scowl, Rayne strode away from the four. If they were an example of what the nobility was like, he wanted no part in it. But spider-like prickles of premonition skittered up his spine when he heard Brayden laugh behind him as he walked back into the ballroom.

5

Taking several deep breaths to calm himself, Rayne fisted and released his hands, then shook them out as he scanned the ballroom. His father was still talking with Thorvin near one of the terrace doors and he caught sight of his mother sitting on a couch, a gaggle of ladies swarming around her. Suppressing his anger, Rayne approached Thorvin and his father. "Father. Thorvin. I was hoping I could talk with you in private for a few minutes?"

"Of course," Theodor said. "I had forgotten you asked to speak with me earlier. You wanted to talk with your mother as well, didn't you? She doesn't seem to be too busy." He chuckled low in his throat. "I'm certain she will be quite willing to step away from the party for a few minutes."

Theodor led the way to where Rowena was sitting, laughing as one of the ladies finished speaking.

"That was quite the unexpected turn in your story, Lady Nora," Rowena said as her eyes drifted up to meet Theodor's. "But, it appears I must leave you ladies for a bit. Perhaps you can tell me how it all ends later." With a graceful motion, Rowena stood. Theodor held his arm out for his wife, and

Theodor, Rowena, and Thorvin followed Rayne into an empty receiving room.

Once everyone was settled, Rayne looked to Thorvin who gave him a questioning look for a minute before the light of understanding lit his eyes and he nodded.

What Rayne interrupted outside the ballroom pressed down on him and it took an effort of will to stifle the urge to blurt out the whole incident. But with Thorvin sitting in front of him, Rayne decided it was best if he told his parents about the plan he and Thorvin had discussed first. After Thorvin left, he would inform his parents about what happened with Ruthie, Brayden, and the young men from Nemora.

He pulled in a deep breath and held it for a few seconds before beginning. "Since I returned, we have kept silent about the circumstances surrounding my disappearance and what I did the last ten years. I know we agreed it would be best to leave my past in the past and you didn't want to cause me further pain. But with no true facts presented, people have started inventing all kinds of stories about me and what happened. Everything from me being possessed by Sigmund, and still being under his control, to the whole disappearance being nothing more than a fabrication by you while you hid me away to keep me safe growing up. The rumors continue to grow and spread. Mother, Father, Thorvin and I discussed this earlier and he agrees with me. Something needs to be done."

Rayne looked between his parents, catching each pair of eyes. "It's time we combat the lies by telling people the truth. I need to be open about my calling as the One's Light Bringer and that means revealing things we thought to keep hidden. If I'm going to be effective as the Light Bringer, I must face my past.

"I think the best approach would be to host some kind of public event. Father, I thought you might give a speech, something brief about what happened during those ten years I was gone. I know it would be better if I told the story myself, but I ... I don't think I can face talking openly about my past to so many people. I need you to do that for me.

"After the speech, Thorvin and I could stage an exhibition

match. I can use the King's Sword and Thorvin would wield another ancient weapon. Then, following the match, I'd reveal what I know about the Light Bringer prophecy, explain what it actually says, and share some of what we've learned in our study of the scroll. I'm hoping that if people learn the truth, they'll stop spreading stupid rumors. But even more important than that, I would be publicly announcing my role as the One's Light Bringer."

Theodor and Rowena exchanged glances. Rowena said, "Are you certain you're ready to let people know what happened? What you did, and who you are? Are you ready to commit to the role of Light Bringer?"

"I have to be. I can't let these wild rumors gain any more credence than they already have and it's time I accepted my calling. I don't have a choice but to be ready."

"Agreed," Theodor said. "We wanted to honor your wishes, Rayne, and so we kept quiet about your past and the prophecy. But you're right; this needs to be addressed. I wondered how long you would let this generation of misinformation continue and I'm pleased you came to the decision to deal with it before we had to say something."

After discussing a time frame for Rayne to regain his proficiency with the sword after not practicing for the last few months, it was decided they would announce the event for one month from now.

"The Feast and Fight Competition is always so popular," Rowena said. "Why don't we do something similar to that. We could have food stands; everyone always loves those."

Thorvin cleared his throat. "If I may make a suggestion?"

Theodor and Rowena nodded.

"I think we should set up an elevated ring in the center of the square where everyone can see when Rayne and I stage the match. It would be a perfect platform for Rayne to give his speech from."

Theodor nodded. "Excellent suggestions. We'll treat the crowd to free food, follow that with my speech and your exhibition match, and then wrap the whole thing up with Rayne's announcement as Light Bringer. I like it. We'll call it a Festival of Truth."

Once they agreed about the arrangements for the festival and the discussion wound down, Thorvin left.

Theodor and Rowena were rising to follow him, when Rayne asked them to remain for a few more minutes. Exchanging glances, they returned to their seats. Clearing his throat, Rayne cautiously broached the subject of Brayden. "You two seem to like Brayden a lot. Tell me, is he someone you trust?"

"We trust Brayden unquestionably, why wouldn't we?" Rowena said. "He's my sister's son. We've know him his entire life. You two played together before you disappeared. Don't you remember visiting him on Nemora? Why are you asking this?"

"I don't know how to say this gently, so I'll just say it. He's not who you think he is. He plays on your affections for him as a nephew and puts on a mask of innocence, but then shows his true colors when you're not looking.

"Brayden and three of his friends from Nemora planned to violate Ruthie this evening in the shed off the path running from the formal dining hall to the kitchen. Apparently, they've done this kind of thing before and they don't see any wrong in that. In fact, they asked me if I wanted to join in the *fun*."

Rowena stared at Rayne, her eyes unfocused and her mouth a pinched line, while Theodor cleared his throat and said, "Son, I hope you realize how serious it is to throw around an accusation like this against someone of Brayden's stature."

Rayne turned and walked away from Theodor and Rowena, his thoughts swirling. He spun back and looked at them, uncertain what to say. Again, he asked, "Do you trust him?"

"We always have. Before you disappeared, he watched over you and after you were taken he was like a son to us, helped us, supported us in our loss," Theodor said. "In fact, if you hadn't returned when you did, we were set to announce him as Adopted Heir Apparent for the throne. We were days away from making it official."

Rayne shook his head and grimaced. "Did he know that?"

"Of course," Theodor said. "We needed to talk it over with him, and Miles and Cailyn, before we made the official announcement. We traveled to Nemora and stayed for several days discussing the details. The week before you returned, he began traveling, garnering support for his appointment. When he learned of your homecoming, and that he wouldn't need to continue gathering support for himself, he volunteered to continue meeting with officials and nobles on Sorial, Amathea, and Arisima as an ambassador for me and your mother so we could spend more time with you.

"He understood that with your return, everything we discussed about his official adoption as heir was set aside. You are the true heir, son of the Kierkengaard bloodline. His claim is only secure if ..." Theodor stopped; a confused look crossed his face.

Taking no note of Theodor's words or confusion, Rowena stood and waved a finger at Rayne, her voice taking on a cold tone Rayne had not heard before. "He's my sister's son. We've never known him to lie, let alone commit something so heinous as to harm an innocent child like Ruthie. He is like a son to us, a good son. He *is* a good son, an honorable son. Brayden is an exceptional youth, worthy of our faith in him. We trust him completely."

Rowena strode to Rayne, her eyes chips of frosted glass. "You have misunderstood. Or, more likely, you are trying to diminish him in our eyes because you're jealous of how popular Brayden is. He is, after all, the most sought after young noble on all seven worlds. He's been a son to us since before you were taken. I really don't understand your need to attack him like this. I warn you, young man, stop this persecution right now. It will not end well."

Rayne looked at his parents, confused and hurt by their response. "Of course. Perhaps I misunderstood. I won't pursue this now, but please be careful around Brayden. I know you think you know him. You probably think you know him better than you know me. He's been a part of your life for the past ten years, and in many ways, I'm still a stranger to you. But please be aware of how Brayden acts around others. Given time and attention, you will see his mask slip. Just please be careful in the meantime. You may not be able to admit it yet, but he is a liar."

Rayne left his parents with a knot of confusion lodged in his gut. If his memories of Brayden when they were children were real, Brayden had not only been deceiving his parents for over ten years, he was dangerous.

Although music and laughter still filled the passageways around the dining hall, the last thing Rayne wanted to do was return to Brayden's party. He made his way to the prep kitchen to check on Ruthie. Although the girl seemed fine, she wouldn't admit to anything that happened earlier. Rayne's heart sank when he realized someone had already gotten to her. Whether it was a promise of reward or a threat of harm, the girl wouldn't say anything to him, wouldn't even look at him. And without her verifying what happened, his words were meaningless. It was his word against Brayden's, and right now Brayden's words held more weight with his parents than his own.

Later that night, Rayne woke from a nightmare. It wasn't one of the usual nightmares from his time with Sigmund. This time he dreamed of Brayden. His cousin was sitting cross legged on a stone floor, bathed in the flickering glow of a roaring fire. Others inhabited the room, but Rayne couldn't see them; they hid in the deep shadows, beyond the glow of the fire. Brayden's hands worked the air as if he was weaving something. And as he worked, a gray cloud gathered above him.

Then Rayne was standing in his parent's bedroom watching Theodor and Rowena sleep. The gray cloud Brayden had made floated into the room through the open balcony doors and settled over Rayne's parents like a blanket.

Next, Rayne was standing on the balcony looking out toward the Cameron Sea. As he watched, a dark, boiling mass arose in the distance. In the blink of an eye, Rayne was in the boiling mass of darkness. It thrummed and hissed around him and he thought he was going to be sick. Voices screamed in terror and pain.

Rayne lifted his hands in front of his face but could see nothing in the dense darkness. But then, a flash of lightning ignited the gloom and he was back on his parent's balcony. Another flash split the sky and he saw his hands clearly. They were covered in blood. It dripped and ran from him, covering the floor at his feet and drooling off the balcony.

A voice pulsed around him. *You cannot escape your destiny, son of darkness. It comes for you and your false god cannot save you. Give up and return to me tainted one. You can't escape; in the end, you will be mine.*

He shot up, wide-awake, sweating and breathing hard, struggling against the blankets that wrapped him in coils of terror.

6

By the next morning, Rayne had forgotten the nightmare. It lingered just at the edge of his mind like a half-seen shadow, but he couldn't pin down what he had dreamed. A sense of foreboding was all that remained.

With an internal snarl, he shook off the feeling and jogged to the library with Boone at his heels. Outside the door to the study he paused to collect his thoughts while absent mindedly scratching Boone's head. He decided he would set aside the worries that clung to him like a second skin; the premonition of darkness, the disturbing dream he couldn't remember, everything about Brayden and his parents and Ruthie, at least for now. This morning he wanted to focus on the day before, on what happened when he prayed on the beach and the One spoke to him.

Rayne knew something changed in him that morning on the shore of the Cameron Sea. He had finally relinquished a substantial portion of the deep rage he harbored for so long, just as he let go of his grief when he visited the compound weeks ago. He had faced the fact of his anger at the One and felt the One's understanding and acceptance. And for the first time since the night Sigmund was defeated, he lowered his defenses totally and gave himself completely to the One, not ignoring the anger, but accepting it and then releasing it. He felt the One's peace merge into the deepest level of himself.

Rayne understood moments of grief and pain, and spells of anger and self-loathing would still rise up to ambush him, and he would have to find a way to expose Brayden. But he knew now that despite the darkness still dormant at his core, the One was with him and he felt the assurance of forgiveness and love. Even in the hardest times when he felt like he was alone, the One would keep his promise. Rayne would never be alone. He breathed out a prayer of thanks and prayed for wisdom to face Bishop Hedrick with patience. It still seemed unreal that so much could have happened since he spoke with Elsie yesterday morning, yet he still had to face the bishop.

He looked down and gave Boone a quick smile seeing the unconditional love in her eyes. Taking a deep breath, he opened the door.

He wasn't surprised when he walked in to the sounds of a disagreement between Shaw and Bishop Hedrick. The two men were so engrossed in their heated discussion they didn't even notice Rayne and Boone standing at the door. He glanced over to Anne, who sat on a high-backed maroon leather chair by the window with her feet tucked up on the seat under her skirt. She didn't try to say anything, just shook her head and rolled her eyes. Oh, it felt good to see Anne roll her eyes like that. It reminded Rayne that there was more to life than nobles, lies, and power plays.

"No, no, no," Bishop Hedrick said. "He does use a human body, but there is an evil presence possessing the body. So, though you might call Sigmund a human, he is not solely human. He is a possessed human."

Shaw shook his head, his brown curls bouncing. "I can't see that. From what we've studied at Aleppo, we believe he is a human who uses dark powers to extend his life and to practice powerful magic. But we have no evidence of anything more, nothing like demon possession. Good grief, I'm not even convinced demons exist.

"Ah, here's Rayne. He's spent more time with Sigmund than anyone else we know. Let's ask him."

Turning, Bishop Hedrick looked at Rayne over the top of his glasses with a guilty countenance. He stood up and bowed. "Your Highness, once again I would like to apologize for my harsh words and behavior the other morning. They were uncalled for and I deeply regret any discomfort I caused you."

The sky-blue eyes peeking over the top of the glasses reminded Rayne so much of Warren, he stared dumfounded for a moment as the image took him by surprise. But he shook the impression away. "Please, Your Excellency, I hold no anger toward you for your words. In fact, after the day I had yesterday, they've lost most of their sting. I do hope, however, that you apologized to Anne?"

When Bishop Hedrick nodded, Rayne continued. "I know you meant to hurt me because you, yourself, were hurting. But the One used the words you aimed at me in anger, to bring me to a deeper understanding of his love and forgiveness. Your words helped me to realize the light I must bring to the people of Ochen is the truth found in the One's own words of forgiveness. Forgiveness not earned, but given as a gift, before our ancestors even came to the worlds of Ochen. Now is the time for the people to learn that prophecy has been fulfilled. The One's chosen Light Bringer has come."

Shaw and Bishop Hedrick stood staring in such open mouthed shock, Rayne couldn't help but grin at their expressions. Still grinning, he walked to the long table in the center of the room and moved the breakfast food and coffee to a small table by the fireplace. After giving Boone some water and food and wiping his hands, he retrieved the scroll from the locked cabinet. Taking care, he unwrapped the protective leather cover before unrolling it across the table. When he got to the seal, the scroll continued unfurling without hinderance, and he heard the intake of breath as Bishop Hedrick witnessed the opening of the formerly inaccessible chapters.

Rayne smiled at Bishop Hedrick. "Anne. Shaw. We've spent the last few weeks reviewing the beginning of the Words in preparation to move forward and study the unsealed chapters.

We can no longer wait. I need to share something with you now. It's time. Look at this." Rayne scanned through the scroll beyond the seal. Finding what he was looking for, he motioned for all three to come and read.

"This speaks of a Son!" Bishop Hedrick shook his head. Shaw and Anne looked up at Rayne, eyes large.

"This is something you have hinted at in our studies," Shaw whispered.

Nodding, his grin growing even wider, Rayne unrolled more of the scroll, scanned, and found another section he wanted them to read.

Rayne closed his eyes and felt the peaceful presence of the One as the bishop and his friends read of forgiveness and redemption through the Son. When he was aware that they had finished reading, he moved to a couple more sections pointing out portions for them to read before saying, "What do you think, Anne?"

Anne looked up into Rayne's eyes with a light of understanding glowing in hers. "This is beyond comprehension, and yet when I think about it, it fits so well with the truths of the little we had known."

Rayne looked to Shaw next. "Shaw, what do you think?"

"We knew blood needed to be shed for forgiveness, but we never truly understood how that pertained to us. We thought it meant that if we worked hard, you know, the idea of blood, sweat, and personal effort, we could earn our forgiveness. There was so much missing from the fragments we had available to study. If the Son's blood was *the blood* shed for forgiveness, then that explains a mystery we have wrestled with for generations."

Finally, Rayne turned to Bishop Hedrick. As the bishop looked up, Rayne saw the sparkle of tears in the old man's eyes.

"This is the fulfillment of what had just been alluded to in the old fragments of the Words that remained to us after the Hundred Years War. The One has provided a way for us to come into a restored relationship with him. Through the shedding of blood, *the Son's blood,* we are accepted by the One. We are no longer condemned."

Rayne nodded. "Yes, and this is the truth you all helped me to see more clearly. I couldn't earn forgiveness for the blood on my hands no matter how hard I tried. No one can *earn* forgiveness, not even the best of people. All forgiveness is a gift from the One. And this is the light, the truth, I need to bring to the people of Ochen. The light of this gift of loving forgiveness, purchased by the blood of the Son, freely given by the One to those who claim the Son as savior."

Bishop Hedrick looked at Rayne, his eyes large behind his glasses. "Yes, very well stated. I look forward to studying together more, Sire."

"As do I." Rayne moved to the food table and after slathering honey on two pieces of bread, piled on bacon, and slapped the pieces together. He took his bread and honeyed bacon breakfast and sat on one of the chairs by the window to eat, followed by Boone who walked over and lay down at his feet.

Looking around at the three who were all now sitting at the long table, he said between bites, "What was that you needed to ask me about when I walked in the door?"

Bishop Hedrick looked at Shaw who nodded, so he proceeded to explain. "We were discussing the true nature of Sigmund. Shaw and his community believe he is just a man, a man of great evil power, but a man, nothing more. I believe he has mentioned this to you already."

Rayne nodded, thinking back to the discussion they had before starting to study the scroll. "Shaw said he believes that Sigmund has a master and isn't the source of the darkness, just a servant of the darkness. His master is the real source. Sigmund is a very powerful human who's used dark powers to extend his life, making him a kind of living darkness. And he fears the Light Bringer because the Light Bringer is prophesied to bind him, whatever that means. Is that about right?"

"That is the gist of it," Shaw said. "But Bishop Hedrick and I disagreed because he believes there is more to Sigmund. Would you like to explain your position Bishop?"

"Yes, thank you. Your Highness, I've studied Sigmund of Bainard's history for many years, ever since the death of King

Samuel, your grandfather. My studies have led me to the con-
clude that he's not human.

"Like Shaw, I believe Sigmund has a master, a being more
powerful than he. But in my opinion, and where Shaw and I
disagree, Sigmund is not human. He is a demon who needs to
possess a human body to function in our world. Once the
demon whom we know as Sigmund finds a desirable host, he
possesses the body of that human and takes control of it. The
human soul shrinks over time and, as Sigmund takes more control, the soul is reduced to a shadow of itself. If he likes the
body, he will use his power to prolong the life. If he isn't happy
he moves on to another host. There are some records existing
that provide evidence of this.

"The body Sigmund currently possesses has been used by
him for generations and it still appears to be young and healthy.
However, there will come a time when he will need to find a
new host, especially if the human body is damaged. So, you see,
Your Highness, he is human in one respect, but something
more in another, something demonic. Because Shaw and I
could not resolve our disagreement we thought to ask you. You
are the only person we know who has spent any time with Sigmund. What do you think? Is he just human and his evil limited
by his humanity, or is he something more than human, with a
deeper capacity for evil?"

Rayne looked back and forth between Shaw and Bishop
Hedrick and thought about the dilemma. If he remembered,
could he help find the answer?

7

Closing his eyes, he forced himself to think back to the year he lived with Sigmund and Ponce. The year of nightmare that his mind refused to revisit.

So much darkness threatened to consume him during that year, so much pain and terror lurked around the edges of his memories of that time. What scared him most though, were the many unaccounted-for periods of time he couldn't remember at all, whole chunks of memories locked away behind self-protective walls that his mind refused to breach.

Closing his eyes, Rayne began sorting through his fragmented memories. At first, they were disjointed and random. But as he focused, striving to remember more clearly, some of the fragments coalesced into a unified memory. He was Wren again, back at Sigmund's manor house, locked in a cage sitting in the center of the great hall. It was hot, so hot, and a large fire flickered and roared in the massive fireplace.

Sigmund's colleagues filled the room, laughing and conversing, drinking. There were tables laden with food and Wren breathed in the aromas drifting on the air as his stomach grumbled its emptiness. He was lying on his left side in the middle of the cage, legs pulled up into his chest with his arms wrapped around them, curled into a small ball. Several guests were gathered around the cage, watching as someone jabbed at Wren with a fireplace poker. Though the prodding was leaving painful bruises, he was too afraid to move and just curled tighter into his ball.

"Lord Sigmund," one of the men standing at the cage shouted. "Are you sure he's still alive. He looks dead to me and Ender can't get him to move."

Terror coursed through Wren sending his heart racing as he felt the potent darkness that was Sigmund approach the cage. "Rise, slave." Sigmund's voice came soft but irresistible.

Harsh lessons had taught Wren the futility of disobedience and, trembling, he slowly uncurled and rose to stand, facing Sigmund. He was dressed in nothing more than well-worn, blood-smeared leather leggings and a slave collar. Fresh blood dribbled from several small slices on his arms and back. Wren met Sigmund's eyes but quickly averted his gaze. Sigmund's smile grew.

Wren blinked and took control of the panic threatening to undo him. *Won't give him the satisfaction. It pleases him too much.* He willed his expression to reflect unfeeling indifference.

Sigmund frowned and then grunted. Waving his hand to catch the attention of the others, he announced, "Come my colleagues, witness how much my property despises me, and yet he obeys. I hate to admit it, but it has taken me nearly six months to achieve this level of compliance."

Several of the guests snickered at the admission but they all walked over to the cage to stare at Wren as if he was some kind of rare display.

"Ponce," Sigmund called.

"Yes Master." Ponce pulled a chain with a key from around his neck and unlocked Wren's cage.

"Out," Sigmund commanded.

Wren hesitated a moment but then ducked through the open door. He moved to stand before Sigmund, submissive, his eyes lowered to Sigmund's feet. He was prepared when Sigmund's slap came; he had hesitated in obeying his master and earned the discipline. And yet, the force of it sent him to his knees.

"That's right," a woman said in a drunken slur. "Teach the creature who his master is."

Wren could feel Sigmund's eyes on him as he climbed back to his feet and resumed the submissive position expected of him, once again watching Sigmund's feet. Wren couldn't suppress a shudder as the feet stepped in closer. He wanted to look up and see what Sigmund was doing but knew better. He steeled himself for whatever game his master had in mind now.

He nearly jumped when he felt Sigmund's hand hover above his head, then sucked in a breath as the sorcerer, taking care to not come in contact with Rayne's skin, grabbed a handful of his hair and yanked, dragging Wren to an open portion of the floor, away from the cage.

"Ladies and gentlemen." Sigmund's deep voice filled the dark corners of the room. "I have decided our entertainment this afternoon will be a hunt." He looked down into Wren's eyes, his own pale and cold. "Kneel, slave."

Wren dropped to his knees.

"A hunt?" the drunken woman slurred. "I'm not wasting my afternoon chasing some swarmy fox or something. It's stupid."

"I never said we would be hunting a fox." A sly grin raised the corners of Sigmund's mouth. "You're right. That would be boring. I have something better in mind. The amusement I offer you today is a hunt for a human. This human. My slave. He's really quite lively, given the chance. And to lead the hunt, I have hired two colleagues, hunters of skill."

He motioned, and Ponce ran to open a door that had remained closed through the morning.

Wren watched in horror as two large creatures stalked into the room. They were dressed in leathers and both had beads woven into thick, long braids. They looked like men with wolf faces, their reddish-brown fur melding into long, thick hair on their heads. They were both tall and broad but one looked older and stood nearly a head taller than the other.

Raising heavily muscled arms over their heads as in victory, the two yelled something in the guttural language Wren had heard Sigmund and his colleagues use many times before. The guests responded in the same language and cheered. The two creatures continued to wave and smile, showing pointed canine teeth. Eventually the larger of the two walked up to Sigmund and looked down on Wren who knelt before him, staring forward, hands fisted at his sides in an effort to control their trembling.

The creature reached down and grabbed Wren's upper arm in a vise-like grip. Then, dragging Wren up to his nose, he began to sniff like a dog searching for a scent as the other creature strode up and began to sniff as well. Wren felt darkness rolling off the hunters, seeking out the darkness that Sigmund and Ponce had been nurturing in him over the past few months. He wanted to escape the evil energy of the hunters, but he couldn't fight the veredium-like grip. After a couple minutes of sniffing and snuffling, the creature shoved Wren back down onto his knees.

"Good blood there, good spirit." The creature who had grabbed Wren nodded to Sigmund, with something that looked like a smile. "And just the right amount of rubiate implanted darkness to make the hunt interesting."

"Excellent." Sigmund turned to the other guests again. "I propose we allow our prey to run while we enjoy a leisurely lunch. I think about two hours' head start should suffice." He looked at the larger hunter who nodded his approval. "And while we're waiting I want to encourage everyone to place bets on how long it will take our hunters to lead us to success. Does the slave have the capacity to elude us for long or will we snag our quarry quickly?"

"Aren't you afraid of losing him?" the man who had been poking Wren asked.

Sigmund laughed. "Where would he go? He's just a worthless slave with no family. Nobody cares if this one lives or dies. Except me. And if he happens to find a local, they know better than to give any assistance to my property. No, he has nowhere to go."

"Oh, yes. That's right. I'd forgotten about his *history*." The man with the poker chuckled.

Then, stepping forward, Sigmund grabbed Wren's hair again, forcing him to look up. "Right slave? You know better than to try and flee from your master, don't you?"

He stared into Wren's eyes for a long moment, feeding the darkness in Wren's core with his powerful force. Then with a snort, pushed his head away in disgust. Looking at the hunters he said, "Remember, you must not kill this one. I believe Ponce has informed you of the need for blow darts only on this hunt."

Nodding, the two pulled long shooters from over their shoulders.

"Marvelous. Ponce, release the slave. Ladies and gentlemen, come, let us eat and drink and place our bets while the boy runs."

Ponce came closer, Wren shivered, and his tongue stuck to the roof of his mouth.

As Ponce reached to grab Wren's shoulder, the memory fragmented. Rayne jumped at a touch on his shoulder. His eyes popped open and with terror raging through him, he sprang up into a fighting stance startling Anne, who stood next to him. Boone hopped up barking.

Breathing hard, Rayne stared at nothing. His eyes closed again, and he groaned. He tried to block the rest of the memory as it tumbled into his consciousness, the running, the hunt, the pain. Two days he ran. Sigmund had been livid. Most of the guests had given up and were gone by the time Wren was dragged back. Then there was pain and darkness. Rayne choked down the surging fear. *I remember.* He was chained to the foot of Sigmund's bed and he was drowning in a black void. But then he heard a woman's voice, Anne's voice. "Don't push it, Rayne. You don't have to do this now."

A sob broke from Rayne as he pulled away from the living nightmare.

Without thinking he reached down and quieted Boone. He squeezed his eyes shut to block threatening tears. Several minutes later, his breathing evened out. Opening his eyes, Rayne looked at Anne and realized what must have happened. "I'm so sorry, Anne. I didn't hurt you, did I?"

Anne shook her head. "No, Rayne. I'm fine."

He shifted his gaze to Shaw and then to Bishop Hedrick, embarrassed by what they must have just witnessed. "Those blank spaces where my memories refuse to surface?" Rayne whispered. "They're best left alone."

"I didn't realize," Bishop Hedrick said, his voice subdued. "I'm so sorry."

Rayne shook his head. "Shaw, you're wrong. Sigmund isn't human. And he's not the only one. There are others ... not human." Rayne stopped speaking, swallowed hard, and looked around. His skin pimpled in expectation that he would see the fearsome creatures appear out of thin air.

Anne moved to the table, poured a glass of water, and brought it to Rayne, who accepted it gratefully.

When he had composed himself some, he said, "I'm sorry, Shaw, but I have to agree with Bishop Hedrick. Sigmund has a power to him, an energy that's not human. It's not comparable to the incredible might of the One, but it is more than human. Demon possession is the best way to explain it. There is an evil in Sigmund and his colleagues, a thing that is not human. I know; I felt it. For a year, I lived with it every day. Tried to fight it as they forced their evil darkness into me. And there were other ... things, other ... creatures." Rayne closed his eyes and shuddered. "It makes me afraid. Even here and now, remembering it terrifies me."

He got up and walked over to the table, poured another glass of water, and downed it. "I know Sigmund is going to come for me again. As far as he's concerned, I'm still his rebellious property and he won't give me up so easily. But even more than that, I'm the One's chosen Light Bringer; he has to stop me from fulfilling the prophecy. The only thing that keeps me from surrendering to the fear that tries to consume me each and every day is the knowledge that the One is stronger than Sigmund.

"The inconceivable supremacy of the One is far more powerful than anything Sigmund can imagine. I don't think he realizes how far beyond him the One really is. And because of that, Sigmund deceives himself. He can't defeat the One. But Sigmund *is* strong. Compared to us humans, he and his colleagues are very powerful."

When Rayne stopped speaking, they all remained silent, lost in thought, and the crackling of the fire was the only sound in the room for a long while.

8

For the next month, Rayne divided his time between training with Thorvin; studying the scroll with Anne, Shaw, and Bishop Hedrick; and trying to carve out some time to spend with Boone, Shalimar and the twins. With such a busy schedule, it was easy to avoid Brayden. Thorvin worked Rayne hard every afternoon and frequently into the evening so it didn't take long to see improvement as Rayne polished his rusty skills. At night, he fell into the deep, dreamless sleep of exhaustion.

Mornings, Rayne met with Bishop Hedrick, Anne, and Shaw for a time of prayer followed by study. His faith and understanding grew as they read more of the scroll and discussed the Words of the One. Bishop Hedrick proved to be quite a scholar. Elsie was right, the bishop was brilliant. There were times when Bishop Hedrick and Shaw argued over an issue but, in the end, they usually came to an agreement, although sometimes that needed Rayne's or Anne's intervention to bring about the accord. Eventually, Bishop Hedrick lost a portion of his stiffness and even asked the other three to call him Jonathan instead of Excellency.

To Rayne's delight, Shaw and Anne were spending time

together outside of the morning study hours. Though Shaw was more than ten years her senior, Anne's mild temperament and Shaw's quiet spirit melded well, and Rayne wasn't surprised when the two were seen holding hands.

Working together proved to be not only profitable, but enjoyable. After Jonathan began to lose his stiff façade and relax more, morning studies often included laughter and light-hearted conversation. The palace kitchen staff continued sending breakfast each morning, but Rayne no longer joined the others for the meal. Ever since Brayden's party, his parents had insisted he join them daily for a private breakfast before going to the library.

⋆

With one week of training left before the festival, Rayne and Thorvin decided to switch up their practice to include the ancient weapons. Thorvin left Rayne in the secluded practice room where they had been working every afternoon for the last three weeks while he went to collect the King's Sword and his own weapon. "I won't be long, Sire."

While waiting for Thorvin, Rayne's thoughts centered on his conversation with his parents at breakfast. His early meals had become a disheartening time of clenched fists and reduced appetite. Each morning, his parents challenged him about why he hated his cousin and questioned him about what happened the evening of the party. Each day, the same conversation was repeated. Although it hurt Rayne that his mother and father still refused to accept his words as true, he understood their position. Over the years while he was gone, Theodor and Rowena had grown to look on Brayden as their son.

"Tell me again," Theodor asked that morning. "What is it you believe happened the night of Brayden's party?"

"Are you sure you aren't confused? After all, Ruthie's story doesn't agree with yours." His mother's painful words battered at his sense of self. "Are you sure your memory isn't playing tricks on you? We all know it's quite shattered."

Rayne cringed at the comment. *Doesn't she realize how much that hurts?*

"You must let go of this vendetta you have against your cousin." Theodor rose from the table and strode to Rayne's side. "He's your own flesh and blood. I think your mother is right, you are confusing something from your past with the night of the party. Think hard, can you remember?"

Like I could forget that night?

"Even when you were children Brayden tried to help you be a better person." Rowena smiled and released a soft chuckle. "You probably don't remember, but to be honest, you were a little terror as a child and often it was your cousin who saved you from harm. He was so protective of you. And then there were the times you accused him of outlandish things and he would just smile sadly, shake his head, and respond with kindness."

Right! Brayden? Only if he had something to gain by the performance.

"He's an extremely bright and capable young man." Theodor returned to his seat next to Rowena. "I don't know that anyone could have done better strengthening our political connections these past few months."

"I will not continue to tolerate your accusations against Brayden," his mother concluded. "Either you stop this now, or something will have to be done to correct your attitude young man."

Rayne wanted to scream his frustration at his parents. *What's wrong with you? You praise Brayden without question. Yet, the moment my words reach your ears, you discount them, jump all over me, and hop to Brayden's defense. Everything I say gets twisted in your minds, then you accuse me of being prejudicial.*

Rayne shook his head. "What are they thinking?" he murmured into the dusty silence of the practice room as his father's final words from this morning resounded in his mind.

"If you don't start speaking of Brayden with respect and honor him as you should, I fear we will be forced to punish you."

Rayne also fumed over how much time Brayden spent

with his parents, especially his father. His cousin had asked permission to sit with Theodor when he held open audiences and his father agreed. Brayden certainly could be pleasant when he wanted, and he seemed to be a welcome addition in the audience chamber, playing his role as the king's nephew to the hilt, charming Theodor's advisors and other officials with his wit and social graces.

Rayne was tired of answering the same questions morning after morning while he felt the sensation of his mother's magic probing him, searching for deception. He feared she was starting to believe the stories circulating that he was still Sigmund's pawn. That he, not Brayden, was the deceiver. He would reach back along her lines with his heartfelt feelings of honesty. But as the days went by and he still hadn't convinced her or his father of the veracity of his words, Rayne began to wonder if there was more to the situation.

Does Brayden have some kind of hold on my parents? He practically lived with them for the last ten years. There must be something I can do to find out. If Brayden is exercising some kind of control, Mother is unaware of it. And she's a master mage. Does Brayden have the skill to place a magic compulsion on them without Mother sensing it? Rayne was struggling with the possibility when Thorvin returned with the weapons.

Seeing the King's Sword for the first time since the night he almost killed his parents put a knot in Rayne's stomach, but after his first hesitation he reached out to take the weapon from Thorvin's outstretched hand. It felt comfortable and right in his hands. A shock of pleasure washed through him when the sword responded to his touch and started to glow.

The bond he remembered from all those months ago ignited, renewing its union with him, establishing again his connection with the power in the sword. The comforting presence of the One cloaked him. Rayne didn't understand the connection between the sword and the One, and how they came together in his spirit, but he was grateful they did. Somehow, he knew a time would come when he would again need that power and peace.

He began to swing the sword in figure eights while

Thorvin watched. Rayne moved slowly and precisely. Without thought, he fell into set patterns as his past training kicked-in. He moved with ease through the basic forms of defense and attack then shifted naturally to more advanced forms. Eight lines of attack followed by another eight lines as he maneuvered through all sixteen possible lines of attack. He flowed into blocking patterns and then repeated the forms again before shifting into his personal technique designed by Thorvin for him alone, adding forms of attack and defense using his hands and feet combined with the sword. He repeated the whole workout again striving for speed while maintaining perfection of movement, exulting in the purity of the dance. As he moved, the conflict that had gripped his mind melted into peace and the soothing sensation of pure muscle movement. Rayne was unsure how long he danced with the sword but when he stopped he was covered in sweat and breathing hard.

Looking up, he noticed Thorvin watching. "How long?" he asked, catching his breath, "How long was I doing that?"

Thorvin shook his head and chuckled. "Long enough. Watching you do that is mesmerizing and a lot less tiring than sparring with you. Let's take a break and go get something to eat. Come on, I'm hungry."

As they walked toward the palace kitchens, Rayne asked Thorvin what he knew about Brayden. Until now, Rayne hadn't talked to anyone except his parents about Brayden and his suspicions, but he knew Thorvin had grown up with Rowena in Inverness and would know about Brayden and his family. Rayne hoped Thorvin could give him insight into the situation.

Thorvin gave Rayne a dark look. "Why would you ask me about him?"

"I just want your opinion. What do you think of him?"

Thorvin released a snort. "I don't think much of him. I know he's your cousin and you're probably pretty close, and maybe you like him. I know your parents think highly of him. But, honestly, I don't trust the power hungry little snot. There's something off about him."

Looking a little abashed at his bold comments, Thorvin added, "Sorry. I should take into account that you might actually like him."

Rayne chuckled, relieved at Thorvin's honesty. "Thanks. I was beginning to think I was the only one who couldn't stand him."

"You too?"

"Yeah. What I don't understand, is how much my parents trust him. They're smart and usually good at reading people. And yet, in spite of that, they trust *him. Completely.*"

His voice lowered with pain, Rayne admitted, "They trust him more than they trust me."

Thorvin nodded. "It does seem that way, doesn't it?"

"Can I tell you something in confidence?"

"Of course, Your Highness."

"The night of Brayden's welcome home dinner, he and three of his friends planned to violate Ruthie. You know, the pretty little blonde girl from the kitchen? I told my parents what happened that night, and they're still questioning me about it. Every morning we meet and every morning, they ask me the same questions. Then they go on about how wonderful Brayden is. I know Mother and Father want to trust me, or at least I hope they want to trust me, so, why don't they? What kind of hold does Brayden have on them that they won't even consider he might be lying?"

Thorvin's brow scrunched in thought a minute. "What does Ruthie say?"

Frustration flashed through Rayne. "She won't speak up. She denies anything happened. I don't know why, but by later that night she refused to talk about any of it."

"That certainly puts you in a tough spot." Thorvin grimaced and shook his head. "I know back when I still lived on Nemora, Brayden's parents, Cailyn and Miles, were good people. I remember Cailyn as a kind and caring person, if a little weak. Your Aunt Cailyn and your mother were always very close. They were more than just sisters; they were sisters and best friends. We used to do a lot together, riding, hunting, going to plays and concerts.

"To convince Rowena that Cailyn's son is capable of what you're accusing him of is not going to be easy. Perhaps for now it would be best to set aside this thing with Brayden. Focus on getting through this next week. Then when the festival is behind you, keep an eye on Brayden. Try to find some convincing evidence to bring to your parents."

Rayne frowned, but agreed with Thorvin. He needed to stay focused on preparing for his exhibition and speech.

After talking with Thorvin, Rayne decided to visit Stevie and Sashi. The last few weeks had been so busy, he hadn't seen much of the twins, and he needed to get away from the palace for a while. He headed into town and down toward Kasper's Blades.

"I'm sorry, but Stevie and Sashi aren't here," Korie said. "They're visiting friends and won't be back until late."

Rayne knew his disappointment was showing when Korie gave him a look of sympathy and said, "Mace and I would enjoy your company if you want to stay and wait for Sashi and Stevie while we work." She smiled a warm, welcoming smile.

"I would like that."

Rayne liked watching the Kaspers work; they were both so talented. He took a seat on one of the tall stools around a heavy wooden work bench where he could see all that was happening. Mace and his assistant were working on a long knife for one of the palace guards while Korie and two assistants were working on a sword for a minor noble. There was a comfortable atmosphere of shared goals in the shop behind the store front as the smiths concentrated on their work, and Rayne found the sound of their hammers soothing. Periodically one or the other of the two would plunge the metal they were working into a bucket of water and the hissing would act as a counterpoint to the sound of the other hammers still striking metal.

When they finished for the day, and the shop was cleaned, Kori said, "Why don't you come up to the living quarters and stay for supper, Rayne? It'll be something simple, but you're welcome to join us."

"Thanks, Mrs. Kasper, but I think I'll just head home. Please let the twins know I was here, okay?"

"Of course, Rayne. I'll be sure to let them know you waited for them."

Rayne wasn't ready to return to the palace after he left the shop, so he decided to take a walk. *At least I don't have to worry about dragging a guard around. But I don't know if that's good or bad. Ever since Brayden's return Mother hasn't cared enough to even wonder if I'm safe or not.* After walking aimlessly for a while, he found himself in Lady Lilith's neighborhood. Old, ghosting memories of pain sent him sprinting back toward the Great Square.

What's wrong with me? Why am I so restless? Time alone with the scroll, that's what I need. Finding purpose in his decision, he jogged back up to the library and spent the next several hours studying the Words of the One to Corylus.

By the time he stopped reading, Rayne's eyes were scratchy and bleary. He rubbed them with the heels of his hands, rolled up the scroll, and put it away. He chuckled when his stomach growled a protest at its empty state. *I should have eaten at the Kasper's. I'll stop in the kitchen and see what's available at this hour otherwise I'll never get to sleep.*

It was quiet in the baking kitchen, but Ruthie was still there cleaning and setting things up for baking in the morning. When she saw Rayne, she bowed. He told her to rise and she looked at him with guilt-ridden eyes before turning back to her work. He wished he could help her, but unless she was willing to tell the truth of what had happened the night of the dinner party, he couldn't. Ruthie made up a plate for him and Rayne, not wanting to sit there with her guilty eyes on him, took it and walked out to a bench.

The evening was cold, but he enjoyed the chill while he ate. When he stopped back in the kitchen to return the plate on his way to his room, it was empty, so he left the dirty dish on one of the heavy wooden work tables.

Although his time with the Kaspers had brought an interval of peace, and studying the scroll had been productive, Rayne was still restless and feeling at odds with things. His parents expected him to join them for breakfast again in the morning and he dreaded the inevitable confrontation.

Life was simpler before Brayden returned. Rayne grappled

with the change in his parents since his cousin's arrival. It was as if with each passing day, they moved farther from him. His mother avoided him and had lost interest in helping him hone his magic. When he asked her about it, she said she was too busy to spend time with him. And his father seemed to grow colder by the day. If Rayne had his way, his cousin would go back to Nemora and stay away from his parents permanently.

By the time Rayne returned to his rooms, Andrew was asleep, curled up in one of the chairs, with Boone sleeping next to him. Rayne smiled at the two as Boone lifted her head and then with a contented sigh lowered it back down and closed her eyes.

Exhaustion dragged Rayne to his bed, but sleep eluded him. Between his nerves over the upcoming exhibition, the thought of people learning the truth of his past, and his concerns about speaking out for the first time as the Light Bringer, he was having a hard time settling. And he still had to make it through several more days before the festival.

The whole stomach churning issue of how to deal with Brayden kept his thoughts skittering like mice around a floor littered with cheese crumbs. He knew Thorvin's advice was good. Focus on the festival first and then on Brayden. But he couldn't let go of the feeling that Brayden was controlling his parents in some way and that his control was getting stronger every day. What Thorvin said earlier resonated with Rayne's own feelings, there was something off about Brayden. Rayne just couldn't figure out what it was.

When he finally reined in his ricocheting thoughts with the decision to leave off worrying about things until tomorrow, something deeper was exposed, an uneasiness in his spirit. Like a vision in a tale, the afternoon he had first spoken to Thorvin about staging an exhibition blossomed in his mind. It came to him so vividly, he thought he could smell again Thorvin's sweat-soaked leather and the scent of flowers blown from the gardens. He was walking back to the palace when the sudden inexplicable cold and premonition of darkness assailed him.

He couldn't explain what was happening to him, but he knew there was a darkness hovering near, something that reminded him of Sigmund. Rayne lay awake for a long time before sleep finally came to him.

9

Rayne knelt on the raised platform set up in the Great Square for his exhibition match with Thorvin. He wore the clothing Sigmund had given him to wear the night he was sent to murder his parents; the night the One saved him. The strangely-tailored, deep purple sleeveless silk tunic that exposed his slave mark, black leggings, and bare feet reminded him of his past and the One's grace in bringing him out of the darkness. Though the chill of the morning air pimpled his skin, he would warm up once he began moving.

Thorvin leaned against one of the supporting posts and watched Theodor as he spoke to the large crowd which ebbed and flowed across the square and filled the surrounding streets. People sat on roofs and on shoulders and strained to see the platform better. Most of those in attendance waved small flags displaying the Kierkengaard insignia.

Food had been consumed in massive amounts and the food stalls were now closed. The people, quiet and attentive, listened while Theodor spoke of Rayne's captivity, his struggle against being forced to kill, his battle against the darkness Sigmund birthed in him, and finally, his freedom from his captors and their evil, brought about by the power of the One to save him. Theodor then went on to speak of Rayne's gifts as a warrior.

"Now free of Sigmund and his evil coercion, Crown Prince Rayne is committed to using those abilities to protect you, his people." He then quoted the ancient prophecy.

"'In the thirtieth generation, the Light Bringer will come from the blessed line. In his sixteenth year, he will cling to the One and he will grow in wisdom and strength to fulfill his destiny and seal the living darkness. He will bring light to the people of the worlds of Ochen.'

"My son, Prince Rayne, your own future king, is the prophesied Light Bringer. He has been called by the One to protect you from the coming darkness and bring light to all the people of Ochen.

"And now, I am most proud to present to you an exhibition match between Crown Prince Rayne Nathan Samuel Kierkengaard, wielding the King's Sword, and Master Swordsman, Lord Thorvin Kraftsmunn, also wielding a weapon of ancient forging."

The crowd let loose with noisy cheers and whistles. Some people stomped their feet while others beat on drums scattered through the square. The cheering continued for several minutes as the citizens of Westvale reveled in the celebration of their returned prince.

It was time. Rayne knelt near the edge of the raised platform praying quietly while Theodor spoke. "I know that I'm unworthy to be your Light Bringer, blessed One, but I believe you called me and I'm trusting you. Give me wisdom to know the words you would have me speak, so people will hear your truth."

To wield the King's Sword in front of a crowd of people was hard enough, but to speak to the eager public watching him now, and take on the mantel of Light Bringer, caused Rayne's stomach to rebel. It was good that he had eaten only some dry bread for breakfast.

The crowd quieted again as Rayne rose. With a nod to Thorvin, he strode to the center of the ring. The match—not a true contest—was staged. Thorvin had planned every move in detail. Rayne and he worked through it so many times during the past week that Rayne could perform it in his sleep. When Rayne grasped the hilt of the King's Sword it responded to his touch as it always did. Exclamations of surprise showered Rayne as the glow of the sword moved up to his hand and bathed his arm, then permeated the air surrounding him. Thorvin's sword responded in kind as a glow sparked, then spread down its entire length.

With a signal from Thorvin, they began the series of moves that would take them through a complete demonstration of Rayne's skills. Rayne centered himself and focused. Even though every move was planned, any mistake with the ancient weapons could result in injury to Thorvin or himself. All their practice paid off when an expectant silence seized the crowd as the two moved with grace and speed, attacking and defending, then backing off only to engage again. They finished with Rayne circling his sword close into Thorvin's, and twisting his wrists with a quick flip that ripped the sword from Thorvin's hands and sent it flying. It was a good move and Rayne grinned when he completed the maneuver.

After Rayne made the final move, before Thorvin's sword had even stopped spinning, Thorvin grinned his approval. "Well done, Your Highness, very well done." Then the large warrior went to one knee and bowed low to Rayne. The crowd erupted once again into ear splitting cheers and raucous noise. Thorvin rose and, with a final salute to Rayne, left the platform.

The moment Rayne feared was upon him. He turned in a circle as the crowd continued their joyous outpouring for several minutes. He bowed deeply toward the raised dais where his parents sat, before dipping his head to the stands where the nobles sat. Turning to the crowds of commoners, he inclined his head again and the people cheered even louder in response. After scanning the crowded square, he raised his hands; the King's Sword still glowing lightly in his right hand. As the level of noise dropped, Rayne began.

"People of Westvale, thank you for your support."

The echoes of loud shouting and the banging of drums

exploded once more, and again Rayne raised his hands for silence.

"You listened as my father, King Theodor, spoke of my past, of how I was raised in darkness. But the darkness wasn't complete. Darkness never is. The One placed a light bringer there for me. His name was Warren. The One made a way for me to be saved from the evil of my captivity. But even more important, he has made a way for all his people to be saved from the darkness of sin and separation, and to come to knowledge of his love and forgiveness.

"In the past, we believed we needed to earn our forgiveness by our own actions, by our own blood, sweat, and effort. But this is not so."

Murmurs and rustlings spread through the crowd at that statement. The idea that forgiveness was something that needed to be earned was deeply ingrained in the minds of the people of Ochen. Rayne paused, then lifted a quick prayer that the people would be open to the truth.

"Because of his great love for his people, the One's own Son purchased our forgiveness for us long ago, before our ancestors even came to Ochen. Forgiveness is a gift from the One, not something we can earn. No matter how good we are, we are not capable of earning it. But the One gives us the gift of forgiveness because the Son already purchased it for us by his own blood. He died the death of a criminal even though he was innocent. But he didn't stay dead. He rose from the dead because he was one with the One."

Now the outcry of the crowd drowned out Rayne's words as the shock of what he said began to sink into their minds and they gave voice to their disapproval; but Rayne had one more point he wanted to make before he was ready to let them go to think through what he was saying. Raising his left hand, motioning for peace, he achieved a level of attentive quiet and began to speak again.

"No one is good enough to earn forgiveness, but it is also true that the Son's gift is so great that no one is so bad that he can't find forgiveness through the Son. I am proof of this. I was living in evil, a hired assassin, a murderer with rubiate darkness growing in me. And yet, the One forgave me and loves me, even me. He offers this gift to every one of you."

The uproar started to build in volume again. Rayne turned in a slow circle, scanned the faces around him, and met eyes when he could. He knew some of the people were thinking about his words, but most were probably too shocked to even consider them yet. And there would be those who would never accept them. But he felt peace in being the Light Bringer and he thanked the One again for allowing him to speak of the gift of the Son and forgiveness.

At that instant, in the blink of an eye, Westvale was bathed in a pure brilliance that couldn't be explained by the shining sun. A hush fell over the square while eyes focused on Rayne and spectators stared in open-mouthed astonishment. He sensed the comforting presence he always felt when the One was about to speak, and in that moment, Rayne closed his eyes and rested in the peace and warmth as it enveloped him. The voice came to him; this time it was not the soft utterance in his head, or even the external voice Stevie and Sashi had heard. Now it boomed like thunder rolling through the streets of the city.

This is my Light Bringer. I have sent him to bring the message of forgiveness through my Son. Listen to him. His words are light in the darkness.

As the rumble faded, silence reigned in the city, but only for a moment. Like the building noise of a crashing wave, the resonance of thousands of voices calling out in unison echoed through the Great Square, the sound intensified as those scattered through streets and alleys joined the clamor.

The presence of the One still upheld Rayne. Yet, as his gaze swept over the milling throng, uncertainty swept over him. *Okay—what do I do now? Didn't think about how I get through the square. Way to go dimwit, now you're trapped.* Then a path opened through the packed square and Rayne understood. A contingent of palace guards were opening a way for him through the crowd to the palace grounds. His father, experienced in these matters, must have planned for this. Relief flowed through Rayne when Noah climbed the steps to the platform and, after a deep bow, waved him over. Still holding the lightly glowing King's Sword, Rayne allowed himself to be surrounded by the guard and hustled to the palace.

10

The feeble, withered old man struggled to remain upright and moving as he made his way across the Great Square of Westvale, the crowd milling and surging around him. He had no fear of being recognized here in his current state and stumbled with a determined expression toward the flag-festooned stand where the nobles sat. Head swiveling and bobbing on a too skinny neck, he scanned the raised platform for a particular young noble.

He detested being reduced to his current condition and resented the handsome, well dressed nobles laughing and drinking while he shuffled on, pain, anger, and frustration bubbling like acid inside him. The guard tried to keep him from approaching the stand, but the old man mumbled something under his breath while writing with a finger on the air and the guard backed away. When he located the noble he sought, the aged man stumbled to him.

Brayden sneered down at the decrepit excuse for a human

being who seemed to want to talk to him. "Ugh, get away from me old man. You stink. I don't know who you are, but you certainly don't belong here."

Holding his breath, Brayden raised his arm to summon a guard to remove the old fool, but the decaying man grabbed it, pulled it down with an incredibly strong grip, and mumbled in Brayden's ear. Horror battled with shock as Brayden pulled back and crossed his arms. He looked closely at the repulsive creature standing next to him.

"It can't be." Disgust wrinkled Brayden's nose. He stared for a moment, doubt lingering in his mind, but he said no more and suffered the man to stay by his side as Theodor began his speech.

𝕴𝕴

Standing next to Brayden, Sigmund writhed inside the now corrupted body he once took pleasure in possessing. He had been proud of keeping it handsome and young for so long. Now he loathed being forced to continue to inhabit the impossibly old and decaying body. The once-beautiful shell was now nothing more than corrupt, dying flesh. He was aware of Brayden's disgust and swore he would find a new host before he had to spend much more time trapped in this worthless husk.

Sigmund's meeting with the Demon Master on the Shattered Continent had not gone well. He hated visiting the Shattered Continent, that huge expanse of land which had been blasted to nothing but barren rock during the Hundred Years War, that scarred land where his master now lived. Not only had Sigmund been deprived of the pleasure of his long-awaited revenge, he failed his master. In response to his defeat, Sigmund was summoned to the slag-heap his superior called home to pay the price for that failure. As punishment for his ineffectiveness at stopping the Light Bringer from appearing, Sigmund's master blasted the body Sigmund inhabited with dark fire, damaging it beyond repair. Now he was forced to find a new host and that thought enraged him. In his weakened physical state, he could accomplish little. He needed to find a new host without delay.

As Theodor stood to address the crowd, Sigmund cursed Ponce for disappearing the night of the slave boy's betrayal. Ponce's desertion had forced Sigmund to travel to the Shattered Continent and face the master's wrath alone. He teetered once again, fighting the ancient body, forcing it to continue existing one painful breath at a time. Ponce's disappearance the night of the failed vengeance was one more reason to hate the boy who had been the cause of Sigmund's humiliating defeat. But once he acquired a new body, Sigmund would search out that cowardly rubiate and make him pay for his desertion.

Without help, Sigmund now struggled alone, trapped in the wasting body. But his hatred would not allow him to miss this *festival*, this celebration of the Light Bringer. It was all so infuriating. *He* had made the prince all he was; Sigmund's training had made the boy strong. By rights, the little slave belonged to him. Even the clothes he now wore were Sigmund's. Sigmund's design, Sigmund's property. Oh, how he hated the One. He had twisted the sorcerer's work for revenge and used the prince for his own purposes.

While Theodor droned on, Sigmund glared at the youth kneeling on the raised platform. He growled his frustration and ground his teeth. He loathed that boy almost as much as he loathed the One himself. It was his fault the demon's beautiful body was now nothing but a corrupted shell. It was his fault that Sigmund's master threatened to ban him from Ochen if he failed again, and it was that boy's fault that Sigmund's perfectly planned revenge had been thwarted. He would not fail again.

What he wouldn't give to possess the boy, to take that young body and make it his own while destroying the soul trapped within. Sigmund licked his cracked lips at the thought of tormenting Rayne's spirit. *If only the boy wasn't so well protected. Couldn't even touch him before, only damage him from a distance. But the pleasure to be had if I possessed that servant of the enemy would make all my pain worth it.*

He could take the cousin now, that one was ripe for the

plucking. Sigmund had nurtured Brayden from the time he was a child and he had grown in pride and arrogance since then. *Yes, the handsome one would be an easy trophy.* He looked up at the haughty young man standing tall and broad-shouldered next to him, considering. *That one is eager to embrace the darkness for the power it could give him. And he hates the prince almost as much as I do.* But the demon didn't want the cousin. He wanted the prince. *How to do it? How to steal him away from my enemy? The One is always so possessive of his people.*

As Sigmund watched the mock battle between Thorvin and the youth, he decided he would find a way to subvert his enemy's will and take the boy for his own. *There must be some way. Thwarting the will of the One and stealing this particular servant would please my master, put me back in his good graces, and it would be so pleasurable. I'd be rewarded well for achieving such a significant win over the One.*

No, taking the cousin now would be unsatisfactory. Besides Brayden is useful. His ability to manipulate Theodor and Rowena and free me from wasting energy to control them, is … convenient. He's done it for years right under the nose of that so-called master mage and he's now quite proficient. There's still much to be gained from that arrangement. No, I'll find a lesser human to take for now, someone to inhabit in the interim, someone I can use until I'm ready to bring the entire Ochen system under the sway of darkness.

Go ahead and rise up little Light Bringer. You can't stop me. You've no idea what I've put in place. The years spent planting my servants in high places and using my power and money to build political alliances. When the time is ripe, I'll make my move.

For now, Sigmund would continue using Brayden. He was a worthwhile asset, cruel and easily controlled. Brayden would help him skip onto Nemora where he would find a new host among Brayden's peers. Many of the young man's friends, being of the same easily manipulated mold, were already primed for control. Sigmund's servants had been working on that world for the last two generations to produce usable hosts and political allies for Sigmund and his colleagues.

While he was losing himself in his future plans, the sorcerer suddenly felt a blast of power slam into his demonic self, the spirit that inhabited the host body. It was the One. The One was claiming the boy as his Light Bringer. Sigmund's demonic self writhed in the host body at the pain his enemy's transcendent presence inflicted.

When the pain subsided, Sigmund glared at the boy again. He vowed to himself that somehow, he would find a way to snatch that gnat of a Light Bringer from the One and possess him.

With that thought foremost in his mind and anger fermenting in his stomach, Sigmund watched as Rayne was escorted by the palace guard from the square. One way or another, Sigmund would have his vengeance on the little princeling. That frustratingly annoying boy may have won this battle, but Sigmund vowed to himself, in the end he would win the war.

11

Once Rayne was safely in the palace, the guardsmen returned to the Great Square as the crowd began to disperse. Rayne turned to Noah, to thank him for remaining by his side, but then noticed the look on Noah's face.

"Are you alright?" Rayne asked.

Noah shook his head, staring at Rayne. He started to speak then just turned to jog after the other guards. Rayne got the feeling that if it was lonely being the crown prince, it was going to be even more lonely being the One's Light Bringer.

He started toward his rooms to change when he heard Brayden's voice behind him. Rayne had done a good job avoiding his cousin the past several weeks and he really didn't want to face the man now. But as Brayden called to him, Rayne knew it would be rude not to greet him. So, with a mental shrug, he turned as his cousin approached.

"Well you've done it now, Little Raynie." Brayden smirked. "You've certainly made a fool of yourself and created a difficult situation for Uncle Theodor and Auntie Rowena with that little speech. What was that all about anyway? Sounded like a bunch of nonsense to me."

Rayne opened his mouth to make a derisive remark about Brayden's lack of brain power when he realized that, as the One's Light Bringer, he couldn't. His words could no longer be just his words. Every word from his mouth would now reflect on the One. *How could you put such responsibility in the hands of a damaged sixteen-year-old kid?* And for the umpteenth time, he wondered why the One hadn't chosen Shaw to be his Light Bringer. Rayne took a deep breath trying to decide how to answer Brayden when his cousin continued.

"And that whole light show and voice thing. How did you manage to pull that off? It was quite impressive, especially for the rabble."

"That was no show." Rayne's jaw bunched as he worked to remain calm. "It was the real thing. The One chose to speak to the people of Westvale and it was amazing and wonderful. Don't diminish it with your lack of belief. If you would be open to an honest discussion of what happened in the square, I would be happy to talk with you about it."

Brayden laughed, and Rayne shook his head.

"You don't really believe that nonsense you were spreading, do you?" Brayden raised his hand in an arc of dismissal and continued to snicker.

"Yes, actually I do. After hearing the voice of the One how could you not believe?"

Brayden looked at Rayne, his eyes growing wide. His smile wavered. "Because I don't believe there is a One. I'm certain that you and your father found a way to stage that little performance for the benefit of the masses, and I won't fall prey to that kind of manipulation. I'm too smart to be fooled by a simple deception. You, of all people, should know that."

Unexpected sorrow rose in Rayne as Brayden walked away snickering and mumbling about the *good joke Uncle Theodor was playing on the masses.*

How could he not see? Rayne asked the One. Shaking his head, he plodded up the stairs to his room. Entering his suite, alarm jolted through him as arms shot forward, wrapping around his waist. He lifted the King's Sword out of the way over his head.

Andrew, oblivious to the sword's danger, had nearly grabbed the blade as he hugged Rayne. "You're so brave. We watched everything from the palace balconies facing the square and heard every word you said. When the One spoke, his voice rumbled through the entire palace. It was amazing."

Shaw and Anne were there, smiling. *They must have watched from the balcony with Andrew.* Once Andrew released him, Shaw came forward and hugged Rayne as well.

"Andrew is right," Shaw said, a knowing look in his eyes. "It took great courage to speak out the truth the way you just did when it flies in the face of our traditions. I'm so proud of you and proud to call you my friend."

Anne smiled in her knowing way and nodded her approval to Rayne.

If Brayden represented those people who would not hear the One's message, Andrew, Shaw, and Anne represented those who would embrace the truth. Rayne couldn't force people to believe. Only the One could soften a heart to see it. All Rayne had to do was present the truth and that was scary enough.

Rayne handed the King's Sword to Andrew. "Please return this to the vault for me?"

"Of course, Your Highness," Andrew said, practically dancing around in his enthusiasm.

After Andrew left, Rayne sat in one of the green leather chairs flanking the fireplace and Boone jumped up next to him, set her paws on his lap, and licked his face. Rayne laughed and all the tension he had been holding melted off his shoulders. He had done it, taken on the mantle of the Light Bringer. Nothing would ever be the same.

He rubbed Boone's ears and told her what a good girl she was.

Shaw and Anne excused themselves, stating that Rayne probably wanted to change, and they would talk with him later. He took a few minutes to play a game of tug of war with Boone over a piece of rope Rayne had knotted in several places. Well, some things hadn't changed. He was still a sixteen-year old boy who enjoyed playing with his dog.

By the time the tug of war game came to an end, Andrew

returned to help Rayne change. He brought a message from King Theodor and Queen Rowena.

"Your Highness," Andrew said, his voice and manner formal. "During the festival, a delegation sent from the Interplanetary Council and made up of representatives from five of the seven worlds, arrived in Westvale. They have requested an audience with the king and queen, and especially the crown prince whom they are calling the Light Bringer.

"His Majesty, King Theodor, desires that you attend a meeting in the small conference room tomorrow morning directly after breakfast. He expects a response to this request to be delivered immediately."

Curious about these people, who they were and what they wanted with him, Rayne said, "His Royal Highness, Prince Rayne will be pleased to attend."

Andrew sent the answer back to the king with one of the other pages.

11

The two men glared at each other—Brayden tall, young, and handsome; Sigmund, feeble and older than should be possible. An undercurrent of heavy, dark magic filled the room and sparked in the unseen realm, as the ancient sorcerer wrestled to keep his power in check. Brayden stared at him; arrogant, oblivious to his own weakness and vulnerability against the power of the elder. Indeed, the arrogance that called up the threat of violence in the ancient being was, in fact, the very thing that protected the young man. His conceit was useful, could be harnessed for the benefit of the demon.

"They were all supposed to be dead, but you failed." Brayden sneered at Sigmund. "You and your big ideas of vengeance. You couldn't even rein in that pathetic cousin of mine long enough to kill Rowena and Theodor, and now he's gone and paraded himself as this Light Bringer character to the masses. Not only have you lost me the crown, my family will be laughed off the continent. How could you let that little idiot outfox you?"

The silence in the room was deafening. Dense as he was, even Brayden recognized the danger in the pregnant stillness; he had overstepped his bounds. Catching Sigmund's eyes, a shiver skittered up Brayden's spine as dark obsidian swirled through the pale silver of the sorcerer's eyes. The man may be ancient, and decaying as they spoke, but he was still more powerful than anyone else Brayden had ever known. Brayden needed to reverse into safer territory.

Then Sigmund spoke, low and intense. "It's the enemy. It's always him. He stands in our way and protects his own."

Brayden stared at Sigmund, his jaw dropping open for a moment, before words spilled out. "You can't really believe that nonsense my cousin spouts. Idiocy. That's nothing more than a myth used to control the commoners. It's not real. There is no One." Brayden chuckled at the very idea.

Sigmund scowled at Brayden. "You're a fool. He's quite real. He's our foe, the only true threat to our plans. If you can't acknowledge his existence, you've proven yourself a bigger fool than I thought you were. Fortunately, I don't need you to think, just do as you're told."

"How dare y—" One look at Sigmund brought Brayden's words to a stuttering stop.

"I? DARE? I *dare* because *you* serve *me*. Think! Who has the power here? Remember who gave you the ability to influence that aunt and uncle of yours. From the time you were a child and you begged me to destroy your cousin, did I deny you? No. It was I who taught you how to make his parents hear your voice with dedication and believe your words as true, while dismissing their own son's words as unworthy of notice. *I* gave that to you, and *I* can take it away.

"*You* are the one who failed in your bid to be officially named Adopted Heir Apparent when I gave you ten years to succeed. If your succession had been announced just days before that infuriating boy decided to defy me, he would have been forced to challenge you for the inheritance. You failed yourself, so don't talk to me about incompetence.

"I tire of this conversation. Order breakfast to be brought here. I loathe having people see me in this decrepit body."

"Why don't you just kill him?" Brayden growled, deep and low in his throat. "Just kill him and be done with it."

"What?"

"Kill the wretched prince. The Light Bringer. The whatever. And be done with it, move forward with our plans."

"Why don't *you?*"

"You know why. If there was even a hint of my involvement, I would lose the crown. No, I can't be linked with any deaths in the royal family, it's too dangerous. So, why don't *you?*"

Sigmund hissed under his breath. "I have certain ... constraints. I can't physically touch the boy, and actual harm to his spirit is forbidden." Sigmund swayed and clutched the edge of a lacquered table. "I am weakened in my current state, punishment from our master for my failure. I must get to Nemora and acquire a new body before I lose this one completely. I can't afford to waste any of my remaining power; it's taking all my energy just to keep this body alive.

"Now, order that breakfast. I must eat to regain my strength, and then you must make arrangements for me to skip to Nemora. You'll have to provide me with a companion; I'm physically too weak to travel alone. The trip from the Shattered Continent drained me."

With teeth clenched and nostrils flaring in the already deformed face, Sigmund pulled himself upright. "Look on me and be afraid Brayden. If this is what our master imposes on me for failure, think what he can do to you." He tottered to Brayden, stood facing him, and wrapped claw-like, icy fingers around Brayden's biceps. "Be still, boy. I must pull energy from you."

Fear turned Brayden's blood cold as uncontrollable, compelling darkness surrounded him. He clamped a hand over his mouth and stifled a scream as his skin blistered where Sigmund held him. Then Brayden found himself lying on the floor and looking up at Sigmund. His upper arms felt as if the skin had been rubbed raw.

"Ah, that's better." The demon sighed. "Remember, you have pledged your loyalty to our master and to me. And though

I may be forgiving, he does not appreciate failure. Do not deceive yourself, the One is our enemy. He is cunning and more powerful than you can imagine. If we are to defeat his Light Bringer, we must find a way to snatch the boy from his protection. That is our only hope. Now get me food; I'm starving."

Brayden sent his page scurrying to the kitchen with orders to bring up food for two. He longed to escape his rooms; the smell of decay coming off Sigmund's corrupted body filled the air and nausea threatened to upturn Brayden's stomach. *Even after pulling power from me, he's decaying by the minute. I can't wait; I must get him out of here.*

"While you breakfast, Sigmund, I'll go make your travel arrangements." Without another word, Brayden held his breath and lunged from his room to the fresh air of the hallway. Seeking to avoid notice, he snuck down the servant's stairwell. Once he gained the shadows of the lower hallways, he hurried through a secret passage, out of the palace, and into the city.

When the page knocked at the door and announced that food had arrived, Sigmund called for him to set the tray down in the hall and leave. Sigmund, now at least able to walk with some stability, brought in the tray, stoked the fire to a roaring blaze, then forced himself to eat every bit of food the page had brought. Brayden would have to fend for himself if he wanted to eat; Sigmund needed the energy.

Three hours later, when Sigmund woke from napping in Brayden's bed, the young lord still hadn't returned. Sigmund narrowed his eyes and circled Brayden's sitting room. His third glass of honeyed sherry sloshed as he turned to the hallway door. *How much longer? It's been hours.* He drummed his fingers against the glass. *If I remain stuck in here much longer, I'll lose my mind.* He paused, pursed his lips. *I know, I'll see what our young princeling is up to. If memory serves, his rooms are next to these. And if anyone does happen to see me, they'd never suspect that the pathetic, old man, wandering lost in the hallways, is really Sigmund of Bainard. This decrepit body is good for that much at least. And if the prince isn't in his rooms, perhaps I'll leave him a message.*

Rayne smiled as he headed back to his rooms with Boone on his heels. With the meeting set for later this morning, his parents hadn't required he breakfast with them. After joining Shaw, Jonathan, and Anne in the library earlier for Lauds, Rayne decided to stop in at the church kitchen to visit Elsie.

"Well if this isn't a pleasant surprise. What are you doing here? Don't you need to be eating with your parents?" She tilted her head and gave Rayne a knowing look Without another word, Elsie fried up a full pan of bacon and cut into a still-warm loaf of bread. When they sat down, she poured two large mugs of milk and asked, "How does it feel to admit the truth of who you are?"

"Strange … and exciting … and terrifying. All at the same time." Rayne met Elsie's eyes. "What do you think?"

"You've certainly given us much to think about. Jonathan isn't the least bit worried; he believes that, given time, people will come to understand and accept what you said. But, I guess that's to be expected since he knew what was coming." She glanced out the window and took a deep breath. "Your words had the ring of truth to them and I am trying to understand what it all means. The idea that the One has a Son is hard enough to accept, but the thought that he would pay my penalty for me is difficult to grasp. It'll take me time. I expect I'm not alone in that."

Rayne nodded. While they spoke about the coming changes the Words would bring about in the church, Rayne downed two of his favorite bacon and honey sandwiches. Thanking Elsie for the meal, Rayne excused himself. Now he needed to return to the palace and change for the meeting with the delegation from the Interplanetary Council.

It was a beautiful autumn day, the air soft with a light chill, the sky a deep azure blue. Though some of the trees he passed still sported random leaves in shades of red and gold, most had already lost their leaves, or held onto a few tattered, brown stragglers that rustled in the breeze. He breathed in the crisp autumn air and kicked at the leaves underfoot, especially when he walked through the many piles. Soon the servants would clear them from the walkways, but this morning Rayne delighted in shuffling through them. The crunching sound they made when they crumbled underfoot tickled his ears, and the acrid scent that permeated the air as they cracked and shattered complemented the autumn chill.

He wondered what Stevie and Sashi were doing this morning and if they had given thought to the message he presented yesterday. He didn't know how most people were responding to his words, but if the few he met on his way back to his rooms now were any indication, at least people were thinking. And that was all he could hope for, to get people to think about the message.

Rayne checked behind to see if a guard was following. He hoped Noah might be on duty so they could talk. Seeing no one, he sighed. Although he appreciated being tail free, he was concerned that Brayden had that much influence over his parents. Once again, the uneasiness that had plagued him for the past week set him to searching over his shoulders, looking for invisible enemies. The muscles in his back twitched, and he fought off the feeling that someone was watching him.

Boone looked up at him and whined. He could tell she sensed his disquiet. It had been simple enough to discount his anxiety as nerves about yesterday's performance and speech, but now that the feeling persisted, Rayne was certain the cause was something more. An almost imperceptible nudge to his spirit prompted him to hurry. Boone raced ahead to the kitchen entrance. The quickest route to his rooms was through the kitchens and up the servant's stairs to the second floor. Nobles and courtiers avoided the servant's stairs, and the staff wouldn't approach him unless he summoned them.

Rayne bounded up the stairs, taking them two at a time but Boone still out distanced him. She topped the stairs and vanished down the hallway toward Rayne's rooms. Within seconds, she was barking an alarm. Rayne leaped the final two steps and charged down the hallway to find Boone growling and snarling at a very old and feeble-looking man who stood in front of the door to Rayne's suite. Her hackles were raised, her teeth bared, and her eyes glued to the man who looked as though he might fall over from fright.

Rayne ran toward Boone, thinking to call her off the old man. But as he got closer, he sucked in a deep breath and slowed. Sigmund's mark seared the skin over his right shoulder blade with an intensity he hadn't felt since the night he had defied the sorcerer. A familiar sensation of dark magic tickled the back of his mind and although it was faint, he couldn't mistake the source. Sigmund. Rayne knew that magical stench too well to mistake it for anything else. But scanning the hallway, he saw no one except the old man, who was now trying to inch along the wall away from Rayne's rooms and Boone.

"Boone," Rayne called. "Here girl." Boone stood fast and refused to move away from the old man.

"Who are you? What are you doing here?" Rayne grabbed Boone's collar, and tried to calm the dog. He struggled to reconcile what he was feeling with what he was seeing, and the dichotomy sent skitters of fear up his spine. The old man smelled like a rotting corpse. *My instincts are telling me that Sigmund is here. But my eyes are seeing a feeble, sickly, old man, teetering against the wall, barely able to stand.* He called up his magic sense, but all he could feel along the searching tendrils was confusion and chaos. Then something rebuffed him.

The man leaned into the wall, hunched over and staring at Rayne with hooded eyes, not saying a word. Rayne wasn't even sure if the old man heard his question. The stranger looked impossibly ancient.

"Can you hear me?" Rayne asked loudly.

Part of him wanted to get closer to the man, to see if he needed help, but a voice inside screamed for him to keep his distance. He grimaced as the burning on his shoulder intensified. Boone continued to snarl and pull at her collar. Rayne had never seen her act this way before. *What should I do?*

"By the seven! What's going on here?" Brayden. The person Rayne least wanted to see. "Stay away from him!"

Brayden's voice was high and angry as he scooted past Rayne and grabbed the man's arm pulling him around Boone.

Rayne's jaw hung loose as he watched Brayden help the strange man down the hallway. Once the two disappeared into Brayden's rooms, his shoulders released the tension they had been holding. After standing and staring at his cousin's door for a minute, thinking how strange the whole incident had been, he shook his head and turned to his own door.

Boone calmed as soon as Brayden and the old man disappeared, and she now looked up at Rayne, wagging her tail.

What was that all about? Who was that old man and why was he at my door? How did he even get into this wing of the palace? Was he lost? Looking for Brayden's rooms and just got lost? But I felt Sigmund's presence. Why? The burning pain in his shoulder evaporated as he entered his rooms.

12

Knowing he was expected to join his parents for the meeting with the Reclamation Committee soon, Rayne called for Andrew as he entered his rooms, wondering where the boy might be. The young page always had clothing set for Rayne and helped him dress, and Rayne now needed his help to get ready. Boone trotted into the bedroom and whined at the foot of the bed. Nerve endings still raw from the incident with the old man, Rayne followed after her. Andrew lay face-up across Rayne's bed, unconscious.

"No," Rayne shouted, his heart seizing in his chest as he rushed to Andrew's side. He reached his palm under Andrew's nose, relieved to feel even, steady breaths. But the boy didn't respond when Rayne called his name or shook him. Rayne needed Anne.

He stopped, shook his head. *No. I need that old man. He did something to Andrew. That's why he was outside my door. And why Boone was acting so strange.* Rayne knew something was off as soon as he had gotten close to the man. *I'll drag that old man from Brayden's rooms and force him to make Andrew right.* Not wanting to leave Andrew alone in his condition, Rayne told Boone to stay, then rushed back out his door and down the hallway to Brayden's rooms.

Pounding his clenched fist on the door, Rayne shouted, "Brayden, Brayden, you no good, two-faced slime. You open this door right now! Brayden! Come on, I know you're in there, open up!"

With all the noise he was making, several curious servants gathered in the hall behind Rayne. Turning to them, Rayne caught sight of Brayden's page standing with the others.

"Go to the library and bring Anne here," Rayne ordered. "Now!"

Turning back to face Brayden's door, he wondered if he should ram the thing with his shoulder. He was about to attempt it when Brayden pulled the door open. Brayden looked like he had just woken up. Dressed in night clothes, he yawned, and ran his hands through his disheveled mess of hair.

"Who dares make this racket at my door? You're making enough noise to wake the dead." His eyes widened as if he just noticed Rayne. "Oh, it's you Little Raynie. What do you mean by pounding on my door and waking me up?"

"Don't play games with me; you weren't sleeping. I talked to you out in this hallway not five minutes ago." Rayne pushed past his cousin, into his rooms.

Rayne scanned the sitting room. The floorplan mirrored his own quarters, except Brayden's rooms were smaller, and his choice of decor set Rayne's teeth on edge. While Rayne's suite was decorated simply, with just a few well-crafted, wood furnishings, and a couple rich carpets in muted tones, Brayden's rooms were ornate. Richly-lacquered and painted furnishings were crammed into every available space. Heavy red and gold flocked wallpaper covered the walls. Rayne's eyes were drawn to a pair of large tapestries flanking the fireplace. Two men, bloody and wearing slave collars, were locked in mortal combat; they reminded him of the deathmatches he had been forced to fight. He shook his head to dispel the images.

Rayne pulled in a swift breath when he entered the bedroom. Tapestries depicting woodland scenes, complete with naked men and women behaving like beasts, hung in abundance, and a bed almost as large as Sigmund's sat in the center of the room. It was built of heavy wood, with posters rising at each corner to brush the red and gold ceiling. Matching patterns of red and gold leaf ran up the four bed posts, making it look as though the ceiling and bed were of one construction.

Setting his shock aside, Rayne ran out to the balcony. Then, still looking for the old man, he returned to the bedroom, knelt and scanned under the bed. The bed clothes sat in a jumbled mess on the floor at the foot of the bed. He walked to the pile and kicked it but found nothing more than a thick pile of sheets, blankets and quilted bed covers.

Brayden followed Rayne into the bedroom and leaned against the wall with crossed arms, scowling at him. Hatred smoldered in his lavender-blue eyes as he watched Rayne searching his rooms. He shadowed Rayne as he returned to the garish outer rooms and proceeded to search any place someone could hide; in cabinets, under couches, behind screens, but to no avail. Rayne could not find the old man. The smoldering remains of what must have been a good-sized blaze sent skitters of foreboding through Rayne. It could mean nothing, the night had been cold, but something about the size of the fire brought back images of Sigmund reclining before roaring flames even in the heat of summer.

Turning to Brayden, Rayne pierced him with smoldering, angry eyes. "Where is he? Where is that old man you helped to your rooms just minutes ago? Where's Sigmund?"

"You must be dreaming, Little Raynie. Or your study of those ancient myths has finally taken your mind," Brayden sneered. "As you can see, I am alone. I was sleeping peacefully until your uncivilized clamor woke me. And Sigmund? Whatever would make you think he's here in my rooms? I don't know what you're trying to accuse me of this time, but obviously you're mistaken. And anyway, which are you seeking, an old man or Sigmund? Or do you think they're both hiding under my bed. Oh, wait! You've already looked there."

A chill skittered up Rayne's spine as Brayden's grin widened into the wolf-like smile Rayne remembered from when they were children. Voices in the hallway drew his attention to the door. Theodor and Rowena walked in with Anne following. Ignoring his parents, Rayne grabbed Anne's hand and dragged her out of the room.

"Rayne, what's wrong?" she asked as they raced down the hallway and into his suite.

"Please. You have to help Andrew. Something's wrong with him. I can't get him to wake up."

Rayne pointed to his page, still lying on the bed where he had left him, Boone now lying next to him, her head on his chest. When Anne approached, Boone jumped down and came to stand by Rayne. Shaw and Jonathan walked in, quietly taking positions next to Rayne, but his parents hadn't followed. They were probably still talking with Brayden. A sinking feeling clawed its way into Rayne's stomach.

Anne gently rested the back of her hand on Andrew's forehead, then felt for a pulse at his wrist. As she was holding his wrist, Andrew's eyelids fluttered open, and he coughed. Relief flooded Rayne and he almost dropped to his knees with the sensation. Anne wrapped her arm around Andrew's back and helped him to sit up, as he coughed and then caught his breath. Studying Andrew's eyes, she asked, "How do you feel?"

The boy shook his head. "I don't know." He looked up at Anne. "What happened? Why are you here?"

"Rayne found you unconscious and called for me. You were still unconscious when I got here and just came to. Do you remember what happened?"

Andrew crinkled his eyes and chewed his bottom lip for a moment. "I remember coming into Prince Rayne's rooms to lay out his clothing for the meeting this morning. I picked out the outfit, and was about to pull it from the wardrobe and lay it out on the bed, but ... but I can't remember what happened after that."

Rayne stepped up next to Anne. "Did you see anyone before that? Someone you didn't recognize hanging around outside my rooms, a very old man?"

Andrew thought again and shook his head. "No Sire, I didn't see anyone."

"Of course you didn't see any old man." A satisfied smirk

split Brayden's face as he walked in, followed by Theodor and Rowena. "There was no old man to see."

Brayden closed on Rayne. "I don't know what kind of game you're playing *little cousin*, but I don't think it's appropriate to scare your parents, and everyone else at the palace for that matter, with tales of nonexistent intruders. From what I've heard, you probably imagined the whole thing in that mangled mind of yours."

"Enough." Theodor stepped between Brayden and Rayne. "Brayden, you are out of line."

Tense silence filled the air. Brayden glared at Rayne, who stared daggers back at his cousin for a moment before turning and kneeling beside Andrew. "It's okay if you don't remember," Rayne said. "Do you feel okay now?"

When Andrew nodded, Rayne rose and faced Anne, Shaw, and Jonathan. "Thank you all for coming right away." He caught Anne's eyes and signed discreetly, *I'll explain later,* then said aloud, "Andrew seems to be fine, why don't you three head back to the library. I'll come by later and talk to you there."

The three bowed their acquiescence and left.

Rayne knelt next to Andrew again. "Are you sure you're okay?" When the boy nodded, he asked, "Do you feel up to taking Boone out for a bit?"

Even though he seemed more subdued than normal, Andrew took Boone and left Rayne's rooms, closing the outer door as he went. Rayne guided Brayden and his parents into the sitting room and once they were alone, he turned to his parents and motioned for them to sit.

Ignoring the offer to sit, Theodor stared at Rayne and, in a cold official voice, said, "Rayne, I don't know what all happened here, but now is not the time to discuss this fiasco. Your mother and I left the delegation waiting in the small conference chamber when we got news you needed us. You will prepare yourself immediately and join us there to continue our meeting in a civilized manner. Then, once we have concluded our business with the delegates, I think it is high time we addressed this discord between you and Brayden."

Taking a moment to cap his emotions, Rayne rubbed his hands over his face, then looked up at his parents. "Certainly Father. Please give me a few minutes to dress. I will join you and Mother in the conference room shortly."

Rayne hated how cold his father's words sounded, but then his response was just as formal. He knew it would do no good to try and confront his parents until after the meeting with the delegation from the Interplanetary Council was over but confront them he would. They needed to know that he was not lying about the old man, and that he had sensed Sigmund right in the palace. Something real had been done to Andrew, and Rayne would not rest until he got to the bottom of the mystery. Brayden was hiding behind his lies, and Rayne burned with indignation at that fact.

Brayden cast a glare at Rayne then turned to leave with Theodor and Rowena. At the door, Rowena turned back to Rayne. "I love you, Son. Even if it doesn't seem so at times, your father and I love you very much." She closed the door quietly behind her, leaving Rayne alone with his thoughts.

13

Stupid! Sending Andrew away now wouldn't rank as one of my bright-est decisions. Rayne struggled with his clothing. How could something so simple as dressing be so confusing? *Why couldn't whatever happened to Andrew have happened after he had set out an appropriate outfit for this meeting? It's morning. Evening clothes won't work. But what will? Which of these outfits are for morning wear? So many clothes to choose from.*

After pulling a couple armloads of clothing from the small room that served as a closet and dumping them on the floor, he found an outfit that Andrew had dressed him in for a similar situation. He wasted no time changing though he grimaced at foregoing his desired bath. *Let's just hope I'm acceptable as is.* Rayne glanced at his simple tunic and leggings sticking out from under a pile of fancy clothing on his bed. *If only I could just wear them; life was simpler when I wore the same clothes all the time.*

Less than fifteen minutes later, Rayne sprinted to the small conference room down the hall from the main audience chamber. Sounds of conversation droned from behind the door, and, with a short bow, the guard stationed there pulled it open. Rayne squared his shoulders and shaking his hands to loosen the tension he held, walked in. More than a dozen people sat around the conference table chatting. King Theodor was seated at the head of the table in a chair that resembled a scaled-down throne, with Queen Rowena sitting to his right.

Noting the seat to his father's left had been left open, Rayne slipped into the chair. A surge of relief filtered through him at Brayden's absence. As Rayne took his seat, the voices quieted, replaced by the scraping of chairs. He looked up to see every one of the delegates rise and bow to him. He swallowed the lump trying to block his throat and fumbled with his fingers.

"We are honored by your presence, Light Bringer," a tall, white-haired woman with a serene smile murmured as she bowed even more deeply.

Rayne dropped his hands to his lap, his fingers continuing their nervous fidget as the delegates stood staring at him. He shifted his eyes to his father for direction. Inclining his head, Theodor said, "Thank you delegates. My son is not accustomed to such displays of honor and he would ask that you all be seated."

Rayne dropped his eyes from his father to study the polished table top. Another scraping of chairs and a rustle of clothing, and the delegates sat. The old woman who had spoken, looked at Rayne with an understanding smile and, in a deep, quiet voice, said, "I apologize if our actions took you by surprise and caused any discomfort. Some of your history has been explained to us since our arrival in Westvale and we understand how your upbringing would leave you inexperienced in areas of protocol. Please do not take it amiss if we choose to honor you. We are just so humbled to be in the presence of the prophesied Light Bringer that I fear we are easily excited."

Rayne smiled back; he liked this old woman. She spoke with an honesty to her words that was reflected in her open brown eyes, and there was a transparency about her spirit that spoke to Rayne of kinship. Feeling a bit more comfortable, he kept eye contact with her. "I am humbled by your honor. Thank you for understanding. Please don't let me interrupt your discussion."

"You haven't interrupted anything, yet," Theodor said. "As the delegates are here to speak with you, we were just catching up with what the Interplanetary Council is currently deliberating on. These men and women met with the council less than a week ago. But now that you have finally arrived, we can proceed."

Theodor looked to the old woman Rayne now suspected was the leader of the delegation. "Madam Ria, would you explain the purpose of this delegation and the reason for requesting this meeting?"

"I would be delighted to do so." Madam Ria motioned to encompass those around the table. "We are a mixed group of representatives from Arisima, Nemora, Corylus, Sorial, and Amathea.

"Three years ago, each of us was touched by a word from the One calling us to Providence, the capital of Amathea. Most of us responded immediately. A few ignored the call. Finally, last year, the One brought the single remaining holdout from Amathea to Providence. Although three representatives from each of the seven worlds were called, the representatives from Glacieria and Veres never arrived; and though we tried, we were unable to reach them. As I'm sure you're aware, Glacieria has become quite inhospitable, and Sorial has cut off all communications with Veres. We weren't terribly surprised when no one came from those worlds.

"Initially, we were unsure of the One's purpose in calling us together, but soon after the arrival of the representatives from Arisima, we learned of the ancient prophecy. We formed this Reclamation Committee under the auspices of the Interplanetary Council to study its meaning and to determine if the time had come for it to be fulfilled.

"Nearly five months ago, while we were together, the One spoke to us as a group. He told us the time had come and we were to call forth his Light Bringer. The words the One spoke to us were these:

"In the fullness of time the Light Bringer will arise. The lost will be found and he will bring to light my seven words hidden on the seven worlds and I will guide his steps. Sing for joy my people, the broken will be restored; the lost will be found. When the broken is restored and the lost is reclaimed, he will bind the living darkness. Know my people, the fullness of time has arrived; the time is now. Arise my Light Bringer.'"

After waiting a couple minutes as the words echoed in the minds of those present, Madam Ria continued, "Of course at about the same time we heard news of the return of the Crown Prince of Corylus and we decided to bring the matter before the Interplanetary Council. They agreed with our assessment that His Royal Highness, Crown Prince Rayne, was most likely the One's chosen Light Bringer, and so they sent us here to meet with you and your parents."

Madam Ria looked to the man seated on her right. "Deven, I think you would be able to explain what is required of the Light Bringer better than I can. Would you be so kind as to tell His Highness what we have come to believe about his calling?"

Deven reminded Rayne of Shaw; he was short with nut-brown skin, medium length, curly brown hair, and eyes so dark they looked black. He was dressed in brown robes similar to the ones Shaw always wore. As Rayne looked at him, he noticed a kind of crystal clearness to the man's spirit that was similar to what he had sensed in Madam Ria.

Deven cleared his throat and picked up the narrative. "Your Majesties." He inclined his head to Theodor and Rowena. "Your Royal Highness and Light Bringer." He inclined his head to Rayne, a small smile lifting the sides of his mouth.

"Madam Ria has asked me to speak of the calling on the Light Bringer as we understand it. We have pieced together his path as best we could, based on information gleaned from texts we studied from Corylus, Nemora, and, of course, Arisima.

"Our understanding is that Words of the One are hidden on each world. Seven worlds, seven Words. Your task is to travel to each world and recover its hidden scroll. Once the scrolls are reclaimed, you are to bring to light their meaning. Something like what we witnessed you do yesterday in the square, a revelation to the people of the One's truth. We believe that each world has its own specific Word, but that all the Words work together. And together they apply to all the worlds of Ochen. As though they were once a unified whole that had been broken apart. Once all seven are brought to light, the threads of this truth will weave together. We think that it is through this weaving of the Words, that you will bind the living darkness. At least this is our working premise. I must admit however, our knowledge is limited, Sire."

Rayne's brow crinkled in concentration. "I'm supposed to find one scroll on each world? Scrolls that have been well hidden since the Hundred Years War?"

"Yes," Deven replied. "We believe so."

"And if they have been hidden so well for so long somewhere on a whole world, how am I supposed to find these scrolls with no clues as to their locations?"

"Well, Sire, the population on each of the seven worlds is largely confined to the continents where the skipping portals are located. Travel and trade have always been easier through the portals rather than across land, or water, so people have always congregated within proximity of the portals.

"The capitals of each world were founded at skipping line portal sites for this reason, and most other cities and towns were then founded on the same continents as these portal cities. Though there may be small smatterings of people on other continents, we believe the scrolls would have been hidden in close proximity to the portal cities.

Rayne shook his head and crossed his arms over his chest. "Even with the populated areas limited by continent, you must realize the hopelessness of finding a single scroll on each world. It would have taken me months to find one hidden scroll in Coronus's library if I didn't have Warren's directions. I can't envision finding six more on six different worlds with no directions." Rayne shook his head again. "No, I don't think this is possible. Could you have missed something? Like directions?"

Raising a finger for attention, a petite young woman with an abundance of curly, auburn hair piled on top of her head, looking almost as young as Rayne himself, said in a voice so soft he could barely hear it, "Sire, if you please, excuse me."

Focusing on her, Rayne smiled when, once again, he sensed kinship. He nodded for her to continue.

"But y-y-you forget, Your H-h-highness," she stuttered and then stopped. She pulled in a deep breath, closed her eyes, and continued so quickly that the words ran into each other. "The prophecy says the One will guide your steps. You don't need directions if he is guiding you."

Rayne looked at the girl in admiration. Not only did she obviously overcome a severe shyness to speak out, but she spoke a truth he needed to hear despite her fear. "What's your name?"

"Blossom. You can call me Blossom; I'm from Derren on Nemora."

"Thank you Blossom of Derren. You make a good point. If the One is guiding my steps, even someone like me can't go too far wrong."

The smile Blossom directed at Rayne stuttered almost as much as her words. She lowered her eyes to her hands resting on the table, and nervously played with two rings on her fingers.

Theodor asked Madam Ria and the other delegates about logistics and plans like time frame, which world should be the visited first, how travel on the different worlds should be arranged, and how many people should accompany Rayne.

While his father was occupying the delegates, Rayne took time to study each of them. He tried to figure which three came from which world, but except for those from Arisima, who all wore brown robes similar to Shaw's, he couldn't decide who came from where.

As he studied them, he contrived to meet each one's eyes and every time he made eye contact, that assurance of transparency and kinship filled him. He attributed this feeling of affinity, or bonding, to the fact that they had all been called by the One, just as he had been called.

One man avoided eye contact; every time Rayne glanced at him, he would catch a quick look of guilt before the man looked away. Curious now, he studied the delegate. He was a large, older man, still muscular with thin, gray hair cropped close to his head camouflaging an area of baldness on the top, and eyes the color of the cathedral's stone walls.

Pressure to find the source of this man's discomfort seized Rayne, tightening his chest. Every other delegate met his eyes with eager warmth, but this man was hiding something. Just as Rayne decided to question the man, his father called for a break, and invited everyone to the dining hall for the midday meal.

Rayne stood to the side of the door as the delegates filed past until the large man moved to leave the room. Touching his arm lightly, Rayne said, "May I have a word with you before you leave?"

Without meeting his eyes, the man nodded, and they stepped to the side as everyone else filtered out into the hall. When they were alone, Rayne walked back to the table and motioned the man to a chair across from him as he sat.

14

ʼʼ

Rayne waited for a couple minutes saying nothing, hoping the man might speak. But he just sat with down-cast eyes, studying his hands the way Blossom had studied hers earlier. Rayne would have to initiate the conversation.

"What's your name?" Rayne figured he would start with a simple question.

Without looking up the man answered, "Travis, Your Highness. My name's Travis Illk."

"I'm not good at playing games, Travis. I wasn't raised to it. So let's just get this out in the open. What are you hiding? I know there's something. You're the only delegate who couldn't meet my eyes. If I can't trust you, how can I be sure I can trust any of the others? What are you hiding?"

Travis ducked his head when Rayne spoke, then sat quietly for a long while. Rayne waited; he wouldn't let the man go until he answered the question. After several minutes passed, Rayne got up and moved next to the window, looking out, watching.

When he was troubled, the old habit came back without thought. And between this silent man and what happened already that morning, Rayne was troubled. He had put his suspicions from earlier aside while he focused on the meeting with the delegates, but now uneasiness wormed its way into his spirit and twisted his empty stomach. And still Travis sat.

Rayne was looking out the window when he heard sniffling behind him. Was the big man crying?

With a sigh, Rayne sat across from him again and Travis finally met Rayne's questioning eyes. Rayne felt the same transparency he had felt from the other delegates as he looked into the tear-stained eyes; he hadn't expected that. The feeling of kinship was here. Whatever Travis's secret was; it didn't have anything to do with the Reclamation Committee.

"You have to tell me. I know you've got some kind of secret and I can't just ignore that," Rayne finally said. "You know I can have you removed from the committee; they would do that if I asked. And, as Prince of Corylus, I could have you arrested as well."

"Yes. And it would be just." Travis looked at Rayne with deeply pained eyes. "I deserve to be arrested, to be imprisoned or any other punishment you would deem proper, even death. Because, you see, I was the man Sigmund hired ten years ago to kidnap you from this palace on your sixth birthday." Travis dropped his face into his hands and silent sobs shook his body.

Rayne's mouth dropped open and he shook his head, stunned by Travis's words. *Could it be true? Could Travis have done what he claimed? Was this man sitting before him still working for Sigmund?*

"Are you working for Sigmund now?" Rayne asked harshly.

"No. No, Sire. Just that once. Ten years ago, when he paid me to deliver you."

"Tell me." Rayne's voice sounded hollow in his ears and his face was a stone mask. "Tell me exactly what you did."

Travis was about to speak when the noise of approaching people sounded outside the door; his parents and the other delegates were returning. Scowling and rubbing his hands over his thighs in agitation, Rayne tried to process what he just heard and decide how to handle the situation.

By the time Theodor entered, Rayne had made the decision

to continue his talk with Travis in private. He stood and addressed his father. "Would you please excuse us Father. Mr. Illk and I have been involved in an important conversation and I beg your leave for us to speak elsewhere while you continue meeting with the other delegates."

Travis interrupted. "No Your Highness, please. I have held the truth from everyone for too long now. Your willingness to shield me from a public confession humbles me; it is more than I deserve. You truly are the One's chosen Light Bringer. But I need to acknowledge what I did ten years ago and face the consequences of my actions. I need to face the truth openly."

The committee members moved to their chairs and began questioning each other about what was happening. Once they were settled, Rayne said, "Mr. Illk, tell us your story. The whole story. From the beginning."

Travis nodded and pulled in a deep breath. "You all know I was the last person to respond to the call of the One. I didn't join you until last year." Travis looked at each member of the delegation, before glancing at Rayne, who nodded for him to continue. "There was a reason I resisted. Many of you know I didn't come to belief in the One until late in life, but what you don't know is the kind of person I was before then. I was the man wealthy individuals hired if they wanted to acquire a specialty slave in a confidential and discreet manner, with no complications. I was good at my work and knew how to keep quiet. I provided a service and was paid very well.

"Ten years ago, I was approached by a man named Marcus Ponce who worked for Lord Sigmund of Bainard."

Rowena gasped and covered her mouth with a hand; Theodor rose from his seat an oath on his lips.

Rayne watched his parents' reactions with understanding. This was as hard on them as it was on him, maybe even harder. For ten years Rayne hadn't known the truth of who he was. He believed the lies Sigmund had implanted. For ten years his parents suffered the pain of knowing their son had been taken without knowing where he was or if he was still alive. But Travis's story needed to be told and heard. "I know this hurts to hear, Mother, Father, but the One has called Mr. Illk to this group for a reason. We need to hear the whole story. Please Mr. Illk, continue."

Rowena and Theodor sat, eyes fixed on Travis as he continued his story. "Ten years ago, Sigmund of Bainard paid me a king's ransom to kidnap a prince. I had never been paid such an excessive fee before and I knew at my age I couldn't continue in my trade much longer. This one fee would allow me to retire in comfort, and more. So I took the job.

"Sigmund made arrangements for easy access into the palace and for a guide to lead me out, so the abduction went smoothly. As arranged, the young prince was already drugged when I got there. I loaded him into the sack I brought and then followed Sigmund's guide through a secret passage and out of the palace. I left Westvale to meet with a manipulator in a cave up the coast, but when I found the cave, the manipulator wasn't there. While I was waiting, the prince began to wake."

At the mention of a manipulator Rowena shuddered. "The wire," she whispered. "I remember the heinous thing. It was still in Rayne's neck the night he returned. I felt the power and darkness in it. The spell that blocked his memories and his ability to speak. I destroyed it that night."

Travis stared at the table for a bit before he began again. "It was his eyes. I don't think I will ever forget your eyes staring up at me. Your pain and fear, Your Highness." He breathed deeply again and continued, his eyes on Rayne's. "The manipulator finally arrived, a horrible excuse of a human being. I was no better. I knew what was being done. I couldn't even watch. I stood there, holding you still for the man, listening to your sobs as that monster did his brutal work, and did nothing to help you. Nothing! And you just a little child! I wanted my money. I ignored your pain for my profit. When the manipulation was done and I worked up the courage to look, you just sat there with empty eyes. I knew the ensorcelled wire was designed to take your memories and your voice, but nothing prepared me for how empty you would look. I'm sorry. I'm so, so sorry."

Travis covered his face with his hands regret pouring off him. After a couple minutes Rayne prompted him to continue.

"Ponce came. I got my payment with a bonus for a job well done. Ha!" He laughed harshly. "A job well done, can you imagine that?"

Travis shook his head, the struggle to keep his emotions in check written in the lines on his face. With a goan, he continued. "I rode away with my money. I left you alone with him. I knew what that fiend was and still I left you alone with him. I rode off thinking to forget. I had done it before you see, put a bad job behind me. Never thought about it again, never let it bother me. But I couldn't get you out of my mind. For weeks, I would wake in the night with your eyes haunting my dreams. When I could stand it no longer, I skipped back onto Corylus to try and find you. I returned to Sigmund's manor, but you weren't there. Everyone was gone. The place was empty and closed up.

"I spent some time questioning contacts to see if I could find what Sigmund had done with you, but I couldn't find a trace of where you might be. I thought at that point he had probably killed you. So, thinking it made no sense to pursue the matter further, I returned to Amathea and tried to move on. But your eyes still haunted me; awake or asleep, they accused me.

"That was when I heard the voice of the One for the first time. Why he would choose to speak to someone like me, I will never understand, but he did. I ended up giving away all I earned from kidnapping you, every bit of it. I couldn't live with that blood money; every time I thought about how I obtained that money, it made me sick. I was no longer the man I had been.

"Then, about five years ago, I took the funds I had left from prior jobs and started a home for orphans. I thought maybe if I could help them, I could atone for the evil I brought to you and so many others. I hoped the pain and fear I saw in your eyes that night would stop haunting me. The One has blessed that home. Many girls and boys who might have died or been sold into slavery otherwise are now living good lives because I couldn't wipe your pain from my memory.

"Three years ago, the One spoke to me again. I ignored his call to join the group forming in Providence; I couldn't accept that I could be part of such a gathering. Then last year, I could no longer ignore his call. I left the care of the children to a young man with a heart to help them and sought out the Reclamation Committee. By that time, I had believed in the One for several years. How could I not? I knew that someday I would have to face the consequences of what I had done.

"And so I came to study the prophecy and to understand that it spoke of Theodor's heir. I knew the royal couple never had another child, and I thought you were dead. I convinced myself that whoever was chosen as adopted heir must be the true Light Bringer. But the prophecy was specific. The more I studied, the more it bothered me. The prophecy speaks of a descendent, not just a political successor. I knew I was living a lie." Travis paused and looked around at the committee members. "I lived with you, studied and shared everything with you. I came to love you as brothers and sisters. All the while believing you were dedicated to a prophecy I had ... already ... destroyed. But the One wouldn't let me go." Facing Rayne again, Travis said, "Then, when we heard the news of your return, my hope was born anew. The One had performed a miracle.

"I'm ready now to pay for my crimes. I will accept any punishment you deem fit for all the pain and suffering I caused you, my prince."

Rayne sat quietly staring out the window with unseeing eyes, hands clenching and unclenching, as Travis ended his story. He trembled with the effort to control his desire to see Travis punished for stealing his childhood, for delivering him into the evil that was Sigmund, and his need to punish the kidnapper who had caused his parents so much pain. But as he nursed his fury, the small interior voice of the One spoke and he felt peace spreading through his spirit, softening his rage. Rayne recalled hearing the words spoken once before, the first time he lifted the King's Sword. *You too have spilled blood. Vengeance does not belong to you.*

Rayne spoke to the voice in his spirit. *What! You mean I*

shouldn't seek justice for what was done to me. Tell me, is it vengeance or justice to demand he pay for his actions; a punishment he justly deserves? Have I judged you by what you deserve? The voice gently replied. *Or have I not instead given you my mercy and grace? Think on this my child, your desire for vengeance arises from darkness; not from light. Trust.* In that moment Rayne knew what he needed to do; he had to trust the One's judgement, not his own. But it was hard, too hard. Letting go of what seemed just and right, and his own self-righteous anger, wasn't easy. The man had caused him unimaginable pain. Rayne struggled, caught between his inability to forgive and his gratitude that he had been forgiven. But, in the end, he knew he needed to trust the One. Letting go of the rage and his desire to crush the man who had stolen his childhood was one of the hardest things he had ever done. But it was the right thing to do. And as he released his need, he felt the One's approval. Joy and peace rose in his spirit.

After Travis finished his story, minutes of silence stretched by; no one spoke or moved. Finally, Theodor rose with a face like stone, cold eyes glaring down at the man who had just confessed to stealing his only son, his heir. The sound of Rayne's chair moving back drew Theodor's attention.

Rayne rose and gazed at his father. His words came in a soft whisper. "Father. Please stand with me on this. Trust me. I know we have not agreed on many things these last few weeks, but I need you to trust me in this. Allow me to judge here even though that judgement officially belongs to you."

Theodor turned, and Rayne willed him to understand. The king's eyes softened, and he nodded his compliance. "I will trust you in this, Son. I, Theodor, King of all Ochen, officially entrust the sentencing for this crime to Crown Prince Rayne." He sat down, reaching for Rowena's hand.

Turning from Theodor and looking directly at Travis, Rayne said, "'No one is without guilt. No one is worthy. The Son alone is without guilt and the Son alone is worthy. He makes us worthy by taking our guilt and giving us his righteousness.'"

He pulled in a deep breath and continued. "The One spoke these words to me when I was so consumed by the darkness of my life I thought I didn't deserve to live let alone be his Light Bringer. He helped me to see that I couldn't earn his forgiveness. It was a gift from him through the already made sacrifice of his Son. He took all my guilt, brought me out of the darkness that was destroying me, and gave me his light."

Rayne paused, swallowing at the weight of the words he spoke. "How could I accept this amazing gift of his forgiveness, when I did not deserve his mercy, and yet deny my forgiveness to others? Deny mercy to you?" Rayne paused again for a moment, staring at Travis. "The One reminded me that vengeance belongs to him alone because only he can see into the heart of a person. And the truth is, if I did judge you, my judgement would not come from a place of righteous understanding, but from a need for vengeance."

Rayne waited a moment to allow his words to sink into the thoughts of everyone sitting around the table and to cap his emotions. "Travis Illk, are you truly sorry for the part you played in the crime of kidnapping the Crown Prince of Ochen—for kidnapping me—ten years ago, and delivering me to Sigmund?"

His gaze on his hands twisting on the table, Travis nodded, but then rasped out, "Yes, yes. Yes, Your Highness, I am truly sorry."

"I believe your life these last few years has been evidence of your changed heart. And I also believe that your repentance was a gift from the One. You answered his call on your life. As I have been given the authority by King Theodor to pass judgement on you, I will do so now.

"Travis Illk, you are forgiven for the crime of kidnapping me as a child." Rayne could hear murmurs around the table and his mother's intake of breath. "And now, having been officially judged, you can no longer be punished for that crime.

"But—Travis—there is still restitution owed to the people of Ochen. The One has claimed you and placed you in this committee of reclamation. I call you now to serve the people of Ochen by serving this committee, and by aiding me in my role as Light Bringer. These are the tasks the One has set for you; I will not question his wisdom."

Now that he had finished speaking, self-consciousness set Rayne's fingers to twitching as everyone stared at him. He stumbled back into his chair and sat down hard. He was aware of the overarching quiet of the room and wondered how his parents were reacting to his words. He looked surreptitiously to his right trying to read his father's expression, but Theodor was closed to him, his father's face a mask, an unreadable blank. Beyond his father, he could only see his mother in profile with no indication of approval or disappointment.

Across the table, Travis sat with his face buried in his hands. But no one spoke and Rayne hoped he hadn't misunderstood the One and made the wrong decision. Then Theodor rose and in a coldly official voice, announced, "We are finished here for today. You are dismissed."

15

As the committee filed from the room, each member reached out to Rayne and offered support and thanks for his mercy. Despite the delegates' approval, Rayne was intensely aware of the silence rolling off his parents. The door closed. He was alone with his mother and father—and the penetrating quiet. He waited.

After several minutes passed in silence, Theodor ground out his displeasure. "Perhaps if you would show as much interest in my judgements during open audiences as Brayden has, you would understand the necessity of punishing those guilty of crimes against Corylus in a proper manner." Theodor stood and began pacing. "The man sits there and confesses to a crime that harmed not only us as a family, but all Corylus—no, the entire planetary system—and you forgive him? Just like that, you blithely forgive that criminal. What were you thinking?"

Rayne cringed as his father's intensity increased with every syllable until his final word was released as a powerful roar. It was the first time his father had raised his voice since Rayne returned, and the disapproval that royal voice projected dropped a rock in Rayne's chest.

"I prayed to the One for guidance." Rayne swallowed hard, his voice barely a whisper. "It wasn't my forgiveness to give, it was the One's."

"You're right. It wasn't your forgiveness to give," Theodor rumbled, zeroing in on just those words. "It should have gone before the Interplanetary Court. Now I am bound by your decision, as is the Court."

Fisting his hands while struggling to keep his voice even, Rayne asked, "Then are you rescinding your promise to back me in this?"

"What?" The word came out as an indistinct growl as Theodor stopped pacing and turned smoldering eyes on Rayne. "When I agreed to stand with you on this, I trusted you would make a wise decision about the man's punishment, something the court could understand and accept. Your decision to forgive him sends the message that you will be a weak ruler. You must never be perceived as weak, especially not by those on the Interplanetary Council, or the judges of the Interplanetary Court."

"Following the voice of the One is not weakness." The old spark of rebellion began to smolder in Rayne. "I thought you would understand my decision. It was based on his guidance and the very words I spoke about forgiveness yesterday. If I, the One's chosen Light Bringer, can't be an example of forgiveness, how can I bring a message of forgiveness?"

With a sigh, Theodor returned to his chair and sat. "If you were just the Light Bringer that argument would be valid, but you are also the Crown Prince of Corylus and all Ochen. You must think things through before you act, Son." Theodor's voice softened, his desire to help Rayne understand evident in his posture.

"I'm sorry if I've disappointed you Father, truly. I will try to do better in the future. Perhaps I would learn more about making proper judgements if I took Brayden's place by your side when you hold open audiences." Rayne let the statement hang, hoping his Father would take up the suggestion, needing to create some distance between his father and his cousin.

Theodor pursed his lips and contemplated Rayne; his eyes

narrowed. He shook his head. "Brayden is a quick study, always has been, as well as a fine student of interplanetary politics. He's already quite an astute politician and I value his judgement. He will be an important political ally for you in the future. For now, we will leave things as they stand."

Rowena had risen when Theodor returned to his seat. She walked across the room and turned to lean against the table by the windows, watching Theodor and Rayne with folded arms. In the quiet after Theodor's statement, she said, "I, like your father, am disappointed in your decision to forgive Travis Illk. You have much to learn if you expect to be a good king. But as the judgement has already been handed down in front of witnesses, there is nothing we can do to change that. In the future, please consult with your father or me, or even Brayden, before you make such rash decisions."

"Yes." Theodor drew out the word. "Speaking of Brayden, enlighten your mother and me. What exactly happened this morning? He said you woke him from a sound sleep. Pounded on his door, created an uproar, and then accused him of sheltering Sigmund. Sigmund? Really? Either him or some old man, Brayden wasn't certain. He was quite confused and upset. And why did you accuse him of having something to do with your page passing out?

"I don't understand this animosity you harbor toward your cousin. He has been nothing but supportive of you since he returned to Westvale, while you have taken every opportunity to disparage him. Brayden is an exceptional young man, a credit to his family. He's bright, eager to learn, and quite capable in all areas of rule. Explain yourself."

Frustration rose in Rayne's chest like a flow of hot lava, propelling him up from his chair and past common sense. With an internal snarl, he released what had been tearing at him for weeks. "Don't you remember what it was like when I first returned? Before Brayden came. How we were a family? You opened your hearts to me because, even though I was a stranger, I was still your son. I felt loved and valued—trusted. I don't think you will ever understand how much I needed you to trust me—how much I still do.

"But that all changed when Brayden arrived. From the moment he returned to Westvale, you two have been different." Rayne paused, walked to the window then turned back to face his parents. "Every morning for the last month I've joined you for breakfast and you've challenged me about my accusations against Brayden. But I haven't changed my story, or backed away from it, have I? I need you to trust that I am telling you the truth, that I wouldn't lie. I know I said I could accept you trusting him more than you trust me, but if I've lied, that's the lie; I can't accept losing your trust to him of all people. It hurts." He shook his head.

"If I can't get you to believe me about Brayden's actions the night of the dinner, I'm pretty sure you won't care for what I have to say about this morning. And that scares me, because I don't know how to reach you where Brayden is concerned. He's dangerous and you refuse to see it."

Rayne wanted to say more, explain about Brayden and the old man, and sensing Sigmund this morning. But each time he spoke his cousin's name, his parent's expressions grew harder, more distant. He felt as if an invisible gulf was growing between his parents and himself. The sensation was so strong; it was like they were being physically sucked away and he had no defenses or weapons to fight that. It tugged up other memories, scarred remains of fear and Aunt Cailyn convincing Rayne to lie to his parents and take the blame for things Brayden had done. Rayne pulled in a deep breath and snapped his mouth shut. Talking was only driving the wedge deeper.

"Well, whatever happened the night Brayden returned, you must have misunderstood and built it up in your mind to something other than what it was." Rowena frowned. "Brayden's side of the story differs greatly from yours and several of the nobles in attendance that night confirm his version of the incident. Ruthie says nothing happened." Rowena raised her eyebrows and waited a moment with a look of quiet expectation. "And ... you have been unable to produce even one witness to attest to your side of the story. We've pointed this out on numerous occasions; according to the witnesses, you were the one who attacked Brayden's friends without provocation. What are we supposed to think?" She paused, her eyes rising to meet Rayne's. "But we're ready to set that aside as it is in the past, as long as you are willing to drop this vendetta against your cousin."

Rowena moved to sit next to Theodor once again and a smile crossed her lips. "You played together so well when you were children. There were so many times when your wild nature would lead you into trouble and Brayden protected you from the consequences. Even now I remember how he tried to lead you to make better choices and be a good example for you. It makes me laugh to think of it now; you really were a troublemaker, and quite the accomplished little liar even then."

"No." The cry erupted like the call of a wounded animal, driven by pain, before Rayne could harness it. "No." Rayne lowered his voice, striving to control his emotions. "I wasn't the liar. It was Brayden. It was always Brayden. He would make the trouble and then force me to take the punishment. He lied then and he's lying still. Why can't you see that?"

Rowena chuckled, a light airy sound. "Oh, Rayne, I think I would remember better than you. My memories were never tampered with."

A potent mix of pain and anger bubbled through Rayne's veins at the lacerating words, hot and demanding. He lashed out. "Your memories didn't need to be tampered with; you were already being controlled. I don't know how, but Brayden's been manipulating you since before I was taken. I remember. Ever since he arrived in Westvale, I've been remembering things. Like how he would lie to your face and smile that big innocent smile and you believed whatever lie he fed you. You *always* believed whatever he said back then, *always* took his side. And you still accept, without question, whatever fabrication he feeds you now. How can you be so dimwitted?"

"Enough," Theodor roared, rising and slamming the table with his fist. "Rayne, how dare you speak to your mother with such disrespect. You insist that no matter what you say, we won't believe you; and then you use that as an excuse for not telling us what happened this morning. How can we even decide to trust you if you won't trust us with your version of what happened? Brayden has already told us his side of the story. He had no problem telling us what happened."

"Telling you *his version* of what happened, which has nothing to do with the *truth* of what happened. You're being used by him. I don't know how, but he's lying, and you would rather believe him than me." Willing his parents to listen to him, Rayne sighed and pleaded, "Won't you at least think about it? Try to search out the truth instead of just taking Brayden's word? Please?"

Theodor and Rowena stared at him, saying nothing, eyes like darkened windows, expressions like stone.

The spark in Rayne flared. Old fear and anger rose, driving him to shout, "Stop being so stupid!"

The room went quiet again. Rowena and Theodor's silent disapproval smothering Rayne.

How could I have lost their approval so quickly? Rayne lowered his eyes to the floor, automatically assuming his old posture of submission as a lump of burning regret grew in his chest.

"Your attitude is unacceptable young man," Theodor's voice was cold veredium. "Go to your rooms and take time to think about the proper way to address your parents and sovereigns. We have suffered your insolence long enough. You are remanded to your suite until breakfast tomorrow morning. At that time, I expect you to have drafted a formal apology for your behavior not only toward your mother and me, but your cousin as well. Go. You are dismissed."

16

Rayne stormed out of the conference room and headed to his suite, stomping and wishing he could hit something. He thought briefly of defying his father, going to the barracks training grounds and losing himself in a sword dance but realized that would be a mistake. His parents were angry enough already and he didn't need to make matters worse by giving free-rein to his rebellious nature and disobeying his father's order.

Not wanting to talk to anyone, he left the main corridor and headed back toward the kitchens to take the servants' stairs up to the second level, like he had done earlier that morning. It didn't seem possible that was just a few hours ago. He felt as if a lifetime had passed since he last climbed those stairs, so much had happened.

He was about to round a corner when Brayden's voice sounded from just ahead. He couldn't quite make out the words but Brayden's presence in this hallway could only mean trouble. He stopped and quietly inched forward.

"You must miss Nemora very much since you've been tied up with this Reclamation Committee for so long. Perhaps you should take a break and visit home for a time."

"Oh no, I c-c-couldn't my lord. My duties on the Reclamation Committee are too important, especially now that the Light B-b-bringer has come. And besides, the s-s-skip is so expensive."

Rayne recognized the voice; Blossom. Brayden was talking to Blossom of Derren. He wondered if they knew each other from Nemora. Knowing Brayden, it seemed unlikely, but he couldn't be sure that they hadn't met before.

"Well, perhaps I could help you with that," Brayden said. "All you committee people take your work so seriously. I am certain you deserve a break. I do have priority skipping rights and would be honored to help someone as important as you Lady Blossom. I'm quite curious about what you people are studying. I don't suppose you would consider joining me in my suite for something to drink? Maybe even a quiet meal? You could tell me all about your important work."

Rayne stepped around the corner and coughed lightly. Blossom startled, then curtsied. Brayden flashed an insolent grin. "Oh. If it isn't the vaunted Light Bringer himself. Such an unexpected honor."

"Miss Blossom, please rise. I need to talk to my cousin for a bit," Rayne said. "Would you excuse us?"

"Yes, S-s-sire. But please, I'm sorry. I got lost in the hall and don't know how to g-g-get back."

Attempting to set the nervous lady at ease, Rayne gave her what he hoped was an encouraging smile. "I'll share my short-cut with you. You're standing next to the kitchens here. Just go back through this doorway, cut through both kitchens and down the hallway opposite. It will bring you out on a pathway. Follow that path and it will take you to the church buildings behind the cathedral. You are staying in church housing, aren't you?"

Blossom curtsied again and nodded, then hurried into the kitchen. Rayne turned to face Brayden, his still smoldering anger rousing the latent darkness within him. He wanted so badly to wipe the leering, wolf-like smirk off his cousin's face. Rayne struggled against the desire to hit Brayden and he curled his fingers into fists. A vision of Brayden at the end of his sword filled his mind and drove Rayne to say coldly, "We need to talk, *cousin*. Perhaps you would care to join me in a practice match at the training fields?"

Brayden's smirk morphed into the full wolf smile Rayne remembered. "I think that would be most interesting and I do seem to have some free time on my hands, now that you have rescued the fair Miss Blossom from my *nefarious schemes*." He chuckled. "Why don't we change and then meet at the far ring, away from prying eyes? We can talk in private there. How long will it take you to get ready without that squeaky little page of yours? About fifteen minutes?"

"Fifteen minutes suits me just fine." Rayne turned his back on Brayden and stormed off, still fighting the urge to punch his cousin. *Right on the nose. Maybe you won't be so attractive to innocent girls with a broken nose.*

Walking into his suite, Rayne was surprised to find Andrew and Boone still gone. *How did Brayden know Andrew hadn't come back yet?*

At least he didn't need Andrew's help to dress for this meeting. He threw off what he was wearing and added it to the crumpled mess in the middle of the floor. Normally he tried to leave things neater for Andrew, but his current state of anger didn't allow for being nice. He located the leggings and the tunic he had worn for the exhibition and threw them on.

Then Rayne stopped. *Shoes? Boots? Barefoot?* His instincts screamed 'no shoes', he was most used to fighting with his feet feeling the ground. But he didn't want to appear less than Brayden and that need to demand a degree of self-respect in Brayden's presence drove him to don his black leather boots. He grabbed a leather cord and pulled his hair back into a tail. It wouldn't do to give Brayden the upper hand by having loose hair. Rayne had confidence in his abilities, but he was also well aware of Brayden's reputation as a master swordsman. He wouldn't give his cousin a needless advantage.

While he was dressing, his father's words surfaced in his mind. *Confined to your rooms until tomorrow morning.* A small, internal voice urged him to obey but he was too angry and too intent on finally having a chance to face Brayden to listen.

Rayne skirted the usually busy paths to arrive at the far practice ring unnoticed. It's location beyond a tree row a fair distance from the main fields, meant it was rarely used. He picked up a practice sword from one of the stands he passed along the way and decided to warm up as he waited for Brayden.

Working through some basic forms, he thought about what he should say to Brayden. He still needed to understand what happened this morning. *He's lying about being asleep; he was in the hallway outside my suite just minutes earlier. And I know he's lying about knowing the old man; he told me to stay away from the feeble old sneak before pulling him into his suite.* Rayne was sure of his instincts. That old man was linked to Sigmund somehow. *I didn't imagine sensing Sigmund; I couldn't have.*

Rayne moved faster as his anger at the whole situation festered, pushing him. He needed to find out what kind of control Brayden had over his parents and what he could do to break that hold. Rayne missed his mother's instruction and encouragement in learning to use the magic energy of Ochen. She hadn't given him any lessons or even sent her mage sense to check on him since the day Brayden had returned. And his father was treating him like a stranger. *Is this all related? Does Brayden's connection to the old man have something to do with the way my parents are acting?* He moved faster and notched up into an advanced form.

Allowing his anger to drive him, Rayne wasn't finding the peace he usually experienced when dancing with a sword. Even back at Coronus's compound, peace always accompanied this dance. But today his anger fed on itself, destroying his ability to think clearly.

Is Brayden doing something to me too? That thought brought him to a sudden stop. As his motion stilled, the sound of clapping rose behind him. *No!* How had he let his guard down so far as to not be aware that he was being watched?

Turning, Rayne grimaced. Brayden stood clapping, his annoying wolf grin spreading across his face. And standing next to Brayden was Theodor. His hands clenched at his sides. His eyes smoldering. His face reminded Rayne of an over-ripe tomato.

Just like when they were children, Brayden got Rayne into trouble again. How many times had he done this when they were kids? Brayden must have known about Theodor's command that Rayne keep to his rooms until tomorrow morning, and Rayne had allowed his anger to goad him into disobeying.

Breathing hard, Rayne hung his head as Theodor said, "I am most disappointed in you Rayne. Though your recent behavior has been offensive, I did not expect you to sink so low as to disregard my command so casually. I wanted to believe you had more respect for me than this. When I chanced to pass Brayden in the hall and he mentioned coming out here to join you, I thought he must be mistaken. But I see, I was the one who was mistaken. I trusted you, and now you put me in the difficult position of needing to punish you once again. What do you have to say for yourself?"

Rayne bristled at the thought that Brayden had tricked him. The two-faced liar hadn't even changed his clothes. He never meant to spar with Rayne, just use the situation to his advantage. After Rayne left he must have waited in the hallway outside the conference room until Theodor came out. Rayne needed to say something to deflect his father's anger, but what? He couldn't use the excuse that Brayden challenged him, he had been the one to initiate the match.

"If Brayden was on his way to meet me for a practice match, then why isn't he dressed to fight?" Rayne asked Theodor. "Ask him why, if you just happened to run into him in the hallway on his way to meet me, is he still dressed in formal clothing?

"He set me up. He must have overheard our argument and then used my anger to goad me into disobeying. After I left to change, he waited for you just so he could stand here now and smile at me in his superior way and then laugh when you punish me. Ask him. Ask him if he really intended to face me."

Rayne let his anger drive him once again. Dropping his sword, he stomped forward, flexed his fingers, and finally realized the satisfaction of feeling Brayden's nose crack under his fist. Blood spurted from the ruin of Brayden's nose, spattering

Rayne's hands and the front of his tunic, running down the front of Brayden's jacket.

Leaning into Rayne and grabbing his shirt as if for support, Brayden hissed into Rayne's ear, "You little snot face. You broke my nose! You actually broke my nose! You're going to pay for this you piece of trash. Maybe not today or tomorrow, but you will pay and with heavy interest."

Then, pushing from Rayne, Brayden said in a loud voice, "Cousin? Why? If I have offended you, please forgive me for whatever it is you hold against me. I hold nothing against you. I'm sure this violence is just a result of being raised as you were. I forgive you."

He turned to Theodor and bowed. "Please, Uncle Theodor, excuse me."

Cradling his face in his hands, Brayden stumbled back toward the palace dribbling blood on the grass as he went. When he faltered, Theodor sent two guards to help him.

Rayne knew it was wrong the moment he hit Brayden. It felt good, but it was going to cost. He had learned long ago to not let anger dictate his actions, just as he learned to be aware of his surroundings. But when Brayden was around, he lost all sense. The realization slammed into him. As long as Brayden was in Westvale, he couldn't stay.

He looked up to see his father glaring at him, disgust written in his expression. Yes, Rayne would have to leave, at least until Brayden went home to Inverness. But who would look out for his mother and father?

"By the seven, I don't understand you Rayne." Theodor shook his head. "You stood there and pardoned that off-world kidnapper. What was his punishment? Oh, that's right, you told him to go on living as he had been living for the last year, serving as a member of that blasted committee. You showed weakness with that decision. Then, you turn around and decide to purposely disobey my direct command by coming here after I ordered you to your quarters. And then, despite everything your mother and I have said, you attack Brayden right before my eyes and break his nose. This has got to stop. You leave me no choice."

Theodor motioned for the two remaining guards to flank Rayne. With anger lacing his voice, Theodor said, "Boy, you are a disappointment to both your mother and me. You lack discipline and self-control and have forgotten how to show respect. As a result, you will spend the remainder of this day and tonight in a cell instead of in your rooms."

Turning his focus to one of the guards, Theodor commanded, "Take *His Royal Highness* to the barracks and lock him in a cell for the night. And I do mean *lock it*. He is to be allowed no visitors while he is there; he is to spend the time reflecting on how he has grieved and embarrassed me today. He can be released in the morning."

Turning back to Rayne, Theodor's voice took on a note of cool condescension. "You said earlier that your mother and I don't know you as well as we know Brayden. Well, you are right. After witnessing this unprovoked violence, I realize I don't know you. And you make it very difficult to repair that breach."

Theodor waved for the guards to escort Rayne to the barracks. Rayne stood watching as his father walked the path Brayden had just taken, shoulders bent and looking suddenly older.

17

Aware that the guards were waiting, Rayne let the last dregs of anger drain from him as he rubbed his temples. He turned to retrieve the practice sword but found one of the men already picking it up. When the guard turned back to him, relief flooded Rayne; it was Noah. But after meeting Noah's eyes, he lowered his head in embarrassment at letting his anger drive him to the point of violence.

With a look of understanding, Noah asked, "Do you want to talk about it, Sire?"

Rayne shook his head. What would he say anyway? But as they started walking, words began to flow. "He's always been like that."

"Who, Sire?" Noah asked as the other guard followed quietly in their wake.

"You know, Brayden. You've seen for yourself these last few weeks what he's like. And don't tell me you haven't noticed. I know you too well to think you could miss his attitude and the way he maneuvers people into doing what he wants.

"I didn't even remember him until he came back to

Westvale. He did this when we were children, you know. He would set me up to be punished for one thing or another. When he's around I can't seem to control my anger. I was wrong; my father was right to punish me."

"May I speak freely, Your Highness?"

Glancing over, Rayne gave Noah a level look. "You don't need to ask, Noah. I value your opinion."

"I haven't known you long, Your Highness. But I do know you would not have lashed out like that if you hadn't been provoked. I think the king was wrong. I've always thought of King Theodor as a fair man who seeks out all the facts in a situation before making a decision. Is it normal for him to trust Lord Woodfield so completely? After all, you did make a good argument that he could be lying."

"Unfortunately, yes. The more I remember from before I was taken, the more I realize how my parents could see no wrong in Brayden. He was always there, and he was always untouchable. Whenever my parents faced a choice of believing him or believing me, he always got their trust and I got punished.

"I think part of the reason my father was so angry with me wasn't because I broke *a* nose, but because I broke *Brayden's* nose. I've been challenging my parents about their devotion to him and I don't think they can tolerate that. I remember being frustrated by this even when I was five years old, and now that I'm old enough to understand, I still don't understand. I'm troubled about the reason behind their blindness where Brayden is concerned." He paused, taking a deep breath. "And I know I was afraid of him when I was five."

As they crossed the last practice field before the barracks, Rayne caught sight of Thorvin working with several men and waved. After shouting a few final commands, the weapons master jogged to the three.

"What's going on here? Are you injured Your Highness?" Thorvin's eyes flicked from Rayne's bloody tunic to the guards.

Rayne huffed. "I'm fine, if you don't count the fact that I allowed Lord Woodfield to drive me to do something stupid again." He shifted his gaze away from Thorvin's. "I broke Brayden's nose right in front of my father."

"Good for you, boy." Thorvin smiled his approval.

"No. Not good. Now I have to spend the rest of today and tonight in a cell as punishment. What is it about me that I keep ending up in cells? Answer me that if you can." With the anger growing cold, disgust with his actions trickled through Rayne and infused his voice.

Thorvin chuckled. "I guess it's just your ability to rub people the wrong way, Your Highness."

"Not funny." Rayne grimaced.

As they headed into the barracks, Thorvin redirected them to his quarters.

"That's not acceptable," the guard Rayne didn't recognize protested. "His Majesty specifically ordered that the prince be conducted directly to a cell where he is to remain until tomorrow morning. Discipline for striking Lord Woodfield and disobeying His Majesty."

"I'll take full responsibility for His Highness." Thorvin cast an irritated look at the protesting soldier. "I know him. He won't be comfortable until he's washed and put on a fresh tunic. Noah, go to the prince's rooms and ask Andrew for some clean clothing."

"Yes sir." Noah jogged out the door.

The other guard, refusing to let Rayne out of his sight, followed Thorvin and him to the Weapons Master's quarters. As Rayne pulled off the bloody tunic, Thorvin poured water from a pitcher into a large bowl and then tossed Rayne a cloth and a chunk of soap. He scrubbed the blood from his hands and arms up to his shoulders, breathing a sigh of relief as the evidence of his anger dribbled into the bowl and merged with the water.

While Rayne was washing, his eyes were drawn to the door when a knock sounded.

"Captain Fontaine," Thorvin said opening the door. "What brings you here?"

"I heard there was some problem with the young prince and that he was here with you." The captain glanced over to where Rayne was washing and with a shudder, quickly averted his gaze.

Rayne caught his reaction and sighed. It wasn't unusual for people to react with revulsion when seeing his back. Between Sigmund's mark and the network of scars, courtesy of Ponce and Coronus, it wasn't pretty.

Captain Fontaine turned back to Thorvin. "What happened?"

"Well." Thorvin chuckled. "It seems our young prince broke Lord Brayden Woodfield's nose."

Captain Fontaine tried to hide the smile that lifted the sides of his mouth by faking an exaggerated cough. But he failed, delight evident in his reaction. Rayne couldn't help but smile back. "I see I'm not alone in my estimation of my cousin. But tell me, if you can, why my parents can't see him as the slimy creature that he is?"

"I'm sorry Sire; I have no answer for that. But I can tell you that there have been numerous complaints from the people of Westvale about the good Lord Woodfield. He's well known for taking advantage of unsuspecting girls, carousing with other young nobles, causing damage to various establishments, and not paying debts in town. Every time I bring one of these complaints to His Majesty's attention however, his whole demeanor changes, like he's not himself. He loses focus, seems disoriented, and reprimands me for attacking Lord Woodfield. In the end, he pays off the people who complained. I've been privy to His Majesty's use of good judgement and wisdom in all kinds of situations; but when it comes to Lord Woodfield, I can't explain it. And it's been worse lately." The captain paused, frowned, then nodded. "Since your return."

Rayne scrunched his brow. "I think Brayden's got some kind of control over my mother and father. Something he's been using ever since we were children. No matter what I say, where he's concerned, my word is meaningless in my parent's eyes. They won't listen to me. Ever since I accused Brayden and his friends of trying to violate Ruthie during Brayden's welcome home party, Mother and Father are angry with me all the time. I can't seem to say or do anything right in their eyes."

He turned to Thorvin. "Have you heard anything about what happened at the palace this morning?"

"Just some rumors, nothing concrete. What happened?"

"I was there and I'm not sure what really happened." Rayne swallowed the lump in his throat as fatigue settled into his bones. "I was on my way back to my suite after seeing Elsie, coming up the back way, using the servant's stairs, when Boone ran ahead. I caught up to her in the hall outside my door. She was really upset, barking and growling at this creepy stranger who was cowering against the wall.

"The whole incident was very bizarre. I was certain I sensed Sigmund, but he wasn't there, just this weird, smelly old man. Boone wouldn't even listen to me at first. Just kept snarling at the man. I was about to ask him what he was doing outside my door when Brayden arrived and insisted I leave the man alone. Then Brayden took him into his suite.

"After that, I went into my suite and found Andrew unconscious on my bed. I tried to wake him, but I couldn't. I was sure that old man had something to do with Andrew's condition. I went to Brayden's suite and pounded on his door, yelling for him to open up. When he finally opened the door, he acted as though he just woke up. He said I was mistaken; there was no old man. I searched his rooms but couldn't find anyone.

"Then Anne arrived with Shaw, Jonathan, and my parents. I dragged her back to my rooms to see if she could help Andrew, but he woke up on his own. When Brayden and my parents followed, I questioned Brayden about the old man, but he denied everything, said he had been sleeping and my yelling woke him.

"But, Thorvin, Sigmund was there. I sensed him and his mark on my back burned like it was on fire. And there really was an old man! I didn't make that up. Brayden is lying.

"Anyway, after all that, I made the mistake of forgiving Travis Illk, the man who kidnapped me when I was six. He gave up his old life and is now a part of the Reclamation Committee we met with this morning. That made Father even more angry and I guess I sort of called my parents stupid.

"Father ordered me to my rooms to cool down and prepare an apology to make at breakfast tomorrow. I was on my way there when I ran into Brayden. He was in the hall outside the kitchens, flirting with one of the delegates we just met, a shy young girl from Nemora named Blossom. I suggested she return to her room. I guess, now that I think about it, Brayden probably knew I would head to my rooms the back way and was waiting for me. I let him goad me into challenging him and walked right into his trap.

"You know the rest. Father was beyond furious when I hit Brayden, angry enough to order me escorted to a cell rather than my suite. So, that's my day, Thorvin. And now it ends with me washing blood from my hands. Again." Rayne grimaced at the memories. "And then spending the night in a cell. Welcome to my life."

"No," Thorvin and Captain Fontaine said in unison. They looked at each other and then Captain Fontaine said, "Please, spend the night in either Lord Kraftmunn's quarters or mine. We'll not have you spending the night in a cell."

"I'm not going to let either of you get in trouble just so I don't have to sleep in a cell. If it got back to my father that I didn't obey this command after I just disobeyed the last one, I would get another punishment and whoever helped me would be in trouble as well. Besides, it's not like I'm not used to sleeping in a cell, right Thorvin?"

"Yeah." Thorvin's focus dropped to the floor. "But I'll stay with you. I want to know more about you sensing Sigmund's presence this morning."

"I'm sorry sir, I can't allow that." The strange guard spoke with an authority that contradicted his rank. "His Majesty specifically ordered no visitors. We've already swerved from his command in bringing the prince here. I won't disobey him more."

"No problem." Thorvin growled, scowling at the man. "I just remembered. I'm on guard duty tonight."

Captain Fontaine sighed. "I too just remembered. Guard duty. Yes. Tonight."

Rayne grinned his thanks to both men as the guard frowned. There was a knock on the door and Andrew hurdled in followed by Noah who held an armful of clothing.

"Sire." Andrew ran up to Rayne. "I'm so sorry. I fear I'm the cause of your trouble. Please allow me to take your punishment; I'll gladly spend the night here in your stead."

Rayne ignored Andrew's offer but noticing Noah balancing a rather large bundle of clothing motioned him to leave the clothes on a chair. Noah sighed in relief as he dropped the heavy load.

Rayne stared at the mound of clothing, his mouth hanging open. "Andrew, I'm only here until morning. How many outfits do you think I'll need? I'm spending the night in a cell, not going to a party."

Andrew looked at the pile himself and shrugged. "I guess I panicked when I heard you were being punished. I wanted you to know how sorry I am about what happened this morning. I'm sorry I can't remember anything that might help you."

"You have nothing to be sorry for. How are you feeling?"

"Actually, Sire, I'm still feeling a little funny. Not really sick, but not really right either."

"Have you told Anne?"

"Yes Sire. She said she needs to talk to you about it. Something about weaving something."

"A weave?" Rayne's gut clenched.

He walked to Andrew and looked into his eyes. The moment he made eye contact, Andrew's eyes took on a glazed look and his body went stiff. In a voice, old and cracking, Andrew said, *Greetings my rebellious little bird. It's been a long time. I'm quite concerned about how complacent you've grown. Far too comfortable here at the palace, in safety, with mommy and daddy. But not to worry. Soon, at a time of my choosing, I will claim what is mine and you will pay for your treachery.*

Immediately after speaking Sigmund's words, Andrew collapsed.

As Rayne stood, locked in fear, staring ahead, Thorvin knelt to check Andrew. Rayne shook his head to break the spell and looked down to Thorvin who gave him a nod. "Andrew is fine, Sire. He is just sleeping."

"That voice." Rayne's heart thrummed into his throat. "The old man in the hallway outside my rooms. He *was* Sigmund. But how?"

Looking down at Andrew again, Rayne asked Thorvin, "Are you sure he's just sleeping?"

Captain Fontaine bent down next to Thorvin and checked under Andrew's eye lids. "Yes, Sire, Thorvin's right, it seems the boy is just sleeping now. Perhaps we should take him back to your suite and put him to bed."

After Rayne grabbed a simple shirt and trousers from the pile, Captain Fontaine and Noah took Andrew and the clothing back to Rayne's quarters. The Captain promised to return soon with food.

18

Rayne finished washing then dressed and combed his hair, tying it back into a tail again. As he was securing his hair, Thorvin turned to the guard. "I don't remember seeing you around before. Are you new to the palace guard?"

The man stood silent, his manner haughty. He gave Thorvin an appraising look and said, "I am new *here*," before turning his focus back to Rayne.

"What's your name?"

"Corporal Parker ... Sir. My name is Corporal Job Parker."

"Well, *Corporal* Parker, you are dismissed. I will see that King Theodor's order is carried out."

Corporal Parker continued to stand like a statue, his face an emotionless mask, watching Rayne with unblinking eyes.

"Corporal," Thorvin growled. "I gave you a direct order. You are dismissed."

"With all due respect Sir, I am obligated to complete the order the king gave me directly. And I must point out that you are not in my chain of command. You are not a member of the palace guard, just an outside consultant."

Rayne, seeing the look in Thorvin's eyes at the young man's comment, touched Thorvin's arm and shook his head. "Come Corporal. Take me to my cell. I'm sure you have better things to do than spend any more time babysitting me."

Rayne walked back through the hallway and down a set of stairs to the lower level where the cells were located, Corporal Parker dogging his heels. The cells were empty and no one was on duty so Rayne walked to the last cell and sat on the cot. Thorvin grabbed the key ring and locked Rayne's cell. He set the keys back on their hook and dismissed the obstinate corporal.

Corporal Parker glared, a stubborn expression etched on his features, as if he wanted to challenge Thorvin again, but then, with a final scowl directed at Rayne, he turned on his heel and vanished up the stairs.

After Parker left, Thorvin said, "he may not think so, but he is required to follow my orders. Why did you stop me from confronting him?"

"He just wanted to do what his king commanded." Rayne shrugged. "I was going to end up here anyway, why make a big deal of it?"

"I didn't like the way he enjoyed having authority over you, Sire." Thorvin retrieved the key and unlocked Rayne's cell.

"Oh, I don't know." Rayne chucked. "It seems to me he was more intent on ruffling your feathers than mine."

"But I wasn't the one he was watching so intently."

"Of course, I was his charge, not you. You're the one who took it all so personally."

"You bet I did," Thorvin growled. "He disobeyed a direct command. I will address this issue with Captain Ellis in the morning."

Thorvin grunted and dragged a chair into Rayne's cell, lowering his bulk onto the hard seat. "Okay, now that we're alone, tell me, what's happening?"

Rayne opened his mouth to speak but then snapped it shut and shook his head as burning tears sealed his throat. After a minute, he said, "I know Sigmund was in the palace this morning. I don't know what happened to him, but the old man I caught outside my rooms *was* Sigmund. He had to be. He must have just left Andrew when Boone and I saw him skulking outside my chambers. He sent that message through Andrew so I would know he can get to me whenever he wants. Brayden must have smuggled him out of the palace before I came looking for him. Which means they're working together. I need to leave Westvale; everyone here will be safer with me gone."

As Rayne was finishing, Captain Fontaine walked down the stairs. A private carrying a large basket of food that scented the air with hunger-stirring aromas, followed him. The captain took the basket and dismissed the soldier before carrying it into the cell and setting it on the cot. Rayne sniffed the air, suddenly aware of the hole in his stomach. Captain Fontaine grabbed another chair and dragged it over. "Did I hear right, you're planning to leave, Sire?"

"I don't see how I can stay. You saw what happened to Andrew. Sigmund is targeting me which puts everyone around me in danger. He just proved he can get into the palace, even right into my rooms. He was staying with Brayden; I know he was."

"Tell me again, what were those words Andrew spoke?" Thorvin asked.

"What does it matter?" Rayne shook his head, suppressing an overwhelming need to scream as a potent mix of fear, anger, and frustration bubbled within. "He still sees me as his property and he's sending me a message. 'You're going to suffer for your betrayal, my little bird', or something like that. I don't know why he didn't act on that this morning; he could have. Maybe it has something to do with him being old now. Or maybe he just wants me jumpy and afraid so I can't function as the Light Bringer." Rayne paused, trying to figure out what Sigmund was doing in the palace.

"The thought of falling into his hands again scares me beyond belief. So, yes, I'm afraid. But, what he didn't count on is that I'm more concerned he might harm the people I care about here at the palace. And that's made me angry. What he's succeeded in doing is pushing me to leave Westvale and seek the scrolls sooner than I planned.

Rayne shook his head again. "Who am I kidding? I had already decided to leave Westvale. It's like you said Captain, Brayden's influence on my parents is more evident now than it was for the last ten years. When I first returned, things were different; Brayden must have realized he was losing his hold on them. I think he needed to come back and, I don't know, do something to strengthen his control. That's why my parents and I were … well … why my parents trusted me and actually seemed happy with me around until Brayden returned. I think my presence affects the amount of influence Brayden needs to exert over Father and Mother. I hope that if I leave, he'll relax his hold, and then maybe, they might be able to see through his lies.

"It's not only that, though, I need to find the scrolls. If I'm the Light Bringer, I have to fulfill the prophecy, right? That's what Sigmund wants to prevent, and I can't let him stop me. Even sitting here now, I feel the pressure to move. So, it only makes sense for me to leave."

The two older men nodded at Rayne's words.

Captain Fontaine uncovered the basket and began to pass out a feast. "As soon as I told the head cook what I needed and why, everyone in the kitchen got busy. They were eager to send you the best of what they had." Captain Fontaine lifted a fork of mushroom stuffed squash to his mouth. His eyes closed, and he moaned his delight before continuing. "Most of the palace staff would do just about anything for you. They are aware of what really happened the night of Lord Woodfield's party and they know what he's gotten away with over the years. They're not stupid. They've figured out that your punishment is connected to you standing up to the king and queen about Lord Woodfield even though Ruthie is too afraid to speak up."

He paused, taking another bite. "I should eat with you more often, Your Highness. This is delicious.

"You see, Sire, everyone knows you treat people with respect regardless of their station. The staff, the soldiers, and even a goodly number of the citizens of Westvale know you care and that has earned their trust and respect. I think you should know that."

"Thanks." Rayne dipped his head. "At least someone trusts me. I just wish my parents did. Maybe if I'm gone and they have time to think about the things I've said, especially if Brayden does relax his control, when I come back things might be like they were before. Maybe then my parents will listen to me."

He paused, then turned to Thorvin and chuckled. "Hopefully more so than our persistent corporal was willing to listen to you."

"Corporal Parker's attitude smacks of insubordination. I've got a bad feeling about him." Turning to Captain Fontaine, Thorvin said, "What can you tell me?"

Captain Fontaine grimaced. "I wish we hadn't spoken so openly in front of the man earlier; I don't trust him. He's one of a small group of soldiers who came from Inverness about three months ago. They all reported to Captain Ellis with assigned ranks of corporal or sergeant even though they were just being inducted into the palace guard. They already have a nasty reputation for inciting arguments among the men and throwing their weight around. I tried to track the origin of their ranks and orders, but I couldn't get any answers. In the meantime, they have consistently been assigned duty guarding the king even though that's supposed to be by rotation."

"You think Lord Woodfield had something to do with their arrival here," Thorvin stated.

"Yes. I think he did, and I believe he's behind the current guard assignments as well. Captain Ellis says the orders come from the king's desk, but he's no more comfortable about it than I am. The whole thing smells."

The three continued talking as they devoured the contents of the basket. The next several hours were spent discussing a variety of topics including the mystery surrounding the guardsmen from Nemora. With his mind fixed on his upcoming quest, Rayne asked questions about the different worlds and both Captain Fontaine and Thorvin proved to be good sources of information.

The conversation wound down and Rayne began yawning. The last couple days had been stress-filled, and now his body craved rest. While Thorvin and the captain continued talking quietly, Rayne curled up on his cot and was asleep almost instantly.

\\

After Rayne had been sleeping for about a half an hour, Captain Fontaine looked over at him and said, "He is indeed a fine young man. It's a shame that Lord Woodfield has influenced his parents against him. He's right, you know, their relationship was different before Brayden Woodfield returned.

"I've served with the palace guard for more than eight years and never before have I seen the king and queen as happy as they were during those months after Prince Rayne's homecoming. Until Lord Woodfield returned. Do you remember how anxious Queen Rowena was when the young prince left to return to Coronus's estate for the scroll? Now she doesn't even seem to care that he's going to skip onto other worlds. It's all so strange."

"Yeah," Thorvin agreed. "And it's been noticed by others. You and I aren't the only ones worried because of the change. I've talked to Bishop Hedrick and he's concerned. But he's hesitant to lay the blame on Lord Woodfield. Like the king and queen, Bishop Hedrick has known Brayden for years and always thought him an exceptional young man. Remember, Bishop Hedrick was unsure about Rayne initially. But since they've been working together, he's come to respect the prince and value his opinion. So, although the bishop knows something is wrong, he's unsure what."

Thorvin's eyes flicked to the sleeping form. "Regardless of the cause of the rift between the king and queen and their son, Bishop Hedrick joins us in our concern for the prince."

"What was it like?" Captain Fontaine asked.

Thorvin gave him a questioning look.

"What was it like training him? After hearing the stories, I quietly checked out that cell under the training ring at Coronus's compound when we were there. How did he live through that as a child and not be more emotionally scarred?"

"Frankly, I don't know how he did it. I looked away so many times while he was growing up. Coronus was so fixated on creating the perfect assassin and Rayne was incredibly talented. To please Sigmund, Coronus drove Rayne into spilling so much blood, even at a young age."

Thorvin shook his head, eyes focused on nothing as memories filtered into his thoughts, twisting his stomach. "The worst was when Sigmund brought him back after keeping him for that year when he was thirteen." Thorvin shook his head. "The boy came back so broken and angry, I thought he would never recover. But Warren and Anne wouldn't give up on him. They fought the darkness and showed him love until he was able to move forward. When Coronus killed Warren, I thought Rayne would fall back into the darkness again, but I guess the One gave him the strength to fight it.

"And training him ... he's the most gifted fighter I've ever worked with. When he was really young the older youths abused him. He tried to fight back, protect himself; it was pathetic to watch him at six or even nine years old try to keep a trained teenager at bay.

"When he was ten, I started giving him some basic instruction. Once I taught him something he would know it and use it. He has a quick mind and even at ten he began to understand combining fighting styles. By the time he was fifteen, that last year at Coronus's, he was unstoppable. But it was hard on him when Sigmund and Coronus called for death matches. He won, but he hated himself for it."

Thorvin stopped for a moment, thinking. He breathed deeply and let out a huff of air. "What was it like to train him? It was an honor. I'm just sorry it took me so long to admit the truth of what I was doing and help him escape that life."

He looked back at the sleeping youth again. "You're right, Anton, he is an amazing young man. Sometimes it's hard to remember he's only sixteen. But then he goes and breaks Brayden's nose."

The two men chuckled and Thorvin continued. "I don't know of anyone else who could have gone through half of what he's gone through and come out on the other side with such resilience and care for others. His heart should be hard as rock, yet he goes and forgives the man who took him in the first place. And … gives that man the honor of serving him. Now that's grace and forgiveness. If this is an example of the truths the One's Light Bringer is called to show to the people, I want to know more."

They talked for a bit longer but then each took a cot in an empty cell to sleep for the night. Both agreed; they would not leave their prince alone.

19

It was after midnight when the dream pulled Rayne from sleep; he sat up with a start. In the half-light of the low-burning lanterns he noticed Thorvin and Captain Fontaine sleeping in the next two cells and smiled to himself at their loyalty. But then he focused on the dream.

In it, he felt again the pain and humiliation of being a slave when Coronus would lead him with collar and chain. It was dark, smoky, and he couldn't see anything beyond gray images. He heard voices, many voices. There was the noise of people working around him and the sound of whips. Time seemed to go on and on; it passed in a swirl of gray fog and gritty smoke.

Then he saw the girl. She reminded him of Anne, slight with blonde hair; but her hair was more honey than wheat, long and wavy. He was drawn to her. But no matter how hard he tried to get close, she always stayed just out of reach. And he could tell she was crying. Then, suddenly she turned to him and he saw her face clearly. Her eyes were large, the color of golden autumn leaves streaked with brown, and set perfectly over a small nose sprinkled with freckles. But then her eyes turned cold, angry, and lifting a knife, she plunged the blade into his chest. The pain seared his heart and burned through him like molten veredium. The voice spoke. *My people are calling Light Bringer. It is time to bring light to Veres.*

Rayne had experienced something similar before, when he was being brought to Westvale to kill his parents. He dreamed and then knew he couldn't kill the king and queen. Now he knew he was being called to Veres. And he knew he would meet the golden eyed girl there. He lay back down with his arms under his head and looked up at the dark ceiling, seeing golden eyes and honey hair until he again fell asleep.

The next morning when he woke, Thorvin and Captain Fontaine were already gone, and his cell door was open. He headed out toward the palace. The morning was cold and the grass was crunchy with ice. Fog, reminding him of his dream, surrounded Rayne as the sun turned the gray mist golden where its rays wormed through the shredding tendrils of fog, turning the remaining leaves into bonfires of color. He was glad he had worn boots yesterday as he jogged up the steps into the palace. Déjà vu sent skitters up his spine as he ran through the kitchens and down the hallway to the second-floor stairs.

But today there was no old man hovering around his door. He glanced toward Brayden's suite and wondered what his cousin was up to and what his connection to Sigmund was. Entering his rooms, Rayne pulled the door shut with a soft click, trying to be quiet in case Andrew was sleeping, but it was a useless endeavor. Boone started barking in joy and whining as she jumped at Rayne, wagging her tail as if she hadn't seen him in months.

He noticed a bath already set up and was wondering if he should take Boone out for a walk before bathing when Andrew came in from the bedroom. "I've already walked and fed Boone. You're running late. You probably didn't get the message, but His Majesty rescheduled today's meeting with the Reclamation Committee to be a breakfast meeting. You need to get ready and head right over."

He waved toward the steaming bath in front of the fireplace. "When you're done here I have clothing set out on your bed."

Andrew seemed his normal efficient self, but Rayne still asked how he was feeling and if he had talked to Anne.

"I'm feeling fine this morning. Whatever happened, I'm over it now." Andrew looked up but quickly averted his gaze to the floor while shuffling his feet. "What did I say yesterday? When I woke up on the way back here, Captain Fontaine told me I said something strange to you, but I don't remember. What did I say?"

Rayne's thoughts raced. *How much should I tell Andrew? He deserves to hear the whole truth from me.* "Are you sure you want to know this?"

Andrew nodded so Rayne continued. "The words were from Sigmund. I knew I sensed him here yesterday. He put some kind of weave on you and you were unaware when you spoke the message to me. You said …" Rayne hesitated.

"Please, you have to tell me."

Taking a deep breath, Rayne repeated Andrew's words. "'Greetings my rebellious little bird. It's been a long time. I'm quite concerned about how complacent you've grown. Far too comfortable here at the palace, in safety, with mommy and daddy. But not to worry. Soon, at a time of my choosing, I will claim what is mine and you will pay for your treachery.'"

Andrew's face went pale. "I said that? I'm so sorry."

"I told you before, you have nothing to be sorry for. This is not your fault so don't you go feeling guilty for what happened. You are the victim in this; remember that."

Seeking to lighten the mood, Rayne said, "What do you think Andrew? Should I use some of that fancy-smelling soap I don't like this morning? I probably need it after not bathing yesterday and then spending the night in a smelly cell? Come on, help me."

Scant minutes later, Rayne was sprinting toward the conference room. As he entered, he pulled to a stop. Everybody else was already there, including Brayden.

A knot formed in Rayne's stomach. Like yesterday, Rowena sat to Theodor's right, but today Brayden sat to Theodor's left and the only empty chair was to Brayden's left. Rayne was forced to sit next to Brayden, away from his parents.

The anger that always coiled just under the surface when he was around Brayden threatened to erupt and Rayne squashed it, reaffirming his decision to leave as soon as possible. As everyone was already seated and obviously finished eating, Rayne ignored the food laid out on a table under the windows and slipped into his seat.

Sitting next to Brayden, Rayne's fingers twitched, his nerves felt raw and exposed. When Brayden turned toward him, Rayne saw the effects of his fist on his cousin's face written in shades of purple and yellow-gray peeking around a white bandage over his nose. *Maybe I should apologize.* One look at the violent hatred spilling from Brayden's lavender-blue eyes choked the thought and sent skitters of fear down Rayne's back.

Brayden turned his attention back to the group and smiled. "As I was saying before my tardy little cousin arrived, there are no hard feelings. One must allow for the enthusiasm of youth. I'm sure little Raynie meant me no harm when he hit me so hard he broke my nose. Though I am mystified at what I could have done to elicit such violence from him. But whatever it was," Brayden turned to Rayne, his face so close Rayne felt his warm breath as Brayden's mouth curled upward at the corners, "I'm quite sorry it led him to lash out with such uncontrolled anger. Perhaps next time he'll show enough sense to talk to me before causing his parents and me such avoidable pain."

An intense urge to break Brayden's nose again, right now, right here, flooded through Rayne. He swallowed hard against the rising violence, realizing he was just responding to Brayden's influence. With an effort, he closed his eyes and said in a weak voice, "We need to pray."

He couldn't believe it, but he actually heard a faint growl come from Brayden. Opening his eyes, Rayne said a bit louder, "We need to pray for guidance before we start this meeting."

Whatever his cousin hoped to achieve by being here and discussing his broken nose with the committee members, Rayne wasn't going to allow it. He needed the meeting to focus on the issue of the scrolls, not his relationship with Brayden.

Rayne rose to lead the prayer, his need for the reaffirming

warmth of the One driving him to stand. Everyone bowed their heads, except Brayden, Rayne noticed. Glancing down at his cousin, Rayne couldn't mistake the anger evident in the whitened knuckles of his clenched fists.

He closed his eyes again seeking to quiet his spirit before praying. The peaceful warmth he always associated with the voice preparing to speak enveloped him, and Rayne basked in that warmth. He lifted praises with a heart washed of the violence that had just moments before threatened to erupt and destroy. He ended by asking guidance from the One for moving forward with the plan to retrieve the scrolls. As he was speaking final words of thanksgiving, the room filled with the light of the presence of the One. *Light Bringer, the people of Veres cry out; go to them. Be courageous. When the cup of wrath overflows, the broken will be reclaimed. The time of judgement approaches.*

No one moved as the voice faded. Silence filled the room and the light returned to normal.

Still standing, Rayne said, "The One has spoken. Both here and now, and in a dream last night. I will go to Veres." He sat back down.

It all happened so quickly. Rayne had thought it would take months of planning and discussion before they even chose the first world to visit. He watched the committee members looking around at each other as if trying to make sense of what just happened. Not only was the world to be visited named, the One had spoken words of judgement.

For Rayne, the need to get to Veres overshadowed the message of judgement; last night's dream had gripped him and wouldn't let go. He would leave the words of coming wrath for the committee to wrestle with while he was off-world. Already they were murmuring among themselves about the meaning of the cup and the broken.

What concerned Rayne most at this moment was his parent's reactions not only to the One's words, but to the announcement that he was going to Veres. But they were seated on the other side of Brayden and Rayne refused to give his cousin the satisfaction of seeing him lean forward to look at his parents. Glancing over from the corner of his eye, he could see the raised veins in Brayden's fisted hands on the table. Rayne was certain if he looked up, he would see Brayden scowling. He felt the heat of anger rising from his cousin.

Madam Ria stood and, breaking the silence, announced, "That was incredible. Well, ladies and gentlemen, I believe the One has set our work before us. He's given us new words to study. Words of direction. And frightening words of judgement. 'When the cup of wrath overflows, the broken will be reclaimed. The time of judgement approaches.' We will have to pray for guidance to understand the meaning of these new words.

"But take heart, my friends, the One is in control. Let us not, in our fear of the words of judgement, forget the first part of the message, the words of direction. 'Light Bringer, the people of Veres cry out; go to them. Be courageous.' With these words, he has revealed his will in the choice of Veres. And, if I understand Prince Rayne's announcement correctly, he also had affirmation of this in a dream and already decided to travel there."

She turned to Rayne. "It appears your next task is to skip to Veres. While you're gone, I think it best we study the remainder of the message. If that meets with your approval."

Rayne nodded in agreement.

A smile of encouragement blossomed across Madam Ria's face. "As you are planning to leave for Veres soon, have you given thought to who will accompany you Sire?"

The thought of putting any of his friends in harm's way soured Rayne's stomach. He had avoided thinking about that question. But here it was, the decision he dreaded.

"I would prefer to go alone, but reason tells me I will need help."

"Why?" Brayden's voice was quiet and tight. "Why would *you* need help? Aren't you some kind of master assassin, a special killing machine? With all your training, I'm sure you're more than capable of taking care of yourself. Isn't the Light Bringer supposed to go on his own anyway?"

"Not really," Deven spoke up, mercifully ignoring Brayden's reference to Rayne's past. "The prophecies do mention at least one person sent to help the Light Bringer, so I don't think he's meant to travel alone. But I think Prince Rayne should be allowed to make the decision who will accompany him."

"Yes, I agree," Madam Ria said.

Rayne waited for his father or mother to say something, anything. But when neither of them spoke, he said, "Getting onto Veres isn't going to be easy. The Sorial merchants have closed the portal to Veres and only those with special visas are granted access to the skipping line. I have an idea of how I might be able to travel there, but I can't do it alone. Father, may I talk with you about my plan? Will you talk with me?"

The need to ask these questions, the implication that his father wouldn't even want to speak to him, tore at Rayne. But his obligation to the people of Veres overshadowed his own pain. The tension between Rayne and his parents was painfully obvious in the ensuing silence. Theodor shifted and turned cold eyes on Rayne and he knew his father was still furious. *This isn't going to be easy.*

In a voice like cracking ice, Theodor said, "I believe my son and I have a matter to discuss. The Reclamation Committee will leave us now. We will reconvene directly after lunch."

Isolation settled around Rayne after the committee members filed out. His parents' disapproval and censure pressed in on him with an almost physical force. Not only had he lost the support of the committee, his defenses were crumbling under the onslaught of hostility Brayden's presence directed at him. *No, this is definitely not going to be good.*

Needing to distance himself from Brayden's animosity, Rayne rose and took up his defensive position next to the far window, his back to the wall. He felt more secure this way, protected. He glanced out the window at the now impossibly clear azure sky and wondered how far he had dropped in his parents' opinion, and just how angry they were. But he found comfort in the thought that his parents' behavior was a result of whatever Brayden was doing, not their true feelings for him. He clung to the hope that deep down, his parents still loved him.

Theodor cleared his throat. "I believe you have something to say to your mother and me."

Rayne swallowed hard. "Yes. Your Majesty, King Theodor." He bowed to his father. Taking a few steps forward, he bowed to his mother. "Your Majesty, Queen Rowena." Then, stepping back, he bowed once again and said, "I wish to say how very sorry I am for causing you pain with my unwarranted outburst yesterday. I regret my words of anger."

Rayne knew he was being more formal than necessary, but he felt as though he had become nothing more than an inconvenience to his parents, and he wanted them to know it. He bowed once again, deeply, to first his father and then his mother. He returned to the security of his position by the window, watching his parents, waiting for them to speak.

"Rayne Kierkengaard, you should be ashamed of yourself, treating your father and me in this manner. I know you are upset about something, but we should be able to talk as family and not strangers." Rowena motioned for Rayne to sit. "Please come, sit with us. You make me nervous when you stand at the window like that."

Rayne couldn't deny his mother, so taking a deep breath he moved back to the table and sat across from Rowena. He didn't understand why Brayden was still here, but hesitated to ask, knowing it would only irritate his parents more. Keeping his eyes cast down on his clasped hands he waited to see what direction his parents would take next.

Her voice soft, Rowena pressed. "I believe you still owe another apology, Rayne."

That's it! Rayne choked. *They want me to apologize to Brayden?*

"You know, Rayne," Rowena continued. "Brayden has been patient with your attitude, and very understanding about you breaking his nose. I don't know what possessed you to behave in such a vile manner to your own cousin. Perhaps that's how you settled things when you were a slave, but that behavior is not acceptable here, especially for someone in your position. I think an honest apology is the least you can do."

Rayne wanted desperately to feel the security of a wall at his back, but he just looked at his hands as he fisted them.

Brayden spoke up. "Auntie Rowena, you shouldn't be so hard on little Raynie. What else can we expect with the kind of upbringing he's had? And he is still so young. We really can't assume mature behavior from someone like him, can we?"

Rayne refused to meet Brayden's eyes. He continued to look down at his hands as he felt the force of displeasure from his parents and Brayden aimed at him. It felt as if something physical was actually pressing down on him. But he could not bring himself to apologize to Brayden. *I can't do it. How can I say I'm sorry, when I'm not sorry?* If given the chance, he would break Brayden's nose again.

Rayne's movements were slow and deliberate as he pressed upward and bowed once more. "I need to again ask your pardon. Your Majesty. Your Majesty. But I *refuse* to apologize for something *I do not regret*. I do, however, regret that I am such a disappointment to you." Rayne paused and pulled in a deep breath. "Therefore, I think it best if I formulate the plans for Veres alone. Once they are set, I will leave."

Pain leaked from Rayne's heart, infusing his words. "It hurts that my presence has become a matter of discomfort for you, so I will not subject you to it any longer. I will vacate my rooms and move out of the palace immediately. Perhaps it would be best if all further communications are made through Thorvin as I am planning to ask him to accompany me to Veres."

While Rayne was speaking, a piercing pain tore through Rowena's spirit. It spiked for only a second, but then it felt distant, like a faraway streak of lightning. *Something's not right. What?* She pulled in a deep breath, but it came hard and she felt as though she was seeing and hearing through a layer of wool. She looked up at Rayne and a tremor shuddered through her, sparking her magic. But then her eyes were drawn to Brayden and he smiled at her. *Yes, dear Brayden. Everything is fine when he's near.* The feeling passed. She sat without saying anything, unaware of two lonely tears tracking down her cheeks.

11

Rayne walked out of the conference room, eyes downcast, hurt, and feeling very alone. He had hoped his parents would stop him, or at least try to talk him out of leaving. Instead they sat like statues while Brayden watched with his wolf-smile as Rayne left.

Rayne had taken his stand and he couldn't back down now. *What have I done? Where am I going to go now?* Even when his life had been so horrible before, he always knew where he was going to sleep.

He wouldn't stay with anyone living on the palace grounds or even the church properties. They might get caught up in this battle and he wouldn't do that to any of his friends. Maybe he could stay with the Kaspers, at least for the next few days. By then he hoped to be on his way to Veres.

When Rayne walked into his rooms, Boone greeted him. He knelt down next to her and buried his face in the rough fur of her neck. Tears began to fall and his spirit cried out to the One. *Does it ever get better? I thought they loved me, wanted me. Sigmund was right. They don't love me. They don't want me. Not while they have Brayden.*

You don't really believe that. The quiet voice spoke. *Your parents love you very much, but they have been deceived and are blinded. They will see the truth when what is broken is made whole. Then you will know their love. Be courageous. Be patient and trust me.*

Rayne wiped the tears from his eyes and stood. *But it's so hard.*

When he looked up he saw Andrew staring at him, his eyes wide. "Rayne, what's wrong?"

Rayne sniffed. "I have to leave Westvale." His voice cracked. "I have to go away for a while, and I can't take Boone. Could you please keep her for me?"

Andrew looked up, his face a mask of stunned disbelief. "What do you mean, you have to go? What happened?"

"I can't talk about it now. Can you take care of Boone? I need to know she'll be okay."

"Of course. I'll take good care of her." Andrew blinked back tears. "What's happening? Why can't you just be here? This is your home. Wait, you are coming back aren't you?"

"Sure, Andrew. This is my home and I will come back. I just can't be here now. Thanks for being my friend and for taking care of Boone."

Rayne started going through his clothes while Andrew watched, sniffling. Rayne wouldn't need anything except some basics. He didn't want to take any of the clothes his parents had given him. But reality hit when he realized the only clothes his parents hadn't bought, were a couple worn sleeveless tunics, one pair of plain leather leggings, Sigmund's strangely tailored tunic, and the fancy woven leather leggings he'd worn with the tunic.

He refused to take the Sigmund's tunic. Not only was it covered with Brayden's blood, it brought back too many memories and its cut exposed Sigmund's mark. He packed his two old tunics, the plain leggings and after a moment's hesitation, the woven pair. *Not much.* He would have to take some things his parents had given him, but only what he absolutely needed. He pulled out a couple shirts with sleeves, a jacket, and the black leather boots. And he would keep what he was wearing. He grabbed several sets of small clothes. It would have to do.

Stuffing everything into a satchel, Rayne walked to the door. Andrew ran up to him and threw his arms around Rayne, sniffing loudly. Even Boone was whining like she knew something was wrong.

"It'll be okay." Rayne put his hand on Andrew's head. "You'll see. I'll be back. The One said broken things will be fixed and I have to believe that means my parents will accept me again when the time is right. I just need to be patient. And keep trusting the One. You do trust him Andrew, don't you?"

"Yes," Andrew mumbled into Rayne's chest. "I'll pray for you every day, Rayne. So you have to come back, you just have to."

"I will." Rayne turned and stepped out the door. With a last glance back, he felt the strangest sensation that he wouldn't see Andrew, Boone, or his rooms again for a very long time.

He almost relented and considered offering Brayden an apology. But for as easy it had been to forgive Travis Illk, Rayne couldn't forgive Brayden. *Travis was sorry for the pain he caused. Brayden takes pleasure in causing pain.* Rayne shook his head and turned away. *No. I won't let Brayden win.*

20

Brayden scowled as he made his way back to his rooms, tenderly touching his still sore and swollen nose. He had met several times with the healers and they assured him the nose would heal fine, but he could barely contain the venomous wrath he felt for Rayne having the nerve to physically attack him. Sure, his idiot cousin was leaving, just as Brayden hoped he would. But Brayden had seen the tears on Rowena's face.

He slammed into his room and scowled at his page, who took one look at him, melted away into the hall, and disappeared. Brayden despised the little wimp.

Sigmund had spent three years helping Brayden construct the distortion blanket starting when Brayden was eleven and Rayne three. It had been Sigmund's idea, a clever piece of distortion magic slowly developed in Theodor's and Rowena's minds, built up thin layer upon thin layer so Rowena wouldn't sense it. Sigmund created it with a dual purpose. Certain layers worked to connect feelings of integrity, love, and trust to Brayden, while other layers connected feelings of mistrust, apathy, and loathing to Rayne. It had proven useful right from the beginning and Sigmund decided to let Brayden continue working with it over the past ten years. It was quite effective at keeping Brayden's image untarnished in the minds of the royal couple. Until Rayne returned.

At this point, the fact that Rowena felt anything other than a curious loathing for Rayne while in Brayden's presence was a major concern. When Sigmund was at the palace, he added to the distortion directed at Rayne and strengthened the whole thing. At first Sigmund refused Brayden's request, claiming his power was too limited in his current condition. But after witnessing the effect Rayne's return was having on the king and queen, he decided that driving the wedge between the boy and his parents deeper was worth the energy expended. Despite the drain on his weakened reserves, he added two even thicker layers of distortion before leaving for Nemora.

Brayden walked over to an ebony sideboard decorated in gold leaf and poured himself a glass of red wine. Swirling the wine absent mindedly, he moved to sit on a loveseat while he calmed his nerves by calling up visions of Rayne's hurt looks all those years ago when his parents began believing everything Brayden told them.

Even before Sigmund started work on the distortion blanket, he showed Brayden other ways to create trouble for his annoyingly perfect little cousin. Brayden enjoyed the game often, and things had gotten so much better once the distortion blanket was in place.

Chuckling and sipping his wine, Brayden thought about the summer when Rayne was five. Theodor, Rowena, and Rayne had visited Nemora for a week and when they were leaving for Corylus, Brayden asked Rowena to let Rayne stay for another few weeks. "Please Auntie Rowena," he pleaded. "We can have so much fun if Raynie can stay. I'll take good care of him. I promise. You know how much you can trust me, Auntie."

Brayden smiled widely as the memory bloomed in his mind, Rayne crying and begging his mother to please take him back home with her to Westvale. It had been quite pathetic. Of course Rowena listened to Brayden and ignored Rayne's pleas. The amusement Brayden found tormenting his young cousin was a sweet savor in his mind. The young wimp was even afraid of shadows. Brayden grinned and took another sip of wine.

One hot and stormy afternoon near the end of Rayne's stay, Brayden dismissed the servants saying he and little Raynie wouldn't need any attendants for several hours. Sneaking past the guards and off the castle grounds was a fun adventure. But dragging his whiny little cousin to the ancient sacrifice stone where Brayden arranged to meet Sigmund had been infuriating. The little goody-goody cried and struggled against his larger and stronger cousin. Brayden licked his lips, seeing again in his mind's eye the image of five-year old Rayne, trembling in fear as tears ran off his chin once he realized he had been brought to the old, blood-stained sacrifice stone. Even Auntie Rowena feared the primitive site. Brayden, angered by the wimp's struggles, squeezed his wrists hard enough to make him cry out in pain. It had been so exciting. And if Brayden's interfering mother hadn't caught them and ended the game before Sigmund arrived, Brayden would have been rid of the little pain back then.

Brayden despised Cailyn. His mother had always been such a weak person. He knew she was afraid of him, her own child. But in this instance, she stood up to him, ordering him to take Rayne back to Castle Inverness immediately. He had made her pay for her interference.

Brayden didn't see Sigmund again until he was in Westvale for Rayne's sixth birthday celebration. He was shopping in town when Sigmund approached him and asked for help with the kidnapping. Brayden was eager to be of service to his old friend and mentor. He waited outside Rayne's nursery, hiding in the shadows when the moronic nurse walked down to the kitchens for a snack before settling in for the night. He still relished the feeling of pride he took in his ability to guide the kidnapper through the servants' halls and out of the palace with no one the wiser.

Sipping his wine again, Brayden allowed the memories to fade.

If only that idiot had obeyed Sigmund like he was supposed to and killed Theodor and Rowena. Brayden ground his teeth as venom heated his blood, then swore as pain radiated across his face. *I want him dead. He should be dead, not breaking my nose. All of them … dead. I should have been crowned by now.*

At least with Rayne leaving, Brayden wouldn't have to worry his presence might tear at the carefully constructed blanket. Rowena's tears were proof of Rayne's ability to reach past Brayden's control and into her spirit. But, at least he hadn't succeeded for more than a moment and Rowena had settled right back into the deception.

When Rayne returned, he had, without even knowing it, begun unraveling all that Brayden worked toward for the last ten years. Brayden was forced to return to Westvale and reestablish his well-crafted position of trust with his aunt and uncle. But now that Sigmund had helped him strengthen his control over Theodor and Rowena, and Rayne was leaving, Brayden allowed himself to relax and poured another glass of wine. He sat back down and considered what he now knew of Rayne's plans.

Veres. He chuckled. *Of all the places he could chose to go, the fool picks Veres. Even if he succeeds in skipping onto Veres, he'll never make it back off that world alive. His father has too many enemies on Sorial, and his reputation as a master assassin guarantees someone will get him into the games.*

Brayden smiled broadly as a plan formed in his mind. He had friends on Sorial. Wealthy friends who were always looking for talented fighters, warriors worthy of participating in their weekly death matches. *All I need is a little more information about my dear cousin's plans, then I'll send a message. Let's see the little brat worm his way out of slavery this time.* Brayden calmed, all was still under control. One minor lapse by Rowena wasn't going to lead to disaster.

Downing the rest of his wine, he walked over to the sideboard and poured himself a honeyed sherry. Thinking of Sorial, the place he had been introduced to the delightfully sweet drink, made him desire the unique taste of the sherry.

Brayden liked Sorial; with his wealth, he could buy anything he wanted there. And the games on Veres were always good for a diversion, especially the death matches. Nothing took his mind off his troubles better than watching a bloody death match with his good friend, Jason Andersen. He swirled the sherry, breathing in its distinctive bouquet. *I could invite Lady Elaine to spend a few days with me at the Andersen House Gaming Complex on Veres. She's always up for a good time. And, if Jason acts quickly, perhaps I can even catch Rayne's first match.* He thought for a moment, but then growled. *No. I can't. What an inconvenience. I can't leave Theodor and Rowena alone in case the nuisance changes his mind and decides to return to Westvale. I know. I'll invite Lady Elaine up to my suite for the afternoon.*

Where is that wimp of a page?

Looking out into the hallway Brayden didn't see his page. What did draw his attention, however, was his cousin's page returning from walking that flea-bait dog. *With Rayne gone, I should acquire his doting little page for myself. That would encourage the palace staff to recognize me as heir.* He huffed out a breath. *And … yes.* His eyes sparkled as he licked his lips. *It's time I moved into my cousin's suite. The rooms are larger than mine.* He sighed. *It will need redecorating though. Rayne has no sense of taste. It'll be easy enough to convince Uncle Theodor and Auntie Rowena to give me the prince's suite. After all, if all goes well, he won't be needing it again.*

※

Thorvin watched from a distance as an obviously agitated Rayne headed toward the Great Square. After talking with Noah, Thorvin had waited outside the kitchen entrance, confident that if Rayne was going to leave, he'd sneak out that way. He didn't need to wait long for the prince to storm from the palace carrying a lumpy travel satchel. After following Rayne then watching him stand in indecision for a few minutes at the edge of the square, Thorvin knew Noah was right. Deciding he needed to intervene, Thorvin jogged up to Rayne, and grabbed his arm. "We need to talk. You're coming with me. No arguments."

Rayne dragged his feet as he followed Thorvin back to his quarters. After closing the door behind them, Thorvin seized Rayne's satchel and threw it on a chair growling in frustration. "Noah was on duty outside the door of the small conference room this morning. He had the foresight to leave it cracked open after your father dismissed the delegates. Is it true? Tell me. Is it true your parents didn't even try to stop you from leaving?"

Rayne stared at Thorvin for a minute then turned to grab his satchel. "I don't want to talk about it." He moved to leave, but Thorvin blocked the door.

"Talk to me son."

Rayne looked up at him with unshed tears sparkling in angry eyes. "Don't call me that old man; I'm not your son." Stepping away from Thorvin, Rayne said more quietly, "Just call me *boy*. That's familiar; I know where I stand when I'm just *boy*."

"Then it's true." Thorvin shook his head. "I hoped Noah was mistaken."

Rayne flung his satchel down to the floor with enough force that it skidded a few inches before settling into a lump. He plopped into a chair and stared at the ceiling, his right leg bouncing an erratic rhythm. Thorvin read the internal struggle on the young prince's face as he strove to control his emotions. He sniffed but held his tears in check and said to Thorvin, "You know, old man, I'm tired. I'm so tired of my life being messed up. But I'm also tired of feeling sorry for myself. I can't do it anymore. I won't. I'm done with crying; I'm done with feeling sorry for myself. It does no good."

With a deep sigh, he closed his eyes for a couple breaths and when he opened them he looked up at Thorvin with fiery eyes. "I have to get to Veres. I can't let what's happening with my parents and Brayden stop me. *I* can't help my parents; they won't even listen to me. The One is going to have to take care of them. But I *can* and *will* help the people of Veres. Will you come with me?"

Thorvin had known for a long time that there would come a moment when whatever Rayne asked of him, he would do. He resigned himself to that fact back when he first decided to betray Coronus and help Rayne. But looking at the determination in the prince's eyes now, and the set of his jaw, Thorvin felt a stirring, not of resignation, but of anticipation.

For the first time, Thorvin began to understand what it meant to be committed to this prince. That he, of all people, would be helping the One's Light Bringer scared him, but it also thrilled him to his very core.

Without thinking about where it all might lead, Thorvin said, "Your Highness, I have just been waiting for you to ask. What can I do?"

Rayne focused intent eyes on Thorvin. "Thanks, old man." He coughed and then continued. "I have a plan to get onto Veres but I'll need help. Can you fix it for me to meet with a few people without my parents or Brayden finding out? I know everyone has spies here, but I don't want Brayden to know what I'm planning."

"I think that can be arranged. Who am I inviting?"

"Stevie, Sashi, Anne, Shaw, and you. I think six people will be a good number to work with and I trust these friends. How soon do you think you can get them together?"

"It's almost lunch time now. Anne'll be in the dining hall. Shaw's probably in the library. I could send a messenger to the Kaspers' shop for the twins."

"No. No messengers. This needs to be kept quiet."

"Okay." Thorvin considered his options. "Wait here. I'll meet with Anne then bring you lunch. After you've eaten, try to get some rest while I contact the others and arrange to meet later. When things are set, I'll come and get you."

"Thanks. With all that happened this morning, I never got breakfast and I'm starving."

"I know." Thorvin chuckled. "I can hear your stomach from here. It sort of brings back old memories."

Thorvin wasn't sure if he should have said that; Rayne still struggled with what had been done to him in the past. But Thorvin was relieved when Rayne grinned. "Yeah, it used to make Sigmund so angry. If he hated my stomach growling so much he should have fed me better." He shook his head and surprised Thorvin by saying, "Thorvin, we're going to do this. We're going to get these seven scrolls, bring them together, and make Sigmund squirm."

As Thorvin headed toward the kitchens, a smile flitted across his face. Yes, there were problems. There was definitely something wrong with Theodor and Rowena. Rayne was right, Brayden was behind whatever was happening to them. He was a snake they would have to deal with. And Sigmund was still lurking somewhere with an agenda that included Rayne and vengeance. But Thorvin knew now that Rayne would be okay. He would face these challenges and come out on the other side stronger. This time Thorvin would be there for him. Maybe he wasn't Warren, but he could do his best to help Rayne face this next test.

21

When Thorvin returned, Rayne was sound asleep, sprawled across one of the chairs, the empty lunch dishes set on a tray on the table. Checking the time, he decided to let the prince sleep a little longer.

He was pleased with his successful afternoon; he had been able to talk to everyone he thought should come to this meeting. Trustworthy friends who would want to be a part of what Rayne was doing, even if they wouldn't skip to Veres with him. Thorvin would take responsibility for whom he invited and if Rayne didn't like it, so be it; the boy needed to learn to accept help from his friends.

The sun was riding low in the western sky, casting long red fingers across Westvale, when Thorvin woke Rayne.

"Your Highness." He shook Rayne's shoulder. "It's time. We need to head out."

Rayne groaned and stretched, then looked up at Thorvin with sleep-laden eyes. "What? Oh, yeah. Did you set it up? Are we meeting now?"

"Yep. We need to get over to the church house. I arranged to meet everyone there. So wake up and get a move on, otherwise we'll be late for our own meeting."

Rayne stretched again and yawned. Pushing upright from the chair he walked over to the sideboard and splashed some water from a basin onto his face before running fingers through his sleep-mussed hair. "Waking up." He pulled his boots on and stood. "I'm ready."

Thorvin motioned for Rayne to stay put as he looked out the door. Once he was certain no one was in the hall, he waved Rayne out. He led the way to the church grounds, stopping from time to time to avoid notice.

$$\text{\bf 11}$$

They walked into the church house that served as the bishop's living quarters as well as dining facility for church staff, official guests, and visiting itinerant monks. Entering through the back door he always used when he visited Elsie, Rayne half-expected to see her there. But the kitchen was dark and empty. He followed Thorvin into the hallway that led deeper into the large dwelling. Rayne had never been past the kitchen before. His eyes were drawn by the golden warmth of the aged wood on the walls and the worn floor. Portraits of serious old men scattered on the wall looked like they had been painted a long time ago. He was wondering where Thorvin was taking him when he heard the hum of voices.

Rayne stopped and grabbed Thorvin's arm. "How many people are here?"

"Don't worry. There are only friends here," Thorvin said as he opened the door into a large formal dining room filled with four heavy wooden trestle tables and enough chairs to seat twelve people at each table. Two of the tables were lit by candelabras and there was an assortment of cold foods set out. The wood paneling from the hall continued into the room making it warm and inviting. But Rayne stood in the doorway confused by the number of people present. He stared at Thorvin who stopped just inside the door.

Narrowing his eyes at Thorvin, Rayne asked, "What's this?"

At that moment, Boone jumped up from where she had

been lying next to Andrew and almost knocked Rayne over with her exuberant greeting.

"Whoa, girl." Rayne reached out to the excited dog. "How did you get in here? You're not allowed in here."

"She is tonight, by special permission of both the cook and the bishop," Jonathan said as he moved to greet Thorvin and Rayne. "This is a special meeting and Boone is part of this select group, so Elsie and I decided we could make an exception and let her in."

Grinning, Rayne bent down and rubbed behind the dog's ears as she wagged her tail in delight. When he rose, Rayne looked Thorvin in the eye. "Okay, old man, what's going on here. I asked you to set a meeting with just four other people and there must be a dozen here. What are you up to?"

"Well, the truth of the matter is ..." Thorvin looked down and shuffled his feet. "I know you want to leave for Veres in the next day or two. And I knew all your friends would want to hear what you're planning and get to say good-bye before you leave. Look around, Rayne. Everyone here in this room would have been hurt if you left without saying good-bye."

Thorvin paused a moment before a knowing smirk curled his lips and he called, "Let's get this meeting started. You said you have a plan. Well, we're waiting to hear it."

"Yeah." Rayne shook his head. "But I didn't think I would have to share it with so many people."

He looked around, a comforting warmth filling him at seeing not only Stevie and Sashi but their parents as well. Elsie and Jonathan were there along with Anne and Shaw. Andrew was sitting next to Noah who looked happy to be sitting next to Sashi. Captain Fontaine was standing, talking to Kori and Mace. But the person whose presence surprised him the most was Travis Illk. The man sat off by himself still looking guilty as he fidgeted in his seat.

Even though Rayne felt awkward explaining his plan to so many people, Thorvin motioned for everyone to take seats. A minute later, Rayne was the only one still standing.

He looked down at Boone, who leaned in next to his leg, looking up at him with open affection. "Okay girl, let's do this." He took a deep breath and plunged in.

"Before I start, you need to understand. Whatever we discuss here tonight goes no further than this room. If news of what we are doing gets out, my whole plan could fail and put those involved at risk. By now, you all know the One has called me to Veres. And as you are all aware, access to Veres is restricted. What I am about to propose is dangerous because everything I know about the games, how they work, and how to get on Veres is based on second-hand, unverified information. To be honest, I'm following my instincts here and hoping for the best."

As Rayne caught each individual's eyes, he saw nods of agreement around the table. He knew they all understood the difficulty of his task, but in the next few minutes they would learn the serious nature of the plan he was proposing.

"Special visas issued by the Merchants Guild on Sorial are required to skip to Veres, and the only people other than the merchants themselves who are issued visas are those involved in the illegal games. These games are well attended by young nobles; as a royal, I would normally have no problem gaining an open visa. But with my father's efforts to stop these games, the merchants would never issue one to me. When Private Matheson kidnapped me on our trip to Warren's Rest, he planned to profit from my abilities by selling me as a fighter for the games. I propose to do something similar.

"My plan is simple. I take on the role of a slave meant for the games with Thorvin as my owner. Stevie and Sashi will pose as his guards, Shaw as his Second, and Anne as his personal healer. The hardest part will be making the right connections on Sorial so we can obtain an open visa. We'll need it to be able to travel freely when we get to Veres and, from what I've learned, they're only issued to the owners of high-level fighters and wealthy nobles. My hope is to obtain the visa, skip, and then avoid participating in the games by leaving the capital immediately.

"After leaving Eleri, we will try to make contact with the rebels. I'm hoping that they will help us locate the scroll. Once we have the Words of the One to Veres we should be able to aid the Verenian rebels in some measure, then, with their help, leave Veres.

"That's it, the gist of my plan."

As he expected, everyone protested his plan and the need to put himself at risk with such a strategy.

He let them talk for a while and voice their worries, but then he spoke again. "If anyone can come up with a better solution for getting onto Veres I would be happy to hear it. Taking on the role of slave again is not something I look forward to doing. But I have thought about this a lot, and this is the one plan I can think of that offers a good chance at success."

The voices settled when Rayne spoke, then continued in subdued whispers as they murmured among themselves trying to come up with another plan. Finally, one voice rose above the others. It was Travis.

"He's right, you know. The only way you're going to get onto Veres is by associating with those running the games. Like everyone else here, I do not like the idea of the young prince putting himself at risk. But if he must get to Veres this is probably the best way. I think I can help with making connections on Sorial. Unless things have changed much over the last few years, I can give you a couple names. And although it has been a long time since I was on Veres, I can supply you with a map of Eleri and the area around the skipping line portals."

"Thank you, Mr. Illk," Rayne said.

"Please, just call me Travis."

"Travis, then. I would appreciate any information you can give us. Names, maps, anything else." Turning back to the group at large, Rayne said, "I think this settles it; this plan is our best chance at getting onto Veres. Stevie, Sashi, are you willing to participate in this and take on the role of Thorvin's guards? I know my plan could put you in danger, so think about it before you answer."

Stevie nodded readily, but Sashi avoided Rayne's gaze. "I don't think I can do this." She bit her lip and shook her head. "I can't pretend you're some slave and not you, I won't be believable. I'm sure to mess up and do something stupid. Isn't there someone else who could be a guard?"

"I would do it," Noah said, setting his hand on Sashi's, "but I don't think I could get out of my duties for an indeterminate amount of time without raising suspicion. Otherwise I would do it for you Sashi."

"I have the same problem," Captain Fontaine said. "I'd like to help, but my absence would be noticed."

Sashi looked like she was going to cry, but she said, "Okay, if you need me, I'll do it."

"Thanks, Sashi," Rayne said. "I'm sure you'll be just fine."

Rayne turned his attention to Anne and Shaw. "Anne, Shaw, what about you two? Are you willing to put yourselves at risk to help me?"

Shaw spoke up. "You know, Prince Rayne, I have been committed to your journey since before I even knew you still lived. Like Sashi, I fear I might do something to put you at risk, but I will do my best to help the Light Bringer in any way I can."

Rayne looked to Anne, his oldest friend, and signed, *what do you think my friend? Are you ready to put yourself at risk again for the slave boy Wren?*

Smiling the small smile that had comforted Rayne so often in the past, Anne nodded. "If you had thought to do this without me and tried to leave me behind, I would have followed you on my own. Oh Rayne, you know you were my strength and my hope when we both thought we were going to die. I would join you even if you were heading into Sigmund's stronghold tomorrow, my oldest and dearest friend."

Rayne nodded his appreciation of Anne's answer. No matter where life took them, the bond they shared back at the compound would forever join them in a special friendship. He knew he didn't need to ask; Anne would always be there for him. But he felt it was important that each person going to Veres be confident enough with his or her decision to be able to make a verbal commitment, a spoken vow. And Rayne knew there was one more person he needed to ask.

"Thorvin. Even knowing you are putting yourself in danger, are you willing to come with me to Veres? Know that I will be counting on you to convince these people you are my master and I am your slave. Can you do this?"

Looking Rayne in the eye, Thorvin said simply, "What must be done, I will do."

"Travis, how soon could you have that information for us?" Rayne asked.

"I can give you the names and draw up the map right now if you wish, Your Highness."

"Good. Then do so. Go over the details with Thorvin as you work and give him the names of your contacts."

After looking around at his friends once more, Rayne said, "Unless anyone can give me a reason not to, I want to leave tomorrow."

Although his statement produced shocked looks, no one said anything.

"Good. Shaw, as Thorvin's Second, you should go to the portal station now, verify what hours are set for the outbound skip to Sorial, and purchase our passes.

"Jonathan, as I seem to be without funds at the current time, do you think the church might be able to cover the cost of our passes? I will pay you back when things are finally straightened out."

"The church would be honored to aid you in your search for the scrolls. Shaw, come to my office and I'll write you a promissory note to cover the passes."

"Jonathan. Shaw." Rayne called after them. "You haven't eaten. Do you want to grab something before you go?"

"I'll get the passes first," Shaw said as he and Jonathan headed up the hallway.

Rayne turned to Travis. "Didn't Madam Ria say the Reclamation Committee has funds available for the search?"

"Yes."

"Since I already asked Bishop Hedrick to cover the cost of the skip, can I rely on the committee to provide funds for the rest of our needs on this trip? Thorvin, how much do you think we will need?"

Thorvin looked up to Travis and they exchanged glances. "What do you think? Allowing for bribes and other unexpected expenses, I'd say about five thousand sommes?"

"You'd better make it seven thousand just to be safe," Travis said. "You can always return whatever is left when you get back."

"Can you get that for us by tomorrow morning?" Rayne asked Travis.

"That shouldn't be a problem, Your Highness." Travis returned his attention to the map he was sketching.

With a sigh, Rayne sat down. He focused on Thorvin and Travis again and asked, "Am I missing anything?"

Glancing up, Thorvin said, "No, Your Highness. I think you have everything covered. Well done. Barring any problems getting through the portal, I think you will have your wish. We should be on Sorial by this time tomorrow."

Releasing the tension that had knotted the muscles of his back, Rayne bent down and scratched Boone's ears again. She sat at his feet leaning into him the entire time he was talking, and he had drawn strength from her unquestioning loyalty. He traced the narrow white streak that ran from the crown of her head to right before her nose, scratching gently down her face with a finger. She moaned in doggie delight at the attention.

Rayne was grateful Jonathan and Elsie agreed to allow Boone into the church house. He looked up, thinking to thank them, but Jonathan hadn't returned yet.

Elsie sat next to Andrew, talking to Anne and Shaw who sat across the table from her. Rising, Rayne moved between the two tables to stand behind Elsie. Once she realized he was there, she pushed back her chair and turned to him.

I'm so sorry." She stood up and wrapped him in a motherly hug. The hug felt good and Rayne leaned into it just as Boone had leaned into him earlier. Elsie was about the same size as his mother but where Rowena was thin and muscular, Elsie was full-bodied and soft. Feeling the constraint of his newly sworn vow to keep his emotions in check, Rayne stiffened and awkwardly placed one hand on her back in response.

Her eyes brimming with unshed tears, Elsie said, "We need to talk."

22

Andrew shifted down a chair so Rayne could sit next to Elsie. When they were settled, Elsie turned to Rayne, her eyes misty with unshed tears. "My poor sweet boy. I can't believe this is happening again. I had all but forgotten how bad it was, and you just a little mite of a boy at the time."

"Um." Rayne swallowed, his eyes fixed on Elsie. "Are you talking about Brayden?"

Elsie pulled her lower lip between her teeth. "Of course, you couldn't know, you wouldn't remember. You were so young." She sat, quiet for a moment, staring at nothing until Rayne asked, "What wouldn't I remember?"

"Oh." Elsie's eyes went wide. "Brayden. Yes, of course Brayden. Brayden and your parents." She grimaced. "That lying little snake." Shaking her head, she looked back up at Rayne. "I never worked in the palace, so at first I didn't know what to believe. The few times I saw Brayden, he seemed well mannered if a bit stiff. I had heard the stories though, things whispered by the staff and told to me in confidence by your old nurse, Martha.

"Before you were born, Brayden was a frequent visitor to

the palace, a favored nephew. He probably spent more time here with your parents then he did in Inverness with his. He was already eight years old when you were born.

"At first he would have nothing to do with you, but by the time you turned three and were walking and talking, Martha told me he would come into your nursery wanting to play with you. It seemed odd to her that an eleven-year old boy would take so much interest in a toddler, but he convinced her he loved his *Little Raynie,* as he called you, and wanted to take care of you."

"Humph." Rayne grunted. "He still calls me that. It's annoying."

An understanding smile touched the corners of Elsie's lips. "Well, your parents encouraged her to allow Brayden to spend time with you. They said it was important for you to bond. That he would be a good influence on you when you got older. She began trusting him, letting him take you for walks, or watch over you in the nursery while she got caught up with other tasks.

"That is until the day she thought to surprise you two with a snack in the gardens and caught him pushing you into one of your mother's rosebushes. That nasty, thorny, climbing one by the arbor. You were struggling and crying, and your arms and face were bleeding. Martha stood and watched for a minute. She couldn't believe what she was seeing. There was no mistake, your cousin was purposefully hurting you … and he was smiling.

"Martha pulled Brayden away, but he shrugged her off and called her some unrepeatable names before storming into the conservatory. She gathered you up and took you right to the healers to tend the cuts from the thorns and the bruises on your arms where Brayden had grabbed you.

"Leaving you with the healers, Martha went straight to your mother to tell her what happened. Brayden, that Nemorian serpent, was already there reporting that Martha had not been watching you properly. He told your mother she had left you alone in the garden and you got tangled in a rosebush. He insisted he did nothing more than try to help you, but then Martha returned, grabbed you, and pushed him away.

"Of course, your mother believed Brayden. She even threatened to banish Martha if she didn't admit her fault.

"Martha told me the whole story when she came to my kitchen the following day. I remember clearly what she said next. 'I know that Lord Woodfield makes a show of caring for the young prince, but he means to harm my little boy, I just know it. I may not get Her Majesty to believe me; she trusts Lord Woodfield absolutely. But Elsie, mark my words, there's something off about that Nemorian serpent and no good will come of allowing him near the prince.'

"After that, whenever Lord Woodfield was around, which was often, everyone noticed the change in your parents. That, coupled with the fact that every day he was at the palace you had new, unexplained injuries, led certain members of the staff to make a pact. Someone would always be near, so you would never be alone with your cousin. No one talked about it openly. They were afraid.

"But the worst was the pony incident when you turned five." Elsie paused, her face going pale as she pulled in a sniffling breath. "Brayden hadn't been around for a couple months and your mother and father were so different when he wasn't in Westvale. The whole palace felt brighter without him here. Your mother told me of the special present she and your father had gotten for you, a beautiful Arisimanian pony. She was so excited the morning you left for Nemora to celebrate your fifth birthday with family.

"Although Theodor and Rowena originally planned to spend several weeks on Nemora, you returned the day before your birthday. Brayden came back with you." Elsie shook her head. "It was a horrible time. Your parents were even worse than before, shunning you and praising Brayden. You were so hurt and confused. Martha couldn't stop crying. It was like a strange gloom covered the city and shadows were growing in places where shadows don't normally grow. Everyone felt it; like the city itself had gone dark." She shuddered.

"I never learned the details of what happened on Nemora, the whole thing was hushed up. But from what I learned later—and please understand, no one here believed the story—Brayden accused you of joining with a group of older boys from Inverness in slaughtering a cow at some ancient sacrificial stone not far from Castle Inverness. It was supposed to be an offering to some demon. Your parents were beyond angry; they cancelled your birthday celebration and gave the pony to Brayden." Elsie paused and took a couple deep breaths before continuing in a voice barely louder than a whisper.

"Oh Rayne, I haven't thought about this in so long; I guess I just wanted to forget it ever happened."

Rayne reached over and gently placed a hand over Elsie's trembling fingers. "It's okay, Elsie. Tell me what happened."

"The week after you returned, your parents threw a party for Brayden. Wanting to show off his new pony, he invited a group of high-ranked nobles and their children. As part of your punishment for what had supposedly happened on Nemora, you were confined to your nursery for the day.

"It was late afternoon when Brayden told your parents there was something they needed to see in the riding ring. When they arrived at the ring, along with all the guests, you were … riding the pony.

"Theodor called for the stable master, Wilson, to remove you from the pony and bring you to stand before him. Wilson and several other witnesses said Theodor and Rowena were like statues made of ice.

"Wilson said you looked so afraid. You trembled as you stood before them and tried to explain. You said Brayden had come to your nursery and told you that all was forgiven. That because your parents felt bad for punishing you, they wanted to make it up by allowing you to ride the pony while everyone else was at the party.

"But that Nemorian serpent denied it all. He even had a couple other boys say he was outside with them the whole time. He told your parents you were lying, just like always, and he wasn't going to cover up for you anymore."

Elsie paused and began wringing her hands. "Wilson said … oh my … Wilson said the king and queen wouldn't even look at you or listen to you. They believed every word Lord Woodfield said. Then …" Elsie stopped again, sniffing and shaking her head.

"Then the king and queen asked Lord Woodfield to set your punishment. Can you imagine that? What a horrible thing to do. Wilson said it was the saddest thing to watch."

Elsie shuddered and drew in a shaky breath. "Brayden said ... he said ... the pony was the cause of your disobedience, so the pony needed to die. Though most of the guests left at that point, your parents forced you to stay and watch as Brayden, personally, killed that poor pony.

Elsie struggled to blink back tears. "You came to me after, even though it was getting dark. You ran into my kitchen and threw yourself into my arms, crying; you were so hurt. You fell asleep with me holding you after crying until you were too tired to cry. Martha came for you then. The whole palace was in shock; it was like the king and queen were total strangers.

"You were such a kind-hearted little boy and it took a long time for you to get over what happened." Elsie straightened with a huff. "A few weeks later, Brayden left.

"Once he went back to Inverness, everything changed; it was like a storm had passed and the sun came out. Your parents were themselves again, loving you. The three of you were the happy family we all knew. But they never acknowledged what happened; it was almost as if they didn't remember the way they treated you and what was done to the poor pony. It was a peaceful time; until you were invited to spend several weeks on Nemora. We were all so worried about you while you were at Castle Inverness." Elsie let out a sigh.

"Brayden didn't return to Westvale until the following spring, a few days before you disappeared."

While Elsie was talking, everyone got quiet. Jonathan had returned from his office and he waited at the door, listening. "I don't remember any of that."

"You were away at that world-wide church council in Easton at the time," Elsie said. "Remember? You left for the conference the day after the king and queen left for Inverness. Your council ended up lasting nearly two months. By the time you returned, Rayne was on Nemora and things were pretty much back to normal. But you must remember the stories. They were still circulating for months after."

The wrinkles in Jonathan's brow deepened. "Now that you mention it, I did hear something about turmoil at the palace when I got back. I never realized what all happened."

Looking down at the table Rayne murmured, "I don't remember." He looked up at Elsie, struggling to reconcile his shattered memories with Elsie's words. "How could I forget something so important?"

"What we need to focus on now, isn't the past," Thorvin said, pushing up out of his chair and pulling attention to himself. "We need to concentrate on making it through Sorial and onto Veres." He gave Rayne an appraising look. "You're not the person you were six months ago, Sire. You're a prince now, with newfound strength. Can you set that aside and once again become a slave? This plan will only succeed if we all play our parts well.

"Elsie's story about Brayden, what he's doing to Theodor and Rowena, and how long this has been going on was hard for you to hear, Your Highness. But you must decide which front you want to fight first. You can't be of two minds and succeed. Do you want to infiltrate Veres? Or would you set that aside to remain here and confront Brayden first? The choice is yours, Sire, I will stand with you whichever you decide."

Everyone focused on Rayne and he closed his eyes to pray, the decision sitting like a hot coal in his stomach. *No matter what I decide, I have to let go of something. I need your help. Please?* After a few minutes, he looked up. "I want to stop Brayden and help my parents so bad, it hurts. I don't know what he's done to Mother and Father, or what he might do to them in the future." He shook his head. "But the One has called me to Veres. I have to trust my parents to his care and focus on what must be done to get onto Veres."

Looking around, he continued. "Elsie, Jonathan, Captain Fontaine, Andrew, you four will have the most access to my parents, please watch for anything that looks like Brayden is increasing his hold, or that he's going to harm them in some way. If so, seek help from the Reclamation Committee." He shifted his gaze to Travis. "They would help my parents, wouldn't they?"

"Without a doubt, Sire."

"As I said earlier, with me gone, I hope Brayden will relax his hold, maybe even return to Nemora."

Rayne turned back to Thorvin. "You're right, I've changed and it's not going to be easy to play the role of slave again. I'm counting on your support to make this happen. And you too Stevie, Sashi, Anne."

Shaw walked in at that moment and announced they had passes to skip to Sorial the next morning.

Elsie waved at the food on the tables. "Come, everyone, please eat. Tomorrow morning will be here before you know it. There is plenty, and I won't tolerate anyone leaving without having eaten his fill. Especially you, Rayne. I've made some of your favorites."

The tables were piled with several loafs of Elsie's standard bread plus two loafs of a specialty sweet bread she made for special occasions. There were three kinds of meat cut into thin slices, and a selection of salads, including one made from red beets and oranges brought in from Arisima that Rayne couldn't stop eating.

Rayne was enjoying his third helping of the salad when Kori, Mace, Stevie, and Sashi, came to say they were leaving. Thorvin walked over and asked if they had anything to wear that would look like the two were dressed in uniforms. After a brief discussion, they determined to stop at a clothier they knew in the district to see if he had something suitable; if not they would get matching outfits on Sorial.

Captain Fontaine and Noah said good-bye and headed back to the barracks. Travis and Andrew came up together, Travis's arm wrapped around a laughing Andrew's shoulders. After saying good-bye, as the two were about to walk out together, Rayne called to Travis. "Hey. Thanks again for your help. Could I ask you to keep an eye on Andrew for me? He's a good kid, and I don't trust Brayden. Between what I've been remembering and what Elsie said, I know Brayden has always wanted everything that was mine. I wouldn't put it past him to try to claim Andrew. Please don't let that happen, okay? Maybe the committee could use him for something?"

Andrew turned back. "What about if I agree to be Lord Woodfield's page if he asks for me. I can keep an eye on him and try to learn what he's really up to. Being his page would get me close."

"No." Rayne shook his head. "I don't even want to think about that. You stay away from Brayden. Do whatever Travis finds for you to do and take care of Boone for me. That will be help enough. I don't want you anywhere near that—what did you call him Elsie—Nemorian serpent."

Andrew's eyes shifted to his feet. "Yes Sire." He called Boone and went out with Travis following. Travis whispered back to Rayne as he walked out the door. "Don't worry, I'll keep an eye on him."

Shaw, Anne, and Thorvin sat for a while longer at the table, talking. Anne was quite comfortable in her role as healer, and she was helping Shaw understand his position and his expected behavior as Thorvin's Second. Thorvin, sitting across the table from Anne, spoke up from time to time adding pointers and more information.

Bishop Hedrick had been called away on church business and Elsie, with the help of a serving girl, was clearing the tables. Rayne asked if he could help and she told him 'no' in firm language, saying clearing tables was no task for a prince. Rayne chuckled. "True. But starting tomorrow I'm going to be nothing more than a slave again and, who knows, I might just end up clearing tables."

Handing the tray she was holding to the girl, Elsie turned back to Rayne. "I don't know why you have to do this. I understand what you said, but I still don't understand why it has to be you. Couldn't Thorvin be the slave and you be his master?"

Looking up at Thorvin, Rayne chuckled. "Look at him, Elsie. Can you really see him as a slave?"

She looked up and with a sigh, shook her head.

"No, and neither will anyone else. I wish I could think of another way to do this. Even if it's just a sham, being a slave again scares me more than I would admit to anyone else. I know this plan isn't ideal, but even though I've been wracking my brain, I can't come up with a better way onto Veres." He gave Elsie a slight smile. "It's okay, Elsie, it won't be for long. Once we've gotten onto Veres, I won't have to play slave any longer. It'll just be for a few days while we're on Sorial."

"Yes. But that's the problem, you'll be on Sorial. I don't trust those merchants. Everyone knows they'll sell anything for a profit. I will worry about you every day you're gone."

Rayne and Elsie hugged again. Thorvin, Anne, and Shaw rose to head back to their rooms. Morning would come soon and they needed to be ready.

23

Rayne looked out from under the deep hood of a long black cloak that covered him from head to foot. He was grateful for the warm garment as he watched a few snowflakes floating down from the fish-scale gray clouds layered over the square in front of the portal station. After a windy night that seemed bent on stripping away every last leave still clinging to the trees, the air now was still and cold.

Portal Square was crowded with both travelers and freight waiting to skip onto one of the other worlds or streaming away from the station, having just skipped onto Corylus.

The portal station in Westvale, the royal city of Ochen, housed portals for skipping lines to Arisima, Nemora, Amathea, Sorial, and Glacieria, making it the largest hub in the system.

The Emporium City station on Sorial, the second largest hub, with portals to Nemora, Corylus, Amathea, and Veres, was the busiest station in the system. The level of trade conducted in Emporium City kept the skipping lines humming day and night, switching from arrivals to departures every four hours.

Thorvin told everyone to come to the station separately in case they were being watched, and then join up right before they were scheduled to skip so they would arrive in Emporium City together. There were always paid informants watching the portals in Emporium City. The merchants didn't like surprises.

Thorvin and Rayne made their way to the square outside the portal station early to be sure they weren't followed. Rayne was absent-mindedly scratching around the veredium slave collar Thorvin had gotten from somewhere, as he scanned the square for their friends. He hated wearing the collar; it reminded him of his past and things he'd rather forget. But he agreed with Thorvin that they needed to look convincing. At least he and Thorvin agreed he didn't need to wear shackles.

Rayne watched as Stevie and Sashi arrived. Tall and athletic, the twins were dressed in matching uniforms like many of the wealthier merchants' guards wore; dark green pants tucked into black boots, white wide-collared shirts, and waist length light green jackets. Both had well-used scabbards strapped at their waists. They looked good, Rayne thought, very believable.

It was getting close to the time they were scheduled to skip, and Rayne was beginning to worry that Shaw and Anne still hadn't arrived when he saw them. Rayne blinked several times and shook his head. He had never seen Shaw wear anything but a monk's robe. *Anne must have done it.* This morning Shaw looked like the consummate wealthy noble's Second. He wore dark gray stripped trousers with a deep green, knee-length, tailored, leather coat over a blousing yellow shirt with gold trim around a low-cut neckline. His recalcitrant brown curls had even been oiled into a semblance of order. Rayne found it hard to reconcile this image with the humble monk he had studied with the last few months.

Anne wore one of her regular dresses, but Rayne noticed the long sleeved yellow shift she wore under the green linen over-dress matched the yellow in Shaw's shirt. Even Thorvin looked his part. Though still wearing his trade-mark black, everything had the look of expensive, well-tailored clothing, from his incredibly soft doe-skin boots to the fancy feathered hat that looked rather ridiculous on the large warrior.

At a nod from Thorvin they all shifted toward the steps leading up to the station building, angling toward each other with care through the rushing, jostling crowd. The station was large enough to house all the portals, including the large freight portals for Sorial, Amathea, and Nemora. The only portal serving outbound customers currently was the small portal for the skipping line to Sorial, and, as usual, it was busy. Despite all the bumping of people traveling to Sorial, and general activity in the station, the companions came together as a group right before the portal.

Rayne followed Thorvin in. He felt the familiar sensation of a sinking stomach followed by a rushing feeling and then he was stepping out behind Thorvin.

Shaw came through right behind Rayne, and following Thorvin's instructions, he immediately moved to hook the lead he carried to Rayne's collar. Shaw hesitated and pulled the lead back, everything in him rebelling at leashing his friend. He drew in a stabilizing breath and reached toward the collar, his hands shaking. Rayne didn't say a word but gave Shaw a hard look which increased his level of discomfort.

Thorvin had warned Shaw that in his position, he would need to control Rayne. He would be expected to treat the prince as a piece of property, not a person. So, as everyone else stepped through, Shaw tugged the lead to pull Rayne forward. If anyone was watching, Shaw hoped his lapse hadn't been noticed and he set his mind to playing the part required of him while they were on Sorial. He hoped he wouldn't slip again, but it was so hard to treat Rayne the way Thorvin said he should. Shaw prayed yet again that his actions wouldn't give them away.

But at least they had arrived looking the part of a wealthy merchant with a small, inconspicuous entourage. Travis said that would be best. Unlike the commoners, the nobles who participated in the games, either as spectators or slave owners, didn't usually flaunt their intentions to the general public. The tended to skip in quietly with a small party. This fit well with Rayne's plan.

11

Despite Travis's warnings none of them was prepared for the stench, the heat, and the overwhelming noise of Emporium City. They had skipped from the fresh, crisp air of a late autumn snow in Westvale, into the intense summer heat of midday under Sorial's two suns. The humidity from the lake Emporium City was built on made everything damp and moldy, and intensified the reek of the city. Emporium City's markets didn't even need lighting at this time of the year as the two suns tracked several hours apart, bathing the city in stifling heat and light well into the nighttime hours for two months.

Less than an hour later, Rayne wished he could remove his sweat-soaked heavy cloak, or at least lower the hood. But the plan called for him to remain hidden, so he was forced to put up with the discomfort. He struggled with the warmth trapped by the weighty garment and the rivulets of sweat that dribbled down his torso as Thorvin stopped at various stalls, taking his time, talking to different merchants.

It was all part of their plan to attract the attention of a master house gatekeeper, the person who could get them an open visa for travel on Veres. Thorvin dropped the names Travis had given him at every stall they visited, mentioning his desire to meet with a gatekeeper. He made it known that he was a noble with a very rare piece of property.

As the afternoon wore on, Rayne pushed back the front of his sweat-dampened hood and glanced up at the sky. He squinted at the harsh light of the large, yellow sun, Xanthe, angling over the tops of the pavilions as it trekked across the horizon. He blinked and looked away quickly, the bright light searing his eyes. Directly overhead sat the smaller, silver ball of Ortrun. Although Ortrun didn't bring tears to his eyes like Xanthe, he remembered Warren's warning. *Though smaller in size, the silver sun of Sorial is more dangerous than Sorial's large yellow sun. Unlike Xanthe's harsh unforgiving light, Ortrun's light is soft. But that gentle-seeming light is deceiving. The dangerous rays can harm your eyes, even blind you, before you're aware of the damage.*

The immense Emporium City Central Market was actually made up of many smaller bazaars that merged from one into the next and into the next. The only way to know which of these a shopper was in, was by the flags surrounding each plaza. Each market had several plazas and flags of specific colors and design indicated which master houses' goods were sold there.

The largest individual market was run by the Andersen family, headed by Lord William. The Andersens controlled both the Merchants' Guild and the Miners' Guild, and their family flags, half red and half black cut on a diagonal, announced ownership over more than half of Emporium City Central Market.

There were also a few smaller plazas set up to sell only certain goods, like weapons or meat or clothing. The various flags of ownership were scattered throughout those sectors. But most of the markets were a noisy jumble of any type of goods. The noise was almost deafening as merchants loudly hawked their wares and customers and merchants haggled over prices.

Birds squawked, pigs squealed, children screamed, and at one point they even passed two auctioneers selling slaves. The heat rose in waves of smell; the smell of spices and unwashed bodies mingled with the smell of livestock. But the most pervasive and distinctive odor came from the water of the lake Emporium City sat on, a smell similar to rotten eggs.

Shouting over the noise, Anne passed everyone except Rayne small cloth squares she had just purchased. They were scented with a sweet-smelling oil to help dilute the worst of the stench. She gave Rayne a sorrowful look and he nodded understanding. Slaves weren't given such luxuries. He almost asked for one anyway; the smells were making him dizzy. He felt funny, as if he was seeing things through a long, dark tunnel. The feeling had come over him several times since arriving in Emporium City, and he looked forward to getting away from the stench, the noise, and the stifling heat soon.

According to Travis's information, they were only a few blocks from the inn where they planned to stay, when Anne stopped at another stall to purchase a lighter weight cloak for

Rayne. Shoved from behind, Rayne stumbled into Shaw as his hood was yanked from his head taking the thong tying his hair into a tail with it. He gained his balance, righting himself as the sun reflected off his midnight black hair now falling lose around his shoulders.

Everyone turned to see who had shoved Rayne, Sashi and Stevie almost pulled their swords, but Thorvin's hand stopped the motion. Whoever pushed Rayne was gone.

"What's this?" Thorvin growled loud enough to be heard by nearby vendors. "Did you do that on purpose boy?"

He stepped up to Rayne who glowered at him. Thorvin raised his hand as if to strike. Rayne promptly lowered his eyes in a submissive manner.

Thorvin continued, his voice loud and cold. "That's better. You try my patience slave; I'm tired of your tricks. One more stunt like that and fight or no fight, I'll take my whip to you. And pull up that hood! I won't have others gawking at you unless I'm profiting from it."

He turned to Anne, still glaring. "Hurry it up woman. I want a cold drink and I need something to eat. Aren't you done yet?"

With a bow, Anne said quietly, "Yes, my lord. I'm sorry to hold you up. I'll be done shortly."

She made a show of paying more than the cloak was worth and not waiting for change as she scurried after Thorvin who was marching rapidly toward the inn. Shaw struggled to keep up with the swiftly moving Thorvin while tugging on Rayne's lead. Once again adopting the role of recalcitrant slave, Rayne fought it every step of the way. Stevie and Sashi gave each other unsure looks as they brought up the rear.

Striding past the remaining stalls while vendors hawked their wares, the tunnel vision Rayne experienced earlier returned. The slave collar cut into his neck and darkness seemed to hover around the edges of his vision. He stumbled when the darkness unexpectedly thickened, making it hard to breathe. The unexpected action caused Shaw to pull up short and he sent Rayne a quick look of apology. Thorvin turned back and growled his disapproval, waving them forward. Rayne shook off the suffocating sensation and after he glowered at Shaw, the monk allowed some slack on the lead.

"You alright?" Stevie whispered coming up behind him.

"Yeah, yeah, I'm fine," Rayne mumbled.

They arrived at the inn Travis recommended soon after, a rather shabby looking, dirty place. Thorvin mumbled, shaking his head in disgust. "This is a problem. Things have changed since Travis was here last. He said it would be clean and quiet. This place is a dump. Well, we're here now so let's make the best of it."

Rayne retied his tail and pulled his hood back up, hiding his hair and features. They climbed the three steps into the inn, Shaw towing Rayne behind as he approached the innkeeper to arrange for a large suite. He also ordered that food be brought to their rooms.

As Thorvin's Second, Shaw was expected to handle his master's slave while making lodging arrangements. Rayne softly clicked his tongue in disgust when he caught Shaw squirming. They had both noticed the innkeeper's obvious appraisal of Rayne, as if considering his worth, while the man took his time fishing keys from a large, dirty apron.

24

Rayne breathed a sigh of relief when Thorvin locked the doors to their rooms. The suite consisted of three rooms; an outer bedroom with a door to the hall, connected to a common room, also accessible from the hall. The third room, another bedroom, was accessible only through the common room. Everyone gathered in the common room, finally able to shed cloaks and jackets. The room was furnished with a scratched and stained table, four wooden, straight-back chairs, a couch, and several uncomfortable looking, well-worn stuffed chairs covered in a dark brown material. Thorvin threw his hat on the floor and looked at it as if he contemplated stomping on the thing.

Rayne was a sweating mess under the cloak. He pulled it off eagerly and threw the damp offending material down onto the somewhat clean looking, wood floor. He was irritable; the collar itched, he was hot and sweating, and now he just wanted something cold to drink. He was about to voice that thought when they heard a knock at the common room door. With a quick glance at Thorvin, Rayne ducked into the inner bedroom, leaving the door between the rooms partway open so he could see without being seen.

Thorvin held up his hands for quiet and nodded for Stevie to get the door. The innkeeper entered followed by a couple servants carrying trays of food and drink. After putting the trays on the table, the innkeeper motioned the servants out, but he hung back, his eyes scanning the room.

"Well," Thorvin growled at the man. "What do you want?" The man gave Thorvin a conspiratorial smile showing several missing teeth. "That slave boy ya come in wiff. Heard ya had a bit of a problem wiff 'im in the market. I know a man what'll take 'im off yer hands fer ya. What wiff 'im being rebellious and all. Give ya a fair price too."

"What makes you think I'm looking to sell?" Thorvin grabbed a sweating glass of ale from a tray and nonchalantly sat on the couch swinging his feet up onto a chair and sipping the cold brew. He looked around sending the message with his eyes to everyone to sit down while the innkeeper chuckled as he craned his neck trying to see into the inner bedroom.

"Not fer sale, eh? Well, mister, ya know you're on Sorial now. Ain't nuffin can't be had fer the right price here. Iffin I could just get a peek at 'im, I bet I could offer ya a price that would tickle yer fancy."

Thorvin glared at the man, who nodded knowingly while scratching an arm pit. "He's one a them fighters, ain't he? Yeah, yeah, ya headed for Veres, sure enuff. Yeah, I bet. Heard the boy's got fire in 'is eyes. Owners 'spect some 'bellion from those what fight. That's it, ain't it? Ya taken 'im to Veres?"

"My business is my own."

Stevie, Sashi, and Shaw found seats while Anne moved easily across the room, watching the man as she walked into the inner bedroom and closed the door behind her. Rayne nodded to her and pressed his ear to the door.

"Ah course, ah course," the man said slowly as if considering. "But if ya was interested in gettin im into the games on Veres ya would need to see a gatekeeper ya know. Ain't nobody gets into the games wiffout seein one and ain't no profit from a fighter who ain't fightin', right?"

"And I suppose you're going to tell me you know one?" Thorvin laughed.

"Well, I might know sumthin'. Ain't makin' no promises, ya know. But I might know sumthin'. Fer a price."

"I'll think about your offer—" Thorvin said with emphasis. Rayne grinned knowing Thorvin was probably pointing toward the door as he spoke. Thick as the man was, he apparently got the message and huffing, left.

"What did you do?" Shaw asked, his mouth hanging open. "Isn't this gatekeeper person the one we were trying to meet? Why didn't you take the man up on his offer?"

"Shaw." Thorvin shook his head. "You have a lot to learn about dealing with people like our innkeeper. Patience. You must learn patience." Thorvin leaned back and closed his eyes.

Sashi stood up and started stalking about the room, shaking out her fingers as if ridding them of spider webs. "Is it me, or am I not the only one who feels like she just bumped against something slimy? Oooh, he made my skin crawl!"

Rayne and Anne had come in from the bedroom and Sashi turned to Rayne. "You can't stay here. We have to get you back to Corylus. This is not good. How did he even know ... why would he even ask ... if we wanted to sell you? Arrrgh!"

Looking at her calmly, Rayne said, "It's a good thing, Sashi. Remember, I'm supposed to be the bait that gets us to Veres. It seems our plan to keep me veiled is drawing attention. Now, we just need to attract the right kind of attention. I hope Travis's old contacts are good and we don't have to wait around here for days."

"That stunt in the market place happened pretty quickly," Thorvin said. "I suspect at least one of those names we dropped was responsible for that."

"What are you talking about?" Shaw asked, frustration adding a squeak to his voice.

"The person who *accidentally* bumped into Rayne. That was no accident. Somebody wanted to see what we were hiding under the cloak." Thorvin got up, grabbed one of the plates, and started to fill it. "I don't know about anyone else, but I'm hungry. Let's eat."

Following Thorvin's example, they all filled plates, grabbed drinks, then got comfortable.

Once everyone was settled, Thorvin began to explain. "According to Travis, there are three master houses, each supported by a minor house, with extensive gaming complexes on Veres. The minor houses oversee the complexes and run the training rings where most fighters start out. These are the second-class fights attended by those who can't afford the exclusive and extremely expensive center ring fights. The big money fights, run by the master houses, are the ones that draw the wealthy and powerful. New talent isn't usually picked up by the master houses. They let their subordinates bring in the new stock so they can gauge the slaves' skills by having them fight in the cheaper games. If a slave shows potential, he's given more training and then sent to fight in the center ring. The center ring is the only place you'll find paid fighters. Unlike the slaves who have no choice, these free men choose to fight because they're good at it and like killing. Of course, the hefty purses they can win is a strong incentive. A talented fighter can retire with a small fortune after just a few matches. If he survives.

"Our goal is to get an open visa that will allow us to travel freely on Veres. Unfortunately, a minor house can't get us that kind of access, only a master house. But those who run the center ring games need to be careful in selecting fighters if they want to please their paying customers. A disappointed fan might decide to attend a rival's complex the next time he comes to Veres. That means we need to impress a master house gatekeeper up front.

"Once we've got the visa, we can pull Rayne out before he has to fight. But to get there he needs to prove to a gatekeeper that he's talented enough to place in a high-value match without competing in lesser fights first. Rayne's got the talent, but we need to get him that opportunity. We were dropping names and making it obvious that I'm confident my slave is skilled enough to move directly into the death matches. We were spreading the word that only master house gatekeepers were welcome to examine our property."

"Yes," Shaw said. "I get that. It's what Travis was saying last night, use his contacts to spread the word. That, and buying lighter clothing, was the purpose behind that incredibly uncomfortable stroll through the markets."

"Right," Thorvin said. "But I didn't expect our presence to be so quickly noted. Someone connected to one of the houses was curious. You see, owners who want to participate but haven't yet been invited to the games, need to catch the attention of a lookout. The gatekeepers pay them to keep their eyes open for any new talent skipping onto Sorial.

"Nobles and true connoisseurs who own high-quality merchandise destined for the center ring, are discreet. They rely on a lookout's ability to spot potential talent. The trick to attracting a gatekeeper from a master house, is to present your fighter quietly and with confidence. And knowing the right people helps.

"If you're not already connected with a master house and have a proven history of bringing them worthwhile fighters, it's almost impossible to meet with one of their gatekeepers. That's why Travis's connections were important. His established reputation can open doors to us that wouldn't open otherwise.

"And to make Rayne even more tempting, Travis and I came up with the plan to keep him a mystery. Make the gatekeepers wonder what we have hidden under the cloak. The fact that we're confident enough to not even allow the lookouts to gage his potential, makes Rayne a very enticing package. We've presented a mystery that only a gatekeeper can unravel, making our slave irresistible. It also helps to keep his true identity hidden.

"Now our Rayne has the skills to move right into a master house fight with no problem. He was forced into death matches at an early age and he's got the experience to handle himself. And we've raised their curiosity to the point where someone will have to invite us to a gatekeeper's inspection. We obviously have something more than a street brawler, we aren't shouting out how qualified our fighter is, or even showing him off discreetly. We're just offering a peek at something of quality to only the right people. And that forced someone to snatch a quick look behind the curtain. Now, it's just a matter of time before we get an invite."

"But didn't we already get an invite from the innkeeper?" Shaw asked.

"Oh yes." A satisfied smile spread across Thorvin's face. "But not the kind of invite we're looking for. This innkeeper is obviously a lookout for a minor gatekeeper. No, we're waiting for an invite from someone who can offer us a much more profitable arrangement. And for as quickly as Rayne was checked out in the market, they must be hurting for good fighters right now. It won't take long, trust me.

"These games are big business for the master houses. The actual cost of a ticket to the fight is minor. They make money on visas, travel, inns, other entertainments; these things add up. But the biggest profits come from gambling. The master house games are frequented by the highest nobles and wealthiest commoners from across the system. It wouldn't be unusual for a wealthy noble to spend thousands of sommes on one visit, not to mention what he might lose on bets. Of course, most come in secret, but everyone knows they do come. Even members of the Interplanetary Council have been known to frequent the gaming complexes."

Sashi jumped up and started pacing again. "This whole thing smells, like the nasty lake we're sitting on right now. Nemora's moons Rayne, I get the jitters just thinking about it. How do you stand people treating you like you're some kind of commodity? I mean they don't even care if a fighter lives or dies just as long as he makes them money. That innkeeper almost broke his neck trying to look into the other room to check you over with his slimy eyes. And someone purposefully pulled your hood down to see you, and not so he could just say hi."

"I know Sashi," Rayne said. "Before, when I really was a slave, it turned my stomach. It was so hard. I hated it and I hated myself because of what I could do. The things I was forced to do." He paused, a shiver running through him. "But now, I choose to allow this because it serves a purpose. I can put up with a lot if it will get us to Veres. And if we have to, we'll just accept a lesser offer and deal with it. But if we can get an open visa by waiting a few days for an offer from a master house, I'll wait."

Sashi shuddered. "Just as long as you don't have to fight in one of those death matches."

"Agreed."

After eating, Thorvin suggested everyone get some sleep. Anne and Shaw cleared the dishes and left them in the hallway so the innkeeper wouldn't have an excuse to come back into their rooms.

Thorvin and Rayne took the inner bedroom. Anne and Sashi shared the other bedroom while Shaw and Stevie camped out in the common room. At first Thorvin insisted they lock the doors between the rooms for security, but it got so hot he finally agreed to leave all the doors open so the meager, fitful breeze coming through the lone window could circulate through all three rooms. The stench was still strong, but that was better than sweltering with no breeze at all.

The next day they headed out to the markets again, this time wearing lighter clothing. Rayne was still covered from head to foot, but the light cloak Anne had picked up for him was much cooler and more serviceable in the heat. Anne sewed one of the scented cloth squares into the inner lining of the cloak and that too helped. He also wore a pair of inexpensive sandals Anne purchased for him yesterday. Slave shoes, cheap and serviceable, but also cooler than boots.

Attempting to avoid the worst of the heat, they went out early in the morning. Xanthe was climbing and Ortrun wouldn't rise for several hours yet. The merchants were still hawking their wares; nothing had changed from yesterday. Emporium City Central Market never closed; it remained open even through the half-light of the night. In Emporium City making money was a nonstop endeavor. After trekking through various plazas that they hadn't visited the day before, and walking for several hours, talking to different merchants, they wearily made their way back to the inn for the midday meal. There had been no contact, no other incidents, and everyone was hot and irritable.

When they returned to the inn, the innkeeper watched Rayne intently as they walked in. He grumbled his frustration at seeing nothing more than a suggestive shape under a black cover and gave Thorvin a disgusted look. But he smiled when they asked for food and drink to be brought up to their rooms again. This time when he arrived, Shaw and Stevie met him at the door taking the trays from his servants without allowing them entry. The man stalked off, mumbling again.

Thorvin's plan was to go back out during the night, when the heat was less oppressive. After they ate, everyone settled in to try and get some sleep during the hottest hours of the afternoon. They would head out around the time Xanthe was riding low in the sky, that way they only needed to contend with Ortrun's lesser heat. This time they planned to do some shopping instead of just walking.

Anne had asked Thorvin if she could purchase some herbs and ointments she couldn't find elsewhere. Shaw wanted to look at books and scrolls.

Stevie said, "If Anne and Shaw get to shop, Sashi and I want to look through that amazing weapons bazaar we passed the day we arrived."

Several hours later, with the stifling heat releasing its grip on the city, and everyone feeling cramped in the small rooms, Thorvin agreed it was time to head back out to the markets. He refused to let the group split up though and growled a reminder to everyone to remember why they were here; it was not to go shopping.

Knowing what she wanted, Anne made her purchases quickly. Less than a half-hour after leaving the inn, they were on their way to the booksellers' bazaar.

Looking around at all the books and scrolls, stall after stall, offering such bounty, brought memories of Warren to Rayne's mind. There were books of every size, some incredibly old, some bound with veredium-tooled leather, and some that looked like they had just been bound. There were stalls of just scrolls. Rayne thought if the Sorial scroll was hidden here at the booksellers' market, he wouldn't find it in a hundred years. If the role of slave did not constrict him, he'd spend time searching out several books Warren would have liked and bought them for the library at Warren's Rest.

Thinking about the compound got Rayne wondering how

work was going there, if the school was open yet, and students were even there by now. As he watched Shaw run from stall to stall like a child in a candy shop, Rayne felt a twinge between his shoulder blades. They were being watched.

Shaw spent well over an hour deciding what to buy and, finally, settled on purchasing two books and a scroll. They made their way down the crowded main thoroughfare with Thorvin holding Rayne's lead as Shaw excitedly showed his purchases to Anne. They were nearing the weapons bazaar when Rayne caught Thorvin's eye. He nodded. Thorvin too was aware they were being watched. He handed Rayne's lead off to Shaw and mumbled quietly, "Pay attention, people. We've got company."

They had only been in the weapons market for a short while when Shaw was approached by a small boy wearing a jewel-encrusted slave collar. As the group came to a stop, the boy looked up at Rayne, his dark eyes curious, then addressed Shaw. "My master sends greetings to your master and would like to invite him to a late supper. If this is agreeable to your master, you are all to follow me to my master's manor. He instructed me to warn you that he would be sorely put out if you rejected his offer."

The entire time the boy spoke, his eyes kept shifting to Rayne who remained a dark mystery under his enveloping cloak.

This was the offer they had been waiting for. Thorvin nodded to Shaw and Shaw said, "My master accepts this generous offer."

Without another word, the boy turned and led them through a confusing labyrinth of streets, leaving the markets behind. Here, rather than market stalls, small shops with tiny yards predominated. A short while later, they passed over a bridge that spanned a narrow strip of the lake. The smell as they crossed almost overwhelmed Rayne and he fought to place one foot in front of the other. Shadowy tendrils of darkness enveloped him, and he felt as if he was walking through a shrinking tunnel that threatened his equilibrium. Once the bridge was behind them, the smell dissipated, and Rayne's head cleared.

The boy jogged without stopping and they now found themselves moving along wider streets, passing large houses.

There was no doubt, wherever they were going, they were heading toward wealth and power.

After following the boy for almost three hours they came to a massive two-story house built of gray stone with sparkling black veins running through it. The mansion was set well back off the road, hidden by large trees and manicured shrubs. The boy led them to the front of the house and up to a set of solid, wooden, double doors painted red. After bowing deeply, he ran off into the half-light.

25

They waited for only a moment before the doors were pulled open by a large man wearing loose black trousers and a form-fitting, sleeveless red vest, cut short at the waist and open at the neck to reveal a slave collar. Without speaking a word, the slave bowed them in, then led the companions toward the interior of the house. After passing several closed doors and another hallway that bisected the one they followed, he led them into a courtyard that was open to the sky above. Blazing torches placed along the walls cast flickering light through the dim, nighttime light. It was much cooler here. Several slaves, positioned unobtrusively among the greenery, were fanning the air, creating a constant breeze.

A man reclining on a low couch covered in a finely woven fabric colored in a geometric pattern of crimson, black, and white, looked up at them with eyes that reminded Rayne far too much of Sigmund. The man was dressed in a long, belted robe of fine red linen with thin lines of black running vertically from top to hem. His chin-length black hair was neatly trimmed and oiled and, as he sipped from a cut crystal goblet, his pale gray eyes roamed over Rayne and his friends as if deciding whether they were worth greeting or not.

After a few minutes of awkward silence, he rose and approached Thorvin. "You must be the owner of the property I've been hearing about." He looked pointedly at Rayne, nothing more than a dark shape in his hooded cloak. "You must have a large measure of confidence in your slave's skill. Expecting a master house to approach you out of curiosity rather than displaying your goods was a gamble. Even now, I see you prefer to keep him a mystery. I applaud your unique approach."

Rayne's skin pimpled; the man walked around him, his eyes boring through the thin black material of the cloak, while Shaw clutched his lead possessively, sending nervous energy pulsing through the leather. Then, turning his attention to the group in general, the man took a few minutes to look each person over with cold appraising eyes before dismissing them. His eyes moved back to Rayne, who stood slightly apart at the end of his tether, and lingered on him as if no one else was worth his notice.

Turning back to Thorvin, the man said, "If it is agreeable, I would have you join me for a late dinner." His gaze drifted to Rayne once more. "I'll have my man take your slave directly to my testing ring; there are cells down there where he can be secured until we are ready for him. After we've dined, if we feel for some entertainment, I might consider inspecting him and maybe even testing him tonight, if it's not too late."

Thorvin eyed the man with a stony expression. "It is not agreeable. We were led here under threat of repercussions if we declined your offer and now you invite me to dine with you before we've even been introduced. This is not agreeable in the least."

The man chuckled softly. "You speak your mind. I like that. I've heard that about you."

He waved his hand with a languid motion. One of the slaves put down his fan, poured a glass of the honey-colored liquid the man was drinking, offered it to Thorvin, and bowing, returned to his fan duty.

"Accept my humble apologies, Lord Kraftsmunn."

Thorvin raised eyebrows and the man chuckled lightly.

"Yes, I know you by reputation. Not many people of note skip onto Sorial without our being aware of their arrival. Allow me to introduce myself. My name is Louvain Andersen. I'm sure you've heard of my uncle, Lord William, master merchant and head of Andersen House. I regret that we seem to have gotten off to a bad start. I had looked forward to discussing training techniques with you. I've been told you are quite proficient at producing superior warriors."

Moving slowly, Louvain turned his attention back to Rayne, circling him like a predator stalking its prey. "You have succeeded in peaking my curiosity; I am most eager to see what you have hidden under this cloak. My eyes in the market tell me he is ... interesting.

A smile slid across Louvain's face and he inclined his head at Thorvin. "Be forewarned though, Lord Kraftsmunn, your reputation has led me to believe I can count on your ability to provide us with a contestant of a certain skill level. I wouldn't have invited you here if not for that. I hope for your sake I won't be disappointed. But, then again, I'm sure you would never have come to Emporium City with anything less than a worthy offering for our ring.

"Lord Kraftsmunn, as a fellow noble, please accept my apology and set aside your irritation. Dine with me. I'll send a slave and have the meal set out immediately. Allow me to make amends for our difficult start."

"I would be honored," Thorvin replied. He turned toward Shaw, Anne, Stevie, and Sashi, and after giving them a quick warning look, mouthed 'cooperate'. Turning back to Louvaine, Thorvin gave him a quick nod before following him through a darkened doorway.

****

As Thorvin and Louvain left the room, a large man stepped out from a dark alcove where he had stood, silent and still in the shadows, startling Shaw. He reached to take Rayne's lead from Shaw and after a moment's hesitation, Shaw handed it over. One of the slaves who had been fanning came forward and motioned for Shaw, Anne, Stevie, and Sashi to follow him, leading them in the opposite direction from Thorvin and Louvain. Shaw looked back toward Rayne as they were leaving the courtyard, but Anne elbowed him. When he looked at her she gave him a quick shake of her head and Shaw lifted a silent prayer to the One to protect all of them.

How does she do that? Shaw wondered as he watched Anne easily handle the whole situation, talking in a self-assured manner to the servants, all of whom wore slave collars.

While Shaw, Stevie and Sashi sat nervously playing with their food, Anne carried on small talk. But as Shaw listened, he realized Anne was gleaning information.

"The Andersen family holds the most power of any family on Sorial and Veres," a talkative, young slave girl said with a proud smile.

"And are these games very successful?" Anne quietly prompted, looking at the girl with widened eyes.

"Master Louvain's family has been profiting from the games ever since they built the complex eight years ago. Master says the Andersen House Gaming Complex is the most successful and luxurious complex on Veres. Master Louvain says it attracts important visitors from the whole of Ochen. It's only about a day and a half travel from Eleri so a lot of people come for just a few days if they want. Master Louvain says he's going to take me there someday. He says it's like a small walled city."

"And Lord Kraftmunn's slave?" Anne asked. "Where was he taken?"

"Oh." The girl shivered. "He would have been taken below the house to the testing ring. There are cells down there. Sometimes Master Louvain orders me to go down and clean the ring after a testing. It can be truly bloody. I don't like to go down there."

"Would Lord Kraftsmunn's slave have been fed?" Anne asked.

"Oh, yes. Master Louvain likes the slaves to be in top condition to be tested. He's going to have to fight to show Master if he's any good." The girl hesitated a moment, biting her lip. "What's he like under that cloak anyway? We were wondering.

Is he truly ugly? Or hideous and strange looking? Or something like that? Why else would your master hide him with that cloak?"

Anne chuckled lightly. "Nothing like that."

With Anne's gentle prompting, they also learned that there were currently twenty slaves serving in the house, twelve of whom were armed guards. The talkative slave boasted that though Louvain wasn't the final gatekeeper for the Andersen's, one day he would be. Shaw admired Anne's ability to put the staff at ease and extract the information she wanted with no one realizing what she was doing.

Louvain challenged Thorvin's small stock of patience. The man danced around every subject Thorvin brought up. Thorvin had approached the topic of the Andersen family's holdings on Veres from several directions and still hadn't learned anything about how many games the Andersen's ran, or where their facilities were located, or what he needed to do to obtain an open visa.

Thorvin shifted his tack and tried to gain information about the testing process and how fighters were judged worthy to compete in the Andersen's top tier games. Louvain just smiled and said Thorvin would witness the process himself shortly. But the man's idea of shortly included a seven-course meal served over a three-hour period before he finally decided he was ready to move on to what he called the evening's entertainment.

Thorvin relaxed a notch once he was reunited with his friends. They had finished eating a while ago and were waiting for him and Louvain in the courtyard. From there, Louvain led them down a long flight of stairs into a seating area surrounding the testing ring. On the way, they passed a balcony that overlooked the ring with a table and several comfortable looking leather chairs. Reaching the lower level, Thorvin was relieved to see Rayne, sitting quietly on a cot in one of five cells lining the back wall, still wrapped in his cloak.

The ring itself was an oval shaped depression, slightly lower than the surrounding area and covered in sand. A short barrier of raised stones separated the sandy oval from the rest of the room, keeping the sand from spreading onto the polished floor.

$$\text{\\}$$

After eating a simple meal in his cell, Rayne had spent the last few hours studying the viewing area surrounding the sandy ring, trying to avoid thinking about what was coming. Tables were scattered across a polished wooden floor and deeply padded chairs with pillows and small blankets were set in small groupings, all facing the ring for prime viewing. Everything was Andersen red and black. The chairs sported deep wine-red cushions on black lacquer frames, while the tables were finished in the same shiny black lacquer. The pillows and blankets were designed to look like miniature Andersen House flags.

Louvain waved a hand toward the sitting area. "As you can see, Andersen House has spared no expense where our guests' comfort is concerned, even when they are just witnessing the testing process. This is but a small sample of the care we have taken to make our patrons comfortable at our main complex, where those of rank and means are entertained by the finest fighters in the Ochen system."

"Please, make yourselves comfortable. If you desire anything while I conduct my inspection, just wave for a slave. They are trained to serve." Louvain grinned as he indicated two scantily dressed young girls in slave collars standing in the shadows along the wall.

At a word from Louvain, the large man who brought Rayne down earlier, moved away from the wall next to the girls. Pulling a ring of keys from a chain at his waist he opened the cell door and waved Rayne out.

Rayne took his time, pacing with slow steps toward the sand-covered ring. Once he reached the edge of the sandy ring, Louvain walked up to him and, looking back at Thorvin with anticipation lighting his eyes, said, "Finally I get to unwrap your package, Lord Kraftsmunn."

Turning to Rayne, he licked his lips. "Remove your cloak, slave."

Rayne complied. He undid the ties at his throat then pushed off the hood with slow, deliberate movements, allowing the whole cloak to drop to the ground. His long black hair fanned out around his bare shoulders as the leather thong holding it in a tail slipped off with the cloak. He stood staring forward with shielded eyes as the man walked around him, assessing, calculating. Rayne was wearing basic black leather leggings, sandals, and the standard sleeveless tunic of coarse woven material in deep green similar to the green of Shaw's jacket and the twins' pants.

Louvain stopped in front of Rayne and, once again looking back to Thorvin, said, "Well he's certainly pretty enough to catch the ladies' fancy, especially with those eyes. They are an unusual color. Interesting." He paused, frowned, then shook his head. "I don't know. He's not very large or impressive. How old is he anyway?"

"As far as I know, he's about sixteen."

"Humph. Young too. Can't have that much experience."

"You'll see." Thorvin's voice was soft but confident.

Louvain gave Thorvin a noncommittal look, shrugged, then turned back. Rayne swallowed his revulsion as Louvain grabbed his hands, and examined the network of scars and rough callouses, obvious evidence of his experience with blades. Looking back up, Louvain commanded, "Remove your shirt, boy."

Keeping his eyes level and his focus forward as if Louvain didn't even exist, Rayne slowly and with a degree of attitude, complied. He suppressed a shudder as the man moved behind him, running cold hands over the scars on his back.

"Rebellious spirit, I see. Not an acceptable trait in a house slave but tolerable in a fighter. Still as troublesome as these scars would indicate?"

Thorvin sighed as if in resignation. "Sometimes."

Louvain stopped at Rayne's right shoulder and ran his

hand over Sigmund's mark. "Thorvin come here. Whose slave brand is this? It's unique, doesn't even look like a proper brand."

Thorvin got up and walked over. "Oh, that. Don't rightly know. He had that when I got him."

"Humph. Magical?"

Thorvin shrugged, noncommittal, and returned to his seat. Louvain circled back to stand in front of Rayne, who continued to stare through Louvain as if he was invisible.

"You will lower your eyes when I look at you, boy!" Louvain scowled. Rayne drew in a deep breath and lowered his eyes. Louvain stepped in close, his breath warm on Rayne's face. Rayne froze. Louvain smiled, resting his palm on Rayne's cheek then running his fingers along his jaw, murmuring, "Very pretty."

Rayne's reaction was automatic and swift. He tore away from Louvain's touch, as old fear speared through him. Louvain's jaw dropped, his eyes springing wide, but then his face reddened in anger. With a curse, he stepped close again and backhanded Rayne with enough force to send him staggering.

"Defiant slave!" He snarled, moving to stand over Rayne. "You will remain compliant while I examine you or I will end this inspection. You will be disciplined, and your master will walk away disappointed. I doubt that will make him happy."

As he was speaking, his gaze swiveled back toward the sitting area where Sashi and Shaw had started to rise before stopping and slowly sitting back down.

Louvain turned eyes crinkled in suspicion to Thorvin. "What's this? I have to ask myself why your people would react in this manner when I've done nothing more than appropriately discipline this uncooperative slave. Tell me Thorvin Kraftsmunn, convince me there is a good reason. Otherwise I might begin to think you're spies. Soldiers sent by that interfering king to investigate our games. Why would these two come to the aid of a mere slave, or is he in reality something more?"

Thorvin sighed and shook his head. "I apologize for my over-zealous employees. They are young and inexperienced. They seek no more than to protect my property. Please, feel free to discipline the slave however you wish. I know he can be quite irritating. I promise my people will not seek to interfere again. But ... I would take it amiss if your discipline left him unable to fight. Like someone recently said to me, 'Ain't no profit from a fighter who ain't fightin'."

Turning back to Sashi and Shaw, Thorvin grimaced his irritation at the two.

By this time, Rayne stood steady, watching the exchange. With an internal snarl, he stepped up to Louvain, close, too close. Threatening. Forcing the man to focus on him again. He needed to redirect that suspicious mind.

But before Louvain could do more than stare with mouth open at Rayne's proximity, the large guard, who had watched the whole exchange with narrowed eyes, pulled out a disciplining rod and strode toward Rayne.

Rayne pivoted to face him. The man plunged forward. His movements smooth and precise, Rayne shifted slightly to the side, allowing the man's own momentum to drive him past Rayne, throwing off the man's balance. In that fraction of a second, Rayne snatched his opponant's arm, twisting it up and flipping him over onto his back, knocking the air from him. As he tried to rise, Rayne kicked the man's chest, driving him back to the ground, while yanking the rod from his hand.

Rayne then turned back to Louvain, whose face was a mask of naked shock. Dropping to his knees, Rayne slid to a position in front of him. Kneeling at Louvain's feet, he bent his head in a submissive posture with eyes to the floor, then lifted his hands, palms up, open, offering the rod to Louvain.

Rayne pulled in several deep breaths, struggling to quell the adrenaline spike brought on by his explosive actions. *Enough. Can't push too far. Just enough to impress.* He fought his instincts and his body's call for action. *Must make him believe. Nothing more than a submissive slave.*

Clapping sounded from the stairs as a tall, well-dressed man with slicked-back, shoulder-length brown hair strode down the last few steps and started across the viewing area toward Louvain. "Oh, Louie," he crowed. "My but that was impressive. What have you here for me tonight?"

The newcomer walked past Louvain, waved the large guard away and went straight to Rayne. Reaching down, he tilted Rayne's head up to look him in the eye. "Impressive." He grinned. "Yes, yes, most certainly. Very nice. This one should be quite an attraction. Have you tested him yet, Louie?"

Louvain growled. "My name is Louvain, stop calling me Louie! You know I don't like it when you call me Louie. And no, I haven't tested him yet. He attacked me. I'll test the slave after he's paid for his offense, if he's still able to stand when I'm done with him."

The newcomer let go of Rayne's chin and turned to Louvain. "Louie, don't be a fool; you're just angry because he scared you. If this slave had meant to do you harm, we wouldn't be talking now."

The newcomer looked back down at Rayne who had, once again, bowed his head. Smiling he met Thorvin's eyes and winked before returning his attention to Rayne. "A rare piece indeed. No, this one is not to be disciplined. Besides, I think his kneeling submission was nicely done."

He walked to Louvain and draped an arm over his shoulders. "We need to talk, Louie, and then I will oversee the testing."

The man inclined his head in Thorvin's direction. "Please excuse us. I need to talk to my cousin in private." He then propelled Louvain across the room and the two of them conducted a hurried, whispered conversation as Louvain kept looking back at Rayne.

The two argued for a bit, but then the newcomer apparently got his point across to Louvain because they walked back to Thorvin and Louvain introduced him as Jason Andersen, son of Lord William and senior gatekeeper for the Andersen House games.

Bowing to Thorvin and giving Rayne an enigmatic grin, Jason said to Louvain, "Test him against Rollo."

26

Jason climbed the stairs to the balcony where he moved to a seat to watch.

Louvain glared at the large slave Rayne had defeated and ordered him to get Rollo. The man wasted no time disappearing up the stairs. Louvain walked back to Rayne who was still kneeling and grabbed the disciplining rod. Sneering at Rayne, Louvain asked Thorvin, "What weapon?"

Thorvin shrugged. "He prefers the long sword, but he can fight with any weapon."

Louvain studied Rayne a minute longer, then a crafty smile split his face. "Rollo uses the long sword. Why don't we switch it up and see what the boy can do with dual short blades?"

Thorvin swallowed his ready protest. The long sword gave this Rollo an advantage of reach that Rayne would lack. But trusting to Rayne's speed and abilities and wanting to appear unconcerned, Thorvin just shrugged. When he returned to the table, Stevie hissed, "What are you thinking putting Ra ... Wren at that kind of dis ..."

Thorvin gave Stevie a hard look and mumbled, "Trust his training, okay?"

Seeing the nasty looks Stevie, Sashi, and Shaw were directing at him, Thorvin left the table to watch from a position at the edge of the ring.

Rollo, a large, well-built man with a shaved head who looked to be in his thirties, walked casually down the stairs from the main level already carrying a longsword. Arrogant, self-assured. Thorvin noticed that this man did not wear a slave collar and he was probably carrying his own weapon. He was a free man who, confident in his abilities, chose to fight for money. He would be a challenging opponent. Rollo glanced at Rayne and smirked. He nodded toward Louvain and then walked into the ring where he stood swinging the sword in loose figure eights, waiting.

With a command from Louvain, the large slave who had followed Rollo back down the stairs, ran to an alcove and selected two short swords from a rack. He returned to where Rayne knelt and handed them to him.

ᴎ

Taking the twin blades, Rayne rose and began to maneuver the swords in circles at either side and then in figure eights across his torso. He knew he wouldn't be allowed much time to get the feel of them. He moved forward one step at a time, bouncing lightly on the balls of his feet, swinging the blades, checking their balance, before stepping into the ring.

"Stop wasting time boy," Louvain snarled.

But with the same look that used to get Sigmund so angry, Rayne just stared at Louvain while he circled the blades a few more times and Louvain fumed.

Rayne wished he had more time to acclimate to the balance of the unfamiliar weapons, to settle his emotions, find his core of balance. But the moment he began to swing the two swords, he found himself struggling against the tunnel-like darkness he had experienced earlier. Oppressive and chilling, it felt as if he was falling through space even as he stood still. He had tried to suppress this feeling of encroaching menace ever since they skipped onto Sorial, but every time he pushed it down, it worked back up in him like bubbles rising in water, persistent, inevitable, irresistible.

The two suns, the heat and the smell of the lake, the sounds of the market place, filled his senses, triggering an acute sense of threat as he swung the blades. A skittering of memory scratched at the surface of his mind, the movements pulling up an internal call for violence and blood, for speed and action.

He had been on Sorial before. With Coronus. He was living the memory, trapped in a spiraling vortex of violence brought on by the movement of the blades, the atmosphere of Emporium City, and the stench of the stinking lake it sat on. Torn between the rage and pain of the encompassing memory and the present.

Growling as the violence of his past took him, Rayne stalked into the ring. He stood still and glared at the target facing him, alert, primed, waiting for the man to make the first move. There, in the target's tensing muscles, in the focus of his eyes, before the man even moved.

Rollo surged forward, initiating a downward stroke. Rayne, already moving, saw it as if in slow motion. Reflexes sparking, he blocked with the left sword. Twisting, he ducked past the descending blade, past harm. Turning into Rollo as he rose, he slashed the shocked man with a swifter-than-thought upward slice, scoring the man's ribs. First blood. Rayne shuddered.

Rollo pivoted to face him, his face a mask of rage and pain. Rayne shifted outside Rollo's reach. Like an insubstantial phantom, he slipped behind the man again. Twin slashes tracked across either side of Rollo's lower back before the man even realized what was happening. A split second later Rayne was airborne. His explosive kick slammed into Rollo's unprotected kidney.

Rollo was on his knees, gasping. Rayne stepped in behind him, right blade frozen at his neck, left blade poised to puncture a lung. And Rayne stood silent and still, now completely immersed in the memory.

Fear and anguish rolled off him. He was in a room, the last strains of music fading. He had killed. Broken the necks of two little girls. Two innocent little girls dead because of him. And blood, so much everywhere. He was drowning in it. Rayne's muscles quivered with the need to move; screamed for him to move, swift and violent.

But he stood. Frozen, pinning Rollo with his blades. Blades that brought death. Everything in him screaming to kill, Coronus screaming, Coronus selling him and then pain. He was falling down an endless black hole.

Rayne looked up and saw his next target watching him from just beyond the ring. Rollo now nonexistent to him.

11

Rayne, silent and deadly, strode toward Thorvin. For the first time since Thorvin had known Rayne, he was afraid. The boy had death in his eyes. Then Jason was on his feet, firing a dart. It caught Rayne in the neck and he stumbled just feet from Thorvin, spun, and dropping the blades from senseless hands, collapsed.

Silence reigned in the room. Everyone paralyzed by the shock of what just happened.

Jason came down the stairs from the balcony. Looking at Rayne's crumpled form he said to Thorvin, "That was quite incredible. I've never seen anyone move like that. It's a shame he's so damaged. Is he always this crazy?"

Thorvin stared blindly at Jason for a moment, then shook his head. "What did you do to him?"

Jason shrugged, his eyes cold. "No need for concern. As I'm sure you are aware, the slaves who excel in the games tend to be obstinate and need to be broken initially. We've found it handy in the past to keep a shooter and a supply of darts on the balcony. He's not the first fighter I've had to put out in this ring."

As the shock passed, Anne hurried to Rayne, but Louvain's big man brushed her aside and picked Rayne up like a limp rag, flinging him over his shoulder and turning to carry him back toward the cells. But Shaw, Stevie, and Sashi confronted the man.

"Put him down," Shaw said. The slave gave him a blank look; then, with a noncommittal grunt, started forward again.

Thorvin shook off his disbelief. "Shaw, Anne, stop. Stevie,

Sashi, remember your place." They looked at him with such uncertainty he groaned. Then, regaining his self-control, he shouted, "Now."

Jason smirked, sending fingers of apprehension along Thorvin's spine. "But your *slave* wasn't exhibiting normal rebellion, was he? I know what that looks like. His reactions were more like those of one reliving some traumatic event of the past. It's commendable your people show such concern for a *slave,* but they shouldn't get too attached. Being in the ring will only make him worse. But then, I expect you already know that."

While maintaining eye contact with Jason, Thorvin pointed to Rayne. "Tell your man to put him down. We need to get him back to the inn."

Jason clucked his tongue. "Such concern for a damaged piece of property. But that won't be necessary. You won't be going back to the inn. You'll be spending the night here as my guests. Tomorrow morning, I will personally escort you to our premiere complex on Veres. In any case, your *friend* should be locked up; he might still be violent when he wakes. We'll send someone to the inn for your things."

Watching as the large man deposited Rayne's limp body onto the cot, Jason said, "Louie, remember what I said. You're not to touch him. As we discussed earlier we need to handle this situation with care. I must talk with Father now, but I'll be back for them in the morning."

Jason returned his attention to Thorvin, a slight smile hovering at the edges of his lips. "You'll be traveling to Veres as guests of the Andersen Family, therefore you will have no need for a visa. Louvain will see to your needs tonight."

Thorvin and the others followed without argument as a thin gray-haired man and a slight girl carrying lanterns, guided them up to the second story of the house where they were to spend the night. Of course, the six armed guards who moved into positions at the bottom of the stairs were incentive to offer no arguments.

At the second-floor landing, Anne and Sashi followed the girl down the hall to their right while Thorvin, Shaw, and Stevie followed the old man down the hallway to the left. After being shown to their room, Thorvin stood by the door a few minutes, listening. When all was quiet, he opened it a crack. Anne and Sashi slipped in.

"What just happened?" Sashi looked to Thorvin. "I mean, what happened with Rayne? It all happened so fast. Did he really just try to attack you? Nemora's moons, Thorvin, what's going on?"

With Sashi, Shaw, and Stevie looking at him for answers, Thorvin shrugged and looked toward Anne who had stopped just inside the door and was leaning against the wall, staring at empty space, her brows wrinkled in concentration.

"I'm not really sure." Thorvin released a deep sigh. "Anne, any ideas what our boy was up to with that last performance? He scared me there for a minute. If Jason hadn't hit him with that dart, I can't be sure he wouldn't have attacked me."

"I can't be certain," Anne murmured. "But I think he was lost in a memory. Do you remember Thorvin, did Coronus ever bring him to Sorial?"

Thorvin squinted at Anne as he ran through memories of Rayne's contracts in his mind. Then a sick feeling climbed his throat and he swallowed hard. He groaned. Four sets of questioning eyes focused on him. "Coronus brought him onto Sorial for only one contract that I know of Anne. Do you remember the first contract Rayne filled after that year with Sigmund?"

Understanding bloomed in her eyes and she nodded once.

"What?" Shaw asked.

Still staring at Anne, Thorvin asked her, "Did he ever talk to you or Warren about that contract?"

"No." Anne's voice came out in a hushed whisper. "He never talked about what happened anytime Coronus took him out. Refused to tell us anything. Especially then."

"Do you remember how violent he was when he came back that time? How he almost killed Rufus? That's when I first came to you and Warren asking for help." Thorvin turned away from everyone and walked farther into the room, into the darkness beyond the circle of light from the lantern, unable to face those around him. "You thought it was a result of his time with Sigmund; and it was. Mostly. But there was more to it that time."

Thorvin stopped speaking for a few minutes, breathing in the darkness. "The Sorial contract included not only the main target but anyone who was with him. It was bad. The clients wanted to make a bloody statement. They offered a significant bonus for each extra body. Coronus … purposefully waited until there were guests with the target. Rayne killed twelve people that night. Two were just little girls." Thorvin stopped, swallowed. "Coronus was so pleased with his profits that he stayed in Emporium City for the next week drinking and partying with the clients."

Thorvin stopped again as the light from the lantern cast moving shadows across his back. The others sat, silently waiting. When Thorvin spoke again, his voice was strained. "That last night on Sorial—as if Rayne wasn't sick enough from the killing—Coronus, that slimy, money-loving piece of crap, sold the boy to some rubiates for the night and then bragged about the added profit. He bragged about making easy money!"

Thorvin closed his eyes and shook his head as he struggled with his guilt at not stopping Coronus. "I ignored Rayne's need for two more years before I finally stood up for him. Two. Whole. Years." Regret and self-loathing flooded Thorvin, turning his voice rough.

"That's in the past." Anne's sharp voice forced Thorvin to face her. "Pull yourself together and focus on what we can do to help Rayne now." Then in a softer voice, she added, "Okay, Thorvin? We need you here now. Rayne needs you here. Now."

Thorvin ground his teeth, pushing back the guilt. Anne was right. He looked at her and realized how many times she had been right, had been a rock for the people around her.

Shaw's a lucky man, Thorvin thought, as Anne reached out to Shaw and took his hand.

"Well," Thorvin said. "Maybe it hasn't worked out exactly as planned, but tomorrow we're going to Veres. I don't like not being able to see Rayne and make sure he's okay, but he's probably going to sleep for a while, we should do the same. There's nothing we can do for now except cooperate with Jason and keep our eyes open for a chance to break away once we're on Veres."

"But do you think Rayne's alright?" Stevie asked. "I don't like the idea of him being alone when he's caught up in this memory thing. I mean, he wasn't acting like himself. What if he doesn't even recognize us when we get to Veres. He didn't seem to recognize you when he tried to use those bloody swords on you after he sliced up that Rollo guy."

Thorvin rubbed his palms over tired eyes. "I know. But except for getting some sleep so we'll be able to function tomorrow, right now there's nothing we can do for him. Unless any of you has a better suggestion. I don't think Louvain is going to let us see him tonight."

"Maybe one of us could try," Sashi pleaded. "Maybe if just Anne or I went down Louvain would let us check on Rayne."

"Maybe," Thorvin said, "But Louvain is suspicious already and Jason is convinced we're spying for King Theodor. By showing any more concern for Rayne than we already have we might be putting him at more risk."

"Thorvin's right," Anne said. "The best thing we can do for now is get a good night's rest. We'll need to be alert and ready to escape tomorrow when the opportunity presents itself. Although without a visa, I think we're going to have difficulties moving around once we get to Veres."

"We'll figure it out," Thorvin said.

"There is something else we can do," Shaw murmured. "Let's pray."

For the next half-hour, they took turns praying aloud for Rayne, for their search for the scroll, for safety for themselves, and a way to help the people of Veres. Then Anne and Sashi snuck back into their room; morning wasn't far off now.

27

Rayne woke, pried open gritty eyes, and attempted to banish the cobwebs from his befuddled mind. He shifted to sit up but sharp pain shot through his skull. He grabbed his throbbing head and groaned. *What happened?* The last thing he remembered was starting to warm up with the twin blades.

Squinting, he looked around. He was back in the cell he had occupied before the testing. *How long have I been out? Is it still night?* Seeing his shirt crumpled on the floor, he reached down to grab it, immediately regretting the action. With slow, cautious movements he pulled the shirt over his head. *Shoes?* He looked around for his sandals. They were gone.

A pottery pitcher and glass sat on the floor near the door. He swallowed. His throat was desert dry, and his mouth felt like cotton. He rose gingerly and with slow, even steps crossed the cell to get a drink. He smelled what looked like water in the pitcher but didn't detect any odor, so he poured a full glass. Taking a small sip, he noticed a slightly bitter taste. But his thirst was so overwhelming, he drank the whole glass down before he even realized what he was doing.

Suddenly dizzy, he stumbled back across the cell and fell onto the cot, instantly asleep again.

Rayne had no idea how much time had passed since he drank the bitter water, but he was aware of someone lifting him and carrying him up the stairs, through the house, and out to a coach. He tried to remember what he was supposed to be doing but his mind was a foggy muddle and he couldn't pull any thoughts together. He wanted to lift his head and see where he was, but his muscles refused to obey. Then he heard Thorvin talking to someone. He didn't recognize the other voice, but he took comfort from Thorvin's presence and allowed himself to sink back into oblivion.

Rayne's body rose then slammed down onto a firm surface. Something soft cushioned his head, keeping it from hitting hard. He opened his eyes and saw Anne's chin framed by a gray, misty sky. His head was resting on Anne's lap. And it hurt. Like some vicious little creature was hammering away with a pick axe inside his skull. He closed his eyes and wished he could drift back into the painless oblivion of black unconsciousness that had buffered him from reality. But then his body bounced again, and his eyes sprang open.

"He's waking up." Anne's voice filtered into his thoughts.

He blinked then forced his scratchy eyelids to stay open, scanning his surroundings while not moving his head. *Oh, it hurts!*

He was lying on the flat, wooden bed of a moving wagon, surrounded by his friends. He wanted to say something, but like the last time he remembered waking, he was so thirsty he couldn't make his tongue cooperate. He tried to work some moisture into his mouth then croaked, "Water."

Anne shifted under him as Thorvin handed her a jug Rayne hoped contained plain water. Then the wagon bounced again and Anne said, "Shaw, pour some into my palms. Rayne, I'm going to try to drizzle some into your mouth. Get ready. Here it comes."

The water was warm but wonderful, its moisture quickly soaking into the dryness of his mouth.

"More?" Anne asked. He nodded, then regretted the movement. Anne repeated the procedure. "Do you think you can sit up?"

"I think so. But my head's throbbing like something's in there hammering to get out."

Wedging his elbows against the rough floor boards Rayne propped himself into a sitting position and Anne scooted to his right moving out of his way. With a moan, he wrapped his hands around his head. He moaned again. "What happened? Where are we?"

"To answer the easier question first, we're on Veres." Thorvin's voice came from his right. "Unfortunately, we happen to be locked in a wagon, on our way to the Andersen House Gaming Complex where you're supposed to fight. And I don't think we're going to escape Jason and his soldiers any time soon."

Thorvin paused and studied Rayne with troubled eyes. "Are you okay? We were starting to worry. You've been out for over a day now."

"No wonder I was thirsty." Rayne looked over at Anne. "Do you think I can have that jug now?"

With a small smile that made Rayne feel her concern, Anne nodded and handed him the water. He juggled it as he attempted to drink while the wagon bounced, jostling him. Despite a generous amount landing on his shirt and leggings, he was able to down enough to satisfy his need. The pounding in his head diminished, and he scanned the wagon interior. "Is everybody okay?"

Sashi gave him an odd look. "We're all fine. But what about you? Do you remember what happened when that creep Louvain was testing you?"

Crinkling his brow, Rayne thought a moment. "The last thing I remember was taking those swords from Louvain's man." He paused, still thinking. "Yeah, that's the last thing I remember. I guess a lot must have happened since then."

"You could say that," Sashi said. "You really scared us."

Rayne dropped his eyes to his hands, questions circling in his befogged brain.

Thorvin cleared his throat. "Sashi's right, you had us concerned. Once you started swinging those blades, you got violent. You almost killed that Rollo guy. When you finished with him, you came at me. I don't know what you were seeing, but it wasn't me. Anne said you were trapped in a memory. Anyway, you started toward me, your eyes dark and distant, cold. Then Jason hit you with a sleeping dart and you went down. Fast. I think they kept giving you something to keep you out, because that was two days ago."

"Did I hurt anyone else?" Rayne looked from face to face, concern rising in him.

"No. Anne thinks the memory you were caught in was from being on Sorial before. With Coronus. Do you remember any of that?"

"No." Rayne looked over at Anne. "Do you think it could happen again? If it does, do you think I might hurt one of you?"

"Honestly, Rayne, I don't know."

All conversation came to an end as the wagon turned sharply and then came to a rocking stop. Rayne closed his eyes in prayer not knowing what might happen. He heard whispers around him and knew the others were praying too.

The sound of two bolts being drawn preceded the lowering of the door. Jason shouted up into the wagon, "This is how things work here on Veres, *Prince Rayne*. Your friends are familiar with this procedure so I'm repeating myself for your benefit. I'm holding a jar of sleeping powder. You might be familiar with this particular powder; I believe you got a taste of it once before back on Corylus. If any one of you gives me any problems, I'll just toss it into the wagon and you can all sleep the rest of the way to our destination. Come out one at a time. You first, Thorvin."

Thorvin met Rayne's questioning eyes and shook his head. "They knew we were coming. Jason already knew who you were before he tested you. But I promise, somehow I will get you out of this." He climbed out the door. Rayne was left to last as Jason called out first Stevie then Sashi, followed by Anne and finally Shaw.

A small vial of liquid was placed on the bed of the wagon and Jason said, "I'm sorry, Your Highness, but you're going to have to drink that before you come out. I suggest you be as cooperative as your friends, unless you would prefer I cause them pain."

Rayne picked up the vial and uncorked it, smelling the contents. Like the water back in his cell, it had no odor. But Rayne suspected it would taste bitter. Knowing he had no choice, he spilled the vial on his tongue and then held it for a moment before relenting and swallowing the harsh liquid. As before, the results were quick. Rayne took one step and tumbled into unconsciousness.

ᚺ

Thorvin growled deep in his throat and yanked at his shackles as he watched two of Jason's men drag Rayne from the wagon and dump his limp body on the dirt road.

"Oh, did we drop His Royal Highness? How careless of us. We're so sorry, Your Royal Highness. We're just so clumsy tonight." One of the men laughed as he made an exaggerated bow over Rayne's limp body "Bow, Sid. Don't you know we're in the presence of Prince Rayne of Corylus. But look at the poor royal pain, lying in the dirt like some besotted old drunk passed out in an alley. We really shouldn't be so careless with royalty especially with the crown prince of the whole Ochen system." They laughed again.

"He doesn't look very royal lying out in the middle of the road, eating dust." Sid kicked Rayne.

They laughed and walked away leaving Rayne where they had dropped him. Sashi shouted angrily from where she was tied to a tree, "You leave him alone."

"Sure, girlie, that's just what we plan to do, leave the royal brat in the road, eating dust." Sid elbowed his friend and they made a rude gesture in Sashi's direction.

Jason shouted at them, "Stop playing around and get him out of there, you idiots! Move that wagon. You're blocking the road. And stop announcing who's here. His arrival is a special surprise for Richard and I don't want that spoiled. Move it."

Thorvin glared as Jason walked up to him. "I don't suppose you would consider a proposition from my family?" Jason said.

"What?" Thorvin growled then paused. Considering his options and what he might gain by playing along with Jason, he shrugged. "I'm listening."

Jason pulled a key from his pocket and unfastened Thorvin's shackles, letting them drop to the ground. "Come. Join me for dinner."

"What about my friends?"

"They're potential freedom could be discussed if we come to an agreement."

"And the prince?"

Jason pursed his lips and shook his head. "He's not up for negotiation."

Looking Thorvin in the eye, Jason asked, "Well? Do you want to hear what I have to say, or should I put the chains back on? I've been authorized by my father to make you quite a nice offer. Join me in my tent. We can enjoy a civilized meal and then discuss business."

Following Jason, Thorvin looked back to see his four companions staring after him, jaws hanging open, and disappointed looks on their faces. *Let them look. If cooperating now can save them, I'll do what needs to be done regardless of what they think.*

Jason's tent reminded Thorvin of the one Rayne used when they traveled to Coronus's compound. But where Rayne's had been simple and functional, Jason's walls were lined with silks and the floor was covered with thick carpets in various shades of red and gray. Glancing into the back room, Thorvin noticed a large bed covered in a plaid blanket.

"Honeyed sherry?" Jason asked as he stood poised to pour a glass.

"Sure, why not."

Jason motioned for Thorvin to sit in one of two chairs set at a heavy wooden camp table. Once they were seated, Jason rang a bell and two slaves appeared, petite Verenian girls with downcast eyes, carrying bowls of warm water for washing and cloths for drying their hands.

"I so dislike eating without having washed first, don't you?" Jason dipped his hands in the warm water and then dried them with a cloth.

The slaves left only to reappear with the first course of food. A salad that definitely didn't originate on Veres. Fruits that must have come from Nemora sat on a bed of greens that must have come from Amathea, dressed to perfection with a spicy sweet concoction. Each of the five courses was more sumptuous than the last and the variety and cost of the meal stunned Thorvin. The Andersen family did indeed have deep pockets and influence. And they weren't afraid to use either. Thorvin realized he was being set up for an offer Jason expected him to accept. But Jason acted the part of a well-bred host by not bringing up his proposition until they sat with cups of coffee and desert pastries.

"Well," Jason sighed. "That was passable for a travel meal. But I think it's time we discussed business. We have a mutual friend, Van Coronus. He speaks highly of your talent for training fighters. In fact, you just missed him. I sent him off-world to *recruit* some new talent for the ring. These Verenian slaves might do for working the mines or menial household duties, but they don't last very long in the ring. In fact, your arrival with the prince was quite timely. Our stock of fighting slaves is rather lean at the moment. Not long ago, we were successful in attracting a well-celebrated independent free fighter from Glacieria. He's quite a favorite; very adept at killing his opponents with flair. The odds against him have grown quite astronomical. Hence the need for Coronus to bring in some worthy new stock."

"Free fighters?" Thorvin asked.

"Of course not." Jason snickered. "They're too demanding and costly on several levels. Except for Yormund. Now he's one free fighter who's worth the expense. He is quite the darling of our patrons. Yormund likes to play with his food before he eats it, if you catch my drift. He loves to hunt and kill. That does draw the crowds, but it also puts us in the unenviable position of needing to find a worthwhile opponent for him on short notice, someone capable of surviving for a bit.

So, you see why I said your arrival was most timely. You have solved a problem for me.

"But you are also in a position to help with the long-term resolution as well. I need someone of your caliber to train the new stock Coronus will be bringing. From what he's told me, you are the man responsible for training his assassins, including the prince. And now that I have seen a sample of his skill, I am convinced you're the man we need.

"The profits we make from the games, including everything from visas to gambling, are quite impressive and I'm sure we could come to an agreement that would benefit both you and Andersen House."

"Wouldn't it be better to just hire already accomplished fighters rather than pay me to train unknown potential. Don't judge what I can do by the prince. He's in a class by himself. I can only work with what I'm given."

"You don't understand. You would be a permanent hire. A constant expense. We could afford to pay you well because, ultimately, it's more profitable than paying for professional fighters. They're difficult to work with, demanding top dollar for each fight and even more for death matches. They can be unreliable if they get a better offer from a competitor or decide to renegotiate their fee just before an important match. Slaves are nothing more than a commodity. They can't command better pay or living conditions or any of the myriad other things those free fighters think to demand. And if one dies, he's easily replaced at minimal cost."

Thorvin swallowed the bile rising at Jason's careless words. He knew that in the past he would have jumped at Jason's offer with no care for anyone but himself. But he had changed. He questioned if there was a way he could help his prince and his friends by playing along with Jason, pretending to accept his offer. But what might he be asked to do? If it involved any harm to Rayne, he would not be able to keep up the pretense. And if he did appear to join with Jason, would his friends understand what he was doing?"

Jason brought Thorvin's internal monologue to an end. "The offer is only good for a limited time. I will need your answer by tomorrow morning. And to assure that you're not disturbed while you're thinking my offer over, you will spend the night here in my tent. Of course, I hope you understand that I can't leave a man of your notable skills free; that might tempt you to some rash action we would both regret."

Jason waved to someone standing in the tent's entryway. One of his soldiers, carrying the shackles Thorvin had been wearing earlier and a length of chain, moved into the tent. Thorvin stood, ready to fight. He had no intention of letting that little man put those chains back on him. Jason chuckled at Thorvin's response, as another guard stepped into the doorway. The man twirled a vial like the one Jason made Rayne drink earlier.

"Are you going to knock me out too?"

"I wouldn't think of it. I'm actually holding out hope you might join us. You see, Coronus explained how effective you were until that royal brat poisoned you with his talk of a One and all that garbage. Coronus fully believes that if the prince were dead you would again become the man you were. Perhaps if I were to silence the boy, you might be more amenable to our offer.

"If I give the word, this man will pour the contents of the vial he's holding down the prince's throat. And, as I'm sure you've already guessed, the vial contains the same drug the prince drank earlier. But with one slight difference. This formulation is twice the potency of the other. Oh, one other fact. The draught is cumulative. Though the prince will be awake by fight time, the boy will be quite disoriented when he enters the ring. Despite his prodigious talent, he'll be in no shape to face Yormund. Oh, poor, poor boy. What a short career. Would you consider our offer then, if the prince was no longer a factor?"

Jason smiled as consuming anger rose in Thorvin, warming his blood and sending heat to his face. "Yes, I see. It's as I guessed. Coronus was wrong. You would despise any who harmed the prince; we could never gain your assistance by killing him.

"And I must admit, I would be loath to lose the potential income that boy could bring to Andersen House. If he is as good as I think he is, we'll profit from him for quite a while, at least until he loses his mind completely to whatever memory it is that haunts him.

"And he's such a pretty boy."

Thorvin's stomach churned at the implications in Jason's words and Jason chuckled in response. "Yes." A predatory smile surfaced. "We profit from more than just the games. The Andersen family stands behind our claim that at Andersen House Gaming Complex anything can be had for a price, *anything.*"

Jason sighed and shook his head. "I see that I don't have to wait until morning for your answer. It was evident as I spoke."

Turning to the man standing with the shackles, Jason said, "Return him to his friends." Then looking back at Thorvin, he waved toward the man with the vial and said, "And if you care about your young friend, don't give me any reason to use this."

28

Thorvin's rage grew hot and demanding, pulling his hands into white-knuckled fists as he left Jason's tent and stalked toward his friends. Fury overriding his common sense, he stopped and changed direction frustrating the guards following him. He ignored the rising protests as he strode over to where the two idiots had dumped Rayne earlier.

Kneeling, he picked Rayne up like a child and carried him toward the others. *How can he be so light? There's nothing to him. He's just a slight sixteen-year old boy with abilities that made him seem older, larger.* Thorvin noticed Jason watching from the door of his tent, but he didn't care. Rayne deserved better than to be treated like a sack of garbage.

Even if Thorvin couldn't do anything more for him under the circumstances, he could at least make sure Rayne slept among friends. Kneeling, he gently lowered him to the ground, then looking over his shoulder, watched Jason turn back into his tent.

After the guard chained Thorvin's shackles to a peg pounded into the ground, he clamped a set of veredium shackles on Rayne. Then, with a self-satisfied grunt, the guard stalked away.

When they were alone, Sashi whispered, "Nemora's moons, what was that all about? Did you actually eat with that snake?"

"Yeah," Thorvin grunted. "I ate with him. He offered me a deal that would make me rich and all I had to do was swallow my pride, deny my prince, and return to the slimy creature I was before. I guess those simple things were too much for an old fool like me because, as you can see, I'm still out here with you."

After that they settled and tried their best to sleep despite the dank, chilly conditions.

Morning came, still damp and gray with a gritty smoky quality to the air that irritated throat and eye. The smoky fog was heavier this morning than it had been yesterday evening. Thorvin was relieved to see Rayne looking at him, alert, more like himself than when he woke up in the wagon yesterday. Rayne closed his eyes and Thorvin knew he was praying. Thorvin noticed, not for the first time, a quality of peace surrounding the prince when he prayed. *He's your Light Bringer. Will you protect him this time?*

Then Rayne surprised Thorvin by opening his eyes and smiling. "Don't worry so much old man. You know I'm never alone. He's always with me."

Slightly angered and unsure, Thorvin asked, "Even the other day when you were going to kill me?"

Rayne bent his head and twined his fingers together. "I'm sorry. I don't even remember it. But no matter what happens, all I can do is keep trusting and moving forward. Otherwise I'll lose my direction. And that scares me more than anything else." He lifted his eyes and glanced at Jason's tent before returning his gaze to Thorvin. "I overheard Jason's men talking. I know I'm going to fight a death match tonight, maybe many nights to come. There's no way they'd waste me on anything less. But I have to hang on to the truth of the prophecy; somehow, I will survive until it's fulfilled. But I also know there are no guarantees what will happen in between."

Rayne shook his head. "I just hope I don't get any of you killed in the meantime. I was right; I should have come alone."

"No," Thorvin said. "We would have followed you if you had come alone. I hope you know that by now."

One side of Rayne's mouth rose in a half smile. "Thanks old man."

"Yeah." They got quiet and Rayne closed his eyes again. Thorvin was glad Rayne was praying. He knew they all needed prayer just to make it through the next days.

Within minutes, the camp began to stir. The prisoners were given a breakfast of dried meat and water. Ample enough fare if not fine dining.

Jason stepped out of his tent, stretching and making a show of patting his stomach. He walked over to the prisoners and looked down at them for a minute before turning to shout orders to his men. This morning everyone was left bound and Jason's men helped them back up into the wagon.

When Rayne moved to follow his friends, Jason stepped in front of him. "Not you. I don't want your friends to get any ideas about trying to save you. Somehow I suspect they would all give their lives for you. It mystifies me, this loyalty. But I think I will remove the temptation by having you ride with me today. We will be at the complex in just a few hours and you might provide some entertaining conversation on the way."

He looked up at Thorvin who watched him from the wagon. "Perhaps your young prince is more amenable than you. Let's see what incentive I might be able to offer him to cooperate with us."

"Don't listen to that snake," Thorvin shouted after Rayne as Jason led him toward the coach. Then two soldiers lifted the back gate and fastened it. Thorvin wondered what kind of deal Jason would offer Rayne. With a sinking feeling he suspected the only deal worth making was for the safety of Rayne's friends. What would Rayne do to protect his friends?

Thorvin settled down with his back to the door, his eyes roving over his companions. Anne sat next to Shaw who had draped his arms around her with the shackles hanging in front, chains spilling onto her lap. Sashi leaned into Stevie and they sat with their legs touching. *Stupid boy. You'd do what you always do, sacrifice yourself to save others.* And for the first time Thorvin prayed. Not cynical or half-hearted words flung into the void, but real, honest prayer.

In just a few hours they would be at the Andersen House Gaming Complex and Thorvin wanted so badly to protect Rayne it hurt. But he knew that it was out of his hands. He was incapable of performing the one duty he had committed himself to ever since that day at Lady Lilith's. And he shook with intense frustration at his impotence.

Rayne stared out the window. Jason's coach was well-made and quite comfortable with high-quality springs. It was certainly more relaxing than bouncing on the wooden floor in the stiff wagon. Similar to the one that Coronus had owned, it boasted padded leather seats, a thick rug on the floor, and leather window shades the color of money. Blue, like sommes. Rayne squinted and imagined the interior papered in sommes and, for a brief moment, he released the tension that held his chest in a vise.

Small pictures were painted on the panels of each door. They reminded Rayne of the tapestries he had seen in Brayden's bedroom and he wondered if Jason thought they were tasteful. Brayden certainly did. But Rayne thought they were in bad taste; something he would feel uncomfortable looking at if his mother was with him.

As the morning wore on, the driver stopped the coach from time to time allowing the horses to rest after each steep incline. Through intermittent breaks in the trees, Rayne could see a river rushing past them, sending cascades of water splashing over a rocky river bed. But the gray smoky mist lent a quality of unreality to the place. Rayne felt as if he was in a dream world, or more likely a nightmare.

Flicking his eyes toward Jason, he asked, "Is it always like this? Always gray?"

"It's the price we pay to process veredium. Perpetual fog and smoke."

"I see." Sorrow for the people of Veres rose in Rayne. He

had thought a lot about the growing slavery problem, but now he realized the problem was bigger than just that. *I want to help them.* He laughed inwardly at the absurdity of his thoughts. *Before I can think of helping the Verenians, I need to help myself ... and my friends.* He turned to Jason. "What's going to happen to my friends?"

Jason sat in silence, looking out the window, ignoring the question. Rayne tried again. "I want them to be free. What can I do to make that happen?"

Finally acknowledging Rayne's presence, Jason turned to face him and chuckled. "Even now, you still believe you're the consummate royal, don't you?"

Rayne sent Jason a questioning look, and Jason shook his head disbelief in his eyes. "You still don't get it, do you? You're as thick as I've been told. You're nothing more than a slave, sitting in my coach, wearing my chains, and yet you think you're in a position to negotiate with me? Well, you're not. I'm going to tell you the truth here so pay attention. Your parents have officially disowned you."

Rayne's heart thudded in his ears and he shook his head. "No, you're lying."

Jason chuckled. "You didn't know that, did you? Well, it's true. It happened just a couple days ago, right after you left Westvale. Your parents have officially named Lord Brayden Woodfield heir apparent. Not only are you no longer a royal, you're nothing more than a commodity. A valuable commodity I admit, but a commodity none the less.

"Even now, you're riding in my coach for no other reason than my desire to separate you from Thorvin Kraftsmunn. And if you weren't destined for the ring in a few hours I would have just tied you to the back of the wagon and made you walk. But that would have reduced the profits I can make on the gambling if you arrive in the ring looking fit."

The coach got quiet again, as they each watched out their windows, Rayne contemplating what Jason had said, numb. He wanted to deny Jason's words, throw them back in the man's face. But he couldn't. Brayden had played him for a fool and there was nothing he could do about it.

As they climbed, the fog got thicker, and he understood they must be getting closer to the place where the veredium was processed. He watched the world rushing by, wondering if he had any chance of escaping. He struggled with the reality of being a slave again. Acting as Thorvin's slave was something Rayne could handle; it was temporary and controllable. And if their plan worked as it should have, their arrival on Veres would have put an end to his need to wear the collar. But Jason's words made things clear, Rayne was property again. He belonged to the Andersen family.

Rayne prayed for the strength to keep moving forward in this situation. He feared the residual darkness that rested, quiescent in his core. Would it surface again, propel him back into violence and blood? Would he fall into a black hole of despair if he was forced to kill again? And he worried for his friends. What would happen to them? Did Jason plan to enslave them as well? Make Thorvin, Stevie, and even Sashi fight in the ring? Rayne knew Thorvin could kill; he had done it before. But the thought that Stevie, and especially Sashi, might be forced to kill for the entertainment of spoiled nobles set his hands to twitching. He focused on the resolve he had nurtured before leaving Westvale and he prayed.

Rayne prayed for power; not just to survive, but to bring about change for the people of Veres. Wasn't that what the Light Bringer was supposed to do? Bring light and change to the people? He felt the warmth infuse him once again. The One was big enough and powerful enough to change a world, to change the whole system, and Rayne clung to that truth. The One would work his will and Rayne would be an instrument of that change.

29

The motion of the coach softened as they rode over a smooth, level portion of road before stopping in front of the gated entrance to the Andersen's complex. Rayne tilted his head to look up through the coach window and swallowed down his dismay. All he could see in either direction, was one immense wall.

Jason chuckled. "Impressive, isn't it?"

After a guard recognized Jason, they were waved forward and passed through the massive gate. Looking back, Rayne watched the wagon continue up the road. "Where are you taking my friends?"

Jason laughed with real mirth. "You should be more concerned with what's going to happen to you. But rest assured, your friends will be well taken care of."

Rayne tried to keep his bearings as they rode past stores, three inns, and what looked like a large training facility. The streets didn't run in straight lines, instead they curved as if the whole complex was designed in the shape of a circle.

Watching him, Jason said, "The streets follow the curve of the wall. What we just passed was one of the lesser rings. We have three here in the complex, our junior partners run the two minor rings, where we stage more affordable fights. You, however will make your debut in the main ring set in the center of the complex. Though it is physically smaller than the other two, the profits earned from one death match there are double what the lesser rings earn in a month."

After a few more twisting turns the coach pulled to a stop in front of a gray stone building that blended in with the fog, the upper levels hidden in the mist. The driver hopped down and gave a hand for Jason to step out. He turned and looked back up at Rayne with expectation. Rayne grabbed the top of the door with his manacled hands and swung his feet out and down, landing next to Jason.

"Well, come on boy." Jason strode toward the building. Rayne shuddered when he noticed that the door was built of heavy wood and near the top was a small barred window. Two large, heavily-armed guards stood at attention, one on each side of the door. With a grimace, Rayne followed Jason in.

They entered a flagstone-paved foyer that opened onto a large training room with racks of practice weapons against the far wall. Jason turned to the left and Rayne followed him down a hall to a room that contained an oversized bath tub, three heavy tables, and several chairs. A series of wardrobes covered the back wall.

Two boys wearing shackles like Rayne's were in the room. The chains of the smaller boy's shackles were draped over a hook on the wall and he sat on the floor staring at Jason and Rayne with fear-widened, golden eyes. The other boy looked up as they entered, disrupting his struggle with a short, pot-bellied man with immense arms, dressed in nothing but leggings and a leather apron.

Walking in, Jason scanned the room before turning his attention to the aproned man. "Leave those two for now. Focus on this one." He shoved Rayne forward. "He's set for tonight's death match and needs special attention."

Tilting his head, Jason examined Rayne with a calculating expression. "Coronus was right. A braid on one side will set your features off nicely." He smiled and pulling a silver-embellished black leather collar from his pocket, threw it to the man without taking his eyes off Rayne. "Put this on him."

"Do you recognize it?" Jason pointed toward the collar the man now held in his left hand as he still gripped the chains of the cowering boy in his right. "It's the one Coronus had made specially for you. Remember? He'll be delighted to see you wearing it again. When he's drunk, which is often, he threatens to dismember you for taking everything from him. I look forward to your reunion.

"Are you wondering how I came to possess this memento from your past? It was a gift from the friend who informed us you were coming, sent with a note giving us the information we needed to capture you." Jason snickered. "You almost got away with it, you know. If not for my friend's timely warning, Louvain would have just sent you here after your testing. You were quite impressive.

"Oh, I almost forgot. My friend asked that I give you a message with the collar. Jason paused and cleared his throat. "Now, how did that go? Oh, yes. 'It has taken longer than expected, but I finally have the satisfaction of informing you that King Theodor and Queen Rowena have officially disowned you. The title of Crown Prince is now mine. Enjoy your new status as a slave for the brief time you have left. And don't worry, little Raynie, I'm taking good care of my new mommy and daddy.'"

A vise seized Rayne's chest, crushing it and stealing his breath, but he kept his eyes down. He would not allow Jason Andersen the pleasure of witnessing any reaction.

"You aren't even surprised, are you? You must have figured out by now. My friend is your cousin, Lord Bray … Oh wait. He's no longer a lord. I shall use his proper title. Crown Prince Brayden of Corylus and all Ochen. The new prince also offered a significant bonus and certain political favors if we assured your death in the ring tonight. But that will be my father's decision. So, you see, it's as I told you earlier. Even if you do survive tonight's fight, you're no longer anything more than another Andersen House possession, like every other slave we own. You have no family, name, or power. No one's going to come to rescue you."

Turning back to the man still holding the struggling boy, Jason's eyes narrowed. He swore. "Chain that boy already. My father will be coming to inspect this one soon. Do you understand?" The man nodded. With a final smile at Rayne, Jason walked out.

Rayne choked down his horror at the message. He couldn't grapple with that now; thoughts of Brayden and his parents would have to wait. He watched closely as the handler dragged the other boy back to the wall and fastened his manacles to one of the hooks.

Rayne tried to size the man up. That Jason felt comfortable leaving them alone said he trusted the man to be able to control trained slaves. Rayne figured the handler must be extraordinarily strong and used to dealing with fighters, but he wasn't going to play along without at least testing him. While his back was still to Rayne, as he focused on hooking the boy to the wall, Rayne turned and sprinted for the door. And ran smack into the torso of the hugest man he had ever seen. Bouncing off the enormous man, Rayne back peddled, bumping into the aproned handler who threw muscular arms around him from behind, pinning his arms to his sides, crushing his chest, and lifting him off the floor.

The large man walked into the room, massive and powerful. He looked down at Rayne and said in a voice that rumbled like shifting rocks, "Little slave must learn his place. You belong to Lord William now. Be good. I don't want to hurt you, Little One."

"Then let me go." Rayne shot back, frustration driving his voice up an octave.

The huge man chuckled, a heavy vibration deep in his massive chest, but shook his head. "Little One has much fire." He studied Rayne, his expression intense, then shook his head. "No, not Little One ... Little Warrior. Sorry Little Warrior. Master says you must fight, and Shin must do as Master says. Now behave for Yuri and things will go easier for you."

Shin nodded to Yuri and he released Rayne who dropped to the floor and pulled a deep breath into his oxygen-hungry lungs.

Shin leaned against the wall next to the door with arms folded and watched as Yuri readied Rayne for his fight. Rayne cooperated. After Yuri removed his shackles, collar, and clothing, Rayne climbed into one of the tubs, shivering at the feel of the cool water on his skin but grateful to finally wash off Rollo's blood. He didn't need any prodding from Yuri to scrub well, he wanted to be clean. Rayne ducked under the water several times after washing his hair to be sure he had gotten all the strange-smelling soap the aproned man had given him out of his hair. The smell reminded him of the smoke that permeated the air around them.

After the bath, Yuri dressed Rayne in black leggings and a snug-fitting, sleeveless, red vest cut short at the waist. It was similar to the vests worn by Louvain's slaves back on Sorial. Again Rayne cooperated, but he felt uncomfortable wearing the too-short, blood colored vest that left his waist bare. He asked if he could just wear what he had been wearing, but Yuri picked up his clothes and threw them in a bin. Rayne suspected he wouldn't see them again.

Once he was dressed, Yuri motioned for him to sit on one of the tables then struggled to run a comb through his tangled hair. With the hair combed, Yuri worked on the braid.

Facing the two other boys Rayne realized they were about his own age. Fear radiated off them as they watched everything with wide eyes. He knew what it was like to be a slave, had lived as one for ten years. But these boys had no idea what was coming; especially the fighting, the killing. They looked like they had just been plucked from their homes. Sympathy for the two overshadowed Rayne's own apprehension and he reached out to them the only way he could. "Hey, my name's Rayne. What's yours?"

The two stared at him, not saying a word. It brought back memories of when he had been so scared that even if he could talk, he would have been too afraid to speak. Figuring Yuri wouldn't allow him to talk much, Rayne wanted to say something that would give the boys hope.

He was still struggling with what to say when words started pouring from his mouth, "Know that you are never alone. The One will never leave you or forsake you. He holds you in the palm of his hand." Rayne clamped his mouth shut. He wasn't sure exactly what just happened, but he was sure that it had never happened before.

"Pretty words," a deep, cultured voice declared from the door. Rayne turned to see who was speaking, but Yuri yanked his hair to keep him facing forward. Yuri stepped away from Rayne and bowed to the man. "Lord William," he said in an unexpectedly high voice before rising and grabbing Rayne's hair again.

"It's all hogwash," Lord William pronounced, his words flat and unfeeling. "You of all people should know that. Royal Prince of all Ochen, vaunted Light Bringer of the One. And yet here you sit, no longer free, abandoned by your parents, unwanted, facing a death match just so I can make a profit. What has the One done for you? Nothing."

Lord William walked in while he was speaking and moved to stand in front of Rayne.

"Our mutual friend, your previous owner, Sigmund of Bainard warned me you had grown quite a mouth on you since I last saw you here on Veres." Lord William grabbed Rayne's chin and looked closely at his eyes.

Without heed for consequences, Rayne pulled back his head and growled up at Lord William. "Why do you all do that? My eyes are like my mother's, okay. You don't have to grab my chin and yank my head to know that."

Rayne braced for the punishment he was sure would come, but instead of striking Rayne, Lord William walked to the boys still chained at the wall.

"I have discussed your history with Van Coronus and Lord Sigmund. I know from personal experience that you are most talented, and they have informed me of your ability to withstand quite a bit of punishment. According to Sigmund and Coronus however, your weakness is a ridiculous need to protect others."

Lord William pulled back a foot and leveled a brutal kick into the side of the smaller boy. The boy cried out in pain and Rayne moved to jump off the table but Yuri stopped him.

"I see that assessment is accurate." Though Lord William smiled, his dark eyes remained cold and calculating. "My games master thinks you have the potential to make me a lot of money. *If* you survive.

"I understand my son has already made you aware of your situation? That Crown Prince Brayden promises to compensate me quite well for my financial loss of you as a fighter if I arrange for your death tonight. Your survival in this fight will not be a result of your ability or the power of your One. Your survival depends on my discretion. A sure and significant profit at your death tonight, or potential for greater profit if you live to fight again.

"Which choice will benefit me most? The answer to that question is what will decide your fate. Your life is in my hands; you live or die at my whim. The One is a fool's myth. It is I who hold your life in the palm of my hand."

Lord William walked away from Rayne. At the door, he stopped and looked up at Shin. "Bring him to the lower cells as soon as Yuri is done."

Yuri finished braiding Rayne's hair, fastened Coronus's old collar on his neck, and then stood back to look at the whole picture. He nodded his approval at Rayne's appearance. Yuri then grabbed a long black cloak like the one Rayne had been wearing before he lost it at Louvain's. He pulled it over Rayne's shoulders and raised the hood. Yuri looked to Shin who motioned for Rayne to follow him out.

They left by way of a back door with steps leading down to a narrow path that wound between several small buildings and a wooded lot. It brought them directly to the lower entrance of the central gaming ring.

But before they entered the building, Shin slowed. He stopped and turned back to Rayne. "Is it true? Is Little Warrior truly the One's Light Bringer? From the prophecies?"

Looking up into the huge man's mahogany eyes Rayne saw a flicker of something. Was it hope?

Rayne nodded. "It's true. That's why I'm on Veres. I'm searching for the scrolls, like the prophecy says. But I guess someone else is going to have to find them now. Maybe there's a prophecy we don't know yet, one that talks about another Light Bringer. It's sad though. I won't get to help my friends or see my parents again. That hurts." Rayne swallowed down the burning pain in his throat, then whispered, "I'll never get to do what the One expects of me."

Shin looked down at Rayne, the skin around his eyes wrinkled in thought. He pulled in a breath as if he was going to say something more, but then turned and entered through the lower door. Shin ushered Rayne into a small cell to wait until it was time to make his appearance. From time to time Rayne would see Shin staring at him with a brow wrinkled in concentration.

Eventually Rayne heard the noisy sounds of excited people coming from above. The crowd he was supposed to amuse with his death was arriving.

30

Lexi was exhausted. No, Lexi was past exhausted. She had passed from exhausted to a state of foggy need a long time ago. Her mind, like her world had become a gray mist of fog and smoke where need dictated every action. And her need to protect herself from any more shattering pain dictated she keep the innermost part of herself tucked away in a safe place. The horror of what happened three years ago when her home was destroyed still haunted her dreams and the need of her people haunted her waking hours.

It should have been her father's duty to protect their people, but it had fallen to her slim young shoulders because there was no one else, just her and Ethan and Silas. And being her father's daughter, Ethan and Silas looked to her to lead.

And now, driven by need once again, Lexi sat her shaggy mountain pony, hidden in a dense stand of pine trees, watching the road that ran along the Eleri River, waiting for Andersen's men and their prisoners. For what seemed like the millionth time, Lexi wondered why the Andersen's couldn't leave the villagers alone, why they and the other mine owners couldn't just pay people to work their mines and processing facilities instead of enslaving the people of Veres, her people.

Pulling in a deep breath as she scrutinized the surrounding woods, she tried to focus on the smell of the wet pines, a fragrance she had loved ever since she was a young child. But Lexi couldn't ignore the faint smoky odor underlying every other scent in the area; the smell of veredium processing, the smell of pain and suffering. A breeze would help dispel the smoky stench, but down in the foothills of the Taliesin Mountains that surrounded the lower stretches of the Eleri River, breezes seldom blew. She would have to wait until the next time she got above the fog line to feel the warmth of the sun or the caress of a breeze.

Movement caught her attention. She waited and watched with narrowed eyes as a group of about fifty people made their way down the valley road, disappearing and then reappearing through breaks in the trees. It would soon be time to act.

In the darkness of the early morning hours a young boy named Peter, from the small village of Rheems, appeared at the hidden entrance to the tunnels beneath Kern House. He had run for hours to ask for help. Lord William Andersen's mercenaries surrounded their village at dusk; rounded up a group of men, women, and children; and claimed them as slaves for Lord William.

The villagers of Rheems believed they would be safe because their village was farther up in the mountains and well off the main paths. Lexi had warned them it was only a matter of time before the mines would need more slaves and they would be sought out. Ethan volunteered to guide them out of the Eleri Valley and into the Upper Taliesin Mountains where many Verenians had already relocated, but they refused, lulled by the false security of not having been attacked. Until now.

As the group got closer she could make out the soldiers, six of them, Andersen's hired thugs. The others, Lexi counted forty-six, were chained together, the villagers from Rheems. The soldiers were riding, the slaves walking. They would be forced to work until their bodies gave out and they died. Then Andersen's men would return to their village. They would return again and again, until the village was no more. Those they took first, the strongest, the healthiest, would last longest in the mines; the less strong wouldn't last as long, so the soldiers would come more often.

But Lexi and her rebels had worked hard these last few years helping any who were willing to move up into the mountains, far from the danger, far from the smoke and the smell of veredium. But even now, so many in the more remote villages of the lower Taliesin foothills didn't see the need to move until it was too late.

This time Lexi would make certain these people and the rest of the villagers from Rheems would escape. But what about the next village? And then the next? Need, deep and never ending, drove Lexi's actions.

She scanned the area as those coming down the road vanished behind the last stand of pines before the road bent and then straightened again, giving her an open line of sight. As soon as the first riders reappeared, she would signal and take her shot. She smoothly raised her bow and nocked her arrow. First one horse then the next appeared this side of the pines and Lexi whistled, the sound similar to the call of a mountain sparrow.

Her arrow took the first man, grazing his upper arm. As he twisted in his saddle, her second arrow found its home in the next man's chest. She hated the killing, hoped always to just wound, but the second man turned as his friend called out.

Ethan had charge of the next two soldiers while Silas, positioned farther up the road, took out the last two. Silas always complained about Lexi not wanting to kill. "If they're not dead, they can come back and then you have to face them again. No, girl," he would say. "Kill them the first time and be done with it."

But her father had taught her life was precious, a gift from the One; and even now, though she questioned the One's existence, she couldn't just kill. Lexi kicked her brown and white pony into motion down the rise, toward the valley road. She couldn't think about her father; she didn't need that distraction now.

By the time she got to them, Ethan was already releasing the villagers. He must have gotten a key from one of the soldiers.

He moved quickly; time was their enemy. They all knew there were more soldiers coming down the valley road. They scouted them earlier. Silas huffed as he dragged the soldiers' bodies from the road to hide back in the pines, all except the one Lexi had wounded. *Silas is right,* Lexi thought. *Now we'll have to deal with a wounded mercenary.* But it hurt; at sixteen she shouldn't have to kill.

Lexi rode up to the wounded man who was sitting on a rock to the side of the road. He glared up at her. "Why don't you just kill me and be done with it?"

She stared at him with unseeing eyes as the words echoed in her mind. *Is this what Daddy wants? For us to just kill him and be done with it? Why didn't he just kill Daddy and put an end to his pain back then?* She had asked herself that question countless times in the last three years. But driving out the thought with a shake of her head she asked the soldier, "Do you want to die?"

"What?" He looked up at her, his eyes dark and hostile.

She repeated the question. "Do you want to die?"

She needed the answer, just one more need among all the needs. But this one was deep; she craved his answer.

"Do you *want* to die?"

"Are you offering me a choice?"

Lexi sat her pony and said nothing as she looked down at the man, waiting.

"I would live."

Lexi released a pent-up sigh. "You are free to go; but leave Veres. If I see you again, you will die."

With doubt in his eyes, the man rose, clutching his arm, and started walking down the road toward the Andersen holdings. He looked over his shoulder from time to time as if he expected an arrow in the back.

Silas, returning after hiding the last body, glanced at Lexi and shook his head, a look of disgust squirming across his face. "Girl, you're gonna get us killed one of these days."

"At least not today old friend." She jumped from her pony, moving to help Ethan with the villagers. As she approached, a woman ran up to her and knelt in the dust of the road. "Please, lady, please rescue my sons."

Lexi reached down and helped the woman to her feet. "What is it you wish?"

"My two sons." The woman began sobbing. "They've taken my boys for their games and the youngest is only fourteen. Their good boys, kind boys, never held a sword in their lives. They'll never last in the ring. Please, my lady, please save my sons."

There it was again, the pressure, the need. Lexi screamed internal frustration *don't you realize I was only thirteen when I inherited this mantle of need.* But outwardly she smiled for the woman. "We'll do what we can. Did they take your sons when they took you?"

"Yes." Unheeded tears dribbled from the woman's chin. "They tied them to horses and left before we started walking."

Catching Ethan's attention, Lexi said, "Have Cai lead these people up above the fog line. You and Silas gather some of the men and meet me at Kern House. I'll have Seren cook up a meal. We'll eat then head for the Andersen House Gaming Complex. I'll not let Matheson maim or kill any more of my people."

Leaving the villagers in the care of her men, Lexi guided her pony down the road until she came to a moss-covered rock that marked the beginning of a well-hidden trail leading down into the lower valley. The pony, knowing it was heading home and familiar with the path, didn't need any guidance from Lexi so she let her mind wander as the pony picked its way down the mountain.

She needed a plan to rescue the boys. She and her rebels had rescued others in the past, but the new games master, Richard Matheson, was cunning and proud. After their last rescue, he vowed to capture the girl who had made a fool of his predecessor, even offered a one-thousand somme bounty for her capture. He also improved security. In addition to increasing the number of guards, Matheson began issuing special passes to gain entry to the complex. Guests were required to keep the passes with them while there, use them to access the rings, and then surrender them to the guards when leaving. With the increased security, the rebels had avoided any confrontations near the complex.

Lexi hated the games almost as much as she despised the slavery in the mines. The Andersen family had built the first gaming center about eight years ago, with the two other master families building gaming centers of their own soon after. But the Andersen's compound was the largest, most luxurious—and most lucrative. Over time, it had grown into a massive complex surrounded by an immense wall. The Andersens spared no expense in creating a prime destination. With richly appointed quarters, extravagant foods made by some of the system's best chefs, and the exciting allure of weekly death matches, it had become a gathering place for the wealthy and powerful. Those who could afford it, paid outrageous sums to stay in the most expensive suites while enjoying the high-stakes games in the center ring.

The two lesser rings, run by the Claymoore family, catered to those who wished to enjoy the bloody sport but couldn't afford the price of the center ring. In addition to the luxury suites and fine dining establishments, there were four taverns where less wealthy guests could spend their money eating and drinking between matches. Three inns and a variety of small specialty shops were dotted through the complex. Anything money could buy was available for a price at the Andersen House Gaming Complex. The gaming complexes represented everything Lexi detested about the Sorial merchants.

When the games first started, the contestants were paid mercenaries who fought for money and prestige. Now only a few of the fighters were free men who chose to earn money by risking their lives in the ring. Most were slaves forced to fight. She had lost a few men to Matheson's cruelty and hadn't attempted to gain entry to the complex in almost six months. But tonight, she would tweak the games master's nose again. It had been too long since she had been to the Andersen Family's Gaming Complex and Matheson's nose was in sore need of some adjusting.

Like most Verenians, Lexi was petite with golden blonde hair and hazel eyes flecked with gold. Despite living below the fog line and not getting much sun the last three years, her skin was golden brown. She last cut her hair the night before her father had been injured and she vowed to not cut it again until her father recovered. Now, three years later, she usually kept the unruly mass of golden curls bound in a bun covered by a hat. Accepting the fact that her father would never recover, she had come to regret her vow. Yet she still couldn't seem to let it go.

Nearing home, she dismounted to lead the pony over a rocky area before back-tracking in a stream. After about a hundred yards in the stream she led him up onto a flat rock that served as the stream's bank. She picked her way through several closely-grown bushes and turned onto the path that led to the entrance of what looked like an abandoned mine.

The abandoned mine was in fact the beginning of a tunnel her father had secretly dug five years ago that led under Kern House. If not for this tunnel, Lexi, her father, and their house-hold staff, would all have died when the manor house burned. Now the remains of the burned-out mansion and the two underground levels beneath sheltered the rebel's headquarters.

Lexi left her pony to the care of Zachary who, with his father Tal, cared for all the livestock. Knocking dust from her pants with her hat, Lexi climbed the stairs into the upper of the underground levels of Kern House. She wanted to clean up before seeing her father.

She thought about how tired she was as she scrubbed the smoky grit produced by the veredium processing from her body. Three years ago, it had not been this bad. The Andersen holdings only included two veredium processing facilities then. But after the attack on Kern House, they built two more and the smoky fog blanketed the area continuously. Lexi could remember the sun shining in the windows of Kern House. Now, when she looked out the cavities where windows had been, she saw nothing but gray haze and muted light through the shattered remains.

Lexi scanned her reflection in the broken piece of mirror she had salvaged from her room above and ran her fingers through the honey-colored hair curling down to below her hips. She only wore it loose when she was with her father. He had always loved when she wore her hair free. And she hoped that somehow, even if he was trapped in the unresponsive body that now imprisoned his spirit, he was still aware that she wore it loose for him.

She exchanged her riding pants and functional brown shirt for a cream-colored dress with a pink ribbon tie at the high waist. It was worn and a little tight, but it served. Her eyes drawn back to the mirror, Lexi turned, trying to see more of herself in the jagged shard and wondered if she would ever own a new dress again. She roughly flung the thought aside as not needed, turned her back on the mirror with a stomp of her feet, and headed out the door to find Seren to see if her father's gruel was ready.

Mealtimes hammered at the raw edges of Lexi's sealed emotions. Each day, two times a day, she strengthened the lock she kept on the door to her heart, her inner self. The room, usually dark, felt like a tomb to her. She carried a lamp in one hand and her father's gruel in the other. It was all he could eat; it slid down.

After his injury, she had tried feeding him other foods, but he couldn't chew and would choke. After trial and error Lexi and Seren had come up with the gruel recipe. It varied sometimes, but basically it was a life-sustaining, thick liquid he could swallow reflexively.

Lexi set the lamp down on the small charred table that used to be in her father's study. Her father, Duke Erland, noble ruler of Veres, loving father, friend of King Theodor. *What a joke.* King Theodor was no friend. He abandoned her father. And the people of Veres. He abandoned Lexi. She had sent him so many messages, especially right after her father's injury, but he never responded. Something must have gotten through, she thought. But, apparently, the king of all Ochen couldn't be bothered by the troubles of a small world like Veres.

Clamping down on her rising anger, Lexi pulled her stool up to the side of her father's large, well-padded leather chair, now set on wheels. Because he sat all day, the padding needed replacing frequently and if it wasn't for Lucius, Justus's old man servant, the thing would smell of waste.

Do you want to die? The question she asked the soldier

earlier surfaced in her mind. *I would live,* he had replied. As she wiped the gruel that dripped down her father's bristly chin she wondered what he would say.

Do you want to live, Daddy? Like this? Please Daddy, I need to know. Please Daddy.

Her father had been a strong man, big by Verenian standards. Always smiling, always telling her about the One. He would talk to her about long forgotten prophecies and cling to hope even when things were getting bad. In one brief moment, a heartless mercenary had stolen him from her, replacing her warm, loving father with an unfeeling replica. So she stopped believing. There was no One, no hope. The prophecies were all lies. Where was the voice of the One for Lexi, for her people? No. There was only silence. There was no One.

She talked to her father as she slowly fed him his meal, watching to be sure he swallowed before she gave him the next spoonful.

"We're going to the Andersen House Gaming Complex tonight, Daddy; me, Ethan, Silas, and the others. I haven't rubbed Matheson's nose in the dirt for a while now. We're going to steal back two boys he's taken for the ring. I don't have a plan yet. Do you have any ideas for me Daddy? ... Nothing today? ... Well, maybe next time."

After she finished feeding her father, Lexi brushed a lock of hair back out of his dull, brown eyes, her fingers resting briefly on his face, and kissed his cheek.

"I have to go now Daddy."

Lexi turned her back on the dark room and as she walked out, swore that someday she would find the mercenary who had done this to her father. For three years she had spoken the same vow every time she left her father's room. She never thought past finding him, or about what she would do if she did find him. She just knew she needed him to suffer.

Over the next hour, several men arrived at the abandoned mine entrance. They came singly or in pairs. By the time they were ready to leave, twelve other rebels had joined Lexi. Counting Ethan and Silas, she would need fifteen passes to gain entrance. Lexi rubbed her forehead. *At least that's not a problem.*

Two spies working for the Andersens had helped her collect twenty in the last few months. Rescuing the boys meant she would need a total of seventeen passes to hand in when they left the complex. With a grunt, she decided to keep the extras just in case and put all twenty into her vest pocket.

As they were saddling their horses, one of the boys Lexi employed as spies came running into the entrance. He stopped, his eyes scanning the large cave-like area that functioned as a stable. When he caught sight of Lexi, he ran up, huffing. "I have ... important ... news, my lady." Motioning for Ethan to continue preparations to leave, Lexi guided the boy past the horses to the back of the tunnel.

"Yes, Kyle, what is it?" Lexi asked after they were out of earshot of the others.

"I was spying out the valley road yesterday, a couple hours south of the Andersen's games, when I saw that fancy coach. The one the Andersens use for special guests. So I snuck in close enough to listen. Jason Andersen's got some special noble named Prince Rayne with him. The guards even called him a royal highness. Jason musta been entertaining that special prince person on the way to the fights because his slaves was fixin' a real elegant meal. I thought you might want to know, so I came here."

Lexi focused her eyes on a point above Kyle's head as thoughts scooted around in her mind. *Prince Rayne? Theodor's son? The quiet boy with the big eyes? I thought something happened to him.* Although the Andersen's games attracted all kinds of nobles, Lexi was not aware of anyone from the royal family attending before. She wondered if this information could be used for the benefit of her people in some way. Sending Kyle to Seren to get something to eat, she waved Ethan and Silas over.

"It would appear my old childhood friend, Prince Rayne Kierkengaard of Corylus will be in attendance at the games tonight." A calculating expression suffused her face as she chewed her lower lip. "I have an idea."

The two men groaned. They were used to Lexi's ideas, her ideas were usually clever and worth executing, but sometimes they verged on the border of insanity. Ethan and Silas looked at each other and then faced Lexi. Ethan said, "Yes, my lady, what do you propose?"

Perhaps it had been kindled by her anger at King Theodor for ignoring the plight of her people; perhaps by her jealousy of Rayne getting to live the life of a pampered royal while her life had been shattered by her father's injury and the injustices perpetrated on her people; but whatever the reason, a little voice inside Lexi said, *steal the prince from right under Lord William's nose*. Lexi liked the idea.

Looking at her co-conspirators, she said, "Lord William takes great pride in offering a safe experience for his wealthy, noble clients, right?" Concerned looks flashed between the two men. Both nodded slow and hesitant.

"And wouldn't his reputation for safety be damaged if something were to happen to someone as important as the Crown Prince of Ochen?" She grinned, releasing a wicked little chuckle.

The two men swallowed and nodded again.

"And ... aren't we infiltrating the gaming complex tonight anyway? Those boys will be in the slave quarters, just up the path from the center ring where the nobles come to be entertained. That's where the prince will be." She nodded and chewed her lip a moment. "Since we're going to be there anyway to rescue those boys from Rheems, I don't see why we can't just grab the prince as well. We'll hold him for ransom."

"No." Silas shook his shaggy head of gray-streaked blonde hair. "That would be foolish. The prince will probably be surrounded by an honor guard. How do you propose we deal with that? We're just rebels by circumstance, not warriors by choice."

Lexi looked at Silas as frustration bubbled in her stomach. "We deal with that the same way we dealt with the guard around that wagon of food we stole last month. We use the mist and the fog in the dark. Just like before, we'll blend in with the guards, take them out one at a time, and then nudge the prize in our direction. Simple."

Silas's brow furrowed and he huffed out a breath as Ethan said, "It might work. It's awfully thick out there today, and it'll be dark in the complex when the games end. It might just work."

"Yes!" Lexi's enthusiasm was contagious. "It will work. And not only will we damage Lord William's reputation, which will hurt his precious profits, we could use the ransom money to help the villagers who need it most. Besides, I owe King Theodor for abandoning my father. I like the idea of taking his son."

The three smiled in agreement and Silas said, "You are a devious woman my lady."

They walked back to the others who were mounted and ready to ride and explained the changes to the plan. Everyone was in good spirits, inspired by Lexi's plan and excited by the prospect of getting to not only rescue a couple boys from a terrible ordeal, but execute a little vengeance on Lord William and King Theodor at the same time. And they all knew how much the ransom money could help their efforts.

31

Rayne couldn't guess what the time might be, but he heard the crowd above his head cheering once again. Whoever the games master was, he certainly knew how to get a crowd worked up. Hearing footsteps, Rayne looked up to see Shin approaching. The huge man was shaking his head and, if Rayne was not mistaken, looked as if he was blinking back tears.

When he got to Rayne's cell, he shook his head again, his shaggy hair bouncing. "Shin should have let Little Warrior go. Now it is too late. Little Warrior must fight mean Khalon warrior from Glacieria. Shin is sorry Little Warrior, it is time."

Shin opened the door and motioned for Rayne to grab his cloak and follow. In the dim light of the lower level, Shin took the cloak and threw it over Rayne's shoulders, still shaking his head and mumbling. He looked at Rayne with sorrowful eyes and pulled the hood up to cover Rayne's head, letting it drop in front, covering more than half of his face. Then Rayne followed Shin's hulking form up the stairs, the clamor of excited voices growing louder as they climbed. At the top of the stairs, Shin walked down a short hallway that ended in a well-lit opening where the sounds of revelry grew intense. Once they reached the opening, Shin stood next to Rayne, motioning for him to wait.

As if in a dream, Rayne heard a strangely familiar voice announce that the main event of the evening would take place shortly. This week's death match.

Several minutes later, the announcer spoke again; his excitement palpable, his voice rising in volume and tone as if he struggled to contain his enthusiasm. "Lords and ladies, what a thrilling night to be here at the center ring of the Andersen House Gaming Complex! I have just received news that we are privileged tonight to witness the very first appearance of an extraordinary new contestant to this ring, or any ring. A talent I have looked forward to introducing here for a long time. Due to the unique nature and remarkable history of this recently acquired offering from the Andersen House stable, the time allotted for betting will be extended, the minimum bet allowance will be raised, and there will be no cap on the maximum bet. This is a once in a lifetime event so don't lose your chance to be part of something unprecedented. Once the contestants have been announced, please take advantage of the changes to the betting structure."

Looking up from under the hood, Rayne gazed out on a medium-sized ring surrounded by a luxurious observation deck. More than three-hundred richly dressed guests were sitting around black lacquer tables like the ones in Louvain's house, while relaxing in deeply cushioned red and black chairs. The whole arrangement spoke of wealth, prestige, and power. Slaves clad in Andersen uniforms of red and black were scurrying to deliver drinks and large platters of food to the noisy attendees who lounged and chatted as they waited for the games master to make the next announcement.

The place was smaller than Rayne expected, with seating for perhaps three-hundred and fifty spectators. But Rayne understood. Though the cost of admission to these death matches was excessive, the true profits were made on the betting, not the number of spectators. The wealth represented by those he saw now was probably staggering.

Scanning the crowd, he saw Jason sitting at a prime, ringside table with several young men and women who were dressed as if they were attending a formal dinner or the theater. Apparently, the center ring at the Andersen's Eleri Gaming Complex was the place to see who was in attendance and to be seen in return. Young nobles, dressed in the most popular current styles, flitted from table to table, talking animatedly. The crowd ebbed and flowed with the movements, colors, and sounds of people enjoying a party. The limited seating just added to the prestige of being in attendance.

Anger coursed through Rayne and he ground his teeth as he observed these spoiled, self-centered men and women who came dressed to impress each other and socialize over food and drinks while others were forced to fight to the death. They reminded him of Brayden. But, of course, his cousin probably had his own private table.

Knowing Brayden sent the information that destroyed his chances for successfully infiltrating Veres, he scrutinized the ring-side tables again. He was surprised his cousin wasn't here tonight to watch his *Little Raynie* fight. Thoughts circling back to the two frightened boys chained in the slave quarters soured Rayne's stomach and he wanted to wipe the smiles off all the smug faces he saw around the ring, laughing, talking, feasting.

Then the games master was walking back to center ring and Rayne groaned when he recognized the man. Private Richard Matheson, the soldier who had kidnapped Rayne months ago hoping to sell him on Sorial, waved his hands and smiled at the noisy onlookers. *Well, I guess he finally got me here.*

"Honored guests." Matheson's voice rang out, loud and clear. "Thank you all for your patience. Your wait is over. Entering the ring from my left, our ring champion. An Andersen House favorite, an ex-master assassin, and killer of more than five challengers here in this very ring. Defending his title tonight." Matheson pointed to an entrance opposite the one where Rayne waited. "Hailing from Glacieria and a member of the fierce Khalon Tribe, I give you Yormund."

Rayne saw his opponent and immediately understood Shin's concern. Yormund, one of Sigmund's hired thugs, stalked down the ramp past the cheering crowd with a grim look of death on his face. He shouted, flexed his massive muscles, and waved at the adoring crowd. If anything, he looked even stronger than Rayne remembered. He still carried his ancient weapon and swung the axe in mighty arcs through the air as it glowed. The spectators cheered their delight.

Rayne turned hopeless eyes back to Shin who shook his head while handing Rayne a well-worn, pocked and chipped, long sword. Rayne could tell right away that the sword was poorly made, brittle with no give at all.

I'm going to die! Panic seized Rayne's chest and squeezed tight. With a last grab at self-preservation, Rayne dropped the sword, reached up and pulled the leather tie from Shin's hair, and mouthing the word sorry, pushed back his hood and tied his hair into a tail. He pulled the hood back up again and retrieved the sword. At least now he wouldn't have to contend with loose hair swinging in his face while fighting Yormund with a worthless sword.

Matheson was speaking again, and the crowd got quiet.

"The challenger in this week's specialty death match is a singular treat acquired for your entertainment by Lord William himself. I am thrilled to present for his first appearance at the Andersen Family Gaming Complex center ring, the disavowed, ex-heir to the throne of Ochen, master assassin of Lord Sigmund of Bainard, son of King Theodor and Queen Rowena, pretender to the title of Light Bringer of the One, Rayne Kierkengaard."

The announcement was greeted with a shocked silence followed by mumbling. All eyes turned to look in Rayne's direction as Shin pushed him forward into the light.

If Yormund had entered the ring as a champion, Rayne entered it as nothing more than a cloaked youth who stumbled his way down the ramp to stand in front of Matheson.

That's right, Matheson, smile. Rayne thought with venom. *But if I survive this, I'll wipe that smile off your face with my sword.*

Matheson grabbed Rayne's shoulder and grinding his fingers into the joint, turned him to face the audience and whispered, "Finally. If you survive tonight, we have unfinished business, you and I." With an animated flourish, Matheson then made a show of removing Rayne's cloak and revealing him to the waiting crowd.

Nudging Rayne, Matheson said, "Turn for the people slave, let them get a good look at you. You saw how Yormund did it. Now you do the same, please the crowd."

Rayne glowered back at the man and refused to move. Matheson looked up at the crowd, turning in a circle, exaggeratedly rolling his eyes and shrugging. "He seems to be a bit shy," Matheson shouted.

The audience was delighted by Rayne's show of rebellion and, laughing in response to Matheson's comment, began calling for the young boys who ran between the tables to take their bets.

Rayne figured if he was going to die, he was not going out as some puppet for the pleasure of the nobles or Matheson or Lord William. Figuring the betting would go on for at least a few minutes he closed his eyes and prayed, *I need you again, my Lord. Your power and strength. You must know that Lord William plans for Yormund to kill me. I don't even have the King's Sword to help me this time.*

Rayne felt the warmth and the voice spoke into his spirit. *Know that I am with you, my Light Bringer. Trust.*

At this moment though, with Yormund ready to tear him apart, Rayne was finding it hard to trust. He knew what the One had done for him in the past but that seemed very far away and fragile now.

But ... he started, then stopped. *But what?* What was he going to ask the One? And knowing he was running out of time Rayne clutched the word the One had chosen to give him. He was not alone. He would trust.

He opened his eyes. Most of the boys who had been scurrying, taking bets, were now standing still, backs against the wall. Looking at Yormund sent skitters of fear up Rayne's spine. He repeated *trust* over and over in his mind as he started to swing his pathetic excuse of a sword while Yormund swung his powerful ancient axe, grinning.

Matheson's voice rang forth again. Rayne was out of time. Yormund was moving toward him and Matheson scrambled out of the ring.

Rayne knew his only hope against the massive Yormund and his axe lay in speed. His speed had been his salvation so often in the past and unless the One decided to fill him with supernatural strength again, speed was all Rayne had in his favor. As Yormund moved directly toward him, Rayne rose up on the balls of his feet and started dancing to his left, trying to keep his sword between his body and Yormund's glowing axe.

Yormund lunged. The man was quick for someone his size. Rayne barely blocked his first swing, an overhead power house of a blow that would have torn through Rayne's right shoulder if not blocked. But Yormund was already countering. Twisting. Pulling his axe in an arc to swing into Rayne's left side. Rayne blocked again. But it cost him. The force of the blow numbed his fingers and he almost dropped the disgustingly brittle sword.

What were they thinking? Rayne squeezed the worn and cracked leather around the sword's grip trying to get his hands to work again. *Pitting me against Yormund without even giving me a decent weapon?* But Rayne knew the answer; Lord William had decreed he die in this ring tonight. Brayden's promised reward for Rayne's death must have been exorbitant.

Rayne circled to his left again, watching Yormund for a tell-tale signal that the man would close on him once more. This time Rayne saw the slight flicker of tension in his eyes and grip as the man moved in. Rayne blocked. He twisted to his left, lowered his blade slightly, allowed Yormund's momentum to propel him forward. Just enough. Rayne swung at Yormund's exposed back. First hit, first blood. But as Rayne danced away from the now enraged Yormund, he wondered at the wisdom of angering the big warrior. *As if that matters now.*

Rayne heard the cheers and cries of the spectators as nothing more than a buzzing in his ears. He knew they were watching for him to make a fatal mistake. That would be all it would take, one mistake. And then Yormund would take pleasure in slowly dicing him into little bits and feeding on his pain.

As Rayne backed and circled in response to Yormund's advances, he realized Yormund was just playing with him. The huge man was obviously aware Rayne's sword was worthless.

With a smile playing on his lips, he pushed Rayne, forcing him to block blow after heavy blow until Rayne could duck away and gain some distance again.

They had traded blows a few more times, and Rayne's sword was chipped and cracked, his arms were shaking from blocking Yormund's powerful swings. Rayne wondered how much longer he and his sword would last. Then Yormund was on him again and this time it was Yormund who drew blood with a quick slice past Rayne's defenses, leaving a trail of blood across the outside of his left hip.

Too slow! Rayne berated himself as he felt the warm stream soaking into the top of his leggings. The crowd erupted, screaming again, enjoying the fight, taking pleasure in blood and pain.

Rayne continued to dance away while Yormund stalked him around the ring. Frustration evident in the man's movements and his face a mask of fury, Yormund charged and struck again with the force of his charge behind his axe. Rayne shifted to catch the axe and push back before ducking away again, when the overly stressed blade broke leaving Rayne with a foot-long stub of a sword.

Taking advantage of Rayne's momentary shock, Yormund screamed as he turned, using the momentum of his body to swing his axe into a powerful overhead arc. Rayne threw himself back, the axe slicing the air where his head had just been before descending to carve a bloody, diagonal track across the front of Rayne's right thigh, slicing through muscle and down to the bone.

Rayne screamed at the sudden agony, knew it was over now. He had lost the advantage of speed and was sick with the pain. He could barely move, and he had no weapon. He saw Yormund back off, smiling, confident.

The big warrior shouted, "Yormund told Sigmund he was better than his little slave boy." He moved toward Rayne again, death in his eyes.

Rayne prepared to face Yormund's attack. He would try to block with the remains of his sword. It was ridiculous and hopeless, but he wasn't going to hobble around the ring away from the man. That would be pathetic. He'd rather die facing Yormund head on. But as he began to swing his stump of a sword to block Yormund's next attack, something powerful plowed into his back, knocking him face down to the ground as the ruined sword went skittering across the sand.

Then Yormund was over him, past him, and Rayne heard a grunt of pain from behind. Twisting, he looked back past a stunned Yormund and up into Shin's sad eyes. The big man had shoved Rayne down and taken Yormund's axe in the chest, saving Rayne's life.

Pushing upright to stand tall despite his wound, Shin took a step forward. He looked down at Rayne and spoke out in a strong voice. "Little Warrior must not die here like this."

Rayne blinked in disbelief when Shin pulled the axe from his chest, blood spraying in ruby droplets over Yormund, the sand, and Rayne. Then, with incredible massive strength behind it, Shin flicked the axe around and drove the axe head into Yormund's chest, burying it. The ancient weapon flickered and glowed and then exploded in a shower of sparks.

Without thought for anything but Shin, Rayne pushed up onto his good leg. With Shin's and Yormund's blood dripping from his face, he hobbled past Yormund's remains to Shin who was now on his knees. Dropping to his left knee in front of him, Rayne asked, "Why? Why did you save me?"

Shin smiled, his face glowing with amazing peace. "Shin happy. Served One. Saved Light Bringer. Filled purpose."

Shock froze Rayne's thoughts. He rose to stand on trembling legs, the ring and the crowd forgotten. He wanted to ask Shin what he knew of the One and if he knew about the Son. Then hands were grabbing him, dragging him back. He was aware of shouting and screaming, the thunderous noise of the spectators around him, bloody sand beneath him. He was lifted from the ground and carried back up the ramp, away from the spectators and their clamor. Then someone was pouring another vial of the bitter drink into his mouth before slinging him like a sack over a shoulder to be carried down the stairs to the room where he had waited earlier. He was dropped to the ground. The sudden pressure on his thigh caused him to scream, spitting out most of the liquid he had been trying not to swallow, as his leg collapsed. Somehow, he caught himself and remained upright holding his weight on his left leg.

Matheson was yelling but Rayne ignored the man, staring forward with unseeing eyes, body quaking. He struggled to understand what Shin had done. Frustration twisting Matheson's face into a hateful mask, he stepped behind Rayne and grabbed the tail Rayne had tied with Shin's leather thong. Matheson pulled back with brutal strength, forcing Rayne's neck into an awkward position. Rayne, trying to ease the pain at his neck and scalp, was losing his struggle to remain upright. The pain suddenly eased, and Rayne's head bounced forward. Matheson had grabbed one of the swords from the nearby rack and sliced through Rayne's hair, taking the tail, and leaving a tangled, shaggy mess behind.

Grabbing Rayne's arm, Matheson jerked him around, almost causing him to fall again. Like a child with a toy, Matheson gleefully waved Rayne's severed tail in his face. "You were supposed to die in that ring tonight. Well, you've beaten the odds again, little princeling. But, no matter, you won't survive much longer. Just because you're injured, don't think I won't send you back into that ring night after night until I'm satisfied you've suffered enough for what you cost me. Then I'll let you die. In the meantime, I'll just take this as a souvenir of your first fight."

Rayne grabbed for it, something in him rebelling at the thought of Matheson taking a piece of him. But Matheson pulled the tail out of reach and pushed Rayne. His leg buckled. Groggy from the bitter liquid he had swallowed, Rayne tumbled to the floor.

Matheson quieted and hid the tail behind his back as Lord William marched into the room. He stalked over to Rayne and looked down at him, his features pulled into a disgusted frown. Rayne blinked up at the man trying desperately to stay conscious and process everything. Lord William was screaming something at him. Rayne grabbed his temples and wondered why everyone was so intent on screaming things at him. He was swimming in a sea of confusion and growing lethargy, uncertain if the fight and Shin's death were real or if he was trapped in another nightmare.

Rayne could barely stand as they pulled him up and clamped shackles on his wrists. Then the cloak was thrown over him and he was partly dragged and partly carried out to the path to the slave quarters. After a few feet, the men released him, pushing him to stagger up the pathway under his own power. The evening was dark with enveloping fog and the incessant gritty smoke. Rayne stumbled forward in a haphazard pattern as he strove to keep weight off his injured leg while cobwebs continued to grow in his drug-fuddled mind. He struggled to see the guards surrounding him through the shifting gray mist. They wove in and out of his vision. He couldn't understand what was happening when, instead of heading back into the hulking building that materialized out of the mist and loomed large in front of him, they suddenly shifted off the path and slipped into a stand of trees.

32

॥

Lexi and the rebels rode to a cave located a couple miles from the Andersen House Gaming Complex. Three small rooms branched off from a large cavern. They used it to store food and supplies as well as extra clothing. The men changed into a varied mix of well-tailored suits they had collected over time. Most were outdated, but the obvious quality of the clothing would be enough to get them past the guards at the gate.

Lexi used padding made from sheep's wool and old pillow cases to fill out the only lady's dress of any quality they had been able to acquire. It was too large for her small frame, but with padding in the right spots and the ties pulled in as tight as they could go, she made a passible looking, if rather lumpy, noble woman. Knowing her honey-colored hair was too distinctive, she stained it with walnut juice to darken the golden tresses. With Ethan's help she pulled the whole damp mass into a semblance of a fancy up do. Good enough. Lexi didn't plan to go into the building that housed the center ring, she only needed to get past the guards at the gate.

They split up to arrive in groups of two or three to throw off suspicion. Once inside the complex, they planned to regroup in a wooded area just off the path that ran from the slave quarters to the center ring.

Ethan suggested using that area because it was near the slave quarters and bordered the path that ran between there and the building where the center ring was housed. Its good location, the added cover of the trees, and the lack of lighting in the area, made it the best place to work from.

Lexi, Ethan, and Silas rode to the complex in a coach she had borrowed from an old family friend. He hadn't asked any questions when she requested it and didn't want to know anything about what she was doing. He just made her promise she would bring it back in one piece.

When they arrived at the gate, while Silas was displaying their passes, Lexi proceeded to play the part of a haughty, spoiled noble. In a loud, high-pitched, whiny voice, she insisted she be allowed to leave her coach near the top of the path by the slave quarters rather than take it to one of the stables.

"I will not pay to have my horses abused by your irresponsible stable boys and I absolutely refuse to wait later while they take their time readying my coach for departure. And I certainly don't want anyone rummaging through my private coach. My people know where to leave my coach. I do this every time I come here. Every time."

She went on to insist they give her total assurance no one would touch it. Silas, who was driving the coach, put on a show of being the long-suffering servant. He rolled his eyes as he handed the men a bundle of sommes. Lexi heard them laughing amongst themselves about the strange tastes of wealthy nobles and the handsome young slave Jason Andersen had brought in earlier.

"Once we see your passes, we couldn't care less where you leave your coach lady," one guard said.

"Just so long as you've shown us the color of your sommes," the other added as he waved the coach in.

After positioning the coach close to the wooded area, Lexi and her men gathered quietly amongst the trees under the cover of mist and smoke. They would make their move when the second match of the evening, the weekly death match, was underway. Once the noise level convinced Lexi the fight was in progress, she sent Silas to the center ring to find out which exit the prince planned to use when he left. She then gave the signal for Ethan and two other men to sneak to the back entrance of the slave quarters while she moved out to distract the two guards stationed by the door. Singing off-key, she staggered as if drunk until she got close to the guards. Letting out a scream, she fell across the path and lay there moaning.

When the guards came to help her, Ethan and another rebel stepped in behind and using sand-filled tubes, knocked them unconscious. Two other men gagged the unconscious guards, tied them, and hid them in some bushes while Lexi and Ethan slipped into the slave quarters.

Lexi and Ethan found the brothers shackled and chained to the wall of a room that looked like it was used for bathing and dressing. No one else was around. It didn't take Lexi long to find a keyring that held the key to the shackles and she released the boys. With a smug smile, she pocketed the ring hoping to create at least a little frustration for the Andersens.

The night was thick and dark when they snuck out the door with the boys and scurried back toward the trees, melting into the dense fog. Lexi was pleased with the way things had gone so far. They could just leave now, forget about kidnapping the prince and get the boys to safety, but Silas hadn't returned. She would have to wait and see what Silas learned. The rebels huddled in the trees, listening to the noise coming from the center ring. Lexi never realized how loud a bunch of nobles watching a fight could get. Suddenly, the sounds coming from the ring turned into a deafening roar and moments later, Silas was running for the trees.

"They're bringing that prince fellow now." Silas's voice vibrated with excitement. "You'll never believe it when I tell you what all happened in there."

"Not now." Lexi motioned for silence. Silas was sometimes too easily excited and when he got excited he tended to talk too much, too fast, and too loud. Lexi needed him to stay focused and quiet until they were out of the complex.

"Which entrance are they coming out?" Lexi asked.

"This way, along the path. But you won't believe ..." Silas started again. but Lexi stopped him. "Save the story for later, Silas."

Lexi wondered why the prince would come out the small slave entrance rather than one of the grand guest entrances. *Must be coming this way for security reasons. Well, the prince's choice to use this path just made our job easier.*

"Are you sure he's coming this way?" she whispered to Silas again.

He opened his mouth to answer when Lexi raised her hand for silence. The door to the cells beneath the ring opened, casting a swath of illumination that merged with the light from the outside torches, setting the mist aglow. Lexi caught sight of a cloaked figure surrounded by several men moving out from the lower level along the path toward the trees. The prince and his men.

The mist swirled, and Lexi caught a glimpse of two guards supporting the cloaked figure. Lexi swallowed her disgust. *That self-centered, heartless royal is falling down drunk! He probably thought it entertaining to watch a man die while he fondled some simpering lady and drank himself into a stupor. Ugh, it looks like his men practically have to carry the drunken fool. Good grief, just look at him stagger.*

Once the door closed and the prince and his men moved away from the light near the building into the surrounding darkness, Lexi whispered, "Go."

Several of her men slipped through the trees, quiet, like phantoms, darker shapes in the dense fog. Each one targeted a guard and after knocking the man out and lowering him to the ground, promptly moved into his position. It only took a minute and if any soldiers were watching, between the darkness and the smoky fog they would never realize that anything had changed in the formation surrounding the prince.

By the time all the guards had been replaced, the group was level with the woods and the rebels veered from the path, herding the prince into the trees where Lexi and the others waited. Noticing that the cloaked figure was stumbling badly, Lexi whispered, "Somebody carry that drunken buffoon. We need to get him and the boys into the coach and get out of here before anyone raises an alarm."

Rayne struggled to keep moving as he was hurried into a stand of trees and then propelled up a hill. He heard what sounded like a girl's voice whisper something about carrying a drunk fool and found himself lifted and slung over a strong shoulder like a bag of grain. Confusion tangled his already muddled and numbed thoughts and he began to wonder what Lord William had commanded these people to do with him and what would happen next.

Searing spikes of pain shot through Rayne's thigh as his body bumped against the man carrying him. Warm blood soaked his leggings from the thigh downward and mingled with the blood dribbling down his side from the slice in his hip. Fighting a losing battle against the effects of the bitter drink and blood loss, Rayne tried to focus enough to insist he be put down. But then he was dumped onto a cracked leather seat in a shadowy coach. Tilting his head back, he looked under the edge of his hood and watched, surprised, as the two boys he had seen earlier climbed into the coach and sat across from him. They were followed by a man who swung in, pulled the door shut behind him, and sat down next to the boys. The man thumped on the ceiling of the coach; a whip cracked and they were moving.

No one spoke as they headed toward the outer gate of the complex. Rayne was sitting next to a rather oddly shaped woman whose dark hair was falling out of what must have once been some kind of fancy arrangement on the top of her head.

As they came to the gate, the lumpy woman flung her hand out the coach window and silently waved papers at the guards. Her driver jumped down from his seat, grabbed the papers and handed them to the men saying, "My lady grows restive. Here are our passes."

After grabbing the passes and giving them a bored look, the guard waved for his partner to raise the gate. The driver wasted no time scrambling back up onto the coach and with the gate still moving, whipped the horses into a canter.

A few minutes later, the driver slowed the team to a ground-covering, easy trot. Rayne was too exhausted and confused to think straight. Too much had happened too quickly, and he couldn't seem to gather the confusing events into a cohesive whole. It was all so jumbled. Had he dreamed the whole thing? Was he still in his cell waiting to fight?

A voice in his mind insisted he needed to ask these people who they were and where they were taking him, but the surrounding quiet seemed to demand silence and the rhythmic movement of the coach began to lull him, dulling the internal voice. Although he had spit out most of the bitter drink when he fell, the residue he swallowed continued to produce the desired result and tendrils of unconsciousness hovered at the edges of Rayne's mind forcing him to give in to his need for sleep. Leaning into the lumpy form next to him, Rayne closed his eyes. The last thing he noticed was that the woman smelled nice.

33

N

"Ugh!" Lexi's voice shattered the silence of the coach. She pushed against the unyielding form to her right trying to shove the prince away. "Ethan! Get over here and help me. I can't move him. He must have drunk himself into a stupor and ... Oh! Ugh! He must have peed in his sleep, the seat's all wet here. Ethan!"

Ethan pulled himself upright in the bouncing coach and grabbed Lexi's hand to pull her up and switch positions. Once Lexi was settled in his seat, Ethan pushed up under the collapsed prince, shifted him into a sitting position, and maneuvered himself into the seat where Lexi had been sitting.

Leaving the disgusting prince to Ethan, Lexi had turned to the two boys to ask their names when Ethan said, "I think we have a problem, my lady. This man isn't drunk, he has no smell of alcohol on him and the wet isn't pee, it's blood."

"What? How could that be? Nobody laid a hand on him." Lexi went quiet as fear streaked through her. "He isn't dead, is he?"

After a moment, Ethan answered, "No, my lady, he has a strong pulse. I don't think he's in any danger. But, from what

I can feel here in the dark, he seems to have a nasty slice just above his left hip. The bleeding's stopped now, but that's what's on the seat, blood. Also, my lady, I think Silas was mistaken. This can't be Prince Rayne. He's not dressed like a noble, he's dressed like an Andersen slave and, my lady, he's wearing shackles. I thought I heard the clink of chains when I was carrying him earlier, but I assumed the prince was wearing a heavy necklace like some of the nobles do."

"That's him," one of the two boys whispered. "Least that's what Lord William called him when they dressed him in those fight clothes; Prince Rayne. And some other names too."

"Are you sure?" Lexi asked.

"Yes, my lady."

"This doesn't make sense." Thinking, Lexi turned back to the shadowy form of the boy. "Was he doing this of his own will? Maybe he likes to play at fighting and paid Lord William to stage a fight to entertain his friends and you just misunderstood. And the injury was an accident."

"No mistake," the other boy said. "Me and my brother both heard Lord William say that he was a prince, but he wasn't a prince no more and that Lord William owned him. And that he was being paid a lot of money to make sure the prince died in the ring tonight."

Lexi shook her head. Nothing about this made sense to her. Looking toward Ethan's shadowy figure across from her, she said, "Do you understand any of this?"

"No, my lady. I'm as confused as you are. We'll have to wait until we get back to Kern House and Silas can explain things."

Lexi chaffed at the mystery. It would be another three hours until they reached Kern House.

Maybe Ethan should wake the unconscious stranger and find out who he really is. Maybe this whole thing is an elaborate trap set by Lord William to find our hideout.

"Ethan, do you think this could be a trap?"

"For us?"

"Well, nothing else makes sense, does it? Think about it. Here we are rushing to our hideout, the place that Lord William's been trying to find for the last three years, with a total stranger we know nothing about. He was supposed to be Prince Rayne, but he's dressed like a slave from the games, and Lord William wants him dead? If he isn't the prince, think Ethan, who might he be? Ethan, we need to wake him up. We have no idea who he is."

The drumming of horses' hooves and the sound of tack creaking as the coach rocked and squeaked filled the darkness. Lexi could imagine Ethan's look of concentration, knowing that, like her, he was considering her words in the silence. She spoke up. "What could Lord William could gain by us trusting this stranger and bringing him to our base of operations? The location, of course." She sensed the movement when he shook his head in the dark and said, "Lexi, that makes no sense either. If that's what he wanted there would be more reliable ways to find where we've been hiding."

Turning to the dark shapes of the boys sitting across from him, Ethan asked, "Can you tell me your names boys?"

One of the boys answered, "I'm Bran and my brother's Alick."

"And you were taken from your home?"

"Yes sir," Bran said. "Yesterday a whole buncha them Andersen mercenaries came to our village say'n they needed new workers. So our village, Rheems, was supposed to pay its duty, they said. We were taken with our mother but then one of the soldiers said the games needed more fighters, and so they picked us two to go with him. Me and my brother was so scared." He sniffled, and then asked, "Do you know what happened to our mother?"

"She was the one who asked us to rescue you," Lexi said. "She's on her way up into the high mountains now and tomorrow we'll send you to her. I know she was really worried about you."

"We was worried 'bout her too," Alick said. Silence descended on the coach for a moment, then Alick spoke up. "You know, that prince fella, he can't be no older than my brother. Maybe sixteen, maybe seventeen. And he was really brave, facin' up to old Lord William hisself when he grabbed the prince's face.

"I thought fer sure old Lord William was gonna hit him but he kicked me instead. The prince, he tried to help me but that old smelly guy with the apron stopped him. I don't think he's with them Andersens."

"Yeah," Bran said. "He seemed real upset when that other man gave old apron guy a special collar for him to wear when he went to fight. Said it was his from afore."

"Yeah," Alick added. "He tried talkin' to us too, but we was too afraid to answer."

"Can you remember anything else about what Lord William said?" Ethan asked.

"Oh, wait," Bran said. "I almost forgot. That prince fella said something about the One, 'bout how he's always with us. And that's when old Lord William came in and said what the prince was say'n was hogwash. That's just what he said, hogwash. And then he called the prince some kind of royal prince and that's when he said he wasn't no prince anymore and called him Light Bringer. Do you remember Alick?"

"Yep, that's 'bout right."

Lexi squinted into the darkness. "Lord William called him what?"

"Light Bringer," Bran said. "Yep, that's right. That's what he said."

The coach continued moving in the silence and the dark fog, as Lexi tried to figure out the mystery surrounding the unconscious man—*boy?*—draped in the black cloak across from her; a deeper shadow in the dark coach. The sounds and movement of the coach lulled Lexi and she drifted off until a change of motion woke her. They were home.

Silas drove the coach right into the abandoned mine entrance and pulling the horses to a stop jumped down. Tal ran up and grabbed the reins from Silas and, with Zachary helping, began to unfasten the horses. Silas opened the coach door and Bran and Alick jumped out. Ethan followed them and reached back to help Lexi down. As she was stepping out of the coach, the stranger stirred. He shifted and moaned lightly.

"I'll get Bran and Alick settled," Ethan said.

"Come to the cavern when you're done," Lexi said. "I'm going to change and check on Father then I'll join you there."

She turned to Silas, her lips in a firm line. "You owe us an explanation, Silas. The man whose blood we're going to have to scrub from that seat before we return the coach can't be Prince Rayne. He is injured though, and needs our help so wake Seren. She can see to his injury. She'll probably want to make coffee for everyone anyway."

Reaching into her pocket, she pulled out the keyring she had picked up in the slave quarters and tossed it to Silas. "I think you'll need one of these. I don't know why I grabbed that, but now I'm glad I did. And Silas," she added, irritation turning her voice gruff, "you were the one who told me he was the prince. So he's your responsibility and will remain your responsibility as long as he's here. I expect you to find out what's going on by the time I see you in the cavern." With a tired sigh, she headed down the tunnel toward the stairs to the lower level of the house.

Ethan rolled his eyes at Silas who shrugged. "I only know what I heard."

Ethan motioned to Bran and Alick, and said, "Come on boys." He led them up the tunnel, following in Lexi's footsteps.

Once the coach stopped, Rayne struggled against an overwhelming lethargy and willed himself to open his eyes. His mouth felt like a desert and every inch of his body hurt. His side was on fire, and his thigh throbbed, deep and unsettling. A lantern cast dim light through the window, and he saw that he was now alone in the coach.

Where am I?

A man poked his head in the door. "I see you're awake. Do you think you can climb out on your own, or do you need help?"

"Water," Rayne croaked. He didn't know if he could move, but his need for water was paramount.

"I expect so," the man said. "We can get water, but first we need to get you out of there. Can you stand?"

Rayne's head throbbed in time with his thigh as he pushed up from the bench and stood wobbling in the coach. Oblivious to the shackles still binding him, Rayne reached for the door frame, missed and panicked as he lost balance and fell through the opening, right into the arms of the man who had been standing there.

"Easy, easy. I got you, son," the man said kindly as Rayne felt strong arms supporting him. "Here. Let's get you sitting and then I can get those things off you."

With the man bearing most of his weight, Rayne started forward in the direction indicated, but as soon as he tried to put weight on his right leg it buckled, and he cried out with the pain of it. The man stopped and increased his support. He yelled back toward the coach, "Tal, can you give me a hand here?"

When Tal came over, the man said, "Let's get this collar and these chains off him, then you can help me get him up the tunnel. We'll take him right to the cavern cause that's where Lexi wants to meet and Seren can look at him there."

The two men helped Rayne to a ledge that ran along the outer wall of what appeared to be a tunnel. He groaned as the men lowered him. While Tal undid the clasp on his collar, the first man pulled a ring of keys from a vest pocket and proceeded to try keys until he found the one that opened Rayne's shackles and they dropped to the floor.

"Who are you?" Rayne's voice sounded like a hollow whisper in his ears.

"I'm Silas and this is Tal," the first man said. "But we'll take care of the introductions after we get you some water and get those injuries looked at."

Silas nodded to Tal. "Ready?"

Tal nodded and the two men linked their arms together making a seat for Rayne. He looped his arms around their necks and hoisted his body up on the sling of arms. Once he was settled, the men carried him up the tunnel. They passed several side passages before entering a large, lantern lit cavern where they took him to an area set with a table and several chairs and lowered him onto a chair.

"Thanks, Tal," Silas said. "Would you mind sending Seren to us before you go back to helping Zachary with those horses?"

"Sure thing, Silas." Tal vanished back into the tunnel.

Silas stood over Rayne for a moment then went back to the wall and grabbed one of several cups sitting near a trickling stream of water. After filling the cup, he brought it to Rayne. "I know you're thirsty but take it slow. This water is chilly."

Rayne moaned in relief as the first sip ran cold and cleansing down his throat. He continued to sip slowly while Silas looked at him, his eyes squinting in confusion. "You *are* the man who was fighting Yormund tonight, aren't you? You look different now, younger. Didn't you have long hair?"

Rayne stared into space for a time, reliving the moments at the end of the fight, seeing Shin's eyes, hearing his words, before being dragged away. "Yes. Shin died to save me."

"Maybe." Silas flicked his eyes away from Rayne. "Shin was big, and strong. And that Yormund was mean. He had a reputation for pulling his swings at the last second, so his hits wouldn't be lethal, and his opponent wouldn't die too quickly. That way he could take his time, inflict more injuries, make his opponent suffer before he killed him. That's why he was such a favorite."

Rayne looked up at Silas with faint hope dawning in him. "Do you think it's possible? Do you think Shin might be alive?"

"Well, honestly?" Silas grimaced and shook his head. "I doubt it. But I suppose it's possible." Silas studied Rayne for a moment. "That was one heck of a fight you put up before that sword broke. I've never seen anyone move the way you did. Was that sword as bad as it looked?"

Rayne nodded.

"What'd you do to get Lord William so mad at you as to put you in the ring with that monster Yormund and not even give you a decent weapon?" Looking at Rayne more closely, Silas added, "You're only a kid. How old are you anyway?"

"Sixteen."

"How'd you learn to fight like that? You must have started when you were ... how old?"

Rayne looked up at Silas with tired eyes. "That's a long story."

"Well, Lexi asked me, so I have to ask you. Who are you? In the ring, Matheson announced you as the Royal Prince of Ochen, He did say you were disowned, but even so, why would a royal prince be wearing a slave collar and fighting a death match with Yormund? So, I need the truth boy, who are you?"

Rayne looked around and watched several men beginning to gather in the cavern before turning back to Silas. "The truth? The truth is, I'm the fool who led his friends onto Veres and now Lord William has them. I don't even know if they're still alive. The truth is ... I am Prince Rayne, Royal Heir to all Ochen, or at least I was until my parents disavowed me. But it's also true that I was raised as a slave and trained as an assassin. The truth is ... I'm supposed to be the One's Light Bringer, but I seem to have failed at that, too. Is that enough truth for you?"

As Rayne was speaking a girl walked up behind Silas. She blinked, and her eyes grew wide. Her face turned a bright scarlet, then she shouted, "You! It's you! Killer! Murderer! Lord William's assassin! Sigmund's dog! You've finally returned. I've waited ... and now you're here. You're going to pay for what you did to my father. What you did to me!"

Looking around, suppressed fury evident in the pitch of her voice and the fisting of her trembling hands, the girl called to the others who were beginning to congregate in the room, "Everyone, come here. Now. I have an announcement to make. Someone I want you all to meet. Ethan. Is Ethan here?"

"Yes, my lady," a middle-aged man with thinning blonde hair answered as he walked in from the tunnel.

"Good! You're all here. I need you all to hear this." With venom sparking in cold eyes, she turned back to Rayne and pointed at him with a shaking hand. "This ... this ... *thing* sitting here is the assassin who destroyed my father, murdered his guards, and burned Kern House. I call for a tribunal, now, immediately. I call for justice against Sigmund's butcher."

34

Rayne had known it was inevitable. He knew there would come a time when he would face the consequences of what he had done as an assassin. But sitting here now, in this cavern on Veres, he closed his eyes and allowed remorse to pour through him like a raging torrent. His accuser was the golden-haired girl from his dream. His actions had brought her pain. Whatever she accused him of doing, he knew she was right. And the thought of that pummeled his spirit. At some point in his past he had done something so painful to her that she didn't even see him as human. He was a thing. And he didn't even remember why.

The One called him to this girl; Rayne knew that. And if the One called him here, then the One was at last visiting judgement on him for what he had been, what he had done. Rayne wondered if the One finally realized the mistake he made when he chose Rayne to be his Light Bringer. Willing to accept whatever punishment the girl called for, Rayne allowed the guilt to wash through him again, obscuring the light of truth just as the smoky fog outside obscured the Eleri River Valley.

He sat numb, unseeing. Then hands were pulling him up.

He heard Silas protesting as he was pushed forward and crashed when his leg gave out beneath him. A woman knelt by his side. Looking up, he smiled when he saw Anne's eyes. But these weren't Anne's eyes. The face wasn't Anne's face, it was older, the blonde hair scattered with silver. And the eyes looking at him were cold; Anne had never looked at him with cold eyes.

"Lady Alexianndra," the woman said. "Much as I agree with you that this *person* deserves to be punished for what he did three years ago, as a healer I'm constrained to see to his wounds. Allow me time to treat and bandage this leg and then let him be tried. And, my lady, I officially request to be part of the tribunal. My husband died in that attack. I have a right to be part of what needs to be done."

"Do it quickly, then, Seren!" Lexi hissed.

Silas volunteered to help Seren. At her request, the table was cleared. With several sets of eyes watching, Silas helped Rayne remove his cloak and the too short red vest. He wanted to protest when Seren said to remove his leggings but knew it was hopeless when she glared at him. "Either you take them off or I'll cut them off. The choice is yours. That right leg's practically worthless anyway."

Silas helped Rayne up onto the table and Seren said in a voice like a winter night, "Lie down."

Seren's hands were not soft and gentle like Anne's but they were experienced and quick. Rayne was unprepared when she poured a liquid that burned like molten veredium on his damaged thigh, shooting pain along his nerves up into his back and down to his toes. He screamed against the pain and struggled to sit up, almost passing out.

But Silas was there holding him down, his face drawn with sorrow. "Sh, sh. Just hang on, the burn'll lessen. I'm sorry. I know it hurts something awful. Seren usually gives us something to dull the pain before she pours that stuff on and stitches us up."

🝔

"Don't you go being sorry for him." Seren said, old anger surfacing. "He doesn't deserve it."

"Ah, come on Seren. This isn't like you. Look at him, he's just a kid."

"You can say that, Silas Compton, you weren't here that day three years ago. I was. I'll never forget this *kid* cutting down Duke Erland's guard. He's no *kid;* he's Sigmund's murderous dog."

With quick, practiced movements she stitched Rayne's cut, aware of his muscles clenching at the pain each time the needle pierced his pale, clammy skin. Ignoring the symptoms of shock, she smeared a healing ointment on his leg before bandaging it. Finished with the leg, Seren said. "Well, let's see your side."

She motioned for Silas to help Rayne sit up and then moved around to look at the slice in his side. As she examined the wound that ran across the top of his hip bone, Seren stepped behind him. She pulled in a sharp breath at the network of old scars across the boy's back, and a curious brand on his right shoulder. Silas leaned over to see what she had reacted to and mumbled, "What kind of person does this to a child?"

Seren knew the boy's back spoke of abuse, indeed, his whole body was scarred, but that didn't change the fact of what he had done here at Kern House. With a shudder, she turned from him and reached into her bag. Whatever he had done, though, Silas was right. After hearing him scream and then seeing his back she couldn't just pour her garlic infused alcohol wash on his side and stitch him again without first giving him something for the pain. Pulling a vial from the bag she set herself to remain objective and moved to face the boy who had killed her husband.

Seren found herself looking into pain-filled eyes the color of mountain violets. She hadn't gotten a good look at the assassin three years ago, but now she saw a young, pale, open face, and a depth of pain she forced herself to ignore. "Here, drink this."

The boy looked at the tincture and then back at Seren with fear-widened eyes, but then he nodded and reached up for the vial, brushing her fingers in the process. Seren shuddered; his fingers were warm. She had always thought of Sigmund's assassin as cold, unfeeling, and reptilian; but the boy was just a boy, and he had warm, scarred fingers.

Rayne compelled himself to meet the cold, golden eyes and accept the tiny bottle. She hated him, he knew. She could give him a vial of poison right now, and no one there would blame her. He drank the tasteless liquid and handed her back the empty container. This time, when he felt the sensation of her liquid running down his hip, the burn of it was dulled by whatever she had given him to drink.

Quietly he sought her eyes again. "Thank you."

She frowned then stitched his side before wrapping a bandage around his waist and upper hips.

When she was done, Silas asked, "Is that who owned you when you were a slave, Sigmund?"

Rayne glanced at Silas, then lowered his eyes to study his twitching fingers. "Yes, I belonged to him from the time I was six until my sixteenth birthday, that was six months ago." Rayne breathed deeply, sadness encompassed him. "I've been free for six months."

Without meeting Rayne's eyes, Seren said, "I'm done now boy. Silas can help you get your things back on."

Rayne was glad that at least he had been able to dress before the golden-eyed girl named Lexi came back in, followed by the man named Ethan and several other men. They quickly rearranged the table and chairs.

Lexi sat at the table with Ethan and Seren while the rest of the group sat together to the right of the table in front of the tunnel opening. They set one chair by itself near the wall where the spring ran, facing the others. Silas helped Rayne to the single chair and then left him and walked over to sit with his friends.

Once everyone was settled, Lexi rose, her back straight, shoulders back. "As daughter of Duke Justus Erland, heir to the Duchy of Veres, and as current reigning noble on Veres, I call this tribunal to order.

"We are here to listen to testimony regarding the murder of Duke Erland's Elite Guard, the burning of Kern House, and the attack on Duke Erland himself that rendered him ... unable to ... move or control his body. Evidence will be presented against this ... this *person* of unknown origin sitting before us now. Is there anyone who will speak for the accused?"

Feet shuffled, and someone coughed, but no one said a word. Then, Silas stood. "I will, my lady."

Silas stood alone, staring at Lexi, as silence pressed down on the cavern.

"Why?" Lexi asked, her mouth firm. "Why would you speak for this animal."

"Because it's right." Silas shifted and rubbed the back of his neck. "Someone should."

"No, Silas, I forbid it. You are a representative of the Erland family and, as such, I will not allow you to speak for our enemy. Is there anyone else willing?" She scanned the room, her eyes cold.

Rayne sat with downcast eyes, watching as his hands continued to twitch, his chopped hair tumbling haphazardly over his eyes while the still-intact braid fell forward over his right shoulder, as silence once again descended on the cavern. Softly and without even lifting his head, Rayne spoke. "It's not necessary. No one should be forced against their will; that's wrong. I'll speak for myself."

"As you wish," Lexi spit out, struggling against the implications of Silas's words. Taking a deep breath, she composed herself to speak with the dispassion of her office. "Let us move forward. According to Verenian law, the accused is entitled to have someone speak for him. In this instance, there is no one willing. Therefore, I now open the floor for the accused to speak in his own defense. Assassin, what can you tell this tribunal of your involvement in the events the night Kern House burned?"

Lexi strode from behind the table and walked up to Rayne. She hated him so much she struggled to cap the fury rising in her. She clenched her hands, wishing she clutched a knife. She was facing the black-haired demon who had haunted her nightmares for three years and she wanted him to suffer. But as she glowered at the slight figure sitting with bowed head, a warmth unfurled deep within her spirit and she heard a small voice. *Mercy, my daughter.* But Lexi didn't want mercy; she wanted justice. She refused to listen to the voice.

"What is your name?" she asked. "Your *real* name. There seems to be some difficulty pinning down who you actually are."

Rayne looked up and said in a soft voice, "My name is Rayne Kierkengaard. But what you want is the name of the assassin from three years ago. Sigmund called me Wren; I was Wren when I ... murdered for Sigmund and Coronus."

"So you admit to killing for Lord Sigmund, and this Coronus person. How much did they pay you? Was it worth it?" Jubilation bubbled up in Lexi at seeing guilt and pain suffuse the amethyst eyes as the force of her words hit. *Yes. Feel my pain.*

Rayne closed his eyes, letting grief wash over him. Lexi's pain pierced him with her need. He prayed to the One to guide him, to help Lexi find relief and peace. Then he said, "No, it was never worth it. I should have just let them kill me. But Coronus was vicious. If I didn't kill at his command, he would not only punish me to remind me of my place as a slave, he would, with no remorse, kill others we weren't contracted to assassinate. Innocents who just happened to be present at the time."

"But you weren't with Coronus the night you came here, were you? You were with Sigmund and Lord William. You stood with them and never said a word, just jumped at Sigmund's command. We all saw you. Now's your chance. Tell us what happened that night, in your own words." Lexi said, her voice now infused with venom.

"I can't," Rayne murmured. "I don't remember."

"You don't remember?" Frustration fueled Lexi's anger. "You don't remember bashing my father's head in with the hilt of your sword? My father! I'll never forget. But you don't remember? How convenient for you." Lexi was right on top of Rayne now, screaming at the top of his bowed head.

Ethan rose and cleared his throat. "My lady. It's late and we've had a long day. I don't know about you, but I'm too tired to think straight. Perhaps it would be better to take a break and get some rest and food. We can continue this after ..."

"I'm. Not. Tired." Lexi shot back, glaring at Ethan. But then she paused. She looked around, embarrassment at her outburst staining her cheeks red. "Please excuse me, Ethan. You're right we've all had a very long day and I think my exhaustion has pushed me into behavior that is not like me. We'll take a break. It's morning and we haven't slept since the night before last. We'll rest until evening, have a meal, and then continue this immediately after."

"Very good, my lady." Ethan nodded.

"What should we do with him?" someone asked, pointing at Rayne.

Lexi pursed her lips, considering. "He truly is dangerous. Silas what did you do with those shackles?"

"My lady?"

"His shackles. What did you do with them? Get them and put them back on him. We'll all be safer if he's chained."

"My lady, he can't even walk without help. What if I just locked him in the storeroom and kept watch?"

"Why do you insist on defending him, Silas? Aren't you the one always telling me I should kill my enemies, so they don't come back and kill me? *He* is an enemy. I'm seeking proper justice. Why do you question me?"

"I don't know my lady, but something about all this just doesn't feel right," Silas said. "If the boy was Sigmund's slave did he have a choice?"

"Well, that's something we'll have to determined, isn't it?" Lexi ground out through clenched teeth. "For now, find those shackles and chain that animal. And for good measure, I like your idea. Lock him in the store room. And Silas, you keep watch."

A short while later Silas helped a shackled Rayne toward the storeroom. "I'm sorry. She's not a mean girl you know, but her father's condition has been a driving force in her life for these last few years."

"What did I do to him?" Rayne hung his head. "I don't remember. There are ... gaps in my memory."

Silas helped Rayne limp into the storeroom and sit on a wooden crate of supplies. "I wasn't here that day, so I can't tell you anything more than what I've heard. I'm sure Lexi is going to tell the whole story when the tribunal reconvenes. Are you willing to wait and let her tell it?"

"Honestly? I haven't looked too hard into the holes in my memory for a reason. Sometimes when I do try, what comes to me is ... well, there's a reason my mind built walls around those memories. They're full of pain and blood. A couple days ago, I almost killed a friend, one of the people who came with me to Sorial. I didn't know what I was doing. Later I learned that the only reason I stopped was because I was hit with a knockout dart. My friend Anne said it happened because I was trapped in a memory and responded to the terror and pain of what I was reliving. But I can't remember." Rayne swallowed and looked up at Silas fear of his past haunting him.

"So, can I wait? Yeah, I can wait forever and still hope to not hear the truth of what I did. I'm afraid of what it might trigger in me. Lexi's right and you know it; you saw me fight. I'm dangerous, a killer. Maybe the best thing is to put me down like any other dangerous animal." Bitterness rose up Rayne's throat and he swallowed hard.

"Now you stop talking like that. What I saw in that ring wasn't a dangerous animal. What I saw in that ring was a courageous and scared boy doing his best to defend himself when he was thrown into a fixed death match. I know what I saw. I've been watching people my whole life; some of them good, some of them bad. I know what you've done and there's no way to change that. But I don't believe you would have killed unless you were forced into it. I don't see a killer when I look in your eyes.

"You know, once I came face to face with that Yormund. I was buying supplies in Eleri and he walked into the shop behind me. Looking into his eyes, I knew I was looking into the eyes of a killer. He was mean, and he was dangerous, and not just in the ring. He did some side work for Lord William. One time they caught one of us, a rebel, a friend. Yormund killed him slow, right in the open area in front of the gates to the complex so everyone could see and hear. Yormund enjoyed inflicting pain and killing. Don't you go comparing yourself with him.

"Well, I guess I should go," Silas said. "I'll bring you something to eat later."

Silas left a lantern so Rayne wouldn't be in the dark. But once Silas was gone, loneliness covered Rayne like a blanket. He missed his friends. Looking around for a more comfortable spot, Rayne realized that between the shackles and his wounds, he couldn't move from where he sat, so he just laid back on the crate and covered his eyes carefully with his arms, crossing his wrists over his head.

Allowing the guilt to swallow him again Rayne almost didn't pray. But then he remembered the words of forgiveness he spoke back in Westvale, after his exhibition match with Thorvin.

The One gives us the free gift of forgiveness because the Son already purchased it for us ...

"I've allowed lies to invade my peace once again my Lord. You've told me you love me and are always with me, but I keep losing sight of that truth. Help me now to cling to you again. My life is in your hands."

The grip of guilt loosened its strangle-hold and Rayne's spirit cried out in praise. He thanked the One for always being with him and for being in control even when the circumstances were dark. Then he prayed for his friends, trusting the One to keep them safe wherever they were and whatever happened.

Then he slept, this time a healthy, natural sleep, not a tincture-induced unconsciousness. And he slept in the peace that he only found when he centered himself in the One.

Rayne didn't know how long he slept but when he woke up he still felt the peace of the One upholding him.

35

When Silas returned that evening carrying a platter of food for Rayne, he stopped at the door to the storage room to unlock it and heard singing. Rayne's voice wasn't loud or very strong; Silas could barely hear it standing at the door. It was clear and young and singing a song to the One Silas remembered from when he was a child. He had not heard the song for many years and he began singing along when Rayne got to the refrain.

A soft, peaceful warmth touched Silas. He never knew such warmth existed. It was inside him and outside him at the same time. Then Rayne stopped singing and Silas felt a pang of deep sorrow. The feeling was so strong, he struggled against the sting of unshed tears. Then he heard the voice. It was full and rich yet quiet as a whisper. *This is my Light Bringer. I have sent him to bring the message of forgiveness through my Son. Listen to him. His words are light in the darkness.*

Silas didn't know what to do with the words; they were new and different. But one thing he did know; he couldn't let Lexi execute Rayne. He couldn't let Lexi snuff out the light.

With new found resolution, Silas unlocked the door and

walked in to find Rayne still sitting on the crate where he had left the boy, head tilted up, face to the ceiling, eyes closed. Silas could never be sure, but when he thought about the moment years later, he seemed to remember seeing an almost imperceptible light surrounding Rayne.

Silas cleared his throat and Rayne looked at him, his eyes full of peace. As if coming from a faraway place, Rayne adjusted his gaze and said, "You've brought me food Silas. Thank you."

His eyes squinted with suspicion, Silas stared at Rayne. "Who are you? Really, who are you? You sit here about to face Lexi's wrath, and most likely an execution, and you sing! How do you do that? And that voice. Was that you too? What is the Light Bringer?"

"You heard the voice of the One. There's nothing else like it in the universe." Rayne pulled in a deep breath. "And I'm his Light Bringer. I still don't understand why he chose me, but he did. He's just been reminding me to cling to the truth that I've been forgiven because his Son already paid my penalty before Ochen even was. If Lexi executes me tomorrow, he'll still work his will and I'll be with him in eternity. Isn't that wonderful?"

Silas wasn't sure how *wonderful* that was because he was sure the One just told him to make certain nothing happened to his Light Bringer. He shook his head. "How am I going to convince Lexi not to execute you?"

"You can't. But if the One has determined that I live, I'll live." A sad half-smile turned up a corner of Rayne's mouth. "I don't know what the will of the One is in this, but he's told me to trust him. I'd still be a prisoner of Sigmund's darkness if not for him. So I do my best to trust the One. But he's chosen a weak and unworthy Light Bringer and I fail more than I'd like to admit."

Then looking at the tray Silas was still holding, Rayne asked, "Have you eaten yet?"

"Yes, my lord." Silas said, surprising both himself and Rayne by using the title. But it seemed right, Silas thought.

By the time Rayne finished eating, Ethan was at the door asking for them to follow him. With Rayne still unable to walk without help, and the shackles making it difficult for him to put an arm up over Silas's shoulders, Ethan volunteered to help Silas get Rayne back to the cavern.

As they walked, Ethan said, "It still hasn't been determined if you're really the crown prince of Ochen. You didn't claim that title, just the name Rayne Kierkengaard. Are you the son of Theodor Kierkengaard, King of Ochen?"

Limping along between the men, Rayne looked over at Ethan. "Yes, I am the son of Theodor and Rowena. I find no need to claim anything that is already mine. I am who I am, whether I make much of it or not. But if Lord William was telling the truth, everything has changed. I've been disowned and my cousin now commands the title Crown Prince of Ochen."

Ethan looked sideways at Rayne. "That's got to be hard to accept, especially for someone so young. How old are you?"

Rayne chuckled lightly. "I'm sixteen. Actually, I'm sixteen and a half now. I'll be seventeen in the spring. Spring on Corylus that is."

"You are an enigma," Ethan said. "Silas was telling us at dinner about your fight with Yormund. You must be an exceptionally skilled warrior to have survived him with a useless weapon. Did you get your training while you were an assassin?"

"Yes. I was kidnapped when I was six years old and raised to be an assassin. Sigmund's ultimate goal was to have me kill my own parents and then be executed for the crime."

They were entering the cavern and stopped talking. Rayne's eyes caught on a new chair set between the table and the large group of chairs. He was wondering who it was for when Lexi asked everyone to please find seats so they could begin.

Once again Rayne sat in the lone seat facing everyone, this time wearing shackles. Lexi didn't want to take any chances and refused Silas's request to remove them. When everyone was settled, Lexi began. "I asked you to tell your side of what happened the night we were attacked. The night my father was injured, his guards slaughtered, and our house burned down. You said you don't remember. How can you not remember?"

Rayne didn't bow his head this time, instead he looked up and faced Lexi with a calm strength and told his story. He didn't know how much of his story Lexi would let him tell, but Rayne knew he had to start at the beginning otherwise they wouldn't understand how he couldn't remember the night that had changed their lives.

"There is much I don't remember. But if you'll give me some time, I'll try to explain what I can."

Rayne took one last look around the room and then turned back to face Lexi, willing her to understand. He spoke in a quiet, calm voice, telling his story plainly. "On my sixth birthday, I was kidnapped from the palace in Westvale. That night, a manipulator implanted a wire in my throat which blocked my memories and my voice. The next morning, I was brought to Sigmund. He inserted false memories in place of my stolen ones and told me I was his slave. I believed the lies; I knew no better. He sent me to a man named Coronus who raised me to be a master assassin.

"The first time Coronus took me out on an assassination, I was eight years old. I failed. Coronus never tolerated failure; punishment ... always followed failure. But to make certain I understood fully what that meant, Coronus whipped me then killed the target and a number of innocent people who were present when I failed. He made it crystal clear that all those people died in horrible ways because of me. It was all my fault. I learned my lesson: kill on command or others would suffer.

"When I was twelve, Coronus decided it was time I earned my keep. By then I had grown stronger and started official training. He used me often because I blended in well and was talented at killing. That made Coronus happy; he could demand top dollar for my services. But Sigmund wasn't satisfied. I was still unpredictable and loathed the killing. So, on my thirteenth birthday, Sigmund took me from Coronus for a year of what he called special training. That year was a time of darkness. In self-defense, my mind began to splinter by erecting walls around certain memories, creating gaps in what I could remember. I leave those walls undisturbed. Probing them is ... dangerous."

Rayne paused. Realizing tears were streaming down his face, he wiped them away, hating the weakness they revealed. He had vowed to be done with his self-pity. But the recalcitrant tears continued to fall so he ignored them and continued, grateful that no one had stopped his story yet.

"I know Sigmund and his colleagues did things ... hurt me in ways my mind has blocked. And there was the darkness. Sigmund's Second, Ponce, was a rubiate and he and his friends used me in the rubiate way, feeding the growing darkness in me as they fed on my blood. I know Sigmund took me off-world, forced me to kill. I tried to defy him. I refused to kill, and he punished me for my rebellion. It was pathetic. By the end of that year I no longer resisted. I killed on command. But my mind walled off chunks of time, sheltered me from the terror and pain of those memories.

"That's why I don't remember, why there are holes. When Sigmund returned me to Coronus on my fourteenth birthday, I was broken. Sick with rubiate darkness; violent. My real self was protected deep in my mind, but outside I was angry and sullen, brutal. So I am sure I'm guilty of whatever you saw me do. I have no defense for my actions other than the fact that I was forced to it. It was never my choice. It was only by the love of the One and the care and love of two friends that I was finally saved from the evil that was consuming me."

Rayne stopped speaking. The only sound was the dripping of the spring at the wall.

Lexi fought traitorous tears that came unbidden at Rayne's story. She couldn't understand how someone could go through so much and just tell it the way he did, with no feeling, ignoring his own tears, like he was telling someone else's story.

But Lexi wasn't ready to let go of her need to get justice for her father and everyone else harmed that night when Rayne came with Sigmund. She steeled her emotions and said, "Now I will tell our side of the events the night Kern House burned. I don't have a sad story of broken memories, but I do have evidence of brokenness."

She turned to a man waiting in the door to the tunnel. "Lucius, please bring in my father."

Lucius walked out into the hallway and then reappeared, pushing a chair on wheels. Duke Justus Erland. He sat unseeing and unknowing, drool drizzling out of the corner of his mouth. Lucius rolled the chair next to the open one between the group of chairs and the table and then sat next to Duke Erland.

Lexi walked up to her father and knelt. "I'm sorry for doing this Daddy. But I need everyone to remember what this assassin did to you." She kissed her father on the cheek, then rose and turned to Rayne again. "Look on your handiwork assassin. This is my father, Duke Justus Erland. Until the night you smashed his skull with the hilt of your sword he was a good man, a strong man, a leader to his people, a loving father."

"That night had begun so normally." Lexi turned and paced away for a moment, gathering strength to tell her story before turning to face everyone again. "Supper was over; we were sitting in the great room. Father was going over some accounts and I was reading, when Lord William, flanked by two of his mercenaries, rode up demanding my father come out to talk to him. He claimed he had a proposition to help resolve the slavery issue." Lexi paused, forehead wrinkled in thought. "I remember the night was light; not like it is now. The smoke wasn't so thick back then and we would have times of clear sky. That night the moon was full and big. Father told me to wait in the great room then he called for his guards, grabbed his jacket, and went out followed by his men. There were four of them.

"As soon as Father walked out, I flung my cloak over my shoulders and ran to the upstairs balcony overlooking the front lawn. I saw Lord William and his men. They sat on their horses, not moving, not saying anything. Father asked what proposal Lord William was offering but he and his men just sat there, looking down at Father and his men. The evening was so quiet, it all seemed unreal.

"Then Sigmund rode out from the tree line with this one

next to him." Lexi pointed to Rayne. "More of Lord William's soldiers moved in, forming an arc behind Sigmund and his assassin. There were so many of them, but they stayed back.

"Sigmund and his assassin joined Lord William and together they rode right up to Father. Sigmund greeted him like they were old friends. But my father knew Sigmund, the things he'd done and his connection with Lord William. He ordered Sigmund and Lord William off our property. He said he wouldn't betray his friend, King Theodor. He had more honor than that.

"Then, without another word, Sigmund beckoned to you, his pet assassin." Lexi turned and looked Rayne in the eye. "You moved so fast it was like you weren't even human. You flew off your horse, drawing your sword as you came. You ghosted through my father's men like a shadow, and everywhere you went death followed.

"I saw Sigmund whisper something and Lord William laughed. They joked while they watched you slaughter our men. Men I had known my whole life, friends. I don't know what they thought so funny and I wanted to scream. But then you were right below me. You look up at me. I saw you in a clear shaft of moonlight. Your eyes were so cold and empty. They reflected the light like unfeeling gemstones. And your hands, they were bloody, dark and black in the moonlight. You saw me there, hiding in the shadows on the balcony, and you didn't tell Sigmund. But then you were moving again, like an evil phantom of death. That's when you killed Jesper, Seren's husband.

"After the guards were all dead, you stopped and stood, like some kind of statue in the moonlight. Sigmund gave you another signal, waved his hand again. At first, I thought he had signaled you to stop because you didn't move, you just stood there, frozen. But then you were in motion again, swinging your sword of death at my father.

"I was so scared I couldn't even scream; I wanted to. I wanted to scream *Daddy, look out.*" Lexi shuddered, staring forward, seeing nothing, caught up in the memory of that night. "But just as you got to my father, at the last second, you tossed your sword of death, twisted your hand, grabbed it the other way, and smashed his head with the hilt. I watched, sick inside, as my father fell at your feet. I thought he was dead."

Lexi stopped, considering, a perplexed look on her face. "I remember. I had forgotten this part. Or maybe I just didn't want to remember. Sigmund was angry with you. I heard him screaming. He waved again and you fell. Then I heard Lord William and Sigmund laughing once more. I always thought you laughed with Sigmund and Lord William, laughed at my father lying on the ground, helpless. But you didn't. I know that now. I can see it again in my mind, so clearly now. They were laughing at you, pinned to the ground. Until Sigmund released you and ordered you back to his side.

"That's when Lord William's soldiers moved, spreading out across the lawn. All this time while you were killing and maiming, they sat still and quiet in the shadows, holding unlit torches.

"With a flash of dark fire, Sigmund lit all the torches in an instant, and then one of Lord William's mercenaries handed one to you. You were the first to touch my home with flames, moving from spot to spot, holding the torch until something ignited. I was even more scared then because you stood right below me again, looking up while you held the flames to a shrub just under where I was hiding. The whole time you never spoke, never said a word. Just stared up at me, the flames dancing in your eyes.

"Sigmund called you to mount. You looked back at him, then up at me again. You threw your torch into the front window beneath the balcony, under me. I remember the sound of glass shattering while I watched you return to Sigmund's side and mount. Then the soldiers all threw their torches into the house and everyone turned and rode away."

Lexi paused, thinking for a minute before continuing. "I heard the servants yelling, but all I could think about was Father. I ran down the stairs, right behind Ethan and Lucius, running through the sparking flames to Father. Lucius held him. He was as you see him now, an empty husk of a man with broken and dead eyes."

Lexi was crying now. She looked up at Rayne, her voice breaking. "Why didn't you just kill him? Look at him, forced to live like this. It would have been kinder to just kill him outright. Don't you understand; you made me want my father dead! And I'll never forgive you for that. Do you know how often in the last three years I wondered if he even wanted to live? If I should just help him die?

"I love my father. *I love him and still I wanted him dead! You did this to us.* And you took the lives of four noble friends, Jesper included."

Still impaling Rayne's eyes with her pain Lexi took a step toward him. "I am sorry for what was done to you, but justice demands you be punished for what you've done to us."

11

Silence followed on the heels of Lexi's words. Rayne heard her heavy breathing and the sound of water dripping. He looked at Duke Erland, Lexi's father, and was struck with the force of what he had done. In defying Sigmund's orders to kill, he had done just what Lexi described more than once. Sigmund punished him for it, eventually breaking the habit. But it shook him to the core, that in his attempt to save lives, he ruined them. Had he left others out there like Lexi's father? Living corpses?

"I'm so sorry," Rayne whispered. "For a time, I defied Sigmund by knocking out unarmed targets rather than killing them. I didn't know."

Seren spoke up. "I agree with Lexi. You may have been forced to kill, but that doesn't change the fact that my Jesper is dead by your hand. Justice demands punishment."

Ethan stood with Lexi and Seren, and asked Rayne, "Do you have anything else to say in your defense?"

"No, even though I can't remember that night, the words you speak ring true. I know I deserve whatever punishment you decide is just. But the One has loved me, forgiven me, and sent me to bring light to the worlds of Ochen. And that compels me to ask you to delay your judgment. Please allow me to fulfill the prophecy. Once that is accomplished, I pledge on my honor as a descendent of King Nathan, to present myself before this tribunal and bow to any punishment you see fit. Please, please, I beg you, let me be the Light Bringer."

36

Silas hopped up. "Lexi, you have to listen to him. He's something special to the One. I'd never heard the One speak before, wasn't even sure he really existed, but he spoke to me today about Prince Rayne and him being this Light Bringer."

Ethan glanced at Lexi and Seren. Both looked hesitant but nodded, so Ethan said, "We would learn more about the prophecy and this Light Bringer. Silas, what exactly did you hear?"

"Well, I was bringing Prince Rayne his supper and when I was at the door to the storeroom I heard him inside singing. I remembered singing the same song with my mother when I was just a little boy. It was about trusting the One in all things. There was something beautiful in listening to the prince's voice. Then he stopped singing and I felt sorrow, as if everything had gone dark and I'd never see the light again.

"But while I stood there, feeling like I'd been abandoned, a kind of warmth began to fill me and then I heard the voice. It wasn't outside talking to me. It was like it was right in my head, soft but strong. 'This is my Light Bringer. I have sent him to bring the message of forgiveness through my Son. Listen to him. His words are light in the darkness.' That's what it said. And, my lady, I just know if we kill the prince and stop his voice, something awful is going to happen."

Hushed murmures filled the room when Silas finished.

Lexi spoke up. "My father believed in the One. But even if he exists, he's done nothing for Veres or my father. I know nothing of this prophecy or a Light Bringer coming to Ochen. My father never spoke of such a thing. Assassin, what can you tell us about this and why it should have any bearing on our judgement?"

"I will tell you the best I can, but one of my friends, Shaw, has studied the prophecies his whole life and if he were here he could explain better.

"The Light Bringer prophecy is very old and though most of the copies were destroyed a long time ago, some were preserved, especially on Arisima. It says that in the thirtieth generation the Light Bringer will come from the blessed line. In his sixteenth year, he will cling to the One and he will grow in wisdom and strength to fulfill his destiny and seal the living darkness. He will bring light to the people of the worlds of Ochen.

"The One chose me to be his Light Bringer. I'm the thirtieth descendent of Nathan. That's why Sigmund wanted to use me for darkness, so I would be too corrupted to serve the One. But the One saved me from that. During the Hundred Years War, each of the seven worlds was given a scroll that has been kept hidden to preserve it. As the One's chosen Light Bringer I've been called to find all seven. When they're brought together, the living darkness, which we believe is the demon known as Sigmund of Bainard, will be sealed. I'm sixteen now so the prophecy is already in motion.

"If I don't unite the scrolls and seal the living darkness, I don't know what will happen. But I do know that if the Light Bringer doesn't bring the light of truth to the people, darkness will continue to grow and the people of Ochen will forget about the One. Even now so many have forgotten without even realizing what was happening. All seven worlds will be without hope.

"This is why I ask you to withhold your judgement, not because I don't deserve punishment, but because I must not fail to fulfill the prophecy for all Ochen. Please set aside your anger toward me until the prophecy has been fulfilled. Help me to bring light to Veres. I give you my solemn vow as Rayne Nathan Samuel Kierkengaard, thirtieth descendent of King Nathan, that I will return and face this tribunal. I will willingly bow to your judgement once my duty as Light Bringer has been fulfilled."

Lexi looked at Seren and Ethan. "What do you think?"

"It is compelling. The prince is unknown to us, but Silas's testimony adds credence to his story," Ethan said.

"I hate admitting it, but I have to agree." Seren frowned. "My question though, is can we trust this boy? His identity was questionable when he arrived. Is he really the crown prince of Ochen? And if not, doesn't that mean the prophecy refers to someone else? If he isn't a descendent of King Nathan, isn't that vow meaningless? There's no one here who can corroborate his story or even verify there is such a prophecy."

"I came to Veres with five friends, others who believe in the One and his prophecy. They put themselves in danger for me. We came for two reasons. To locate the Words of the One to Veres and to collect evidence of the slavery and abuse happening here. My friends are now Lord William's prisoners because of me. But if we could rescue them, they would verify the truth of my identity and the prophecy."

"Rescue five strangers from Lord William?" Lexi snorted. "Do you even realize what you're asking? Don't you think we've tried to rescue our people before? If the Andersen's have them, your friends were probably taken to the Eleri Mine Complex. Security there is tight."

"If we came up with a good plan to rescue not only my friends, but the other slaves as well—and hurt Lord William in the process—would you consider it?" Rayne asked.

"What do you have in mind?" Lexi asked.

"Well, honestly, nothing yet. But your plan to rescue the boys was simple and effective, and if I learned anything from Coronus, it was that the best plan is the simplest plan, less to go wrong. If you're willing, I'd like to learn more about the Eleri mine and veredium processing, anything that belongs to Lord William. Maybe together we can come up with a simple and effective plan on a larger scale than the one you pulled off at the complex."

Ethan's eyebrows shot up. "What do you think, Lexi, Seren? Do we postpone our sentencing and see if we can succeed in rescuing some friends and finding a scroll of prophecy?"

Lexi shook her head. "I know I'm going to regret this. I don't trust him and he's dangerous. But if what we've been told about this prophecy is true, I owe it to all my people to allow this Light Bringer person to pursue the scroll. It's what my father would do; he always sought to honor the One. And if he were able to speak now, he would say think of the people of Veres first.

"If the assassin can help Veres, the need of my people constrains me to do what must be done. Even if it's granting a postponement of sentencing to the murderer who killed our men, reduced my father to his current state, and burned my home. But know this," Lexi focused on Rayne, fire in her eyes, "if you do anything to threaten my people in any way, I'll kill you myself without waiting for this tribunal to reconvene. That is all I have to say. Ethan? Seren?"

Ethan tilted his head to Seren. She looked hard at Rayne for a minute, then said, "You're not what I expected. And no matter what we decide here today, it won't bring Jesper back. Like Silas, I was raised to worship the One, but I gave that up a long time ago. Maybe that's why the Eleri River Valley has grown so dark, too many of us have forgotten. My vengeance can wait. I will hold you to your vow young man, but I can wait."

"Our people are suffering from slavery and darkness," Ethan said. "If the One truly exists, and if he's seen fit to send light into our darkness, I will not gainsay him. I, too, can wait for sentencing. Silas, where are those keys? I think we can remove the shackles."

Silas arranged for Rayne to bunk in the room he and

Ethan shared. Neither man was particularly happy when Rayne woke early the next morning to pray, but they accepted that someone working for the One probably needed to do that kind of thing. After praying, Rayne asked Silas about a bath and a change of clothes. He needed to get out of the stinky, bloody, ragged clothes from the ring.

"I'll see what I can find. Should have something for you by later this morning." Silas said.

A few minutes later, Seren stopped by. "Here," She handed him a rough, wooden cane. "You need to keep weight off that leg. This should help."

ҡ

Ethan, Silas, and Rayne talked quietly as they sat eating breakfast at one of the two heavy, oak trestle tables in the cavern which, Rayne learned, the rebels used as a general-purpose room. Rayne was enjoying the first cup of coffee he'd had in days while Ethan explained how they got coded messages to and from the two spies working as guards for Lord William.

"It's a simple system. Neither has to go out of his way to leave or receive messages, just stop at an old dead tree whenever passing between the mine and Eleri."

"That's the capital of Veres, right?" Rayne verified what he remembered.

"That's right." Ethan nodded. "The guards make the trip often, so it doesn't raise suspicion. Then other members of our group rotate to pick up or drop off messages from our end. It's worked well so far, and as long as everyone's careful, I'm comfortable with leaving that format in place."

"How often do the messages get picked up? Does the weather ever ruin them before you can read them?"

"Good questions." Ethan grinned. "We try to check the drop a couple times weekly and we use leather scrapes and indelible ink made from crushed Brooksedge berries and veredium dust to write the messages. That way if they sit in the tree for a few days, or get wet, the messages don't get ruined."

Rayne gave a brief description of each of his friends as

Ethan wrote them in old Verenian, a language the merchants and their mercenaries didn't know. Being off-worlders, Rayne's friends would stick out, but Ethan wanted his spies to be certain the five were still together.

"We also need to be sure which of the Andersen's mines your friends were taken to," Ethan said as he wrote. "They're probably at the Eleri Mine. That would make the most sense because that's the Andersen's closest mining operation. It's just past the gaming complex where you were, and they always need more slaves there. But before we make any plans, we need to be sure."

"How many mines do the Andersens own?"

"Three. The Sharna Mine down where the Sharna River splits from the Eleri, and the Griffin Mine in the mountains east of the Eleri River are also Andersen holdings. The two other master houses have smaller mines and gaming complexes farther up the Eleri River Valley and down the Sharna River. They don't make the profits the Andersens do, but still it's lucrative enough to go to the trouble of the extra travel.

"There are also numerous precious metal mines scattered through the valley and in the mountains, but they're much smaller and rarely use slaves."

Lexi entered the cavern and walked toward them, but when her eyes met Rayne's she turned and sat at the other table, keeping her distance. He wanted to get to know her, but he knew she wasn't ready to accept him, and she might never be. Ethan finished writing the message, wrapped the leather into a small ball, and tied it with some twine. It now looked like a small brown lump.

Ethan wiggled his eyebrows at Rayne. "Nice, isn't it? Looks like nothing more than a random nut. Not something unwanted eyes would find interesting."

Later, after Ethan and Silas headed out to check the tree drop and leave their message, Rayne limped through the tunnel trying to find his way back to his room. Before Silas had left, he took Rayne to a secluded alcove where he washed in a small tub and changed into the clean clothes Silas had found for him. As Rayne headed back to the general-purpose room, now dressed in simple brown trousers, work boots, and a loose fitting, blue shirt, he got disoriented. He realized he was heading in the wrong direction, away from the house, toward the outer entrance. He stopped and turned around. Leaning against the wall, he was dreading the thought of limping all the way back when he heard Seren.

٦ٮ

"What are you doing out here?" Seren glared, still uncertain if she could trust the strange young man she just found wandering near the tunnel entrance.

Rayne looked up to see her carrying a basket with plant clippings. He gave her a lopsided half smile. "I guess I ... well, to be honest, I'm lost."

"You've walked a long way; you're almost to the stables. That leg needs rest, not exertion right now." Releasing a resigned sigh, she set her basket down near the wall. "Come, let me help you back. I was planning to check on your injuries when I got back anyway."

Seren pulled Rayne's right arm over her shoulder and they moved slowly back up the tunnel. Glancing at her from the side of his eyes, he said, "You remind me of my friend Anne. She was originally from Veres."

"How did you come to meet this Anne if she was from Veres. Verenians aren't allowed off world; haven't been for almost eight years now."

"She belonged to Coronus, the man Sigmund hired to train me. He brought her from Veres to be the healer at his compound. He was impressed by her skill even though she was young, so he bought her from the Sorial merchant who owned her. She showed me kindness; she risked punishment to treat my wounds after Coronus beat me the first time."

"This Coronus would punish his healer for treating wounds?"

"She unlocked my cell without permission. She's always been brave. One of the bravest and kindest persons I know. Because she was important to me, Sigmund brought her with us when we traveled to Westvale to kill my parents, King Theodor and Queen Rowena. Anne knew I planned to defy Sigmund. And even though he vowed to torture her and kill her slowly if I failed, she still supported my decision to save the king and queen.

"Thinking of her in Sigmund's hands almost made me give up. But then, once I entered the Queen's Garden, I started to remember things from before Sigmund kidnapped me, and the One helped to be strong. If not for him, I would not have had the strength to stand against Sigmund that night."

"You would kill your own parents? How could a child do that?" Disgust soured Seren's stomach.

"I didn't know they were my parents at the time. My own memories were blocked and all I knew was what Sigmund planted in me. I believed the implanted memories were real. At the palace, when I started to remember things, the returning memories confused me. I thought they were illusions and I was going crazy."

Seren shook her head. "I never heard anything like this before."

By then they had reached the cavern and Seren guided Rayne up to the lower level under Kern House to the room Silas and Ethan shared. Leaving him sitting on one of the beds, she went for her healer's kit and returned a few minutes later. As she checked Rayne's thigh, she struggled with Silas's words about the song the prince sang. Grunting her frustration, she huffed out the question that had circled in her mind ever since Silas had spoken, "That song you were singing, the one Silas talked about, can you tell me the words?"

"I can sing it for you if you like."

"Since Silas talked about it, I keep thinking back to when I was a child; before the dark smoke and fog covered the valley." She paused. *I don't trust him ... and yet ...* "I would hear your song."

Rayne closed his eyes and sang softly for Seren. It was a simple song, a song of the One's care for even the little birds. Rayne sang the first verse and the refrain. Seren remembered. It had been so long since she last prayed but now she felt a warmth within. When Rayne stopped singing she understood what Silas meant. Something seemed to go dark when the young man's voice stopped.

Surreptitiously, Seren wiped at a tear, not wanting Rayne to see. But he still sat with closed eyes. He looked so young and so peaceful, Seren had to force herself to remember this was the silent assassin who killed Jesper. *Don't be fooled. He's Sigmund's assassin.*

"Well." She huffed. "You look to be doing okay. No signs of infection on your hip, it's doing quite nicely." Seeing a discoloration around the thigh wound though, she shook her head. "I'm not so sure about the leg, though. We'll have to keep an eye on it. You need to keep the weight off it. The thigh is going to take time to heal, the cut is deep and there's a lot of damage. I had to put in a lot of stitches. If you don't rest it, it's going to take even longer, and if it doesn't heal right, you may have a limp."

Seren spread ointment across Rayne's thigh, then bandaged his side and leg again. She left him with the admonition to rest.

37

The next several days passed in a fog of frustration for Rayne as he waited for Ethan and Silas to return. He tried to help Seren with meals but just got in her way, so she sent him back to Silas's room to "take care of that leg." He went down the tunnel to help Tal with the livestock, who sent him back upstairs saying, "You're no help limping around with that cane, so go lie down and take care of that leg." He kept running into Lexi who just waved him away and growled, "stay away from me," every time. He tried to rest but he was bored and longed for something to do other than 'take care of that leg'.

By the fourth day, Rayne decided he'd had enough of the cane. He was determined to walk under his own power and left it against the wall in Silas's room. Walking was painful, but he had learned a long time ago to tolerate pain, what he could no longer tolerate was the inactivity and weakness.

After grabbing a chunk of bread for breakfast, Rayne stood in the hallway off the kitchen, trying to get his bearings. To his left were stairs leading down to the lower level. There, beneath the kitchen, was the great cavern where the rebels congregated and where Rayne had faced the tribunal. A sizeable tunnel ran from the cavern, past rooms carved out of rock where supplies were kept, and through the area that served as a stable before surfacing at the disguised abandoned mine entrance.

Part of the level where he now stood was the cellar for the manor house and had originally been used for storage. Directly before him was a hall with rooms to each side, some served as bedrooms, some as storage. Silas's room was on this level.

Another set of stairs opposite those going down to the cavern, rose to his right. Curious about where they led, Rayne gritted his teeth and managed to work his way up to the next level. The stairs ended at what looked to have been a kitchen and pantry area. It was part of the original ground level of the manor house, and though many of the rooms were charred, some remained intact. The house still smelled faintly of wet, old smoke.

Hearing voices, Rayne followed the sound up the hallway. His eyes were drawn to several paintings still hanging on what had once been brightly painted walls. Light shown from a doorway ahead to his left.

As he got closer, he realized he only heard one voice; it belonged to Lucius. The man was washing Duke Erland's bare chest and arms and talking to him as if the duke could hear and understand everything he was saying. Rayne backed away, uncomfortable at witnessing the activity.

To his right was another stairwell. This one, larger and grander than the small staircase he had already come up, rose to the next level. He moved with slow, careful steps to the grand staircase and climbed. There was much more damage here and when he reached the top floor he found himself gazing out at swirling gray mist where a roof had once been. Rayne moved forward, drawn by a desire to see the view from an opening ahead. He recognized it as the balcony Lexi described when she talked about the events of the night her world was destroyed.

As Rayne stepped carefully over some rubble, he discovered he wasn't alone. Lexi was here. Crying softly. He heard her sniffling and was about to turn back when she whispered, "It's okay, you can stay."

He moved forward, onto the balcony and rested against an intact but heavily charred railing. Below, the smoky fog clung to the remains of what looked like bushes and small trees, skeletons in the mist. Behind, Lexi sniffed again.

"I'll leave if you want," Rayne offered.

"No, please. I ... I don't want to be alone right now."

The two remained, still and silent, for a long time, then Lexi said, "Can I ask you something?"

"What?"

"When you spoke of your life, you spoke with no emotion. Aren't you angry? How can you just accept what was done to you? I mean you're going to be punished for what you did here ... probably be executed. Don't you want to scream at the One and tell him you hate him because your life has been so horrible?"

"Yes," Rayne said slowly, staring out at the mist-shrouded skeletons of scorched trees. "Not that I hated him, but because I hated the guilt in me. I hated me, not him. And I screamed at the One in anger because he allowed the things that brought me to the point where I hated myself. Not long ago, I stood alone on a windy beach and yelled ... and cried ... and told him how unfair it all was. I finally screamed at him for not protecting me and keeping me pure, so I would be worthy to be his Light Bringer."

"And did he answer you? Give you a reason why?"

"He reminded me how, even though he didn't stop the evil that was done to me, he held me through it. And gave me his love and protection when I needed them most. He gave me a message of light for the people of Corylus and all Ochen and helped me to understand that even someone like me could find forgiveness through the Son. He accepted me, bloody and dark as I was, and offered me light. That was more than I could ever imagine."

"But you're not forgiven." Lexi shook her head, loose tendrils of hair bouncing. "I don't know who this Son is, Father never spoke of a Son. But I haven't forgiven you. I will see you executed for what you did. So how can you say you're forgiven?"

"You haven't forgiven me, that's true. But your forgiveness is human, here and at this moment. The One's forgiveness is divine and eternal, reaching into the very spirit. Even if you kill my body, my spirit still lives on. Only now, instead of living on in darkness and separation from the One, my spirit will live on in the presence of his steadfast love and care.

"I know it's hard, but even in the darkest times you need to trust the One to work his perfect will, even if you can't see the outcome here and now. He's had to remind me again and again to trust. I still fail. But I know he's here with me even when I don't feel his presence, or I do something stupid, or I forget to trust.

"My best friend and teacher, Warren, taught me these words from a hymn he loved, 'Though I the cup am drinking which savors now of bitterness, I take it without shrinking. For after grief God gives relief, My heart with comfort filling. And all my sorrow stilling.'

"Growing up in Coronus's compound was hard. If not for Warren being like a father to me, I don't think I would have survived. I thought I would die when Coronus killed him. But the One did still my sorrow and fill me with comfort. It didn't happen right away, but in time."

"I don't know if I can forgive the One, or you," Lexi said. "I can't do it. Trust like that."

"When the time is right, and if you're willing, he'll help you."

Rayne sat on the railing looking out at the gray day while Lexi sat on the wooden floor with her legs pulled up, her chin resting on her arms, quiet. They sat that way for a long time in the chill gray light. Then they heard voices calling for them; Ethan and Silas had returned.

ᴎ

By the time Rayne climbed down to the lower level and made his way to the cavern, Lexi was already talking to Ethan and Silas. When Rayne limped in, Silas looked up at him and smiled. "We found your friends." His smile drooped when Rayne stumbled, and a groan escaped his closed lips.

"What are you doing walking without a cane. I don't think Seren would be happy about that. She tends to take her healing responsibilities very seriously. Come, sit down, and we'll share what we've learned."

Rayne eased into a seat and Silas sat next to him, Lexi across from Silas, and Ethan across from Rayne.

"It's like we thought. All five of your friends were taken to the Eleri Mine. It's good they were kept together," Ethan said. "One, Anne, is working in the processing building. They know she's an experienced healer so they're keeping her above ground in case their healer needs her assistance. The others are all below ground in the mine. Kemp, one of our men, has been able to speak with Anne and take messages from her to your friend Thorvin. Unfortunately, he's been giving the guards trouble. He ended up on the wrong end of a whip last week. He's had a hard time adjusting and the guards are watching him closely."

"That sounds like Thorvin," Rayne said. "He's good at giving orders, but not at being ordered around. I hope he can hold out a bit longer until we can get them out of there."

"Anne is concerned about Shaw. She's afraid being kept below ground is taking a toll on him. Is it true people from Arisima need more sunlight than other people?" Ethan asked.

"I don't know. We never talked about it. We normally have plenty of sunshine in Westvale so it was never an issue. But if that's the case, it's even more important we get them out as soon as we can. Do you have any ideas?"

Ethan pulled out a leather map. "Kemp drew this for us. It's the layout of the mining facility. This sketch shows the above ground layout, and this lower sketch shows the underground layout. Kemp says there are usually thirty-two guards on the property at any given time, working in three shifts; twelve guards on duty during the two day shifts, eight at night.

During the day, three guards oversee the tunnels where the digging is going on, another one is stationed at the top of the shaft, and two more at the mine entrance where the ore is loaded onto wagons. Two supervise the processing and two more are stationed at the gate. Another two patrol the walls.

"At night, the slaves working the mine are locked in three large rooms at the end of a side tunnel. One guard is stationed at the top of that tunnel and one at the three doors. Another two patrol the processing building. About twenty slaves sleep in rooms on the second floor there, including your friend Anne. Two more guards patrol the perimeter and two cover the gate. The guards change shifts every eight hours."

Ethan pointed out the locations of the mine entrance, the processing building, the stables, guard house, and a small guard shack, on the map Kemp had drawn.

He also showed them the main complex road that led from the stables past the processing building, where processed veredium was loaded before passing the mine entrance, where raw ore was loaded. After the mine entrance, it made a ninety-degree bend then exited through the gate to pick up the Mine-River Road which ran straight to the Eleri River where the veredium was loaded from the wagons onto river barges.

"How far is the river from the mine?" Rayne asked.

"Less than a mile." Ethan answered.

"Is the smoke and fog usually worse around the mine?" Rayne's brow creased in thought.

"Yes."

"What if there was a fire down at the docks? Is there some kind of alarm so the guards up at the mine would be summoned to help fight it?"

"Yes, they have a loud alarm bell for emergencies." Ethan sucked in a quick breath. "What are you thinking?"

"And guards, are there many guards around the dock?"

"No. No guards. No one would be stupid enough to try and steal from the Andersens."

"Until now." Rayne grinned, devious thoughts circling in his head. "But I don't want to steal the veredium, I want to fire the docks and sink the barges, especially any that are fully loaded, create enough of a diversion to pull guards from the mine. I remember Coronus always talked about dividing and conquering. If we do this right, we should be able to draw most of the guards from the mine to the docks."

"Hey," Lexi said. "That's good. I like that. Ethan, why haven't we thought of this before?"

Ethan gave her a level look. "Because we haven't been audacious enough to try a rescue of this magnitude before. Or maybe it's because we haven't been crazy enough to anger Lord William this much. Burning his docks and sinking his barges, not to mention stealing his slaves, is definitely going to bring Lord William's wrath down on us. We've never taken things this far before. If we pull this off, it would certainly cut into the Andersen's profits. Yeah, I like it too. But we have to be prepared because this will absolutely enrage old Lord William."

"Well that gives us a diversion, what can we do with it?" Silas asked.

"Is there some way we could keep the off-duty guards in the guard house, so they don't interfere?" Lexi asked.

"Lock them in?" Ethan suggested.

"What about put them to sleep?" Rayne raised his eyebrows. "That's been done to me a few times and I can vouch for the effects, if we could get our hands on some sleeping powder or tincture."

"As a healer, would your friend Anne know how to make something? Maybe Seren knows." Excitement built in Lexi's voice.

"Anne also has ability to manipulate magic energies," Rayne said. "I'll bet she could come up with something. Then one of your spies could get it to the guard house."

Ethan nodded. "Our other man, Alec, has already been collecting and hiding weapons down in the tunnels. He said he figured sooner or later we would be planning something at the mine and having the slaves armed would come in handy. I assume your friends know how to handle themselves in a fight?"

"Thorvin is a master and experienced, Stevie and Sashi have been raised handling swords. Shaw and Anne wouldn't be much help in a fight though."

They continued refining their strategy over the next two days. Once they had a workable plan, Silas took a message to the dead tree drop, explaining what they intended. They needed to know if Anne could come up with something to put the off-duty guards to sleep and if Kemp or Alec would be able to get it to the men.

It took another three days to get a reply from Kemp, but the response was positive. The resident healer had gone to Sorial for a friend's wedding and would be away for the next two weeks. Anne had been relieved from her processing work and assigned his duties. She now had free access to his rooms and supplies. A sleeping tincture which would be undetectable in any liquid was already prepared and Kemp just needed to know when to put the plan in motion.

Rayne smiled at the news. He was sure the One had a hand in paving the way for Anne. Everything else was in place. Ethan sent out word to the rebels to gather at Kern House. Allowing for everyone to arrive, in four days' time, they would put their plan in motion.

38

Rayne sat in a stand of trees off the road that ran between Eleri and the Eleri Mine, his horse shifting beneath him as it munched on a tuft of grass. He had been given strict instructions to stay in the saddle.

"The stitches look good," Seren had said early yesterday. "But the muscle beneath is going to take some time to heal. I don't think it's a good idea for you to participate in this rescue. You should stay off the leg and give it a chance to heal properly."

Lexi glowered at him and said, "You're nothing but an annoying burden if you can't fight." She shook her head, disgust twisting her mouth. "If you get down off this horse and can't keep up, I'll be more than happy to leave you behind for Lord William to reclaim."

Now, almost twenty-four hours later, he waited with the four rebels assigned to bring empty wagons from the stable to the mine entrance. Wagons that would transport the rescued slaves who couldn't walk without help up the Eleri River Road.

Silas's group had left Kern House earlier the afternoon before, to be in place and well-hidden before sunrise. Armed with bows, arrows for flaming, axes, and a good supply of oil, they would provide the distraction by attacking the dock and barges.

Once the guards responded to the alarm, Ethan's people would ride to the mine entrance. If all went according to plan, they would meet with the newly-armed slaves coming from below. If things did not go well, they'd go down into the mine to help the slaves escape to the surface.

Lexi's people, hiding near Ethan's group in some overgrown shrubs by the wall a hundred yards from the entry gate, were assigned the task of freeing the slaves at the processing house.

With the sun rising in front of him, a shallow brightening of the gritty fog, Rayne wondered if the sun ever appeared in the smoke-shrouded and fogged valley, as trees and shrubs took shape in the half light. As he waited, Rayne thought back to last afternoon. By late in the morning yesterday, all the rebels had arrived. There were about twenty-five people gathered in the cavern, mostly men, but Rayne noticed a couple women in the group as he followed Lexi, Ethan, Silas, and Seren into the room. Ethan explained the plan and then divided the people, assigning them to their respective groups based on their skills.

Each group leader then reviewed their specific responsibilities and answered any questions. When everyone was comfortable with the plan and their part in it, Lexi announced it was time to eat.

Unsure of his reception and struggling against the overwhelming desire to remain invisible as he noted more than a few belligerent looks aimed at him, Rayne pushed up onto unsteady legs. "Before we eat, we need to ask the One's blessing on what we are about to do."

He paused for a moment to gather his thoughts and to be sure he had everyone's attention, then continued. "Some of you already know me from the tribunal the other day, but for those who weren't there, my name is Rayne Kierkengaard. I was the Crown Prince of Corylus and all Ochen. I am the son of King Theodor and Queen Rowena. And … I was the assassin who burned Kern House, killed Duke Erland's guard, and injured the duke." Angry murmuring filtered through the group.

"I'm here now as the One's Light Bringer. That's more important than any other fact about me. The One called me here and I've come in response to that call. I know we need his protection and guidance if we're going to succeed in getting everyone from the mine up to the high mountains.

"I also know that darkness has invaded Veres and the One wants to restore light and hope to you all."

Then, bowing his head Rayne prayed. "Most powerful One, we praise you and we thank you for all that you have done in the past and will do in the future. I am humbled by how you work your perfect will through imperfect people. We seek your power now to uphold us in our weakness and give us strength in what we are about to do. Most loving and caring One, Father of the merciful Son, we thank you for loving us even though we are not worthy and caring for us when we stray. We seek your love and care as we move forward with this plan to bring people out of the darkness of this mine and lead them up to the light and freedom above the fog line. We beg your protection in what we are about to attempt and trust you to be with us now and always."

Rayne was finishing his prayer when the room brightened, and as he spoke the final words, warmth infused the cavern and the voice of the One echoed.

This is my Light Bringer. I have sent him to bring the light of truth to Veres. Listen to him. His words are light in the darkness. The voice softened. *I am well pleased Light Bringer. Be true. Be courageous. Trust.*

The comforting warmth lingered in Rayne still. Even now, almost a day later, he rested in the peace of the One's protection. Muted golden sunlight battled the ever-present gray fog and the morning brightened around him. If all was proceeding as planned, Kemp would have drugged the off-duty guards by now.

Except for the hushed sounds of horses and muffled tack, the men around him sat in silent expectation, listening for the alarm to sound from the dock. Once it rang, they would wait until the guards rode out in response, then move in through the gate and head to the stable.

Rayne was beginning to wonder how much longer they

would need to wait when the demanding clarion of an alarm bell sounded from the direction of the river, shattering the quiet morning. Within minutes, eight men raced past where Rayne and his crew sat hidden in the trees. The distraction was working; more than half of the on-duty guards were on their way to the river. Rayne and his people kicked their horses into motion and rode through the now unguarded gate. Following the main road, they turned to their right and passed the mine entrance where Ethan and his men were confronting several of the remaining guards.

There were no guards at the stable, just three men who worked with the mules and drove the wagons. When they saw the rebels approaching, they threw down their weapons and raised their hands in surrender.

While two of Rayne's people tied the men and took control of the stable, one of the women in his group saddled three horses and handed the reins to Rayne. He turned and rode back to the mine entrance. Two wagons were already there and some of Ethan's men were shoveling veredium out of them to make room for the rescued slaves.

Rayne's heart leaped when he looked toward the gritty black-gray hole that was the mine entrance and saw Thorvin striding toward him followed by Stevie and Sashi supporting Shaw between them. Without thought, Rayne was off his horse and limping toward his friends. A grin split Thorvin's dirty face and he jogged forward. When he reached Rayne, he dropped his sword and grabbed him in a bear hug that lifted him off the ground and threatened to break ribs. Then Stevie, Sashi and Shaw were there, and everyone was hugging.

Ethan strode up. "We don't have time for this now! We have to move! You can greet each other when everyone is safe! Rayne Kierkengaard, get back on that horse. Now." With a quick warning look, Ethan was off, striding away to help people into the wagons.

Rayne couldn't stop smiling, thankful and relieved at seeing his friends. "I have horses for you," he said to Thorvin, Stevie, and Sashi. "Shaw, you and Anne will have to ride in a wagon or walk if you're able."

Suddenly, Anne was there; she threw her arms around Rayne from behind and planted a kiss on his cheek before stepping up to Shaw and pulling his arm over her shoulder.

"I heard. I can help him." She and Shaw started toward the wagons.

Unasked questions reflecting in his eyes, Thorvin helped Rayne mount before mounting himself. Rayne looked around at his friends again, joy bubbling up inside as he drank in the sight of them. The first wagon started moving. It was time to go.

"Thorvin. Sashi. Stevie. This is going to be dangerous. That's why I insisted we put you three on horses. I told Ethan you would be able to fight, if it came to that. Our goal is to get these people up into the higher Taliesin Mountains where they'll be safe. But the going will be slow and Lord William's men will try to stop us. Are you up to fighting?"

Thorvin growled, Stevie nodded, and Sashi said, "Just try to stop me. By the seven, I have a score to settle with those guards."

Lexi strode by, sending the men who had gone to the processing house with her to the lead wagon. Cai, a long-haired Verenian and two friends from his village, Mistal, knew the mountains better than anyone else. They would ride point, guiding everyone up the valley road.

When they left the Eleri Valley Road near its end point, the wagons would be abandoned. Everyone would need to climb the hidden paths on foot, something Rayne dreaded. The rebels spread out around the four wagons and the rag-tag band of walkers who followed the wagons.

Now the hard part began, escorting close to four hundred people up the valley road and into the mountains without getting caught or killed. Lexi, Ethan, Rayne, Thorvin, Stevie and Sashi formed a rear guard, positioning themselves behind the last of the walkers.

Once they caught up, Silas and his archers would join Rayne and his friends there. If trouble arose, the men and women stationed around the wagons would fall back to strengthen the rear guard.

There was no talking, just the noise of wagons and harnesses creaking, the periodic sound of hoofs striking rock, and many feet shuffling on the dusty road. The day brightened enough for Rayne to see the road ahead. They had traveled a little over three miles before halting to give Cai time to scout ahead.

The next half-mile of road was narrow, hemmed in by rocky walls as it followed the curve of the mountain. As far as Rayne could see, it looked clear, but anything could be hidden beyond where the road curved and the dusty fog swirled, dropping visibility even more. Ethan and Lexi had expressed concerns about the need to travel this section of road, but there was no way around it.

Tension built. Rayne shifted in his saddle. Fearful murmuring grew. Anxiety blanketed Rayne as they waited for Cai to return. But then, like a phantom, he emerged from the dark mist, waving them forward. The company moved into the rift. The walls seemed to press inward as Rayne followed the Verenians into the dark shadows. It was almost as if the narrow pass collected the gritty fog and smoky mist. Then the mist brightened, the walls opened. Rayne released the tension he had been holding in his shoulders and stretched his back, relieved to be out of the pass.

Though they were through the pass, they had yet to face the real danger. That would come when the mercenaries from the gaming complex caught up to them. The complex was only a couple miles from the mine, and it wouldn't take long for the tricked guards to send for help. Fear propelled them onward as they attempted to put distance between themselves and the coming mercenaries.

Beyond the pass, the road veered closer to the river and the grade grew steeper. The river roared, churning as it rushed past on its journey down into the valley. They climbed upward and with each steep stretch, they moved with slower steps. Another mile and the road evened out again. The roar of rushing water faded as the river swung away from the road.

The caravan pulled to a stop allowing everyone to rest and catch their breath after the last climb. In the relative quiet, the pounding of hooves echoed. Horses were coming up the road. Fast. The rear guard pulled up to wait as the rest of the band quickened their pace, limping forward on tired legs. Those who could, ran. Rayne peered into the fog, now brightened by the midday sun. Relief flooded through him when he recognized Silas and his men. But there were fewer of them now. Rayne counted only five, including Silas. There had been seven with Silas when he left Kern house yesterday.

Silas and his men skirted past the rear guard and while his men continued forward, Silas turned back and reined in between Lexi and Ethan, his face smudged and weary. He nodded at the two without saying a word.

The day wore on; with each mile they climbed, the smoky fog grew thinner. Rayne could almost make out the ball of the sun through the misty air when, once again, they heard the sound they feared. Horses. Coming fast. As before, the rear guard dropped back. Silas's archers took up positions behind them. Matheson emerged out of the thinning mist, leading more than two dozen mercenaries wearing Andersen red and black.

When they were a few yards away, Lexi rose up in her stirrups and called out, "Stay back. My men will shoot. And you will be their first target Richard Matheson."

Matheson reined up, leisurely crossed his hands over the pommel of his saddle, and leaned back while his soldiers fanned out behind him.

"I finally meet my mystery lady face to face." His voice was relaxed and friendly and he smiled at Lexi as if they were two old friends who happened to run into each other while out riding. "The elusive young woman who has caused me so many headaches. You really are quite lovely, not what I expected." He released a loud sigh. "I would prefer to talk, get to know you better, rather than play the part of target for your archers. Why don't you have them stand down and we can converse like civilized people, you and I."

"We have nothing to say to each other," Lexi said.

"Come now. We can avoid unnecessary violence if you'll just cooperate. It's really quite simple. Before this escalates into something we'll both regret, you will leave Lord William's property here, and I will let you go. You and your rebel friends will be forgiven for your little indiscretion today. The slaves stay, you go. As I said, it's really quite simple. And I can guarantee they will not be punished for your ill-advised actions. Honestly, you're not in any position to refuse my offer."

"Matheson!" Rayne drew the man's attention as he moved up next to Lexi.

Matheson's smile grew wide. "Well, well, well." After studying Rayne for a minute, he returned his focus to Lexi. "Now I understand. You were the one who stole this piece from us when you took those boys. Nicely done; I salute you."

"Lexi, he's putting on a show, talking like he wants to make a deal. He's just waiting for you to drop your guard. Don't negotiate. It's playing into his hands."

"Lexi, is it?" Matheson paused, a look of concentration wrinkling his brow before he continued. "Of course, Lady Alexianndra Erland. It makes perfect sense. You're the one I've been wanting to talk to, my lady. You and your fellow rebels. I know we've had some disagreements in the past, but can't we put that behind us? I'm sure we can come to an agreement. Perhaps, in time, even negotiate for the freedom of these wretches you seem so concerned about."

"Don't believe him," Rayne growled. "He'll say anything to get what he wants and then turn on you."

Fury flashed across Matheson's face. "I'm not talking to you slave boy." Matheson composed himself and turned his attention back to Lexi. "Now, what were we saying? Oh, yes, my proposal. You will leave Lord William's property, including this piece of damaged goods," Matheson waved at Rayne, "and, in return, I'll allow you and your fellow Verenians to ride away unharmed. I'll even throw in your off-world friends. Think about it, girl, you're not going to get another deal like this one again. You and your happy band of worthless rebels get to go free."

"Enough!" Rayne's shout rang out. "He's just baiting you to keep you talking. He's not about to give anyone amnesty. Lord William wouldn't allow it. Never." Rayne kicked his horse forward, pulling his sword.

"No," Lexi yelled. "You'll block the archers."

But Rayne had achieved his goal. The stalemate was broken; everyone was moving. Thorvin and the twins were right behind Rayne. They angled past him and barreled into Matheson's soldiers, swords swinging. Rayne heard the hiss of arrows as the archers, taking advantage of the confusion, fired, nocked and fired again before dropping their bows and pulling swords. Leaving the fleeing slaves to Cai and his friends, the remaining rebels turned to face Matheson's men.

Rayne charged after Matheson who yanked his horse's reins hard around and, leaving his soldiers to fend for themselves, turned back down the road and spurred his horse into a gallop. Matheson hadn't gotten far when Rayne, came alongside, kicked out of his stirrups, and pushed off from his horse to tackle him to the ground. Lexi followed, pulling up to watch as Matheson and Rayne drew swords and circled each other. Matheson feinted at Rayne, a confident smirk blossoming on his face when he saw Rayne favor his right leg.

"I thought so." He grinned. "When we pulled you out of the ring, you couldn't even stand. I see you're still feeling the effects of Yormund's kiss. He liked to do that, slow his opponents down and play with them before killing them. I always admired his style."

Matheson circled to his right, sword centered, forcing Rayne to do the same. Rayne shifted with care, limping, avoiding putting his full weight on his weak leg. He knew he was moving slow, too slow to take Matheson. But if he tried to move faster and the leg buckled, Matheson would have him. Rayne knew his greatest strength was his speed but now every move was hampered by his weakened right leg. If he could just hold the man until Thorvin got to them, Thorvin would take Matheson down. *I just need to keep him here.*

Then he saw Lexi. She was off her horse and quietly approaching Matheson from behind, twin short swords in her hands. *Keep his focus on me*, Rayne thought. He lunged but came up short as his leg refused to take his weight and he had to pull up. But Matheson must have heard Lexi, because rather than respond to Rayne's aborted lunge, he turned into Lexi, swinging as he moved. She caught his blade with crossed blades and flung upward to break his balance. He wobbled for a second, but he was too strong and anticipated her move. Using brute force and his weight, Matheson pushed against her blades. She dipped her swords quickly and pulled back gaining distance, keeping her blades forward. He followed her, smiling, stalking, putting on a show of enjoying the game.

But then Rayne was on him, drawing Matheson's attention back to himself. As Matheson raised high right, Rayne moved in swinging upward to come in under Matheson's blade and block, balancing on his left leg. But Matheson aborted and backed away, forcing Rayne to move. Again Rayne tried to engage, only to have Matheson move away, compelling Rayne to keep using his right leg. The abuse was sending shards of shooting pain through Rayne's thigh with every movement.

Then Lexi was there, forcing Matheson to face her as she came at him again, swords swinging. But with two strong blocks, he turned both her blades, pushing them away. Stepping in with a quick motion, he smashed a fist into her chin. Lexi went down hard, and Matheson moved in for the kill.

When Matheson's sword rose over Lexi, Rayne screamed and lunged for the man, falling into him and bearing him to the ground. They rolled, Matheson ending up on top. With a confident smile, he pulled up and smashed his left knee into Rayne's right thigh with the full weight of his body behind the blow. Pain, sharp and deep forced a scream through Rayne's lips as the blow landed full force on his already stressed stitches, sending sharp pulses of pain down his leg and up into his hip. Matheson drove his knee into Rayne's leg again. Silver sparks flashed behind Rayne's eyes and he struggled with nausea, grasping at consciousness.

Smiling in triumph, Matheson pushed up to stand over a stunned Rayne. But as he was rising, Lexi barreled into him. Her slight weight was no match for him though, and regaining his balance, he grabbed her arms roughly and lifted her off the ground, growling. "You've caused me enough trouble already, girl. I had thought to keep you alive to see how you faired in the ring, but you're not worth it."

He shook her like a rag doll, her head whipping with the force, then released his grip on her left arm long enough to back hand her, stunning her. Matheson grunted as he wrapped both hands around her throat bending her over backward as he tightened his grip, squeezing.

Lexi's hands flailed, beating against his arms with weak effort, and Matheson laughed, his eyes wide with excitement. "Go ahead, fight it girl. I do so enjoy the ..." His words turned into a gurgle.

Rayne, shaking off the webs in his brain, struggled upright. Seeing one of Lexi's short swords within reach, he grabbed it and stumbled behind Matheson. He caught Lexi's eyes as she watched him approach. He could see her weakening in Matheson's relentless grip. Rayne, adrenaline coursing, raised Lexi's sword to shoulder height and with all the fear and anger in him, thrust the blade straight into the back of Matheson's neck driving it forward with enough force to propel the point completely through.

Rayne let go of the sword and took one trembling step back. Breathing hard, he dropped his hands to his knees and holding his weight on his left leg focused on Lexi.

"Lexi," he breathed out. "Lexi?" Louder. But she lay crumpled, unmoving, unresponsive.

Still quivering Rayne called up his magic, remembering his mother's lessons. *Be careful Son until you are better trained.* She had told him. *When you send a quest into someone, you are opening a line of energy that runs both ways. You are as open to that person as he is to you until you learn to block and protect yourself.*

His mother stopped training him soon after the warning, before he learned even the basics of blocking. But seeing Lexi lying there so still, Rayne knew he had no choice. Closing his eyes, he pulled energy to himself and sent a tentative questing tendril into her.

Rayne sensed her heartbeat, strong and steady. He was aware of the relentless pain and anger she carried so close to the surface, her drive to help her people. He was tempted to follow that deeper but knew it would be an invasion. Moving outward again he was aware of her breathing, deep and steady.

Suddenly it caught in a gasp. His eyes popped open to be impaled by twin beams of golden light, Lexi looking up at him with wide, shocked eyes.

A bonding warmth blanketed them both and they were in another place, standing together with a presence Rayne recognized as the Son without knowing how he knew this. Eyes of love gazed on them and the voice, like a soft flowing stream, lifted them, speaking into their hearts.

My beloved Light Bringer, protect Lexi, for her heart and yours are one. She is yours and you are hers. My gift to you of love.

Lexi, protect my Light Bringer, for his heart and yours are one. You will always know the truth in him, and know him in truth, because you are his and he is yours. My gift to you of love.

39

Then Rayne was back on the road, Lexi staring at him, her jaw hanging open, Matheson's body next to them. Lexi moved first, pushing up, rubbing her neck as she went to catch her horse's reins. Rayne straightened watching her. She mounted. Pulling up next to Rayne, Lexi's angry eyes locked onto his and she hissed, "What did you do?"

Rayne shook his head, not sure himself what just happened.

"We need to talk," Lexi said as Thorvin and Ethan arrived and Thorvin jumped down, sword drawn.

Looking from Lexi to Rayne and then down at Matheson's body, Thorvin growled, "You two okay?"

Lexi glared at Rayne who after a moment broke eye contact and looked up at Thorvin. "We're fine."

Turning her horse's head and nudging it forward, Lexi cantered back up the road to the waiting company. Ethan looked after her retreating form then down at Thorvin before spurring his horse after Lexi.

Rayne's leg was oozing around torn stitches; every faltering step sent daggers of pain stabbing through him as sweat beaded on his forehead. Thorvin rounded up his horse and helped him mount. "You don't look okay."

Turning his horse, Rayne swallowed rising bile and said, "I'm fine."

The fight with Matheson's men had been fast and lethal, leaving all the mercenaries dead. Five of the rebels were nursing wounds, but fortunately, nothing serious. The archers helped even the odds and Thorvin, Stevie, and Sashi fought with an intensity brought on by what they suffered at the hands of Lord William, the Andersen family, and their mercenaries.

Lexi and Ethan cantered past the rear guard and the wagons to join Cai up front. Thorvin and Rayne took up positions with Stevie and Sashi, the four merging with Silas and the rest of the rear guard.

The afternoon wore on and they kept moving, taking only short breaks after each steep section of road. If anyone dropped behind, one of the rear guard helped the straggler to a wagon.

As the hours passed and they continued climbing up the valley road, Rayne was grateful there were no more incidents. He hoped it meant Lord William was back on Sorial, and if he was off-world, no one else would pursue them until he was alerted. By then, Rayne hoped everyone would be safely up in the mountains.

He refused to think of the problems he and his friends would encounter getting off Veres and Sorial once he got the scroll. That would be a concern for another day, just like his parents' disowning him. First, he had to make it into the upper mountains and find a hidden scroll with no idea where to look. For all Rayne knew, he could have walked right past it down in Eleri.

It was growing dark when Cai announced they would be leaving the road shortly and picking up the path into the mountains toward Mistal. At this elevation, the woods surrounding the road were still predominantly hardwoods with firs and a sprinkling of tall pines mixed in, looking like ghostly goliaths in the darkening fog. The company came to a halt at a point where two massive rocks rose out of the ground. The gurgling of the river was muted in the distance; it tracked farther down the curve of the mountain.

"These are the Sentinel Stones," Cai said. "They mark the beginning of the path we'll be following. From this point, everyone will need to walk. Not far ahead is a clearing where we'll camp for the night. Those who are able, please help those too weak to walk on their own."

After unhitching the mules, they pushed the wagons off the side of the road where a sharp embankment ran down to where the river flowed, hidden by trees and scrub. They sent the wagons hurtling into the rocks and trees below, listening as they crashed and broke up. The Andersens wouldn't be using those wagons again.

Standing a short distance from the road near the twin rocks, Rayne faced off with Thorvin. "It makes sense," Rayne said to a growling Thorvin. "The horses and mules are too valuable to just let go; they need to be taken back down to Kern House. I'll join the other wounded who've volunteered to take them. You know I can't walk up the path. I'll just slow everyone down. You know it."

Shaking his head as Anne and Shaw walked up, Anne supporting Shaw, Thorvin said, "No way. There's no way I'm letting you out of my sight until we're back on Corylus. Besides, it's too dangerous for you down there now. No way. I'll carry you if I have to. But you're not going back down into that valley. You're supposed to be looking for the scroll. How are you going to find it if you don't even look up in the mountains, which Shaw says are sacred to the people of Veres. He says that if the scroll is hidden anywhere, it's probably up in these Tale Mountains."

"Taliesin Mountains," Shaw corrected. "Thorvin's right. You must come up with us. Otherwise Sigmund's already won."

Frustration turning his voice rough, Rayne sputtered. "Yes, you're all right! But look at me. I can barely stand. I can't put any weight on my leg and I tore Seren's stitches fighting Matheson. What do you want me to do?"

"Come," Anne said gently. "At least come to where Cai

and his friends are setting up camp. They're building a fire and Cai has supplies stored up here so soon we'll have a warm meal. Instead of standing here looking like you're going to fall over any moment, let us help you to the fire. Then we'll see what can be done. I'd like to at least look at those stitches before you decide anything. Besides, I think Thorvin will burst if he has to wait any longer to hear all that's happened to you since we were separated."

Relenting, Rayne let Stevie and Thorvin pull his arms over their shoulders, help him walk between the Sentinel Stones, and up the path.

With the light fading, Anne wasted no time unwrapping Rayne's bandage to check his stitches. The wound had broken open. Fresh blood soaked the bandage and ran down Rayne's leg spotting his trousers with a rusty color. The wound looked clean, painful and torn, but clean, and the bleeding had slowed. Anne concentrated on pulling energy to her and sending healing into Rayne's leg.

Looking up at Rayne, she shook her head. "I'm afraid my ability isn't doing much for you. Veres is so magic deficit there's not enough energy to work with." She wrapped Rayne's thigh with clean bandages Shaw had gotten from Cai. "I've done all I can for now. It'll heal, but the scar's going to be a nasty one. Whoever treated you did a good job. Your biggest problem is the way the muscle was cut. The cut is deep and that's going to take time to heal. You need to keep weight off the leg and let your body repair. You must be patient. No more fighting; let others take that burden for now."

She sighed, her eyes running over Rayne, then smiled. "My dear friend. Now that we can finally talk, I want to say it's good to see you again. When Jason took you, we all feared the worst."

"I was afraid I had lost you." Rayne looked around and sighed in relief to see his friends safe. But then his face fell, and anger burned in his chest. "We were betrayed. They knew I was coming; that's how they knew who we were right from the start. Brayden sent word to Jason Andersen."

"That Nemorian serpent!" Sashi said, spitting angry.

"When we get back to Corylus you've got to tell your parents what he did. He almost got you killed! They'll have to listen to you if we all go together and tell them, won't they?"

Rayne shook his head as his fury was submerged under rising sorrow. "No, I don't think so. Whatever he's doing to them, he's been working at it for a long time. I don't think it'll be that simple, even if I almost died. He ..." Rayne thought about telling his friends that his parents had disowned him and named Brayden crown prince, but he wasn't ready to face that yet. He'd tell them later.

"Nemora's moons," Sashi whispered. "I didn't think about that."

"I'm sorry, son," Thorvin said. "I know this is hard on you. Once we're done here we'll go back to Westvale and sort this all out. But in the meantime, what I want to know, is who was capable of doing this kind of damage to you?"

Silas walked over and stood behind Anne, quietly listening.

Looking into the crackling fire Rayne said simply, "Yormund, it was Yormund."

Thorvin snorted. "Sigmund's fighter? What happened? I know you and I know what that man's capable of. Under normal circumstances, you should have been able to take him. So, what happened."

Silas, sputtered then spoke up, his voice edged with excitement. "He could have taken that monster if he had a decent weapon. But they stuck him in the ring with a pathetic excuse of a blade against Yormund and his ancient axe. It was fixed from the start. Lord William wanted the prince dead. Someone must have paid him a lot of money for him to sacrifice a fighter like Prince Rayne in his first fight.

"Oh, but you should have seen him fight. I couldn't believe my eyes at first as I watched this slender sprig of a kid stand up against the ring champion. You've got to be joking, I thought. This kid has no chance. But then I saw him move. It was something to see, him darting in, drawing first blood, moving around that Yormund like some kind of phantom. I never saw anyone fight like the prince. Until that pathetic excuse for a sword broke. Even all those oblivious nobles got quiet when that happened. Nobody moved or said a word. Then Yormund charged and slashed the prince's leg. Everyone watching knew you didn't stand a chance after that."

"What happened then?" Sashi asked, her eyes pinned on Silas.

"Well …" Silas paused, letting the tension build. "Yormund backed off to gloat. He knew what was coming. I heard that about Yormund. How he'd entertain the spectators by slicing an opponent's leg so he couldn't move, then play with him until he got tired of the game. The audience liked that about him. Well, he came at the prince like death. And Rayne, slight as he is, just stands there holding that foot-long excuse of a broken sword. Waiting for the blow …"

"I got hit from behind and shoved to the ground," Rayne mumbled, staring into space, picking up the story. "I turned to look behind me, see what happened. And there was Shin, taking Yormund's axe in his chest. He took the blow meant for me. But he was so strong, so big. I couldn't believe my eyes. Shin pulled the axe from his own chest, flipped it in his hands like it was nothing more than a feather, and then buried it into Yormund, the whole head. That ancient weapon began to flicker and burn and then the thing exploded in a sea of sparks."

Rayne shook his head, seeing again the look on Shin's face. "I tried to get to Shin, ask him why he saved me. But then Matheson and his men were carrying me away and Matheson poured another one of those vials in my mouth to knock me out again. I never got to talk to Shin, never got to thank him. He saved my life."

"Who was he?" Anne asked.

"One of Lord William's guards. I literally ran into him when I arrived at the slave quarters in the gaming complex. And bounced off him too. He was huge; the largest man I've ever seen."

Rayne paused, remembering, then said, "Enough about me. What happened to you?" Rayne soaked in the sight of his friends' faces. It felt so good to see them all again.

"Just the normal everyday things that happen to people

who hang around with you, Your Highness." Sashi winked at him. "Let's see ... hum ... we were kidnapped, chained, forced to work underground. At least most of us were forced to work underground. Someone, who shall remain nameless, used her wiles to get a nice easy job in what passes for sunlight on this world."

Cai was walking past at that moment. He stopped and said, "Just wait, off-worlders. We'll climb above the last of the smoky fog tomorrow. The next morning you'll be above the fog line and then you shall experience the beauty of sunrise in the Taliesin Mountains. Don't judge our world by what's happening in this valley. I look forward to watching your faces then." Cai strode off promising to wake them all early the morning after next so they could watch the sun rise.

Silas chucked. "Cai was born and raised in these mountains and, if you couldn't guess, this is where he loves to be."

"Then why does he stay in the valley?" Anne asked.

Silas's smile faded. "I first met him a couple years ago. His brother had come down from the mountains to visit the portal city of Eleri, thinking it would be a fun adventure. But weeks passed and when he didn't return, Cai came looking for him. Cai learned that his brother had been taken as a slave to fight in one of the minor rings at the Andersen's complex and that he was killed there.

"Ethan was the one who found Cai days later, drunk, looking ripe for the plucking, with Andersen's men eying him up. Ethan couldn't leave him like that, so he brought him to Kern House. He's been helping us ever since. Usually he acts as our guide when we send refugees up into the mountains. But he's turned out to be a good friend and a talented fighter too."

"And what about you, old man?" Rayne turned to Thorvin. "Heard you had some trouble with the guards."

Thorvin grumbled and looked down at the floor. "I never knew what it was like, to feel so trapped and helpless. To be looked at like property and treated like less than dirt. The guards enjoyed inflicting punishment and for the first time in my life I felt the bite of a whip. It was a painful and humiliating experience; I'll never think about slavery the same again. I only had to endure it for a few days." He looked at Rayne, his eyes dark and intense. "But you, Your Highness. Never again will I allow you to put yourself in a position where you have to wear a collar or be subjected to such brutality. I don't care what goal you seek. Don't ask me. I won't do it. You're my prince and I'm committed to your protection."

Thorvin paused for a moment, his eyes distant, then added, "But if I can do anything to end this horrible practice that does not interfere with my vow to protect you, I'll do it."

Fingers brushed the back of Rayne's neck and hunching his shoulders he looked up to see Sashi standing behind him, fingering his ragged hair. "What ever happened to your hair? It looks awful, like it was chopped by a blind man with blunt shears who missed the braid."

"That was a gift from Matheson." Rayne shivered, recalling again those moments after Shin's death. "He wanted a trophy, something to remember me by. So, when they carried me from the ring after my fight with Yormund, and I was in no shape to stop him, he took a sword to it."

Thorvin looked at Rayne, suspicion growing in his eyes. "Speaking of Matheson, Sire, how did you manage to kill him when you couldn't even stand?"

"I couldn't have done it without Lexi's help. She kept attacking him. And once he thought I was no longer a threat, he focused on her. He was so intent on killing her, he never noticed me. It was a fatal mistake."

Rayne thought back to those moments after Matheson's death, seeing the Son and the words he spoke. But Rayne said nothing about any of it to his friends. He needed to talk to Lexi first.

Then Cai took up a position in front of the fire and called for attention. "Everyone, please get as comfortable as you can. The food will be ready soon. After we've eaten, you should all try to get some sleep because tomorrow is going to be a long, grueling day."

Rayne felt self-conscious as his friends seemed intent on seeing to his comfort. Anne scrounged up a blanket. Thorvin, Stevie, and Sashi cut pine boughs for him to lie on to soften the rocky ground. Shaw sat with him quietly talking about the history of the Taliesin Mountains and why he thought the scroll would be hidden there.

Once the meal was ready, Sashi brought Rayne a bowl of the soup Cai's friends had made, and Anne brought Shaw a bowl. Shaw said a blessing and the companions sat together exchanging more stories of what happened while they were apart.

After they had eaten, it didn't take long for everyone who wasn't on guard duty to fall asleep.

40

When Rayne woke the next morning, he was surprised to find Thorvin sitting beside him, awake. "You gonna pray?" Thorvin asked gruffly. "Do that Lauds thing you and Shaw do?"

Rayne nodded. "I planned to. Why?"

Thorvin grunted, avoiding Rayne's eyes. "I'd like to join you."

The hint of a smile flitted through Rayne and he suppressed a grin. "Well then give me a hand up, old man."

Sitting up, Rayne saw Anne already talking with Shaw. Stevie and Sashi were walking over with Silas. Together they greeted the morning with praise and thanksgiving for being together again and for protection on the road yesterday. They prayed for the men who had died and their families, and for guidance in the days to come. Then they sang a hymn most everyone knew, somewhat.

After Anne checked Rayne's leg and infused some healing energy into it, he sat alone, watching the flickering flames of the newly rebuilt fire. His friends went to see if they could do anything to help Cai get ready to move out after breakfast.

Aware of a presence behind him, Rayne turned to see Lexi staring at him. He said nothing, waiting for her to speak first. She hesitated, and he thought she might just walk away, but then she drifted over to where he sat, propped up, surrounded by the scent of pine.

Hostility and uncertainty battled in her eyes and she hissed, "We need to talk."

Rayne nodded. Lexi stood without moving, studying him a few minutes longer, then sat on the log Anne had used earlier. She played with tendrils of honey hair that had fallen from under her hat and trailed over her shoulders, twisting them around her fingers and then letting them bounce loose. Rayne sat quietly, watching the activity of the camp as he waited for her to be ready to talk.

"What am I supposed to do with you?" Lexi groaned, frustrated by her inability to control the emotional storm raging inside her. "You come into my life, shatter it to pieces. You disappear. And then, three years later you return. I thought I'd never see you again, never have the satisfaction of punishing you for your crimes. Finally, I think. Finally, I can get justice for all the torment you caused; justice for my father, my people, myself. But then you turn into something so different than the inhuman monster I always believed you to be, like some kind of mythical shape-shifter. And even though I still want to hate you—need to hate you—I can't.

"Then yesterday, after you saved me, I ... oh ... I don't even know how to say this. Somehow I ... connected with you, saw your memories, knew your remorse and horror at your past ... touched your pain." She shuddered. "How did you do that?" Then, eyes open wide in wonder as she felt again the presence of the man from the vision. "But no, wait, don't answer that yet. First, did you see that person? Right after I opened my eyes, you were looking at me and then I was someplace else, with you and another person."

"That was the One's Son. Did you hear his words?"

"Yes." Lexi's whisper was so quiet, it barely sounded.

"What do I do with you?" She asked again, a tear tracking down her cheek unnoticed. She looked into Rayne's amethyst eyes knowing now the depth of pain he hid behind them. She didn't know what happened in that moment before she opened her eyes after Matheson tried to kill her, but she now knew Rayne in a way she knew no one else. She had seen depths in him that shattered her need to punish him. She knew how much he suffered already. She didn't know how she knew this, she just did.

Did you hear his words? Rayne had asked her. But how could she tell Rayne what she had heard. It was too hard, too revealing.

Then Rayne was speaking again. "'My beloved Light Bringer, protect Lexi, for her heart and yours are one. She is yours and you are hers. My gift to you of love.' Those were the words I heard."

Lexi gasped, not wanting to admit what she heard. It was tearing her heart open, exposing her need to hate and her bitterness. But with an effort of will, she tore the rip in her heart open further. Touching again the faith of her childhood, she prayed to the One to help her release the pain and hatred, and the need for vengeance that had driven her for so long. And she cried at the release and the influx of love that warmed her spirit.

When the emotion passed, Lexi opened her eyes again to see Rayne next to her, his arm around her shoulders. She cried again, this time with the knowledge that the One was working in her, cleansing the hatred from her heart.

She wasn't ready to accept the words of love the Son had spoken, wasn't even sure she could accept Rayne as a friend. But Lexi let Rayne hold her, feeling the warmth of him next to her. Resting in his strong presence. After a bit, she looked over to him only to find herself drowning in his incredible eyes. She steeled herself and asked, "Okay. Now, tell me how I could be in your memories the way I was yesterday. How did you do that?"

He shifted to watch the fire for a minute, a sad smile lifting a corner of his mouth. "It's something my mother was teaching me."

Returning his gaze to Lexi, he continued. "Mother was teaching me to use the magical energy of Ochen. I'm not strong like she is, but I have enough natural talent to make training worthwhile. At least she used to think so." He paused. "Anyway, yesterday when you looked so still and wouldn't respond to me, I was afraid Matheson had killed you. I opened a line of energy so I could sense if you were okay. But I don't know enough to block someone following the line back to me. That's what you did, you followed my sense tendril back into me. I'm sorry if it scared you."

Lexi met Rayne's eyes. "It was kind of scary. I really don't want to do that again. But it changed everything. I saw you, inside you. How do you do it, keep going after what's been done to you?" She pulled in a deep breath and released a sigh. "I can't ignore what I felt. I can't hate you anymore." Lexi stared up at him a moment. "But I can't stop hating you either. It can't be that easy. It can't be." Then she jumped up and ran away.

ᚼ

Rayne watched her disappear beyond the fire and smiled. He was still thinking about his conversation with Lexi, when Thorvin walked up holding a sturdy looking, five-foot tall staff that had been trimmed and somewhat smoothed. "Here," he said. "This should help you walk."

Rayne reached out, wrapped his hands around the wood, and pulled himself upright. At the motion, a shudder ran through his body; a premonition of loss. He shook the feeling and moved forward using the staff to keep most of his weight off the right leg. It would do. Rayne appreciated being able to move without needing someone to help him.

"Thanks, old man. This is good. At least now I don't feel so helpless."

"And you can always use it like a staff if you need a ready weapon," Thorvin joked. But Rayne nodded as once again the strange sensation of loss whispered through him.

It was still early when Cai had the group organized and moving up the path again. The morning passed slowly. As they climbed, the hardwood trees, ash and mountain beech, gave way to dark needled pines and firs. The smoky flavor of the air faded, replaced by the fragrance of pine needles and old dried leaves; while the fog thinned to faint tendrils. Rayne felt the warmth of the sun on his back as he struggled to maneuver around yet another rocky outcropping on the path. Walking with the staff was tiring, he was using muscles he hadn't even known he had and was already stiff and sore. But he took satisfaction in being able to move without help.

When they reached a large clearing, Cai called for a break. Rayne eased down onto a large rock, groaning. He looked around for his friends and was glad to see them all scattered amongst the Verenians. Thorvin was talking to Cai and a couple of his men; Shaw and Anne, holding hands, were with Silas; Stevie was talking to one of the girls they had rescued from the mine, his hands chopping the air for emphasis. It looked as if they were already acquainted and Rayne wondered if they had worked together in the mine. Then Rayne spotted Sashi talking to Lexi. *I'd like to know what those two are talking about.*

Seeing Lexi alone, Sashi decided it was time they talked. She had been hoping for this chance, but Lexi seemed cold and unapproachable so Sashi hesitated. Although she was used to dealing with nobles in the shop, except for Rayne and Thorvin she didn't know any personally and was unsure the proper way to approach Lexi. But she wanted to get to know the Verenian. They looked to be about the same age and Sashi thought she would enjoy having someone her own age to talk to, especially if that someone was a girl. She spent far too much time around Stevie and his friends and she longed for feminine conversation. Though Anne was terrific, she spent most of her time with Shaw.

Lexi's eyes were similar to Anne's but even more golden

and seeing her up close for the first time, Sashi was startled when she realized that the color was actually the result of amber flakes scattered like a sunburst in hazel eyes. The girl was even more petite than Anne and had masses of honey colored hair pinned up in a bun. Giving Sashi a thin smile, Lexi invited Sashi to sit with her.

Unsure but determined, Sashi plunged forward. "I know we haven't been introduced, and I'm not familiar with the protocol here on Veres. But I don't know if normal conventions need to be followed after we've fought together anyway. I mean, we did fight in the same fight, but not together. I mean you rode off and fought with Rayne. I mean fought with Matheson ... oh, I'm sorry. I'm making a mess of this. I'm Sashi, one of Rayne's friends from Corylus. I just wanted to introduce myself and I thought maybe we could talk. With us being about the same age, well, I thought it would be nice ... you know ... um ... to talk ..."

Sashi trailed off unsure what to say next but she was rewarded when Lexi smiled shyly and said, "I would enjoy having a girl my own age to talk to."

Ethan walked up to them with a question for Lexi and she said to Sashi, "Perhaps when we make camp tonight we can sit together for a bit?"

Sashi flashed a grin. "As one woman to another, I look forward to spending time in conversation this evening." After a quick bow, Sashi turned, walked to where Rayne was sitting, and plopped down on a fallen log.

When Sashi sat next to him, Rayne wanted to ask what she and Lexi had been talking about but Sashi was more interested in telling Rayne how unendurable Stevie could be. Rayne laughed at Sashi's story about how Stevie tried to hide his attraction to Emma, the girl he was now talking with, by being rude and obnoxious to her when they were forced to work together in the mine.

As the afternoon progressed and the company continued

to climb, they left the fog below. Here in the higher elevations, the air was clear and crisp under a deep blue dome of sky. The path snaked around the crown of the mountain and when they rounded a bend revealing a panorama of mountains and valleys, Rayne stepped to the side of the path, enthralled by the sight.

Fog shifted down in the valley below, spread out like a pale lumpy blanket in shades of gray. Mountains covered in dense deep green forest rose from the gray mist like phantoms, while others rose even higher, their dark rocky summits dusted with snow. Light clouds moved over the landscape casting shadows, mottling the sun-stroked pines and firs. One moment they were black with shadow, the next, lime green and golden in brilliant sunlight. Rayne closed his eyes and allowed the muted sounds of bird songs and shuffling feet to soothe him. The smell of the pines was fresh, and a fitful breeze ruffled his choppy hair, lifting the braid and then dropping it again.

Then he felt it; a tug deep within. Rayne's eyes popped open, drawn to a peak off to his right. Its crown was higher than the mountain he stood on, sharp and dark against the pale sky. The glint of sun on running water and deep, dark green patches of forest, broken in places by large masses of sharp-featured, gray rock faces, pulled at him. Silas was passing behind. Rayne called to him and Silas moved off the path to join him.

"What mountain is that? Does it have a name?" Rayne asked.

Silas squinted across the valley. "I'm not sure. Is it important? Do you need me to ask Cai?"

"Yes."

Though most of the company had already passed the place where Rayne stood like a rooted statue, he didn't need to wait long before Silas returned with Cai in tow. By that time, Thorvin had walked back to Rayne. After giving him a questioning look, the large man also stood, gazing at the facing slope.

Rayne stared unswervingly at the mountain and his gaze didn't shift even as Silas and Cai approached. "That's the mountain?" Cai asked.

"What can you tell me about it?" Rayne asked, eyes pinned on a sparkling stream about halfway up the side.

"That is Mount Caarwyn. It's sacred to our people."

"Can we go there? Can we get to the source of that running water from here without going to Mistal first?"

Cai hesitated for a moment, concentration puckering his brow. "It will be hard for you. We'll have to skirt that smaller mountain between and then the path up Caarwyn from this face is steep and rocky. There is a small village near the water's source about a day's walk from here. For you, two days, maybe three. Why are you asking this?"

"Because." Rayne hesitated. "Because something is drawing me there and I think it's the scroll. Everything in me is being pulled, like slivers of metal to a lodestone. This is what we came for; I have to go there."

"You're speaking of the One's scroll to Veres?" Cai asked. "When you talked about this back at Kern House I thought you were talking of myths and legends until we heard that voice."

Lexi followed Ethan over. Now, also gazing at Mount Caarwyn, she said, "At first I thought you were lying when you spoke of sacred scrolls. Then, when we heard that voice, I thought I was imagining things. But we all heard it. I wouldn't have believed the One was anything more than an old myth a month ago, something my dad believed but I no longer accepted. Now I'm not so sure. After all that's happened, I think we need to listen."

"If you wish for him to go to Caarwyn Rill, my lady, I'll guide him. My men can lead the refugees the rest of the way to Mistal. Would you have me guide him my lady?"

"We'll be going with him," Thorvin said. "I'll let Shaw and Anne and the twins know that we're splitting off."

"I would join you too," Silas said.

"I too will go with you," Lexi said. "I've always wanted to visit Mount Caarwyn and I want to see what this *Light Bringer* is going to do there. Ethan, you're in charge."

They continued along the path with the rest of the company until they reached a smaller, steeper trail that branched off to their left, leading down into the valley. Rayne was concerned when they descended into thick woods and lost sight of Mount Caarwyn. Cai explained that once they crossed the valley floor and were through the woods, they would skirt the side of the smaller mountain blocking their view. "You'll not only be able to see Caarwyn again, we'll be much closer."

Excited by the thought of finding the scroll, Rayne struggled to control his frustration. Despite his eagerness to reach Caarwyn, no matter how he tried, he couldn't seem to move with any speed. His anxiety continued to mount as Cai called for frequent rest stops. Though everyone told him to sit and rest when they stopped, no sooner did he sit, then he would hop back up saying, "I'm fine, let's keep moving."

By the fourth time Rayne refused to heed Cai's admonition to rest, Thorvin threatened to tie Rayne to his back and carry him up the mountain if he didn't listen to good advice.

His fists clenching at his powerlessness, Rayne hopped to his feet, but he couldn't even pace. He felt as if he couldn't do anything. "I hate this. It's my fault we have to waste all this time stopping. I don't like being weak; it makes me angry, I feel as if I will burst with it."

In a calm voice, Anne reminded Rayne, "Weren't you the individual who told us that the One works his will in his own perfect timing. Be patient, my friend. We will arrive at our destination when we arrive, and your anger will do nothing to make the trip any shorter. Or more bearable."

Rayne hung his head shamed by Anne's gentle reproof. He sighed. "The One knew what he was doing when he gave me a friend like you. Someone who's not afraid to let me know when I'm being an idiot."

Anne smiled at Rayne with affection. "And you should be grateful! Rayne, breathe deeply. Enjoy the beauty around you. The destination will come in its own good time. But don't discount the blessings of living in the moment and the knowledge gained in the journey."

Rayne chuckled. "When did you get so smart? Oh, I know, you've been hanging around Shaw too long. You're starting to sound like him. You know, dusty, old man language."

"And what exactly is that supposed to mean?" Shaw asked, attempting to hide a grin.

"What? It's a complement! I'm saying good things about both of you."

Then Rayne and his friends laughed. In her gentle way, Anne had eased the tension Rayne's frustration initiated. He signed *thank you* to Anne who smiled back.

With Rayne's impatience dissipated by the light banter and laughter, he found himself moving easier. Rayne had allowed his irritation to create more difficulties by trying to move faster than he was able. Once he moved with patience, his balance improved and he maneuvered better. Seeing him advance with less effort, Cai waited longer before calling for the next rest.

By early afternoon they were almost across the valley. Soon they would be climbing the side of the smaller mountain and picking up the path that skirted around it to bring them to the base of Caarwyn. Cai called for a final rest stop before leaving the valley floor.

Rayne leaned back on a large, flat rock, enjoying the warmth the sun had infused in the silver-streaked, gray stone and the earthy scents surrounding him. Just beyond where he reclined, a stand of ferns grew almost as tall as he. Every time the breeze picked up, the fronds rustled. It was a soothing sound. The whole area was peaceful. The sun streamed through breaks in the trees and, if he positioned himself just right, the warm rays felt especially good on his left hip where his wound was almost healed. Water splashing over rocks beyond the tall ferns tinkled and chuckled and, taking advantage of the rest break, Rayne closed his eyes, breathing in the beauty of the moment.

Thoughts of the Words of the One to Corylus filled his mind and he wondered what this second scroll would be like. Would it be the same? Different? Would it have a sealed portion? Footsteps filtered into his consciousness. Cracking his eyes open slightly Rayne was surprised to see Lexi approaching. He opened his eyes fully as she stopped in front of him.

"May I sit?" She pointed to a corner of his rocky seat. He sat up and patted the rock. "Of course, it's not like I own this rock or something."

She sat so close to him, Rayne was reminded how sweet

she had smelled that night in the coach. It seemed like a lifetime ago. Now she smelled of leather and sweat, but it wasn't bad. In fact, he thought, she still smelled kind of sweet, like fresh mown hay.

Rayne knew he should say something; but didn't know what. He dropped his gaze to his hands and fidgeted with his fingers, lacing and unlacing them.

Lexi was quiet for a while, just sitting, not saying a word. Suddenly she turned to him and said, "I like your friends. Watching you laugh and jest earlier was nice, normal. It's been so long since I could just enjoy life without everyone's needs dictating what I had to do. So long since life was *normal*. With all that's happening, I find myself thinking maybe things will get better."

When Cai called for them to start moving again, Lexi stayed by Rayne's side. He glanced at her from time to time wondering about the words the Son had spoken to them yesterday and what they might mean. They seemed to bind Lexi and Rayne in some way. What was the One's will in this, Rayne wondered? Why did Lexi's words contain the extra line, *You will always know the truth in him, and know him in truth?*

He played the words over in his mind, strange words. But he let those thoughts go as Mount Caarwyn came into view once again. *Tomorrow. Tomorrow I'll be there.*

41

Rayne woke to the refrain of a whispered, "hurry."
It was predawn dark, and Cai was shaking everyone awake with the admonition to hurry. Rayne bolted up reaching for his sword, sure that somehow Lord William's men had found them. But then it registered in his sleep-muddled mind. Cai wasn't calling them to battle; he was excited and full of anticipation. *Dawn on the Taliesin Mountains,* Rayne remembered. Cai was calling them to what he had referred to last night as they were drifting off to sleep, as a *wondrous sight not seen any place else in the whole Ochen system.*

With the dark forms of his friends rising around him, Rayne reached for his staff and pulled upright. He followed Cai and the others, moving past the embers of last night's cook fire and back down the path toward a rocky outcrop they had passed last evening just before setting camp. He stopped near the edge of the overlook, surveying dense forest below in the nascent light. Flowing like waves, reminding Rayne of the Cameron Sea on a rainy day, milky gray fog swathed the forest, deeper charcoal tendrils marking the Eleri River course. Rayne was aware of Anne and Shaw stepping up behind him.

Shades of lavender, rose, and gold were beginning to emerge in an aura around the point of brightest light on the horizon. Deep purple and smoky blue were daubed on clouds that swept across the sky in horizontal lines. Rayne stood in awe as the light around him brightened in hues of lavender and blue.

As he watched, Rayne's eyes were drawn to golden flashes shooting from the wondrous colors. They sparked and moved and sparked again, and Rayne realized they were living things. They flew like swallows but so much faster, and they were coming closer. He began to hear their calls, high and sweet, yet chirpy at the same time. Then the tiny creatures were swirling around him. They were about the size of the dragon flies he had seen on a lake once long ago, but they looked like sparrows, with translucent wings that sparkled and flashed in the light of the rising sun.

There were hundreds of the tiny creatures chirruping and swooping and soaring around Rayne and his friends. Without volition, Rayne dropped his staff, gingerly shifting some weight onto his right leg. He closed his eyes and lifted his hands toward the sunrise, palms cupped open, and thanked the One for the beauty of the moment. Then he felt them, like whispers of movement on his arms. The creatures were landing on him, first one then two, then he was covered in a living cloak of sparkling gold. They twittered and talked amongst themselves, their wings glinting myriad colors in the light.

Rayne sensed the change in the air when his friends moved away. He now stood alone at the edge of the overlook. He opened his eyes and gazed out over the valley as he stood robed in the gilded light of the singular creatures. Joy filled him, and he basked in the golden glow that surrounded him and vibrated within him with the flutter of wings.

Then, as if of one mind, the creatures all took to the air, wings whirring and flashing, flying back toward the rising sun before disappearing in the distance. All was still and silent. Serenity enveloped the overlook, spreading outward from Rayne to touch each person standing there in that wondrous moment.

Rayne stood watching after the disappearing golden creatures for a few minutes. The pigment saturated colors painting the clouds muted into washed out pastels of color as birds gave voice to their sunrise songs, greeting the day.

Looking back over his shoulder, Rayne said to Cai, "You're right. I don't imagine anything can compare to sunrise here. That was incredible."

"What?" Rayne asked, wondering if he had dirt on his face or something, as Cai stared silently at him, mouth gaping. "What?" he asked again when he realized that Cai wasn't the only one staring.

"I've never experienced anything like it," Cai whispered. "Sun Sparrows this close. They're rare, and when they do appear, they stay up high and we just see their wings glinting. And to hear their voices?" Cai shook his head. "You truly are blessed of the One."

Uncomfortable with his friends gawking at him as if he was some kind of rarity, Rayne bent to pick up his staff and then turned back to Cai. "I suppose we should be moving."

The group snapped out of their stupor and turning, headed back to camp. No one spoke as they walked back up the trail, everyone still immersed in the peace and joy brought on by the sparrows. Cai and Lexi worked to rekindle the fire while Stevie and Sashi gathered wood. Anne filled a pot with water Cai had brought up from a stream the evening before. Still wrapped in the afterglow of the Sun Sparrows, Rayne sat on a fallen tree a short distance from the cook fire, singing softly.

Claiming he needed to smooth the wood more, Thorvin took Rayne's staff. Silas followed him up to the broad top of an up thrust rock that overlooked the camp. The two sat in companionable silence while Thorvin worked his knife over rough places, and Rayne sang.

After Rayne's song ended, Shaw walked up to him. "May I sit with you a bit, Sire?"

Rayne nodded. "Sure."

Shaw sat quietly watching Anne as she hung a pot over the fire Cai had coaxed back to life. "This has been some adventure,

Sire," he said. "From the lows of being a slave in an underground mine to that glorious moment with the Sun Sparrows this morning. I'm so grateful the One called me to experience this with you." Then, clearing his throat as a light blushing suffused his cheeks, he continued. "He's allowed me to meet the most beautiful and wisest woman I have ever known. And come to care for—no, I must be honest—come to ... love. Rayne, you're the closest thing to family Anne has. I know she thinks of you as her little brother. So, I would like to ask if you could give your blessing for me to ask her to wed?"

Rayne turned knowing eyes to Shaw and then looked back at Anne who watched them from the far side of the fire, her lower lip caught between her teeth.

"If that is her wish, I couldn't be happier. You are two of my closest friends and seeing you happy together is a blessing." Then smiling slyly, Rayne added, "But I can't say I'm surprised."

Shaw laughed and waved Anne over. She looked at Rayne, hope and question swirling in her eyes. Chuckling inside, Rayne plastered a stern, cold expression on his face and said, "I hear you want to leave my service, healer?"

The look of shock on Anne's face sent Rayne into a fit of laughter.

"No ... No ... that's not..." she stuttered, confusion suffusing her features. "We ... you ... of course we want to stay with you. We were hoping to marry after the scrolls are recovered."

Stifling his laughter, Rayne looked at Shaw with raised eyebrows, "I thought you were just asking me if you could *ask* Anne, but it appears you've already done that. I really have no say in the matter at all, do I?"

"Only because we knew you wouldn't object and that you would be happy for us," Anne said. "And because I do think of you as my brother. My beautiful, amazing, and wonderful brother; the best brother in the whole world. The kindest and nicest ..."

"Enough," Rayne said. "Enough with the flattery."

As Anne sat between Rayne and Shaw, Lexi walked over. "May I join you?"

"Yes, please join us," Rayne said. "You can be the first to hear the good news. Shaw has requested my permission to ask Anne to marry him and I have given my blessing. Isn't that wonderful?"

Confusion drew Lexi's brows together. "Why would he have to get your permission?"

Leaning forward to talk around Rayne, Anne said, "Because he's my adopted brother and the only family I have." She looked back at Rayne, affection shining in her eyes. "Do you remember Rayne, when we thought we were going to die in Westvale? Isn't it amazing the blessings the One has brought us since then?"

Sashi bounded up behind Anne, Stevie following in her wake. "Did Shaw ask him?" Sashi blurted out. "What did he say? Can we talk about it now?"

Rayne gave Anne a hurt look. "Was I the only one who didn't know about this proposal? I'm cut to the heart."

Anne laughed, exuberant and happy, then threw her arms around Rayne. "I love you Rayne. I couldn't have asked for a better brother. My life is so full." She grabbed Shaw's hand and pulling him up, dragged him to the fire to get some breakfast and discuss their future.

Sashi sat where Anne had been sitting and asked Lexi, "Do you have any brothers or sisters?"

"No."

"Well then, since Anne can adopt Rayne, I think Stevie and I should adopt you. Of course, Anne and Rayne grew up together, but that doesn't matter. I've always wanted a sister." A cunning look spread across Sashi's face. "We can gang up on Stevie. Yeah, I like the idea of having a sister." Sashi blushed. "Oh, I've done it again. Stevie says my mouth runs away with me because I say things without thinking. Nemora's moons, my lady, I'm sorry if I've offended you."

"No." A small grin worked its way out on Lexi's lips. "Actually, I think it's kind of great that you would think of me like that. I always thought it would be lovely to have a sister. And please, call me Lexi. We have fought together, after all."

"And I think it would be *lovely* if everyone would come and eat so we can get moving," Cai cut in, his voice high in imitation of the feminine voices. "That is if you still want to get up Caarwyn today?"

Sashi jumped up and grabbed Lexi's hand. "Come on, Lexi. We can get to the food before Rayne even gets his staff."

Cai smiled as Sashi dragged Lexi past him toward the cook fire, both giggling, and Stevie followed shrugging.

Thorvin walked over and handed Rayne his staff. "I guess I'd better return this to you. But by the time you get there, your breakfast might just be gone."

"Thanks." Rayne swung the staff and took off, moving in a kind of galloping run, calling for Lexi and Sashi to wait.

"Come on you two, we older folks should get a move on before the food is all gone." Cai chuckled.

"You aren't much older than they are," Thorvin said to Cai as they strode to the fire.

"Well, let's just say I no longer have that amount of boundless energy."

"Exuberant, aren't they?" Thorvin waved at the retreating figures.

"Yes," Cai replied. "It's good to hear Lexi laugh. She's been through so much. I must admit though, seeing her on friendly terms with the prince surprises me. I didn't think I would ever see that."

"She did seem kind of cold initially. Why was that?"

"As one of the three leaders of the tribunal called in judgement against the prince, she'll have to be objective when he's sentenced."

"Sentenced? What are you talking about? What tribunal?" Thoughts of Rayne's history stirred up feelings of misgiving in Thorvin as he dished hot cereal onto a metal plate and grabbed a cup of coffee.

"Oh. Maybe I spoke out of turn." Cai scooped hot cereal onto his plate. "I assumed Rayne told you."

"He didn't tell you, did he?" Silas squinted at Thorvin as

he grabbed his own breakfast and coffee. "This should be interesting."

Cai sat on one of the logs they had placed around the cook fire yesterday evening and watched Lexi, Sashi, Stevie and Rayne talking while they ate, a short distance away on some rocks. Thorvin and Silas sat down near him and Cai said, "Don't know how I landed in the middle of this, Thorvin, but I'll tell you what I know. If Silas wants to add anything he can. But if you want to know the full story, you should talk to the prince." Cai took a deep breath and cleared his throat. "Three years ago, Lexi and her father, Duke Erland, were attacked at their home by Lord William and one of his allies, Sigmund of Bainard."

Thorvin groaned and shook his head, he knew where this was going.

"Sigmund wasn't alone that night. He brought a teenaged boy with him who already had a reputation as an accomplished assassin. I was still living in Mistal at the time, so I wasn't around when this happened. But from what I've heard, it didn't take this boy long to wipe out Duke Erland's guard, leaving their bodies scattered on the lawn. He then cracked the duke's head with the hilt of his sword and left him alive but trapped in a body that can't talk or walk or do anything else on its own. The young assassin then led Lord William's men in torching the manor house. Needless to say, Lexi was devastated by the attack and vowed vengeance on the silent assailant who caused such pain.

"A few weeks ago, we came up with a plan Lexi hoped would bring our cause before King Theodor. Silas, maybe you should tell this part. I wasn't with you that night."

Silas picked up the story, "One of our informants brought news that King Theodor's son, Prince Rayne, was at the Andersen's complex. Of course we assumed he was there as a spectator. We kidnapped him, not realizing we were actually saving him. He was wearing this hooded cloak and we thought he was drunk because he was staggering when we grabbed him, didn't realize he was injured and drugged. He passed out when we got him into the coach, so we never got a good look at him.

"But the next morning at Kern House, Lexi came face to face with the prince and recognized him as Sigmund's assassin. She called for a tribunal. The young prince confessed his guilt and agreed he should face punishment, but then laid claim to the title of Light Bringer and struck a bargain. He vowed to return and face sentencing once he fulfilled the prophecy and brought the seven scrolls together. The tribunal agreed, but Lexi and Ethan, as two of the three sitting in judgement, will be responsible to set sentence when the prince's vow to return is fulfilled."

Thorvin ground the heels of his hands into his eye sockets. "It never ends." He groaned at the knot twisting in his gut. "That nightmare still surrounds Prince Rayne. He can't seem to get a break."

"He told us some of his story," Cai said. "I think that's one of the reasons the tribunal was willing to postpone sentencing. The whole Light Bringer thing is like something out of myth for us. We haven't worshipped the One here on Veres for a long time. If Silas hadn't spoken up about personally hearing the One's voice, I'm not sure Lexi, Ethan, and Seren would have agreed to Rayne's proposal."

Cai shook his head. "A real shame that. I can see Prince Rayne is something special, maybe even this Light Bringer he claims to be. But it's equally true that he's Sigmund's young assassin from that night. I'm glad I'm not one who has to make a ruling on his punishment."

Cai got up and turning back reached down to pull Thorvin to his feet. "But from what I saw this morning, I think the One has a plan for your prince. And it looks as if he's working on softening Lexi's heart. Now if that happens, it would be a miracle indeed."

Some of the tension Thorvin had been holding bled away. "The One does seem to have a way of turning circumstances around for Rayne. I guess I have to take the advice he keeps giving me and trust. But do me a favor, Cai, don't tell any of our friends about the tribunal. I think if Rayne wanted us to know, he would have told us himself."

Cai nodded, then headed to the fire to pack up.

Silas clapped a hand on Thorvin's shoulder. "For what it's worth, I think the prince's story has had an impact on Ethan, Lexi, and Seren. I don't see how anyone could come to know Prince Rayne and not realize what a good heart he has. I don't think it's so hard to trust the One to work this all out right in the end."

Then Silas followed Cai to help break camp and head out.

42

From the moment they set foot on Caarwyn, Rayne felt the curious quality to the air, like it was softer, different, rarefied. The trees almost seemed more alive, vibrant, as if aware people were passing beneath.

The companions spoke little, moving forward quietly, until they grew accustomed to the sensation. When they did speak, it was in soft tones and whispers as if needing to respect the pulsing energy surrounding them. The trees grew to immense sizes, leaves like flower buds beginning to unfold. Numerous smaller trees tucked in amongst the giants were in full bloom with flowers of cream, pink, or lavender, brightening the understory. Flowers bloomed in clumps; white nodding heads, bright yellow stars; blue, purple, and yellow cups. The colors of the flowers, the fragrance, even the way they moved in the breeze all seemed intensified, powerful. They spread out and covered whole areas looking like woven blankets of color.

With the day warming toward midmorning, they reached a point where the only way to go was straight up. Cai, Silas, Lexi, Thorvin, Stevie, and Sashi scrambled up the rocky face. Once they had climbed past the vertical rocks, they looped a rope around one of the giant trees to act as a control and tied it off to another. Cai fashioned a harness at the end, making a kind of seat before tossing it down to Anne, Shaw, and Rayne. Shaw insisted on riding the contraption up first to make sure it was safe. Once he was secured in the harness, Cai, Thorvin, and Stevie pulled him up while Silas watched over the edge talking to Shaw and shouting directions.

Shaw used his feet to push off the rocks as he was hoisted up and pulled over the rough edge. The system worked well, so they lowered the rope for Anne to come next, followed by Rayne. He discovered that the staff could be used to help him "walk" up the rocky face but holding the heavy wood parallel to the ground was a struggle. By the time Rayne was pulled up over the lip at the top, the muscles in his arms and shoulders were jumping from the exertion.

Because the harness and rope worked well, Cai used the device several times to cut out long sections of the path. It was nearing sunset when they faced yet another vertical rise and Cai called for one more rope climb. Rayne watched the others scramble up the rock face using hands and feet to ascend. Cai, Silas, and Thorvin climbed up one side of the sheer rocky incline while Lexi, Stevie, and Sashi scaled the other. The sound of their voices, talking and joking back and forth while they ascended, drifted down to Rayne. Though what they were doing was dangerous, they were enjoying the activity, and Rayne wished he could share the experience with them instead of sitting below waiting to be dragged up.

As before, Shaw went first, followed by Anne, and then Rayne. He walked up the incline using his left leg and the staff while the harness pulled him slowly higher. He was exhausted, his arms shook from the weight of the staff. Each time he shifted it upward, the burden seemed to grow heavier. The end dragged, scraping against the stony face as it pulled toward the ground below. He gritted his teeth, determined to keep going.

Then Thorvin's and Cai's strong arms were there helping him up over the hump of the overhang. "Hold steady," Thorvin said. "We're going to flip you and bring you up and over on your back, so you don't bang up your leg." Thorvin and Cai turned Rayne so his back was against the rock. He looked out over the valley far below as they pulled him up and over the rock.

Rayne pushed the harness off and flipped onto his stomach, ready to confess his exhaustion, when he saw houses set in a bowl-shaped clearing. They had made it. He was looking at the village of Caarwyn Rill.

Built of logs, the houses would have blended into the towering trees surrounding them if not for the colorfully painted veredium roofs. There were about eighty houses in all, tucked in among tall shrubs and set in a semi-circle around a central clearing and a community well. The peaked roofs sloped sharply from high ridgelines downward almost to the ground and ranged in color from bright yellow to deepest purple. The light of the lowering sun shone in broken rays over an immense garden plot, and a well where people were drawing water. Several children ran around the well screaming, chasing a baby pig.

The trees here were even larger than below. There were towering pines and firs competing with hickories and ancient oaks with immense trunks. It was remarkable to see trees of this size so high up the mountain.

Stevie held Rayne's staff out to him. He grabbed the end and Stevie pulled him upright as three men and two women approached from the village. Rayne blinked and blinked again, certain his eyes were deceiving him. *I must be dreaming.* One of the men was huge. He couldn't be, but he had to be ... "Shin?" Rayne whispered in disbelief.

It was Shin. And yet, it wasn't Shin. This man didn't possess the broad warrior's shoulders, and he had some gray sprinkled through his short black hair. Shin's hair had been completely black and shaggy on his shoulders.

Confusion muddling his thoughts, Rayne shook his head. "Shin?"

The men and women came to a stop in front of Rayne, but then Thorvin stepped between as Cai said, "Greetings elders of Caarwyn Rill. It is a great pleasure and honor to see you again."

The man who looked like Shin continued to stare at Rayne while saying, "Greetings Cai of Mistal. We have not seen you here in Caarwyn Rill for many months. To what do we owe the honor of this visit?"

Though the words were not words Shin would use, the voice sounded like Shin's, deep and powerful, sending shivers up Rayne's spine. Though he knew he was probably speaking out of turn, Rayne needed to know. "Are you related to Shin?"

The man bowed his head but didn't speak and Rayne felt the same kind of disapproval he had grown used to from his parents after Brayden's return. He had broken protocol.

Then the man raised his eyes and stepped past Thorvin to stand in front of Rayne. Gazing down on Rayne, the man surprised him by saying, "Welcome, Light Bringer, we have been waiting for you. I am Elder Jiro, Shin's twin brother and honorary Third Elder of Caarwyn Rill."

Rayne wasn't sure what to ask first: Did Shin still live? Did Jiro know what happened to Shin after Rayne had been taken from the ring? How did Jiro know Rayne was the Light Bringer? Making a quick decision, Rayne asked, "What do you know about the One's Light Bringer?"

Jiro chuckled deep in his throat. "I know much that would surprise you young one. But what you are really wondering is how I recognized you. I knew you were coming. And, never before have I met anyone carrying within him the light of the Sun Sparrows. There is no mistake. You are the One's Light Bringer and it is my honor to welcome you to Caarwyn Rill. Even if you are young and impulsive and speak out of turn.

"Allow us the formality of proper introductions and then we can talk." Jiro looked to the others who had walked over with him and dipped his head to a woman with white wispy hair that looked like a halo around her head. She stood no taller than Rayne's shoulders but looked him over with sharp brown eyes that glinted golden when the angled sun's rays caught them. "Elder Tegan is First Eldest, and as such, deserves much honor. She will make the introductions for Caarwyn Rill."

First Eldest Tegan's voice was deep and strong for someone who looked so fragile. "Elder Powell is Second Elder, next oldest after me."

Second Elder Powell was tall for a Verenian, with only a smattering of gray in his wheat colored hair and the most golden eyes Rayne had seen. It didn't seem possible that this man was almost as old as First Eldest Tegan; he didn't look old enough.

"Elder Owain is Fourth Elder, next oldest," Tegan continued. Rayne bowed to a heavy-set man with kind brown eyes, whiskery jowls, and a huge smile. Rayne liked him immediately, he seemed friendly and open.

"You have already met Third Elder Jiro, and this is Afon, she is the youngest of us, Fifth Elder." Afon was just about Rayne's height and she surveyed him with golden brown eyes that reminded Rayne of a bird's eyes, sharp and quick. He couldn't tell for sure the color of her hair. She wore a cream-colored cap that covered her entire head. But she smiled, and the smile reminded Rayne of Anne.

Rayne tried to remember what his parents had taught him about good manners. "It is an honor to meet you First Eldest Tegan, Elder Powell, Elder Jiro, Elder Owain, Elder Afon," Rayne said as he bowed to each elder in turn. "Please, allow me to introduce my friends and fellow travelers."

First Eldest Tegan harrumphed and gave Rayne a sharp look. "Young one, it would be best if you held your tongue. Does not custom dictate that the elder in authority make the introductions while youths speak only when spoken to?" Her eyes shifted between Thorvin and Silas as if she expected one of them to take charge.

Silas looked to Thorvin who cleared his throat and bowed. "Please excuse what must seem disrespectful to you, but the young man in front of you is the one in charge. He is Crown Prince Rayne Kierkengaard of Corylus and all Ochen. Do not judge him by his impetuous nature and youth; he is unusually wise for one so young."

By this time curious people from the village had gathered behind their elders and whispers began to sweep through the crowd. Elder Powell turned to the villagers and raised his hands. "People of Caarwyn Rill, it is almost time for the evening meal. Disperse and prepare yourselves. If deemed appropriate, we will introduce our visitors then."

With necks craning back to watch the visitors, the residents moved toward their houses still whispering among themselves.

Rayne nodded for Thorvin to make the introductions. The elders acknowledged Cai as someone they already knew. They also greeted Lexi, Silas, and Anne, as fellow Verenians. The twin's identical looks, their red hair and green eyes drew out exclamations of appreciation.

"Begging your pardon, First Eldest, fellow elders," Elder Jiro said. "It is growing dark and I must speak with the Light Bringer. May I request that our visitors be allowed to join us at the Elders' House where they can rest and be refreshed, and we can talk? As Elder Powell has indicated, it is almost time for prayers and the evening meal."

First Eldest Tegan and Elder Powell nodded their agreement. Elders Owain and Afon led the way toward the center of the village while Jiro walked between Rayne and Thorvin. They skirted the garden where early vines, spring greens in a rainbow of colors, as well as onions and a couple other plants Rayne couldn't identify, were growing. They passed another smaller garden where herbs scented the evening air with their varied fragrances. The elders turned onto a small path leading away from the gardens and past several houses to a large building set off by itself. It was surrounded by a dense stand of tall fir trees, their needles so dark they looked almost black with a slight purple cast.

The roof of the Elders' House sloped downward from a sharp peak like the village houses, but rather than extending all the way to the ground, it ended on both sides in sweeps where it met the incoming roofs of two large wings. The front of the building was stone, but the rest was of log construction like the village houses. And, like those, its roof was brightly painted veredium, in a shade of burnt orange.

Rayne and his friends followed the elders up three steps

made of great rectangular pieces of cut rock and through large double doors leading into a generous open space. An immense stone fireplace covered more than half of the far wall. Tables lined the side walls, with chairs stacked next to them. The hall was clean and bright with whitewashed walls. Large windows in the wall behind them, now in shadow, would let in ample sunlight during the day.

Jiro took the lead and led them through a doorway into the left wing where small rooms branched off from a central hallway. Bowing to the other elders, he said, "With your permission, First Eldest, fellow elders, I would like to speak to the Light Bringer alone for a few minutes."

Tegan inclined her head in agreement.

"Please excuse us," Jiro said to Thorvin. "The Light Bringer and I must talk. I will bring your friend back shortly."

Thorvin, looking unsure and nervous as Rayne was walking out, began to protest. But knowing he needed to talk to Jiro alone, Rayne said, "It's okay, Thorvin, I'll be fine."

Rayne followed Jiro to another room, farther up the hall. Though furnished like the room where his friends were waiting, it was smaller. The outer walls were built of round logs. Though they were rough and still retained bark on the outside, inside they were smoothed and stained a deep reddish-brown. Jiro waved Rayne to one of two large chairs made of woven branches covered with tapestry throws. Walking to a small table also made of woven branches with a beautiful prismatic lantern and a pottery pitcher with matching mugs set on it, Jiro lit the lantern and asked, "Would you like some water?"

Grateful for the offer, Rayne accepted a mug. Jiro pulled a chair similar to the one Rayne sat on around to face him and taking another mug of water for himself, sat across from Rayne.

It was disconcerting for Rayne; his eyes and ears told him he sat across from Shin, but he knew otherwise. He also knew he needed to tell Jiro that his brother was dead, and that he died protecting Rayne.

But before he could work up the courage to say anything, Jiro looked at him, his eyes deep with compassion, and said, "Your heart cries for my brother, as does mine. Take comfort that he is now in the presence of the One. I am aware of how he died. Shin gave his life to protect the One's Light Bringer just as he knew he would."

Rayne stared at Jiro, confusion blocking rational thought. "How?" It was the only word he seemed able to pull out of the web of his confusion.

A sad smile flitted across Jiro's face before vanishing. "My brother and I have always been connected. When we were children back on Glacieria we would often read each other's thoughts. Perhaps it would be best if I tell you our story from the beginning. Then you will find it easier to understand.

"The people of Glacieria are divided into three tribes of power, each made up of several clans who bonded together in the past for mutual strength and protection. Shin and I were born into the Michi tribe, the only tribe of power that still worships the One.

"At birth, our parents dedicated my brother and me to serve the One. Even as a small child, Shin had a warrior's spirit, while I was drawn to the quiet life of study and books. But though we followed two paths, they were always intertwined by our commitment to the One and our connection as twins. Nearly twenty years ago, Shin and I moved to Veres. Though our missions differed, both charges involved helping the Light Bringer when he came to Veres.

"When we arrived, we were drawn to Caarwyn. We settled here with the people of Caarwyn Rill and were welcomed as part of their community. Then, about six years ago, not long after the powerful merchant families began building their large gaming complexes, Shin moved down into the river valley. He felt called to get a job working for the Andersen family at their Eleri gaming complex. The job was hard on him and he experienced much sorrow at what he was forced to do. Over the years, Shin watched many young men sacrificed for the pleasure of the wealthy, while he waited for the Light Bringer, you, to appear.

"Three weeks ago, as I was praying, I felt Shin's spirit calling. I left the mountain and traveled down to the Andersen House Gaming Complex. But when I got there, I couldn't find Shin.

"Yuri, the man Shin worked with, saw me. He said I needed to leave, that Lord William was searching for Shin and he was very angry. He believed my brother knew the whereabouts of an escaped slave he was anxious to find. Yuri told me Shin was down in Eleri, gravely injured. A family he had grown close to over the years was hiding him. He also said I should not be seen and that I should hurry. I went to Eleri, avoiding the main road and any Andersen soldiers I saw.

"By the time I arrived, Shin was very weak. He told me that the Light Bringer had come, and he was not what we expected. Rather than a scholarly elder, he was a slight youth with eyes the color of mountain violets and hair the color of midnight. A warrior. He told me you had been forced to fight the ring champion, Yormund. I knew of Yormund, a fellow Glacierian, cruel and dangerous. Shin knew you were supposed to die in the ring that night. As you were fighting, words you had spoken to him rang in his heart. He understood then, that you were the one he waited for all those years, and protecting you was what he needed to do. His only regret was that he didn't realize who you were sooner so he and Yuri could have helped you escape before you were forced to fight.

"You see, we expected the Light Bringer to be an elder and a scholar, not a child warrior. He told me he was leaving your care to me because he accomplished the task the One had set for him, and now it was my turn. He was content to die in service to the One.

"He gave me a message for you." The skin at the corners of Jiro's eyes crinkled and a slight smile lifted his lips. He said to tell you, 'Little Warrior Light Bringer do not be sad for Shin. Shin is going to the One. Shin is glad he met you before the One called him home. Someday Shin and Light Bringer will meet again. Then there will be joy, not pain. You will no longer need to battle; but you will be filled with light.'

"It was—it still is—hard to lose my brother. But he wanted you and me to know he was content to serve the One and to help you even at the cost of his life. He went home with the One soon after we spoke. With the help of his friends, I was able to bury him with a simple ceremony. He had several friends in Eleri, including Yuri, and the ceremony was well attended."

Thinking back to that moment in the ring when Shin saved him, sorrow cracked Rayne's voice. "Another person is dead because of me. I tried to talk to him after he saved me. I wanted to ask him why, but they wouldn't let me." Grieved by his inability to protect so many people, Rayne choked back a cry and he shook his head. "No matter what I do, I always manage to bring pain and death to people. People I never knew, people like you and Shin, and Lexi and her father, even my parents are in danger because of me. Shin should have just let me die in that ring. The One could have called forth another Light Bringer, maybe a scholar like you wanted. I'm so sorry."

Jiro looked at Rayne, concern softening his features. "Do not diminish Shin's sacrifice. He had known for the past six years he would forfeit his life to save the Light Bringer. He found peace in that calling. Do not say you should have died; that makes Shin's death meaningless. Live fully as the One's Light Bringer, serve him and his people as you are meant to do. In this way, you honor Shin's gift and you honor Shin's life as well. That is what Shin would want you to do."

Jiro and Rayne sat without speaking, Rayne recalling Shin's final words. Then Jiro said, "Even with what Shin told me, your youth took me by surprise. When he spoke of your fight with Yormund, I imagined someone larger, a more mature if still young, warrior. You need to know it was a great honor for Shin to name you Little Warrior. He would not bestow the title lightly. I found it strange that he would tie the words little and warrior together. Now, after meeting you, I understand why he did."

"I'll never forget him and what he did for me," Rayne said. "I'll try to honor his memory by working to fulfill the prophecy and living a life honoring the One."

Jiro focused his dark eyes on Rayne's amethyst ones, probing their depths. "That is enough. No man can do more than what he is given to do. I am content."

After another few minutes of quiet reflection, Rayne asked, "How did you know I was touched by the Sun Sparrows? How could you know?"

Jiro's wide smile split his face and standing up, he gently grabbed both Rayne's hands and turned them palms up. Rayne's eyes opened wide when his sleeves fell back and he noticed for the first time a faint glow of golden light highlighting the scars on his wrists, the ones Ponce had put there over the years. Now they blended together into a muted reminder of the golden light that enveloped Rayne when the sparrows landed on him.

"We were climbing and hiking all day in the sunlight. I hadn't noticed."

"The light will shine brighter in the dark," Jiro said. "Through the Sun Sparrow's tiny golden glow, the One reminds you that darkness will never win as long as there is even a small light."

"But how did you know?" Rayne asked, still not understanding how Jiro could know about the faint glow.

"When the One called me, he said, 'You will know my Light Bringer by this: Even the little sparrows will acknowledge him. He will bring the light of my Words to Veres. In the darkness, he will be a beacon for the people, pointing them to the Son.'

"I wasn't sure about you or the light until just this moment. But Shin had been certain even without the Sun Sparrow light, and I trusted his certainty, until I was sure for myself."

Rayne looked down at the faint golden light surrounding his hands, still grappling with what his eyes were telling him. Jiro broke him out of his thoughts. "But come, I'm sure your friends are concerned for your absence. Let us not keep them waiting any longer."

43

As they walked out into the hallway Jiro said, "Do not take offense if the other elders, especially First Eldest Tegan and Elder Powell, seem cold to you and do not readily accept you as Light Bringer. The people of Caarwyn Rill are very steeped in traditions. Authority is bestowed according to age. Our elders are respected because we honor the wisdom gained by long life.

"For many generations the elders have taught that the Light Bringer would appear as an aged scholar with great wisdom. Lacking any written Words from the One, they clung to smatterings of old prophecies and pronouncements passed down from previous elders. Your youth will challenge their preconceived notions of what the Light Bringer should be. It is easier for me to accept because Shin and I came from Glacieria and were exposed to prophecies preserved there. Shin believed you were the chosen Light Bringer. And now I have seen the Sun Sparrow's light. Yet even with that, I struggle to adapt my prior beliefs of how the One's chosen Light Bringer would appear, to the reality of you. It will not be so easy for the other elders."

Walking back down the hallway, Rayne noticed people bustling about in the large room where they entered earlier, setting out the heavy, age-darkened, oak tables and chairs that had lined the walls. Rayne's stomach growled at the mouth-watering aromas coming through the door.

Jiro laughed. "The villagers of Caarwyn Rill are setting up the gathering space; we will eat soon Light Bringer."

"Rayne. Please call me Rayne."

Jiro nodded in acquiescence.

As Rayne walked in the door of the room where the others were waiting, First Eldest Tegan was speaking. "And so, for the last four-hundred years Caarwyn Rill has been a place of study."

Shaw nodded eagerly. "Yes, like the communities of study on Arisima. That is how we knew the prophesied Light Bringer was coming at this time."

Owain picked up the train of thought. "The coming of the twins from Glacieria, Jiro and Shin, was a turning point for us. We knew the Light Bringer would follow soon after and they would recognize him."

Turning to Jiro, Owain continued. "Elder Jiro, what do you think? Is this youth truly the Light Bringer we have been awaiting?"

Jiro nodded. "Yes, as Shin said, this young man is indeed the One's chosen Light Bringer." Then he embarrassed Rayne by grabbing one of his hands and, pointing out the glow showing past his shirt sleeve, repeated what he had said earlier. "'You will know my Light Bringer by this, even the little sparrows will acknowledge him. He will bring the light of my Words to Veres. In the darkness, he will be a beacon for the people, pointing them to the Son.'"

Elder Owain smiled and Elder Afon's eyes got as large as full moons. But Elder Powell looked unconvinced. First Eldest Tegan frowned and said, "But he's so young."

Shaw rose and quoted to the group, "'And in the thirtieth generation the Light Bringer will come from the blessed line. In his sixteenth year, he will cling to the One and he will grow in wisdom and strength to fulfill his destiny and seal the living darkness. He will bring light to the people of the worlds of Ochen.' This is one of the prophecies we have studied on Arisima for generations.

"We know Prince Rayne, the son of King Theodor, is the thirtieth generation from King Nathan, the blessed line. He is now in his sixteenth year and has been growing in wisdom and the strength of the One in ways that have amazed me. He may be young, but he is the chosen Light Bringer. He has already taken on the mantel of Light Bringer on Corylus. We who travel with him can all attest to the One acknowledging him there."

"Yeah," Silas added. "The One spoke to us here on Veres too. 'This is my Light Bringer. I have sent him to bring you the message of forgiveness through my Son. Listen to him. His words are light in the darkness.' That's what he said, and I've never heard anything like his voice before."

"These words are new to us. We will consider them and their import," First Eldest Tegan said in a reserved tone. "In the meantime, I believe our people have already assembled in the gathering space for prayers and the evening meal. You are welcome to join us."

With her back stiff and straight, First Eldest Tegan led the way into the large room. The tables and chairs had all been set and a fire licked huge logs in the fireplace. Beautiful prismatic lanterns like the one Rayne had admired when he spoke with Jiro cast vivid light in myriad colors sparkling off the ceilings and walls.

Rayne had never seen anything like the lanterns before. With just tiny wicks, the cut glass lanterns threw an amazing amount of the colorful light. Each of the eight tables set around the room was lit by only one but their combined light shown like a full sun was blazing on the ceiling.

When the elders entered the room, all the villagers stopped what they were doing and stared. First Eldest Tegan raised her hands for silence. "Before we begin our evening prayers, my friends, I will introduce our visitors."

Tegan pointed out each person as she made introductions. "I welcome first a friend you all know, Cai of Mistal. Lady

Alexianndra Erland, daughter of Duke Erland, and Silas, a friend of Cai's and Lady Alexianndra's are all fellow Verenians."

Murmuring flowed across the room, but with a stern look from Tegan the voices quieted, and she continued. "From Corylus I would like to introduce Lord Thorvin Kraftsmunn; Shaw Radinajan, originally a native of Arisima; Anne Parsons, who was originally a native Verenian; brother and sister Stevie and Sashi Kasper. And this young man," she gestured in Rayne's direction, "is Prince Rayne of Corylus."

The whispers of many voices rose in volume like the sound of strong wind filtered through pine boughs, as questions were voiced between the villagers. Another stern look from the first eldest quieted the room once again. With the introductions done, Tegan waved the travelers toward the tables. "Please join us for prayers and our evening meal."

Tegan nodded to Powell who led the people in two hymns of praise and thanksgiving Rayne had never heard before. He glanced at Shaw in question, but Shaw shook his head and shrugged.

After the hymns, Tegan prayed. "We lift our praises to you most holy One, ageless, eldest of all things and most-wise ancient father. By your will Caarwyn was brought into existence, our home and our safe place. We thank you for the wisdom and guidance you have bestowed on us through the years by your chosen elders. In your mercy, you have preserved Caarwyn Rill across the ages, to this very day. We offer our thanksgiving for all the precious blessings you have given this village including the special gift of food we are about to share."

Elder Powell led everyone in a final hymn; the moment was past and people began to stir. Large platters and bowls of steaming food were brought out from the kitchen by several young adults who set them on tables before returning to the kitchen to carry out more serving dishes. Younger children set plates and cups on the tables while teenagers came around with pitchers of water.

Jiro invited Rayne and his friends to make new acquaintances by sitting scattered among the people of Caarwyn Rill.

"I must warn you, though," he said, shifting his feet, "We take our seats by order of eldest to youngest. First Eldest Tegan has requested you follow our tradition as best you can."

Rayne watched as his friends moved to take seats when those of similar ages took theirs. Finally, Stevie and Sashi sat, leaving Lexi and Rayne standing with the other youths. When the teenagers who looked to be about their age began to sit, they took seats as well. Rayne, finding a chair next to Owain had been left open, happily sat next to the friendly elder.

The food was simple but plentiful and Rayne ate to full. It felt good to eat at a table again. He kept studying the lanterns and finally asked Owain, where they came from.

Beaming with pride, Owain answered, "Why, we make them ourselves. The village of Caarwyn Rill has been known for making the most beautiful lanterns in the whole Ochen system for almost six hundred years; ever since the community was founded."

But then Owain's face fell. "At least until this whole nasty business with Sorial began. Now we have no off-world market because the merchants won't recognize us." Smiling again with irrepressible joy Owain continued. "But we haven't let that stop us. We keep making the lanterns. Someday this will all be worked out, so we keep crafting the most beautiful, brightest lanterns and sell what we can locally. The rest we have been storing for the past five years. But, someday." He sighed. "Someday people will remember us. And then our lanterns will once again be in demand through the entire system."

While Rayne talked with Owain, Lexi, seated two tables over from him, watched him furtively from the corner of her eye. She struggled with the emotions he stirred in her. It had been bad enough when she had felt the link and connected with him after he killed Matheson, that quick glimpse into the inner Rayne. Sensing his regret and grief over his past and his desperate need to be loved, his pain at some kind of insurmountable rift between him and his parents. She didn't understand it, but he carried the situation like a weight.

But then the One had spoken into her heart. At least she thought it must be the One. And the words he spoke! 'Lexi, protect my Light Bringer, for his heart and yours are one. You will always know the truth in him, and know him in truth, because you are his and he is yours. My gift of love to you.'

Our hearts are one? She shuddered. *No! I can't love the monster who ruined my life!* She stopped and considered for a moment. *But he isn't a monster, is he? I know that now. But love?*

Looking back over at Rayne, she had to admit she was attracted to him. He wasn't large and heavily muscled in the way most warriors were, like Thorvin. But he was well built, like a mountain panther. She had noticed that even back in the cavern. How could she not, when Seren had taken his shirt off? And his eyes were so deep and ... *stop that!* Lexi berated herself.

Then there were the Sun Sparrows this morning and the way they turned Rayne golden with their light. She couldn't deny that she too had felt the warmth and glow spreading out from him over everyone as he stood on the overlook with his eyes closed and his arms raised. And how humble he was about the whole thing. No, he definitely wasn't the monster she had expected.

Looking back over at Rayne she noticed how hacked up his raven black hair was from when Matheson had chopped his tail off with a sword, leaving the long braid still dangling on the side. *He should get someone to straighten it out, cut it even and take off that silly braid. He would look even more handsome. STOP IT! STOP IT! STOP IT!* Lexi turned away from Rayne. She would not let go of her pride so easily.

Tegan rose from her seat next to Thorvin at the head table. "It is time for sharing. Does anyone have a song or story he or she would like to share tonight?"

Owain stood and announced, "I would like to share a song in honor of our visitors from Corylus. It is said the best ale on the seven worlds comes from Corylus. Well, we haven't been able to enjoy that particular pleasure for many years now, but we make a pretty tasty ale here in Caarwyn Rill. I invite all who would, to fill their glasses, mugs, tankards, or jugs. And when everyone is ready, I'll begin."

One of the heavy oak tables was moved against the wall near the main doors and people lined up at a large tapped barrel set on the table. With much laughter and high spirits, the villagers filled all sorts of containers from small glasses to large tankards. A few men actually filled jugs with the deep brown brew. The heady aroma of dark ale began to drift across the hall.

Stevie was one of the first in line, carrying a large empty glass to the barrel. He stopped next to Rayne on the way and said, "You're not going to turn this down like you did that good ale in Highreach, are you? There's no ice-cold mountain water here now."

Thorvin, coming up behind Stevie, said, "Come on *boy*, let Stevie and me make a man out of you. Here." He thrust a mug into Rayne's hand and helped him to stand, pulling one arm over his shoulder. "Come on, let's enjoy Elder Owain's song."

Shaking his head and laughing, Rayne allowed Thorvin to help him to the barrel and fill his mug. Chairs were moved around so everyone could watch Owain, who was already downing a rather large tankard himself. People moved about the room, congregating with friends or relatives in a more loose-knit fashion then the restricted form taken during the meal. Rayne soon found himself sitting between Lexi and Thorvin.

Once everyone was somewhat settled, Owain began singing a rather noisy drinking song that involved much guzzling of ale, and shouting and stamping of feet, on every refrain. He had a deep rich voice and he danced and winked his way back and forth in front of his appreciative audience. Once he even grabbed one of the ladies sitting in front and twirled her across the floor, dipping elegantly, before twirling her back to her seat amid much loud applause and laughter.

The song ended with a rousing cheer and calls for encore from everyone. Owain agreed but only if everyone emptied their chosen vessels and filled up at the barrel again. Thorvin volunteered to fill Lexi's and Rayne's mugs. Rayne noticed Tegan and Powell were not participating in the fun. They stood to the side, against the wall by the fireplace with stern expressions while talking in muted tones. He marveled at how different Owain was compared to the two. He looked around and found Jiro enjoying the festivities with Cai and a woman from the village, and, after some more searching, saw Afon standing in line waiting to fill her tankard.

Thorvin returned with the mugs and Rayne passed one to Lexi. Their fingers touched for a moment and he found himself looking into her gold flecked eyes. This time she didn't turn away so quickly and Rayne quirked a half-smile at her.

Stupid, he thought as he turned quickly away. *She probably thinks I'm stupid for even thinking she could like me.*

Owain began his song again. And then another. Rayne was thoroughly enjoying the drinking parts this time and before the song was done, he realized his mug was empty. He thought about asking Thorvin to fill it again, but then people were clearing the area, wiping down the tables and chairs and pushing them back against the walls.

Looking to his right where Lexi was sitting, he gave her a loopy grin and was not disappointed when she kind of smiled back. He noticed her mug was empty as well. It had been a wonderful evening and Rayne was sad it was coming to an end.

When he reached for his staff to stand, he was surprised when he almost fell. His balance was not what it should be and he plopped back down on the chair. His eyes felt scratchy and tired. But then Thorvin was beside him with the staff and a helping hand. "I do believe you're drunk, Sire."

He laughed as Rayne tried to focus on his face. "Yes, you are indeed quite drunk. Well, it's no wonder considering you downed six of those mugs and I don't think I've ever seen you drink before."

"Wha ... I only had two."

"And how many songs did you drink through?"

"Two, two songs. Yeah, two songs," Rayne mumbled, though everything seemed rather fuzzy.

Laughing heartily, Thorvin said, "Yep, his Royal Highness

is definitely drunk. The singing has been going on for almost three hours and you, my prince, have had six mugs. Here, let me help you up to our room."

On their way out of the gathering space, Thorvin stopped by Anne and asked her to make sure Lexi also had help to her room. "It seems the young lady and our prince decided to see who could drink more. We'll have to watch these two in the future."

Anne looked over to where Lexi was leaning in her chair, "Yes, I see what you mean. I'll get her to our room. At least Stevie and Sashi used common sense and stopped after two glasses. So not all of our young people were foolish tonight."

Shaw added, "I'm surprised at Prince Rayne; he doesn't normally drink."

Thorvin chuckled. "Well, the boy is growing up after all."

"Hey, I heard that. Doan' call me boy," Rayne mumbled.

Smiling, Thorvin steered Rayne toward the wing where they had been given rooms for the night. "Of course, Your Highness, I won't call you boy."

Thorvin helped Rayne up to their room on the second floor, just above the room where Rayne had talked with Jiro. Rayne collapsed onto a bed.

⟡

Thorvin carefully pulled Rayne's boots off then his jacket and covered him with a blanket. Thorvin grunted and pulled the blanket back, staring at the golden glow that surrounded Rayne like a cocoon. "What a marvel," he whispered as he lowered the blanket again.

Shaw, Stevie, Cai, and Silas quietly entered the room while Thorvin was helping Rayne to bed.

"That is truly incredible," Shaw said, pointing at Rayne. "Do you know, Cai, will that light be with him permanently now, or will it fade in time?"

Cai shook his head. "I don't know. I've never heard of anything like this happening before. Jiro knew about it, so when he noticed the glow on His Highness' wrists, he knew what it was. But even he didn't have more to say. It truly is amazing how much brighter it gets in the dark. I hadn't noticed it during the day, but now I can't see how we could have missed it."

"Well, I hope he can turn it down some so we can sleep," Stevie said through a yawn.

Thorvin stood next to his bed for a moment, looking at Rayne. He grimaced. "This isn't going to work." He stalked to Rayne's bed and pulled the blanket over his shoulders and up to his chin to block out most of the light. Once they were settled, Thovin put out the lantern and climbed into his bed. A faint glow emanated from Rayne's blanket, but it was soft and soothing and soon the room was filled with the sounds of quiet snoring.

44

Rayne opened his eyes to soft, pine-filtered sunshine streaming in through two large windows in the wall beyond his bed. With a groan, he closed his eyes again. He grabbed his blanket, pulled it up over his head, and turned over.

He wondered where exactly he was. He couldn't remember getting into bed last night. In fact, the last thing he remembered was Lexi's smile. *Oh, yeah, that's right. We were singing that song about the drunk cow and the angry rooster ... I think.* His head pounded like a beaten drum and attempting to think made the pounding worse. Then cruel hands were pulling the blanket away.

"No! No!" he begged, yanking the end of the blanket back to his chest and rolling over onto it. "No, leave me be. Give me back my blanket and leave me alone."

"Good morning, sunshine," Thorvin rumbled in his ear in a sing-songy voice that sounded scary. *Good old Thorvin. He can make anything sound scary.*

Thorvin pulled the blanket out from under Rayne, flipping him over in the process. Rayne groaned again as he flung his arms over his eyes.

"You missed Lauds boy; slept right through it."

Opening one eye, Rayne groaned again. "When are you going to stop calling me *boy*. You've promised a million times to stop it, yet you keep doing it. You have no respect. And stop yelling."

Letting go of the blanket, Thorvin sat on the edge of Rayne's bed and reached for a cup of something from the night stand. "Here, drink this, *Your Highness*."

Rayne propped himself up on one elbow and sniffed at the cup. "Yuck! That smells awful! You want me to drink this?"

"Trust me. It'll help your head."

With a deep breath, Rayne grabbed the cup and holding his nose with one hand drank the contents of the cup down as quickly as he could, almost choking on the last of the liquid. Tears streamed from his eyes as he handed the cup back to Thorvin. Whatever he had just ingested, it tasted similar to coffee but it was thick and laced with some combination of herbs. When it first hit Rayne's stomach he thought the drink was going to come back up, but it settled and he began to feel better. The pain in his head diminished and he felt less fuzzy.

Looking around the room Rayne realized he was in the last of five beds set in a row along one wall with night stands next to each bed, and a lantern set on the middle night stand. The other side of the room was a mirror image. The walls and floor were of whitewashed wide wood planks, except for the outside wall which was smoothed logs, the same as in the other rooms.

Five other beds looked like they had been slept in, but Thorvin was the only one still in the room with Rayne now.

"Where's everyone else?" he asked Thorvin.

"Downstairs. Eating breakfast. Come on, I'll help you."

Rayne pulled on his boots, taking special care with the right one, and grabbed the jacket Thorvin was holding for him. After he got his jacket on, Thorvin pulled him upright and once Rayne had a grip on the staff, helped him to the door and down the stairs into the gathering space where they had eaten yesterday.

The other companions were sitting around the one table still set out. From the look of things, they had already finished eating. He sat down between Stevie and Silas and was handed a plate heaped with slices of bread and a mound of bacon. Anne smirked with a knowing look as she handed him a honey jar.

Rayne smiled his thanks back at her and began to make up his favorite breakfast sandwich. But his stomach lurched and with a groan, he dropped everything. It was depressing. He finally had bread, bacon, and honey again, but he couldn't stomach eating it. So, he just nibbled at a piece of dry bread and took tiny sips from a cup of black coffee.

He was finishing his bread when Elders Jiro, Owain, and Afon emerged from the door leading into the other wing. Rayne remembered someone telling him last night that was the elders' private wing. Except for the kitchen which was just beyond the door, the rest of the wing was reserved for the village elders. No one else was allowed back there without permission.

As the three walked to the table, Sashi rose from her seat and began clapping. "Thank you again, Elder Owain, for a wonderful evening. Your songs were brilliant."

Elder Owain bowed as well, his eyes twinkling. "And I thank you my dear. It warms my heart to be appreciated."

Thorvin grumbled, "I don't think your First Eldest Tegan or Elder Powell were impressed by your singing, Elder Owain."

With a rueful expression, Owain nodded. "Yes, Lord Kraftsmunn, you have grasped the situation well. I was reminded this morning that elders should, of necessity, maintain decorum at all times. In fact, Elder Afon and I are here as a penance for our behavior last night. To make amends, we have been charged with your care while you are with us. Although neither Elder Afon nor I perceive this as a punishment,"

A shy smile worked its way out on Elder Afon's red face. "We both are quite delighted to act as your guides while you are here."

Looking to Jiro, Thorvin asked, "And what about you Elder Jiro? Are you being punished also?"

Shaking his head, Jiro said, "No, I am here because I

volunteered to be here. Along with Elder Owain and Elder Afon, I too look forward to getting to know you all better."

He paused for a moment looking around at the group, then with a broad smile lighting his eyes, said, "I have something special planned for this morning. Outsiders aren't normally allowed access to Caarwyn Rill's healing spring, but because of Prince Rayne's injury, I have obtained permission from First Eldest Tegan for you all to join Elders Owain, Afon, and me in visiting the spring this morning. Although it's not a hard or long hike, I have arranged transportation for Prince Rayne. I believe the rest of you are capable of walking?"

After receiving nods all around, Jiro continued. "First Eldest Tegan has also agreed to provide you all with new garments so you won't have to wear your dirty clothing once you have spent time in the spring. The water brings healing and warmth and it would be a shame to put dirty clothes back on after the experience. And while you are wearing your new attire, we can see to it that your dirty clothing is cleaned and repaired."

"Clean anything sounds wonderful at this point." Sashi sighed. Anne and Lexi nodded their agreement.

"Oh, I don't know." A look of wide-eyed innocence crossed Stevie's face. "I mean, what's wrong with what we have on?" He made a show of sniffing his arm pit before twirling into a fake faint on the floor.

Anne and Lexi giggled, but Sashi rolled her eyes. "Nemora's moons Stevie, you're so immature."

Elder Owain laughed out loud, a warm, friendly sound. "This is just what I hoped for, youthful spirits enjoying life. Oh, I am so glad I'm being punished."

Laughing, Sashi skipped over to Elder Owain and gave him a hug. "I really like your attitude, Elder Owain. People who can't smile or laugh are so boooring! I'm glad you're going to be with us today. Maybe you can even sing while we're walking."

"Oh no," Owain said, folding his hands in front of his round face. "I will refrain from singing until First Eldest Tegan and Elder Powell have forgiven me for last night's performance."

Then, with a mischievous look, he added, "But it *was* such fun, wasn't it?"

"How did you ever get to be an Elder?" Rayne asked. "You're nothing like First Eldest Tegan or Elder Powell. Don't you have to be serious to be an elder?"

"Not at all." Afon spoke up. "It is strictly a matter of age. Unfortunately for First Eldest Tegan and Elder Powell, Elder Owain and I tend to be very young at heart in spite of our age. This is not the first time we've had to do penance for indecorous behavior and it probably won't be the last. Even Third Elder Jiro, who is younger than we are, is more likely to behave more circumspectly then Elder Owain and I."

"Then how did Third Elder Jiro get to be Third Elder if he's younger than you?" Rayne asked.

"It's an honorary position the last first eldest placed on Jiro before he died. When he realized the One had sent Elder Jiro and his brother Shin to us, and that Elder Jiro was a scholar, he felt it was the proper course to take," Afon explained.

"Prince Rayne's transportation will be arriving any time now so Elders Owain and Afon and I will wait for you out front," Jiro said. "Just come out when you're ready."

A short while later, as everyone assembled at the foot of the Elders' House steps, a man led a very shaggy, brown and white pony pulling a small cart toward them.

"Ah," Jiro exclaimed. "Here is your transportation, Your Highness."

The man came to a stop in front of Jiro. "Now you be sure to take good care of my Posey, Elder Jiro. You know how much she means to me."

Rayne looked at the shaggy pony and its cart with suspicion and said to the man, "No disrespect, Sir, but are you sure Posey will be able to pull that cart with me in it?"

The man scowled at Rayne and huffed. "You and two more of you without a problem. No worries young sir. Posey may be small but she's strong; she's mountain pony through and through. As long as you're gentle with her, she'll do what needs to be done."

With a final admonition for Jiro to take care of Posey, the man stalked off.

At first Rayne was unsure about the arrangement, but once they started moving he realized the small pony had no problem pulling his weight. Jiro led Posey, so Rayne didn't have to do anything except lie back and enjoy the ride. He took advantage of the situation, leisurely studying his surroundings. Most of the hardwoods were left behind soon after leaving the village and they were now moving through heavy pines and dark-needled firs with little growing beneath their heavy canopy. The fragrance of pine needles impregnated the air and the sun filtered through the high branches in shafts of muted light. The rustlings of small creatures and birds shifting about in the trees lulled him.

There was one birdsong in particular that caught Rayne's attention. The tiny creature seemed to follow them as it sang a full sweet song over and over again, a series of rising notes that ended with a whistle. The melody reminded him of the woods around Westvale and he felt a twinge of sorrow as the recollection stirred thoughts of his parents. His stomach clenched with the hurt of being renounced. He still hadn't told his friends about that; he couldn't face admitting to them that he was disinherited, and Brayden was now crown prince.

How could they do that to me? I thought they loved me. Realization barreled into him and dropped into the pit of his stomach like a rock. *How long has it been since I prayed for my parents?* His time on Sorial and Veres had been so full, but that was no excuse. He closed his eyes and began to pray for his father and mother. But after only a couple minutes, he started to sense Lexi's father's need like a pressure in his mind.

Unsure how to pray for the duke, Rayne asked for guidance. He knew Lexi struggled with guilt over thinking it would be better if her father died rather than continuing to live the way he was. But Rayne couldn't pray for death; it just didn't seem right. He prayed for wisdom to know how to pray and trusted the One to bring his will to pass in his perfect way.

As Rayne prayed, the aromatic scent of the pines faded. In its place a stench of decay and hopelessness rose. The atmosphere turned dark and heavy as a long-buried memory took hold like a strong current dragging him below the surface of the Cameron Sea. His heart beat with a violent intensity and his breathing became shallow. He lost himself in the terror of the memory. It rose up like a specter from the year he had spent with Sigmund.

He was in a shadow-filled, loathsome hole beneath Sigmund's manor house. The stench of his own body and excrement stung his nose and he felt again the cold clammy red clay his face rested on. He couldn't move. He remembered. His mind worked. He could see. He could hear. But try as he would, he couldn't move even one finger. He was trapped.

Then he heard Ponce's voice from somewhere above him, "What do you think Master? He's been down there three days now."

"That long? Truly?" Sigmund's voice thrummed with power. "I suppose that's long enough to know that the paralysis spike functions well." Sigmund released a contented sigh. "It's been so long since I used one, I had forgotten how effective a tool it is. Elegant, but draining; it does require quite a large expenditure of energy to properly place a spike.

"That was a marvelous stroke of inspiration on your part, Master Sigmund."

"Naturally. It was an excellent solution to the situation created by our disobedient little bird." Sigmund chuckled. "And it has also provided an amusing, if odiferous, form of punishment for the boy as well. His failure to perform as instructed embarrassed me in front of William. I can't have that now, can I?"

"If we leave him down there much longer, he might die, Master," Ponce whined. "And I want to play with him again tonight. It's been three days. Have you made your decision?"

"Yes. I've decided there's no need to return to Veres. William's recalcitrant duke isn't going to give him any more problems. The spike will continue to be quite effective until it is destroyed, which will be never."

From the corner of his eye Rayne saw Sigmund's hand motioning in the air the way it did when he was executing a weave. Even in his state, he could feel dark energy pulsing from Sigmund as he pulled power into himself, redirecting it. Suddenly Rayne could move again. Only he couldn't move. Now his body was willing, but he didn't have the strength to do more than lift his head and drop it again, back onto the slimy clay earth.

"Send a servant down for the slave. He will need cleaning up before he will be ready to come into our presence this evening. In fact, send Alrick down for him. Have Alrick bathe him several times and make sure the hair is shiny clean before dressing him for company."

"Company?" Ponce asked.

"Special company tonight," Sigmund said. "A very old and powerful friend. I would like him to examine our little Wren. Yes he ..."

The rest of the memory faded. Tall, dark pines again surrounded Rayne, and fresh mountain air filled his lungs as he sucked in a panicked breath. Jiro was looking down at him, anxiety creasing his forehead. Thorvin's concerned face came into focus and Rayne, heart still beating a frenzied rhythm, realized he was asking a question. "... okay?"

Rayne caught just the last word, but he nodded. "I'm fine." Then shaking the haze from his mind, he added, "I'm sorry if I scared you. I must have drifted off. Just a nightmare, it was just a nightmare. I'm fine."

"Nightmare or another memory?" Thorvin asked, his eyes boring into Rayne. "Jiro said you began breathing hard and whimpering. Was it Sigmund again?"

Rayne hung his head still struggling with what he had just relived. "Yes," he barely whispered. "I think I remembered something. And no, I don't want to talk about it."

Looking back up, embarrassment sent heat up into Rayne's face. Everyone was staring at him with varying looks of alarm. His friends were at least somewhat familiar with his past, but the elders, Silas, Cai, and Lexi looked alarmed. *They probably think I'm crazy.* He caught Lexi's eye and a connection sparked in his mind. If what he just remembered was real, he knew the truth of what happened to Lexi's father. But he wouldn't say anything until he was certain, so he repeated, "I'm fine. Let's keep moving. Please."

A few minutes later they stopped in front of a tiny building. Built of wood stained a beautiful golden color, it sported two identical, adjacent front doors, fashioned out of the same amber-hued wood and painted with a pine tree design.

45

Breaking the silence Rayne's episode triggered, Jiro said, "Here we are. I need to explain some rules before we enter." The companions gathered around Jiro, giving him their attention. "This hot spring is sacred to the people of Caarwyn Rill, so I must ask you to refrain from pranks while we are here. The bath house door to the left is for men and the door to the right is for women. The spring itself is screened, one side for women and the other for men. Please abide by the restriction.

"Lexi, Anne, and Sashi, Elder Afon will enter with you and explain what you need to know. Cai, Silas, Thorvin, and Prince Rayne, please follow Elder Owain. He will direct you and answer any questions you may have. I will join you once I take care of Posey.

"We planned to spend a couple hours here for you to enjoy the hot spring before continuing up to a high meadow where we will have lunch. Once again, as this is a sacred place, please keep talking to a minimum and voices low."

The ladies followed Afon in through their door and Owain led the men while Jiro walked to a small fenced area to set Posey free to graze.

The bath house was simple on the inside, just a few wooden benches and cubicles for their clothes. Rayne bit back a comment when Elder Owain, Cai, and Silas stripped completely. Shaw's face turned a serious shade of red, but he stripped as well, and, with a shrug, Stevie followed their example. Thorvin, seeing Rayne's hesitation, said, "You going to be okay with this? I know you don't like people seeing your back. You want to leave your shirt on?"

"No," Rayne replied. "It's okay."

Jiro walked in as Rayne was pulling off his shirt and Rayne froze, feeling exposed. Jiro politely made no comment as he walked past Rayne. Silas, Cai, Stevie, and Shaw had already trailed Elder Owain through a low door into a darkened area. Thorvin and Rayne followed with Elder Jiro.

Rayne's eyes grew wide at his first glimpse of the hot spring. Small, trimmed shrubs and tiny trees of varying heights were scattered in organized disarray around the half of the spring on their side of an opaque screen that separated the ladies' bath from the men's. Beyond the shrubs, a short distance from the spring, rose huge pine trees whose boughs overshadowed the pool casting the whole in a mottled, shaded light. Rocks of diverse sizes and colors ranging from pale blue to deep burgundy surrounded the edge of the spring. Some rose to heights that dwarfed Rayne while others were submerged to be used as seats in the water. Several small prismatic lanterns were set on rocks at various levels giving off muted light in the shadows. Steam, rising in the air with wispy white tendrils, gave the whole a dreamlike feel.

But more than the beauty, the heat struck Rayne. As he limped through the low opening out to the pool it enveloped him, drawing droplets of sweat out onto his skin. Selecting one of the submerged rocks to sit on, Rayne hobbled toward it appreciating the ease with which he could move through the water despite his injury. The moment he lowered his body into the hot water he felt aches and pains easing. Once seated, he wrapped his hands around his thigh, gently kneading the muscles beneath the newly re-scabbed wound. He relaxed into the warmth and the gentle embrace of the water, smelling a faint metallic scent mingling with the fragrance of the pines.

"What's the distinctive odor?" he asked Owain, who was sitting near him.

"The healing minerals in the spring. It is the combination of heat and minerals that makes it so effective. You should spend time here each day you are with us, to speed the healing of your leg."

Few words were spoken over the next two hours as everyone alternated between soaking in the hot water and laying on wooden benches in the mottled shade. There was a fountain near the pool with cool, fresh drinking water and Jiro and Owain encouraged everyone to drink as much as they could to help flush poisons from their bodies. From time to time, Rayne heard the murmur of voices from the other side of the screen, but it was impossible to tell who was talking, the voices were so low.

The morning passed quickly, and Rayne blinked in surprise when Jiro announced that it was time to leave. Owain whispered through the separating screen, alerting the women.

The elders had gifted the companions with simple clothing, wide-legged trousers that tied at the waist; tunics that fell loosely to the top of the thighs with long, wide sleeves; and long, robe-like, sleeveless over garments. The tunics and trousers were tan while the over garments were a deep green, almost black.

Thorvin growled about the length of the over garment and the wide sleeves on the tunic. "Impossible to fight wearing this." But with a grimace, he complied and dressed. When the women joined them in front of the bath house, they were wearing the same deep green outer garments but underneath they wore simple shifts of the same tan material as the men's tunics and trousers.

Time in the hot spring had done much to ease the pain in Rayne's leg. And though he still needed the staff, walking wasn't as painful.

Jiro harnessed Posey and soon they were ready to continue up the path to the clearing where the elders insisted they must eat the midday meal. They traveled for only about a half-hour before they rounded a clump of rocks that looked like fingers pointing to the sky and Rayne saw why Owain insisted they eat there. The mountain fell away beneath them in waves of green to the valley below. Interspersed among the evergreens and hardwoods were flowering trees that looked like clouds of white and pink. Part way down the mountain side, the scattered trees gave way to fields of grasses and flowering plants. Swaths of red and yellow colored the slope, intensified by the surrounding greens.

Blankets were already spread in the high meadow with baskets of food set out on them. Seeing Rayne's look, Owain winked at him and a broad smile split his face. "Always make prior arrangements for food."

Though the meal was made up of leftovers from last night's supper, the food was tasty and filling. After spending a morning at the healing spring, everyone had a healthy appetite and they all ate well. The tranquil atmosphere from the spring lingered and no one seemed inclined to talk much.

When they were done eating, Jiro showed Stevie and Sashi a path they could take that would circle them up around another lookout and then back to this meadow. They took off with Cai and Silas following. Anne and Shaw sat on one of the blankets holding hands and talking quietly with the Elders. From time to time Rayne heard Owain's generous laugh or Afon's lighter chuckle. Thorvin, left his outer garment on the blanket near Rayne and, still grumbling about the stupid clothing, walked off looking for a place to work some sword forms.

Rayne laid back, his hands behind his head, letting his mind wander as he watched white fluffy clouds drift across the brilliant sky, until he heard a throat clear. Shading his eyes with one hand, he looked toward the sound and saw Lexi. Pointing to a spot next to him on the blanket, she asked, "Would you like some company?"

Rayne sat up and shifted over. Lexi sat down next to him, looking out into the distance. He glanced over at her profile as she focused on the panorama of the valley spread out before them. Time spent in the sun was turning Lexi's skin an even deeper shade of honey brown and Rayne noticed her tiny nose was now covered with a smattering of freckles.

At that moment, Lexi turned to him and his heart raced. He was staring into the incredible golden eyes he had dreamed of all those weeks ago. She startled as their eyes met and then quickly turned back to the panorama, chewing her lower lip. Rayne had already discovered that when Lexi was nervous, she would do that, chew her bottom lip. It reminded him of Elsie. Rayne remembered seeing her do the same thing on occasion, when she was deep in thought.

ᴎ

"I wanted to ask you something." Lexi hesitated, glanced at Rayne, then turned back to look out over the valley once again. "When you thought that Matheson had killed me, and you did that sense thing? And I followed your line back? You explained the next day that was how I suddenly knew ... well, I was in your head. I saw things, felt things. I learned a lot about you in just an instant."

Lexi looked back at Rayne, eyes searching his. "I don't know how to ask this exactly, but ... what happened between you and your parents? I mean, not to pry, but I know it's something that's pressing on you so hard." Lexi's voice lowered. "I mean, the pain I felt in you was so raw and deep. It scared me. But at the same time, I ... I don't know why, I wanted to help you."

Rayne stared out over the valley, not acknowledging Lexi's question for several minutes. She began to wonder if he had even heard her or if he was angry because she invaded his thoughts.

But then he spoke, his voice soft and sad. "The night I returned to Westvale, after Mother destroyed the wire; flashes, impressions from my childhood before I was taken flooded my mind. But like the rest of my memories, what I now have is fragmented. I guess there will always be gaps, holes to be filled. But over time as things have triggered recollections, some of the missing pieces have begun filling in."

Lexi looked over to see Rayne twining and untwining his fingers as he spoke. In the sunlight, the Sun Sparrow glow was barely visible. But knowing what to look for now, Lexi could see it pulsing as Rayne spoke. It highlighted all the scars on his wrists and hands and she shivered thinking about how he came to be so scarred.

"I didn't remember I had a cousin at first; but I do. Brayden. He's older than I am, about eight years older, I think. When he returned to Westvale a few months ago, memories of him began to surface. I'll never understand why, but even when I was only four or five he hated me."

Rayne turned to Lexi, his eyes dark with sorrow. "I mean he really *despised* me. I don't know why, what I might have done to him to make him hate me so, even back then. Anyway, he's the one who told Lord William I was coming to Veres, the reason we were captured. And he's the one who paid Lord William to make sure I died in the fight with Yormund.

Turning, Rayne looked back over the valley. "Brayden has always had some kind of influence over my parents. I don't know how he does it because my mother is a master mage and my father is not easily manipulated. But whatever he's done to them, he's been doing it for a long time and they're completely unaware. And it's all because of me, to create a rift between my parents and me. He was about to be named official Adopted Heir Apparent when I returned. He must have been furious then. Now, he's somehow convinced my parents to disown me and give him my title. He wants that power, that position. But more than just wanting it, he wants to take it *from me*. For him it's always been about taking everything *from me*.

"I haven't told my friends any of this yet. I can't face that. But now you know. What those boys told you the night you rescued us from the gaming complex is true. Lord William told me my cousin is now Crown Prince of Corylus and all Ochen. I'm not a prince anymore; I'm not even a son."

Rayne paused, shaking his head, sadness pulling the corners of his mouth. "Right before I left to come here, the rift between my parents and me had grown so severe that I moved out of the palace, trying to ease the tension. I hoped that if I left, Brayden would loosen his hold on them. But it was hard to leave; I had only been back for such a short time. For the first time since I was five, I had a normal life. I felt the love of parents. But Brayden took it from me; he couldn't even let me have that."

Rayne breathed deeply and then released the air slowly, like he was letting go of more than just a breath of air. "But the One called me to come here. I had to set the situation with Brayden and my parents aside until I fulfilled my role as Light Bringer. And now I'm also committed to face your tribunal after I've recovered all the scrolls and bound this living darkness thing. I may never see my parents again. It's so hard." Rayne looked over and caught Lexi's eyes. "Because of the way we connected, you more than anyone else, know just how much it takes for me to keep moving forward when my heart wants to turn and run back home, confront Brayden, see my mother and father again, help them. And ... feel *wanted* again."

Lexi, seeing the depth of pain and need in Rayne's eyes, dropped her own heart guard a notch and said, "My mother died when I was born so I never got to know her. I guess that's why my father and I were so close. We were the only family we had. He always made me feel so wanted and loved, that I never had to doubt his feelings."

"When I first returned to Westvale, after those ten years of believing Sigmund's lies, before Brayden came back, I felt that way. Loved. Wanted. Now, I just want that back. Brayden can have the throne. I don't care about that. Let him be crown prince; let him be king. I don't need those things. But I do need my mother and father to care about me again. Growing up believing Sigmund's lies that I had been despised by parents who never cared for me, made feeling the love of my real parents so much more precious. To lose it after such a short time hurts."

"When my father was injured ..." Lexi paused and looked at Rayne. Then sucking in a deep breath and working to ground her emotions, she continued. "When my father was injured, I lost my father *and* my best friend. I miss him so much. I still talk to him just like he can hear me."

"Maybe he can," Rayne said.

"Is that wishful thinking on your part?" Lexi's eyes

flashed, and familiar anger bubbled in her chest. "So you don't have to feel guilty?" Then she stopped, and her eyes grew wide as the hot anger went cold. "I'm sorry. I'm probably going to struggle with my feelings about you for a while yet. It's like you're two different people; the despicable ghost I lived with for so long, and the you I'm coming to know. Anyway, I hope you're right and he can hear me. I like to think he knows when I sit with him and that he's missing me while I'm away now."

Looking around, Lexi's thoughts turned to memories of outings with her father. "I would love to bring him up here. I don't think he's ever been up on Caarwyn, but I know he would love it. I wonder if the healing spring would help him in some way. I mean, if we could get him up here."

"Do you pray for him?" Rayne asked.

"I used to. When he was first injured, I prayed all the time. But then I grew angry with the One. He never answered my prayers, so I just stopped praying. Until you came and things started to change. It was like I forgot there was such a thing as prayer. The mining guild kept getting stronger, the smoke heavier, and the fog thicker. I think we all stopped praying, like there was a veredium ceiling between us and the One. I knew my father taught me about the One, to have faith and trust him. But after the anger took hold, the One just seemed so unreal."

"Have you started praying again?"

"Some. After hearing his voice and then what happened to you and me when we saw the Son. I'm afraid though. I think he must be angry with me for denying him all this time."

A broad smile lit Rayne's face. "He forgives. That's what the Son has done for the One's people. He paid the penalty for all those things we've done that separate us from the One. So even if we ignored him for a long time, or lived in darkness, or even had the darkness growing in us, once we acknowledge the Son, he accepts us. We feel his love. I don't know what I would do if I didn't have the One's love, especially now. I know he loves me and wants me, despite my history and the brokenness that still haunts me. That doesn't mean I don't still want my mother's and father's love, I do. But for now, when they're so cold and angry with me, he's my strength. As long as I trust him, in spite of everything, I find peace and joy in living for him."

"But you're his Light Bringer. Doesn't that make things different for you? You're special."

"No, not really. I'm no more special than anyone else. All of the One's people are set apart for a purpose. I just have a different job than most people. But I'm a normal person. The One doesn't love me any more than any other of his children. He loves you just as much as he does me and that love is immense beyond measure for all of us."

"Well, if he loves his people so much, why does he let awful things happen? My father believed and look what happened to him. Look at you. What about all the terrible things that happened to you? You never wanted to kill people, or hurt my father, but you're still going to be punished for doing what Sigmund forced you to do. And it doesn't look like Sigmund's going to be punished any time soon."

"I can't change what happened in the past, but I can choose how I will live in the future." Rayne glanced back over the expanse before them then settled his eyes on Lexi again. "I know it's hard and I can't say I really understand, but Warren used to tell me that the One works a perfect will and his plan is grander than anything we can understand here in this life. Sometimes it seems unfair. Sometimes to work his perfect will, his people suffer here. But when we pass from this life into eternity, all that we suffered here, the pain and injustice, will seem as nothing compared to what we will experience then. I mean, I don't know anything about childbirth, but Warren said it's kind of like that. When it's happening, its painful; but after the baby has come, all the pain is forgotten in the joy of having the child."

Lexi sat looking out over the valley, thinking about what Rayne said. Everything was so confusing. So many things had happened in the last few weeks. But the thing that surprised her the most was how her feelings for Rayne were changing. She felt a peace sitting with him now. It felt good. Right.

Lexi glanced over at Rayne sitting with his eyes closed, head tilted to feel the sun on his face. She wondered what it must have been like to grow up the way he had, with so much pain and horror. Thinking about it sent a shudder through her. She wasn't ready to know more about that part of him. The moment when they connected after Matheson's death was enough for now.

Stevie, Sashi, Cai, and Silas returned while Rayne and Lexi were talking. After waving to Rayne and Lexi, the four joined Anne, Shaw and the Elders in their discussion.

As Rayne and Lexi sat talking quietly, dark, churning clouds building to the west drew Rayne's attention and he heard a distant rumble of thunder.

"It looks like we might see a storm. We need to get back down the mountain," Jiro said as he and the others walked over to where Rayne and Lexi were sitting. "Do either of you two know how far Thorvin might have gone?"

"Thorvin just went to practice some sword forms," Rayne said. "I doubt he went far."

"I suspect if *you* called for Thorvin, he would come running," Anne said to Rayne with a silly grin pasted on her face. He grimaced back at her, not feeling comfortable yelling. "Come on, Rayne, you're not still afraid of him after all we've been through?"

Looking somewhat embarrassed, Rayne said, "It's not Thorvin. It's yelling I'm not so sure of. Oh, Anne, you should know. I just started talking aloud a few months ago. I've never yelled. I've screamed; I admit that. But I've never yelled. Well ... except maybe once at my parents."

Stepping up behind Rayne, Sashi put her hand on his shoulder. "That's not the same thing. You never learned the pure joy of an unrestrained yell as a child. Come on, Stevie, we've got more work to do."

Stepping around to Rayne's front Sashi reached down and took his hand, pulling him to his feet. "You too, Lexi," she said.

Once everyone was standing Sashi let out an ear-splitting yelling kind of screech. Holding his hands to his ears, Rayne asked, "Is that what you want me to do?"

"Naw," Sashi shook her head, grinning. "That just felt

good. Now, for yelling. It's not a scream. It's probably more like what you did when you talked to the people of Westvale after your exhibition."

"But the One helped me be heard then."

"True. But you have a voice now and you have lungs. Take a deep breath and then call out for Thorvin."

Unconvinced, Rayne tried. "Thorvin," he said loudly.

Sashi shook her head and wrinkled her nose at Rayne. "That was pathetic. Try again."

"Thorvin," Rayne said a little louder.

Sashi growled. "Okay, this isn't working. Everyone we're all going to shout for Thorvin and teach Rayne how it's done. Yes, you too Shaw," Sashi said in answer to Shaw's incredulous look.

"You guys too," Sashi pointed to Jiro, Afon, and Owain. Owain smiled large and nodded.

"Rayne, take a deep breath and let loose—loud! On the count of three, everyone call out for Thorvin. Let's show our childhood-deprived friend how to yell. One, two, three." Sashi gulped a chunk of air and signaled. A cacophony of noise filled the air as shouts, yells, and screams for Thorvin sounded just as he rounded one of the rock outcroppings and walked into the clearing. He stood watching as the group kept yelling until Rayne noticed him standing, looking at everyone as if they had lost their sanity. Shrugging, Rayne grabbed Sashi's arm, spun her around, and pointed to Thorvin. She stopped yelling and soon the others followed her example as they turned and saw Thorvin.

"You guys miss me or what?" Thorvin smirked.

"They were teaching me how to yell," Rayne shouted, unable to keep a grin from surfacing. "That was fun." He glanced at Lexi who had a huge grin plastered on her face.

Looking around, Rayne realized the silly act of yelling together released a tension that had been present since he and his friends arrived on Sorial. Sharing the moment created a bond even stronger than the one they had when they left Westvale. Everyone was laughing and smiling at the uninhibited noise, enjoying the spontaneous activity.

"Well, getting wet is not going to be fun," Thorvin raised his eyebrows and pointed to the growing cloud mass Rayne had noticed earlier. The group scrambled to gather their things and load up the cart. Once Jiro harnessed Posey, Rayne climbed in among the picnic paraphernalia and the group made haste back down the mountain toward the healing spring.

They were getting close to the shelter when the first, cold raindrops began falling from a sky that boiled in shades of gray and black. Lightning flashed, turning the huge trees around them into glowing sentinels, imprinting their eyes with after images before dropping back into the obscurity of the surrounding woods.

Jiro struggled with Posey who was becoming increasingly nervous. A bolt of lightning struck a tree near the path, igniting the surrounding area and slinging shards of wood as the tree splintered and thunder crackled and roared overhead. Then the sky turned a solid gray as rain beat down in earnest.

By the time they got to the bath house at the spring they were soaked. Posey stood trembling in front of the structure. Everyone grabbed something from the cart and ran into the building. Rayne lowered himself to the ground and limped up to the wild-eyed Posey, gently rubbing her nose and speaking to her in a crooning voice while the others scrambled to empty the cart. With Rayne taking care of Posey, Jiro was free to help transport the picnic supplies and soon the cart was empty. The fury of the short but intense storm ebbed as the worst moved off to the east and Posey started to relax.

Feeling bad for the little pony, Rayne stayed with her even after the cart had been emptied. Jiro came back out. "I'll take her to the pen."

"I'm soaked anyway," Rayne said. "Why don't you go back in. I'll take her over in a few minutes when she's calmer. I'll be fine."

With a slight bow, Jiro thanked Rayne and headed back into the bath house. Rayne continued talking to Posey as he rubbed his hand over her soft nose and down her neck. As she relaxed she started to lean into him and chuckling he gently nudged her back saying, "I can't even hold myself up and you think I'm going to be able to hold you up. Come on, girl, let's get you to your grass."

Balancing on his left leg, he unharnessed Posey and left the cart in front of the bath house. He grabbed his staff, and led Posey to the enclosure, his muscles more cooperative than they had been for days. Fear that the fight with Matheson might have done irreparable damage to his thigh had become a constant companion and now relief filtered through him.

Once Posey was released and the gate shut, Rayne leaned against the fence watching the patch of sky above his head clear and listening to water dripping in a mesmerizing rhythm from the giant pine trees surrounding the bath house. It was peaceful now. The atmosphere smelled of lightning, pine, and rain. The rain had cooled the air and Rayne shivered as goosebumps pimpled his arms. It was refreshing.

46

Drinking in the serenity after the storm's passing, listening to the calming sounds of water dripping softly in the quiet woods, Rayne felt the warmth that usually preceded a word from the One seep into him. Deep in his spirit he heard the voice. *My Light Bringer, it is time. You must go to the Sacred Grove. Seek out the guardian. She will reveal herself to you alone. Be courageous and strong; trust that I am with you always.*

When Rayne entered the bath house, his companions were gathered in the small entry foyer, talking about the storm and the close lightning strike. He waited for a break, then said, "Elder Jiro, the One just spoke to me. It's time. Will you take me to the Sacred Grove?"

Jiro, Owain, and Afon turned to Rayne, their eyes widened in alarm. "How do you know about the Sacred Grove?" Jiro asked. Then the light of understanding flashed in his eyes. "The One told you. That's how you know."

"What's the Sacred Grove?" Thorvin asked.

"It is a place of spiritual power. Until now, it was known only to the elders of Caarwyn Rill," Afon said. "It is a guarded secret. As part of our initiation when we become elders, we spend a night in the Sacred Grove praying for a word of wisdom from the One."

"The only way you could know about the Sacred Grove is if the One himself told you. No one who has this knowledge would have spoken about it to anyone except another elder," Jiro said, his eyes still wide. "So, yes, I am willing to take you. But you must obtain permission from First Eldest Tegan to enter the grove. That will probably take a couple days. She will claim the right to examine you once she learns you have asked. No one is granted permission to enter the grove unless examined by the First Eldest."

Early the next day Jiro, Owain, and Afon once again took Rayne and his companions to the hot spring. When they returned to Caarwyn Rill, Cai, Silas, Stevie, and Thorvin were invited to join several of the young men for an afternoon of hunting. Afon took Lexi, Anne, and Sashi to explore the village, leaving Shaw and Rayne at the Elder's House with Jiro and Owain.

First Eldest Tegan and Elder Powell sent word they would examine Rayne the next evening. If all went well, Jiro would take Rayne up to the Sacred Grove the following morning. Alone.

The following day, after a third morning spent at the healing spring and a hearty lunch, Thorvin paced the floor in the room the men shared. Stevie and Shaw sat on their beds watching while Rayne stood by one of the windows, looking out at the forest.

"Why can't I go with you?" Thorvin growled. "Every time I leave you alone, you get into trouble. How am I supposed to protect you if you keep leaving me behind? No, I'm coming with you, Sire."

Resting in the aura of peace that enveloped him since the One had spoken after the storm, Rayne turned to Thorvin. "Trust the One. I'll be fine. He told me to go alone. It's what I must do. And you know we need to respect the traditions of Caarwyn Rill. So, Thorvin, I'm asking you not as your prince, but as your friend, please help me by not arguing. Accept my decision."

Rayne stared intently at Thorvin, willing him to understand. Finally, throwing his hands in the air Thorvin relented. "Yes. If that's what you want. I'll support you. But if I sense any threat to you, I can't guarantee I won't follow."

A small smile lifted one side of Rayne's mouth. "I would expect nothing less."

A knock sounded on the door and Shaw opened it to find Sashi, Anne, Lexi, and Afon waiting in the hall.

"We need His Highness for a bit," Anne said. She stuck her head into the room. "Rayne, would you please join us?"

"What's this about?" he asked.

Anne raised her eyebrows and gave him a look that said, *no arguing now, young man*. "Please come with us."

Shrugging to the others, Rayne grabbed his staff and followed Anne. The ladies led him to a downstairs room and shut the door.

Turning to him, Anne said, "You know we love you, Rayne, and accept you just the way you are. But we can't let you meet with First Eldest Tegan and Elder Powell without at least trimming that nasty chopped up mess you call hair. And you need to dress in a way that befits the crown prince of Ochen. So, please have a seat. We have work to do."

Afon laid out clothing while Anne took a pair of shears to Rayne's hair. Sashi and Lexi kept up a friendly banter to keep him distracted so he would sit still for Anne. When she finished the rest to her satisfaction, Anne grabbed the braid still dangling along the side of Rayne's face, the last remnant of his long hair. She drew it up, in front of his face, with questioning eyes.

"With your hair so short now, I don't think this looks right. The decision is yours ... but ..." Anne turned to Sashi, Lexi, and Afon. "What do you think ladies, keep it or cut it?"

"Cut it!" they exclaimed in unison.

Rayne reached out, grabbed the braid, and ran his fingers over it. "I should be happy to get rid of it. Though it's been a part of me since I was eight, it doesn't invoke good memories. I'm not the me I was when Coronus would braid it, not by a long shot."

Taking a deep breath, Rayne said, "Cut it, Anne."

It only took a second, one snip of the shears, and it was off. Anne held out the severed braid to Rayne. "Do you want to keep it?"

Shaking his head, his lips flattened into a tight line, Rayne said, "No, burn the thing."

Anne handed the braid to Sashi. "Well, you heard the prince. Burn the thing."

"Yes ma'am!" Sashi jumped up and ran out to the gathering space where a fire was kept burning all the time. In a few minutes, she was back. Just in time to be ushered from the room with everyone else so Rayne could change.

⚡

While they waited for Rayne to call them back in, Lexi asked Anne, "You were one of the two friends Rayne had growing up, weren't you?"

Anne nodded.

"What was he like as a child?"

Anne closed her eyes and sighed deeply. Then looking Lexi in the eyes, she said, "I don't even know where to begin. What was Rayne like as a child?

"At first, he was sweet and scared and so defenseless. The first time I saw him was soon after Sigmund had sent him to Coronus for training. I was ordered to take meals to a new trainee who would be living in the cell below the training ring. I had no idea why a trainee would choose to sleep in a cell when there were rooms available on the second floor. I was so surprised when instead of a hardened older boy, I found this scared, six-year-old, mute child locked in the cell under the stairs.

"Angered over something, Coronus had beat him and thrown him in there with no care for the wounds on his back. Can you imagine what that was like for a six-year-old child who couldn't even speak?"

"Yeah," Sashi added in a small voice. "I saw the cell once. It was awful, not much bigger than a cage with only a thin mat to sleep on. I cried when I saw it. And that was where he slept for ten years."

Afon drew in a sharp breath. "That's impossible. No one could be so cruel to a small child."

"Possible and true," Anne said, looking at Afon. "Prince Rayne has been through more in his short life than most people would experience if they lived many lifetimes. And most of it was horrible. Coronus was awful, but Sigmund was inhuman."

Rayne opened the door and waved them back in. "Okay, ladies, what do you think. Am I dressed and fixed enough to meet with First Eldest Tegan?"

"Handsome as ever." Anne smiled her approval.

Lexi agreed. Prince Rayne looked very fine now that his chopped hair was neatly trimmed and the strange braid cut. Afon provided trousers and a tunic similar to what Rayne had been wearing, but these were of a finer weave and the over garment was of a deep plum color highlighting Rayne's amazing eyes, making them look larger and of a deeper amethyst color. *Handsome indeed!* Lexi's gaze took in his arching eyebrows, fine nose, and firm chin. Then he was looking straight at her as if he knew what she was thinking. Quickly averting her eyes, she said, "I suppose he'll do."

Her eyes flashing, and with a full grin lighting her face, Sashi grabbed Rayne's elbow and turned him to face Lexi. "Oh, come on Lexi. I saw you looking at him a second ago. That look said much more than *he'll do*! Admit it."

Lexi raised her nose in the air and feigned disinterest. "Well, if you insist."

But after listening to Anne talk about Rayne's early experience under Coronus, her heart wanted to reach out to him and ease the pain she knew he carried. Then Sashi leaned over and whispered in Lexi's ear, "You should have been with us in Highreach when he came out of that cave wearing nothing more than his small clothes. Nemora's moons, boy did he blush!" She wiggled her eyebrows and a knowing smirk brightened her face. Lexi swallowed hard and her eyes grew wide. Everyone started giggling.

꒔

Uncomfortable with all the giggling and looks thrown in his direction, Rayne excused himself to go back up to his room. Half way up the stairs he realized he left his staff in the room with the ladies. Not wanting to go back in there, he decided he would send Shaw for it.

Later, after Shaw had retrieved the staff, and Rayne walked into the gathering space for supper, things weren't much better. Now, all four ladies kept looking at him and whispering behind their hands.

"What's going on with them?" Rayne asked Shaw, figuring if anyone knew what all the strange behavior was about, it would be Shaw. Stevie and Thorvin didn't seem to understand the ladies the way Shaw did.

Hiding a chuckle behind a cough, Shaw said, "It's you, Sire. It seems Lady Alexianndra has taken a liking to you and our Anne and Sashi are delighted with the idea."

"No." Rayne screwed up his eyes and wrinkled his nose. "I think there must be a misunderstanding. I don't think it's possible for Lexi to like me, you know, *like me*, in that way. She's just being nice because she has to."

Shaking his head, Shaw said, "I think it's you who are mistaken, Sire. I'll take the ladies' side on this one. They have been chatting about it ever since your hair cut."

Rayne didn't have long to dwell on Lexi and whatever was happening there. As he was finishing the meal, Elder Powell came up to him. "First Eldest Tegan and I are ready to examine you, child."

Rayne stood and inclined his head to Elder Powell. "I'm ready."

Thorvin rose and Rayne could see anger in the man's eyes. He was probably upset that Rayne had been the one to bow. Elder Powell should have bowed to Rayne as crown prince of all Ochen. *But Thorvin doesn't know the truth. I'm not a prince.*

Rayne raised his hand slightly and shook his head. Thorvin got the message and sat back down. Grabbing his tankard of ale, the big man took a generous swig. Rayne followed Elder Powell down the hallway to the same small room where he had met with Jiro the day they arrived. The furniture had been rearranged. First Eldest Tegan was sitting behind a table and Elder Powell joined her as she waved Rayne to a straight-backed chair set a few feet from the table, facing the elders. Rayne leaned his staff against the wall next to the door and took his seat. A prismatic lantern was set on the table and there was a low fire burning in the fireplace to combat the evening chill.

Folding her fingers together and resting her chin on them, First Eldest Tegan gave Rayne a level look. "With your lineage, you must expect to be shown deference in every situation, but here we don't put much stock in titles. We esteem age and wisdom. You have none of the former and I am unsure how much you have of the latter. As wisdom usually comes hand in hand with age, I suspect you have little of that as well."

Tegan paused, eyes glued to Rayne like a hawk's on its prey, as if she was waiting for him to attempt to refute her statement. He decided to ignore the slight and wait to learn what else the first eldest would say before responding. It seemed a wise choice as she harrumphed and then continued. "At least it would seem that someone has taught you to hold your tongue in the presence of your elders. Something not always evident in one so young. I give you credit for that.

"This meeting has been set to determine if we should give you permission to visit our Sacred Grove. I find myself concerned and dismayed that you even know about the grove. Elder Jiro tells me you claim to have been told of it by the voice of the One. Is this so?"

"Yes, First Eldest."

"How can you be sure what you heard was the voice of the One?" she asked. "When I became an elder, as our tradition dictates, I spent a night in the Sacred Grove hoping to hear a word from the One. Though I felt a warmth in my spirit, I never heard a voice. What makes you so certain?"

"I'm certain because he's spoken to me before. And every time he has, his words have proven true. They have remained faithful to what we have studied in the Words of the One to Corylus and other ancient texts. When he speaks, I am embraced by his warmth and love."

First Eldest Tegan sighed and shook her head with a look of disapproval. "Here in Caarwyn Rill elders and experienced scholars would be entrusted with studying the Words of the One, not children. I suppose you think you're something special, because of your royal heritage."

"I'm not special. That the One chose to show me his forgiveness amazes me still. All I can do is accept and trust. The truth is, I should have been condemned and punished, but instead he led me to faith in his Son and unfathomable forgiveness."

"Then it is true," Elder Powell said, his eyes rounding as if he had just made a discovery. "You weren't raised in the palace, were you? You were the assassin with Sigmund three years ago, the night Kern House was attacked. It was you who injured our Duke Erland."

"Yes." Rayne met Elder Powell's eyes. "I am that assassin. But you need to understand, I did not work *for* Sigmund, I belonged *to* him. I was his slave."

"You were Sigmund's *slave*?" Tegan asked, her voice barely a whisper.

"Yes. I was his property."

"And you murdered people for him?"

"Yes."

Clicking her tongue, Tegan said, "With such a history, how can you expect us to allow you to set foot in our most holy place, our Sacred Grove? You're nothing more than a youth now, how old were you when you started shedding innocent blood for that sorcerer Sigmund? You can't be much older than fifteen or sixteen. How old?"

Rayne sighed, closing his eyes. Would his history always haunt him? It lived in memories remembered and forgotten to rise up and ambush him unaware. And it lived in the judgement he faced from people who saw him as nothing more than what he had been, an assassin. But Rayne understood, if he wanted to visit the Sacred Grove he needed to face the judgement before him now. But, however it worked out, he would answer First Eldest Tegan's and Elder Powell's questions truthfully.

"Coronus, the man Sigmund hired to train me, sent me on my first assassination when I was eight." Rayne studied his fingers, nervous energy driving him to twine and untwine them as he heard the sharp intake of breath from both elders.

"On my sixteenth birthday, the One delivered me from the darkness. He rescued me from the life of an assassin and the horror of belonging to Sigmund. I am no longer what I was."

After several minutes of silence, Tegan said, "What convincing reason can you give us for allowing someone like you, someone raised in darkness and blood, access to our Sacred Grove?"

Rayne felt the building warmth, he leaned into it, accepting the embrace. The One would work his will; he would do what Rayne was incapable of doing, softening the hearts of the two elders.

The voice spoke in the silence of the room, commanding yet compassionate. *"Elders of Caarwyn Rill. You have held firm to your traditions, seeking to honor me; I call you now to hold firm to the words of truth I will speak through my Light Bringer. You have kept your Sacred Grove safe; I call you now to accept that my Sacred Grove has been kept safe all these centuries to preserve it for the coming of my chosen. My Light Bringer is before you. Honor him. His words will be light in the darkness. If I have chosen to forgive and honor him, what is that to you? Have I not the right to choose whomever I will?*

Silence settled back over the room. After several minutes as the warmth faded, First Eldest Tegan whispered, "I understand now. The voice of the One is singular and undeniable. Your Highness, forgive our doubt. We do not have the authority to withhold permission from the One's chosen Light Bringer. I will ask Elder Jiro to escort you to the Sacred Grove tomorrow morning. Can you forgive us for so blindly following our traditions that honored only age, that we almost missed the honor of serving the One's Light Bringer and recognizing his wisdom?"

Rayne rose and bowed deeply, drawing surprised expressions

from the two elders. "It is you who honor me, by allowing an ex-assassin access to your Sacred Grove. The One's forgiveness has changed me, but it hasn't changed the facts of my past. There is nothing to forgive. I thank you for sending Elder Jiro as my guide tomorrow morning. It is what I had hoped."

As Rayne started for the door Elder Powell rose and said in a plaintive voice, "But we have no Words to study, only our oral traditions passed down from elder to elder. When you find the scroll, will you give it to us?"

Rayne shook his head. "I'm sorry, but I must take the scroll for now. All seven scrolls must be brought together to bind the living darkness. But each world will be given copies of all seven scrolls once they are reclaimed. I hope that, in time, all the people of Ochen will be able to read the Words and they will never be lost or forgotten again. And I promise, the first copy made of the Words of the One to Veres will be sent to Caarwyn Rill.

"There are others, like the scholars on Arisima, who never completely lost the Words, knowledgeable people like my friend Shaw. While I'm at the Sacred Grove, talk to him. Shaw would be happy to discuss the One's Words with you; it is a thing that gives him great pleasure."

Turning back to the door, Rayne grabbed his staff, left the elders, and returned to the gathering space.

When Thorvin saw Rayne enter the room, he knew something had happened. The radiance from the Sun Sparrow light highlighting the network of scars on Rayne's wrists and lower arms was shining even more brightly. It glowed through the fabric of his tunic, a golden light so soft yet so brilliant it was visible even in the bright light of the prismatic lanterns. As the villagers began to notice, people turned to stare at Rayne with awed expressions.

Elder Jiro rose and walked to Rayne. "You have your answer then?"

"Yes," Rayne answered softly. "We leave in the morning."

47

It had stormed in the night and again in the early hours of the morning before Rayne and Elder Jiro left for the Sacred Grove. Rayne decided his leg felt strong enough to walk, so they left Posey and her cart in front of the elder's house.

Drops of rain still cascaded from sodden branches, soaking the two when they brushed against them. An intermittent breeze periodically caused whole branches to drip over-sized beads of chilly water down Rayne's back sending shivers through him. In an effort to keep dry, they walked single file down the center of the path. The cool of the morning was giving way to the warmth of what promised to be a hot day for so early in the spring. Rayne and Jiro walked without speaking, each caught up in the silence of his own thoughts. They followed the same path they had taken the past several mornings to the hot spring, but now they passed the bath house and turned onto a small trail that branched off to circle the side of the mountain. Jiro followed it into a secluded valley where he led Rayne through numerous wooded copses, and fields of grasses and flowering bushes. The air cleared and warmed toward midday heat before the trail ended at a sheer cliff face.

Jiro skirted along the smooth, charcoal gray rock face to an area where an abundance of large berry bushes grew. With a look of concentration, he examined the wall, feeling along the face. Eventually, moving two towering bushes aside, he found what he was looking for, a narrow cleft in the dark rock.

Jiro turned sideways and worked his bulk through the opening. Rayne turned also and, with the walls hemming him in, followed. They moved through the rocky crevice for about thirty feet before it opened on a hidden glen. When he emerged, Rayne sucked in a deep breath. The air was clear and fresh, and yet, it had a flavor to it. Inhaling reminded Rayne of biting into a sweet, crisp apple. He felt the power of deep magical energy that had been absent outside the glen. Here, life was powerful. Turning in a circle, Rayne gasped at the size of the trees surrounding him. They were near to double the size of any he had seen yet. Pines so large around it would take several men reaching fingers to fingers to circle them, oaks that towered as tall as the pines but were even more immense in girth. There were beeches and hickories and firs and trees Rayne couldn't name.

One in particular caught his attention. Although not as tall as the others, the tree was covered in blossoms the color of his mother's eyes. The leaves were just beginning to unfurl from golden buds in shades of amber and yellow green. It was the most beautiful tree Rayne had ever seen and he felt compelled to reach out to the golden bark. It was mainly a honey brown color but, like Lexi's eyes, was sprinkled with golden flecks making the whole trunk look like gold.

As Rayne started toward the tree, Jiro reached out and grasped his arm. "I must leave you here. When you are ready to return, I will be waiting outside. May the One go with you, Light Bringer."

Then Jiro was gone. Rayne was alone, but he knew he wasn't alone. He could feel the presence of the One. But he also felt something else, *someone* else. He moved to the tree, drawn toward it as if in a dream. He reached out and touched the bark but pulled back with a start; it was warm. Extending his hand to the tree again, he rested his palm against the warm trunk. Looking up through the branches, everything was amethyst and golden and warm.

Gazing past the tree, Rayne saw others like it growing in a line up the side of a wooded hill, like soldiers marching, one after another. Without volition, he moved from tree to tree, laying his hand on each one he passed.

Rayne didn't register when the bell-like sound started. But, as he moved forward, he was hit with the realization that he had been hearing it for a while. The farther up the slope he moved, the louder the sound became until it was chiming all around him. It was beautiful and soothing, yet insistent and demanding at the same time, like someone calling and expecting a response. But Rayne didn't know the response. It reminded him of the calls of the Sun Sparrows when they landed on him.

Reaching the top of the hill, Rayne saw thick forest falling in waves of light green and yellow all around him. Looking behind, he realized, if not for the line of gold trunks, he would never find his way back to the cleft in the rock. Here, at the apex of the hill, he stood at the base of the last and largest of the golden trees with the amethyst flowers.

As he ran his hand over the bark of the final tree, the chiming stopped. The sudden silence seemed so empty, Rayne wanted to call to the source of the sound and ask it to sing again. In the silence, he heard gurgling and looking around the trunk of the golden tree, he saw a spring of water bubbling from the ground between the roots.

Abruptly aware of an intense thirst, Rayne knelt at the spring and cupped water up to his mouth. It was icy cold and crisp like the snow he tasted the day he and Warren had gone sledding with Cole and Tyson.

The next thing he knew, he was lying on a soft, grassy spot with his back to the tree trunk, the stream gurgling to his left. Images of Warren filled his head and the need to see him again, just to talk to him, flooded Rayne. His eyelids drooped, and deep restful slumber claimed him.

When he woke, everything seemed the same as when he had fallen asleep. He didn't know how long he had slept. It could have been just a couple minutes, or it could have been days. It felt as if time itself had lost all meaning. He drank a few more handfuls of the icy water and then followed the stream away from the golden tree. It led down in a gently rolling direction into the deeper woods he had observed from the top of the hill. Here the trees were so thick, not much grew beneath the ancient giants except scattered patches of varied mosses and ferns peeking through a deep layer of aged brown leaves.

Rayne felt vibrant and alive. He barely used his staff. Energy surrounded him, embracing him and filling him. The bell-like music started again. He felt the other presence; it was close now. Was it the source of the chiming? He continued following the stream as it tumbled over rocks seeking the lower valley, surrounded in a muted light of golden green.

He had no idea how long he walked but growing tired again he stopped and drank more water. Looking back up from the stream he saw her. She was standing on a small knoll watching him. Her lips moved and after watching her for a minute, Rayne realized she was the source of the chiming.

She reminded Rayne of the golden trees, tall and lovely with amber hair and eyes. She was so much taller than Rayne, thin and tall. She seemed almost ephemeral to him, like she would vanish in bright sunlight, and yet there was something that spoke of ancient life as well.

As Rayne stood staring in frozen wonder at the creature, the chiming changed pitch and he began to hear words in the music. She was speaking to him. Calling to the One's Light Bringer. But he wasn't hearing exactly, it was more like he just understood in his mind, not through his sense of hearing.

"Come Light Bringer of the One, come follow." She repeated the words several times until Rayne took a step toward her. She turned and began walking away from the stream. He hesitated for a minute. If he left the stream, Rayne was afraid he would never be able to find his way out to the cleft again. She stopped and looked back; Rayne followed.

They hadn't gone far when the graceful creature bowed low to pass through an opening in what looked like a gigantic, densely-woven hedge, and led Rayne into a dwelling carved out of the thick growth of shrubbery. Looking around, he pulled in a sharp breath when he saw a circular hearth set in the center of the dwelling. A low fire burned on the hearth, and above the fire, a pot simmered.

The bushes and trees that made up the enclosure formed a tight ceiling with a smoke hole in the center. The walls, if they could even be called walls, were of interwoven living branches that all curved outward from the ground and then back inward forming a domed ceiling.

Rayne felt as though he was inside an inverted living bowl made of branches and leaves. He saw no dried or brown leaves, just the fresh green and yellow growth of spring. The floor was packed dirt, swept clean. To the one side of the fire was an alcove with a bed built of thin branches woven in an intricate design and worked around strong, heavy branches which formed the frame. On the near side of the fire to the right of the door, a table sat with two chairs. The table and chairs were golden like the trees Rayne had followed up the hill. They looked as though each had been carved from one large trunk. To Rayne's left was a cupboard holding cooking supplies, another pot, and several jugs and woven baskets. The whole dwelling spoke of peaceful comfort.

After looking around, Rayne turned his attention back to the creature who had led him here. Once again, he was aware of how much she reminded him of the golden trees. Green and golden leaves were plaited through her honey colored hair which fell in loose curls to below her hips. She wore a finely woven shift of deep brown with tiny beads set in a pattern of small amethyst and blue flowers that looked almost alive. Her eyes were deep amber, brightened by pale yellow flecks. And now that Rayne stood next to her, he realized she was nearly twice his height. "Who ... what ... are you?" he asked, his voice soft and hushed.

Smiling she chimed something he couldn't understand and seeing his confusion, she laughed lightly, a sound that reminded Rayne of ice crystals dancing against each other in a breeze.

"My name is beyond your ears, little newcomer. You may call me Ari." This time she spoke in the common language instead of chiming.

"You speak our language?"

"I have not spoken the newcomer language in a very long while; but I remember. Good fortune to you and welcome traveler." Ari spoke the cross-world greeting with laughter-infected words. "But come, Light Bringer, would you share your name with me?"

"My name is Rayne."

"Oh, a good name." Delight shown from Ari's eyes. "Like the refreshment the One sends from the sky so all living things may drink and live. A very appropriate name indeed."

"Well ... It is spelled different."

"That is fine Refreshing Rayne. The thought is still good. You must be hungry. The One told me you would be here for the late meal, so I have made enough food to share."

She led Rayne to the other side of the cupboard where a spring splashed down over a small mound of rocks into a tiny pool that vanished out beyond the green wall.

"Wash yourself so we may be revived."

Rayne washed his hands and face, shivering at the icy coldness of the spring. Ari handed him a towel woven of soft plant fibers.

Ari washed also then led Rayne to the table bidding him sit while she went to the cupboard and returned with cups and bowls and a loaf of brown, crusty bread. Ari took a pitcher to the spring, filled it with the frosty water, and brought it to the table, pouring cups for Rayne and herself. She then took the bowls to the simmering pot and filled them. Her movements were all fluid, like flowing water, graceful and purposeful at the same time. He enjoyed watching her and as she turned back from filling the bowls she caught his eyes and smiled. Her smile was so filled with compassion and tenderness that Rayne could have cried at the sensation of love and total acceptance he received from Ari.

Still smiling, Ari sat in the other chair and asked, "Would you thank the Creator Father for these gifts he has given us?"

Rayne nodded, then tilting his head back and with eyes closed, he quietly prayed, "Most wonderful giver of all gifts, blessed Creator Father, One. Ari and I humbly thank you now for this gift of food you have given to sustain us. May we never forget every good thing is a gift from your hand. We thank you for life, for every breath we breath, and we thank you for the gift of your Son, forgiveness we don't deserve."

"Well done Light Bringer." Ari nodded once.

They ate in silence for a bit. Rayne found the soup to be a curious union of the flavors of berries and greens combined with an herbal seasoning that joined the flavors. The bread was coarse and strong, filled with nuts and seeds, but tasty, with a hint of honey. It made him think of Elsie and his parents. His sadness must have shown on his face because Ari asked, "What makes the Light Bringer so sad? I would think you would be joyful with the task given you."

Rayne met Ari's eyes. "I *am* joyful for the One's hand on me and the gift of being his Light Bringer. It's unbelievable that he would allow someone like me to serve him in such a way. I've been a vessel for darkness, used for evil purposes, and I'm too young and have so much to learn yet. But my failings and history always drive me back to the One. And always I'm humbled by his loving acceptance.

"Yet, there is so much in my life that's still in turmoil. There's evil surrounding my parents and friends and I can't protect them. I fear I'll fail the One. I know how weak I am even though I try to hide my fear and weakness from my friends. And I've hidden other things from my friends. I've been angry with the One and I don't always trust him like I should."

"Yes, you are indeed quite young." Ari nodded, her eyes probing Rayne's and her expression serious. "And you do have much to learn. Yet the Creator Father chose you for a reason. You may be young, but there is great strength in you. And, in spite of what you say, I sense you have a good measure of faithful trust in the Creator Father, whom you call the One. This is your greatest strength. Cling to the One and he will sustain you. You will not fail."

"Are you the guardian I came to find?" Rayne hesitated, uncertain how to proceed. "The guardian of the scroll?"

"Now you are showing your youth; rushing things, being

in a hurry. You asked me earlier what I am. If you can be patient, I will explain."

Rayne bowed his head. "I'm sorry. You're right. Since the One has brought me to this point, I will rest in his will and be patient."

Ari inclined her head and chuckled, a light tinkling sound. She paused and closed her eyes for a few minutes before beginning.

48

Ɨ

"Eons ago, long before you newcomers arrived on the worlds you call Ochen, we ancients had great civilizations on the seven. We worshipped the Creator Father and gave him praise for the gift his Son would give for all peoples when he dwelt on the world you called home before traveling to Ochen."

"When the newcomers first arrived, we ancients embraced them as fellow worshipers of the Creator Father and welcomed them to our homes. We showed them the connecting lines between the seven that the Creator Father had given us in the distant past. And we shared the secrets of surviving on each world. But as your numbers increased, our people decreased. We no longer gave birth and our numbers dwindled. Although we were long lived, our time was coming to an end and the Creator Father called us to him. The worlds of Ochen now belonged to the newcomers.

"At the time you name the Hundred Years War, the Creator Father called the last of our people together here on Veres. He warned us of the coming war and how it would be followed by a time of forgetfulness, when the newcomers would no longer esteem his Words as true or keep them safe. Though many would still worship, their worship would be empty because they would not know the One or the gift of his Son. But in his mercy, the Creator Father had determined to preserve an existing copy of each of the seven Words to be taken from the newcomers and kept in hiding.

"And though the newcomers would be doomed to forget him and live in darkness, the One promised that he would keep for himself a remnant of believers to hold to the ancient truths and pass down the prophecies from generation to generation. Until his chosen time of judgement.

"He then told us of his plan to bring his light back to the newcomers. When the time of judgement approaches, he said, a chosen Light Bringer will arise to reclaim the Words of the One to each of the seven worlds. Out of darkness the chosen will arise with light enveloping him. He will unite the Words and bind the living darkness.

The Creator Father called to himself seven guardians from my people. To us fell the task of guarding the scrolls until the Light Bringer would arise to reclaim them. That time has come. You have arisen, and my time of solitude is finally over. I am ready to be united to my people once again. I am filled with joy at the thought of that reunion. I am also pleased to have served the Creator Father, and to know that your people will once again come to worship him in truth."

Rayne sensed the loneliness laced through Ari's words and realized the price she had paid in waiting alone all those years for the One's Light Bringer to come. But he also sensed the joy she looked forward to when she would finally be reunited with her people now that her task was done. He was, yet again, humbled at being a part of something so vast.

Thinking back, Rayne said, "But there was no guardian on Corylus. Warren showed me the scroll. It had been in Coronus's library for years and Warren just happened to find it."

"With the One there is no 'just happened'. All has transpired according to his perfect will. And it was his will that the first scroll would come to his Light Bringer accompanied by a teacher, someone to lead you into the truth of the Words. The guardian on Corylus remained until the coming of that teacher. Once he was aware of the scroll, the guardian's mission was complete. Without that preparation, you would have been too lost to the darkness to embrace the Son. The Corylus guardian was my husband. We both made the commitment to protect the scrolls knowing we would be apart for a very long time. I have thought of him every day. He is with the Creator Father now, and soon we will be reunited."

Ari remained quiet, staring into space for a few minutes but then shook herself back from the thoughts that had enfolded her. "Come Light Bringer; let us rest. In the morning, I will take you to the scroll."

Although Ari insisted Rayne take the bed, he refused, and she relented. Rayne took the blanket she gave him and curled up in front of the fire near the table and chairs, allowing Ari the privacy of the sleeping alcove. He thought with all the excitement and the expectation of finding the Veres scroll tomorrow, sleep would elude him. But sleep claimed him quickly, encompassing him in a dreamless warmth.

The sun was already streaming through the smoke hole when Rayne woke to the smell of grain cooking and the sound of tiny bells chiming. Ari was singing in her bell language as she bent over the pot, pulled it from over the fire, and stirred berries and nuts into the bubbling grain. Realizing he was awake, Ari smiled at him. "A good morning to you young Light Bringer. After we have eaten I will take you to the scroll. I feel almost young; I am impatient with the need to rush after so long a time of waiting."

Rayne returned Ari's smile. "Good morning to you as well, Ari. Whenever you are ready, I'll be ready too. In the meantime, I would like to spend some time in prayer. If you'll excuse me, would it be alright if I went outside for a bit?"

"Of course, take your time. Breakfast will be waiting when you return. But don't go far, it is easy to lose one's way here in the Sacred Grove. It is quite a large place."

Rayne ducked out the doorway and taking Ari's advice stayed close.

No words, no petitions seemed to come to him, so he just

quieted his spirit and rested in the presence of the One. The air around him surged with energy and then, naturally and easily, like a stream running downhill, Rayne found himself thanking the One for his power and his guidance.

Warmth enveloped him and the voice came. *Your enemies are moving, my beloved Light Bringer. Caarwyn Rill and their lanterns must journey to Mistal. In my perfect timing the light has arisen to dispel the darkness.*

The voice faded but Rayne felt the urgency of the message. He ducked back in to Ari and asked if they could go now. She looked at him in confusion. "Don't you want to eat first?"

"I don't have time. The One just told me I need to bring Caarwyn Rill and their lanterns to Mistal without delay. Something must be happening there. I'm sorry to rush you, but I don't think I can wait. I have to go."

"Well, you can't go on an empty stomach. You need food for energy and I have just the thing." She went to her cupboard and pulled out a wrapped package. "These are traveling rounds, little baked loaves filled with nuts, seeds, and berries. They are filling, sustaining, and you can eat them on the move. I'm sorry I don't have more but take these. I won't be needing them anymore."

She grabbed a leather bag with a long strap from a shelf and placing the package of travel rounds and a skin filled with water from the spring inside, handed it to Rayne who threw it over his shoulder. Then Ari pulled her pot from over the fire, banked the fire and grabbed a shawl. "I'm ready. Come."

She ducked out the door and led Rayne up around the enclosure and through an opening in a second hedge beyond her home. Ari's movements were swift and Rayne struggled to keep up with the pace she set. But he wouldn't give in to weakness and pushed forward. He was grateful when a short time later Ari stopped in front of a small cave.

"This task is for you alone Light Bringer; I cannot enter with you. The light you need now lives within you and it will brighten the way you must go. I will wait here."

Rayne plunged into the dark opening and as soon as the darkness surrounded him, he began to glow brightly. After a quick scan, Rayne saw there was only one way to go. The cave was actually a tunnel. It ran straight for a long while with no branching but then he came to a fork.

"Which way? Which way?" he mumbled under his breath. Trying the branch to his left, he only walked a few feet when his light began to dim so he backtracked and entered the right fork. His light kept bright and sure; this was the way. And then the tunnel opened up into a huge cavern. The Sun Sparrow light pulsed brighter, sending shafts of golden illumination up to a high ceiling. Crystalline structures reflected the radiance back in myriad colors. Moving forward, scanning the walls for another tunnel he realized there was no way out except for the way he had come. To his right was a stone ledge carved into the rock wall, about the height of his shoulders.

Walking to the ledge he saw a leather satchel similar to the one Warren always kept near where he hid the Corylus scroll. Moving forward, he gently reached out and ran his hand over the dark, aged leather. A soft almost nonexistent glow emanated from within the leather bag. He had located the scroll to Veres. Even though he felt time was against him, Rayne opened the satchel and unwrapped the glowing scroll.

The moment his hand touched the bindings on the scroll, a pulse of power shot outward in every direction, causing his Sun Sparrow light to explode, washing over him with a brilliance that forced him to squeeze his eyes shut. Rayne wasn't sure what just happened, but somehow, he knew everything had changed.

He rewrapped the scroll and placed it back in the leather satchel. As he turned to head back out, warmth infused him once again and the voice spoke. *Well done my faithful Light Bringer. Be strong and of good courage. Trust. Your light will save Mistal and strike a spark on Veres. All the worlds of Ochen have awaited this moment.*

Rayne stood silent and still as the One's warmth filtered through him. He almost cried out as the warmth intensified at his right thigh, searing, and yet banishing the pain and weakness at the same time. He felt the muscles knit together and power infuse the whole leg. A new strength permeating his being,

Rayne lifted the staff that had been his strength and support the last several days. His eyes ran the length of it and he thought of the work Thorvin had put into shaping and smoothing it. And he wondered if he should keep it. But then, leaning it next to the ledge where the scroll had rested for the last thousand years, he walked out of the cavern without a backward glance.

Ari was standing off to the side, staring into the distance, singing to herself when Rayne emerged from the tunnel.

"Did you feel something when I was in there?" Rayne asked.

"Yes." A calm peace lit her features as if she too had been touched by the Sun Sparrows. "The Creator Father's chosen has reclaimed a scroll."

"But that didn't happen when I touched the Words to Corylus the first time."

Ari studied Rayne with wise eyes. "How old were you when that happened?"

He thought for a minute, recalling Warren's support after he had failed on his first assignment. "I was eight when Warren first showed me the scroll."

"Ah, but you see my dear Refreshing Rayne, that was different. You did not reclaim the scroll from its guardian; your mentor shared it with you. Your belief was newly forming, like an infant, a nascent bud. Now, you are older, stronger in your faith, and filled with Sun Sparrow light. Therefore, the burst of power was strong. I felt it move through me. The living darkness will have felt it as well. Take care, child; your enemies will know you have reclaimed a scroll."

Rayne stood still, staring at Ari. "You mean what happened was felt away from here?"

"Oh my! The force of that release of energy will have been felt on all seven worlds. But come, it is time for you to go. If you are willing, I can have us back at the crevice almost in an instant, but this method of travel is hard for newcomers to endure. You must trust me and be brave and not open your eyes no matter what. Can you do that?"

Rayne nodded. Ari leaned over him and wrapped her long arms around him. "Close your eyes tight and hold on."

Rayne closed his eyes and immediately felt a rushing, his clothes and hair fluttering as though a powerful wind was buffeting him. He was glad he hadn't eaten anything. It felt like a floor had fallen out from under his feet and his stomach lurched as he plummeted downward. He held so tightly to Ari he was afraid he might break her ribs, she seemed so thin and fragile.

But then the sensation stopped and Ari was saying, "I am proud of you young Light Bringer. You have done well with the transport, better than most newcomers I have traveled with. Now, open your eyes. The cleft leading out of the Sacred Grove is before you."

Rayne opened his eyes and looked up into Ari's.

"Although being a guardian has meant a thousand years away from my loved ones," Ari said, "I am glad the One chose me for this task. It has given me the chance to meet you. After all this time, it would have been a wonderful gift to get to know you more. But things have now been put in motion and the Creator Father is calling you back to Caarwyn Rill just as he is calling me home."

Tears pooled in Ari's eyes and she swallowed hard. "We will not meet again until we are both with the Creator Father. Keep well Light Bringer; hold to your faith in the One and be strong."

She paused, her eyes widening as she sucked in a breath. "The One has chosen to show me some of what you must yet endure." Reaching out she cupped Rayne's cheek, her long, fine fingers resting on his hair, and looked deeply into his eyes. "When all seems lost, remember the lost will be found and the broken made whole. Never stop trusting the One; he is always with you. I know you will do well."

Rayne hugged Ari gently. "I too am glad we had this chance to meet. Even though our time together was short, you made me feel loved and accepted. You'll never know how much I needed that right now. I'll never forget what you've done for me."

They hugged once more and then stepped apart. Rayne wrapped his arms around his body and blinked back tears as

Ari faded into a misty shadow of herself. Waving a final good-bye, she vanished.

He stood still for a moment watching after her then waved to the spot where she had been. "Thank you, Ari; be at peace now."

With a final look around, breathing in the splendor and sweet savor of the place, Rayne turned his back and entered the cleft, leaving the Sacred Grove behind. He wondered briefly if he would ever see it again. Then he was out. Elder Owain was with Elder Jiro and they were running toward him, waving their arms, and shouting.

49

Sigmund writhed within his new host body, frustrated by the uninspired nature of his boring new assistant, Milo. He cursed Ponce again for abandoning him. *Where is that scrawny deserter hiding, anyway? When I finally find the little rat, he's going to pay for his betrayal in blood and pain.* But Sigmund missed Ponce. The man was a mastermind of organization, but even more, Sigmund missed his ability to play creatively. Ponce had taken pains to delight Sigmund with the quality and variety of his entertainments. This new assistant was dull.

Milo's skills at organization and business were quite good, perhaps even better than Ponce's. While Sigmund was away meeting with his master, Milo had followed through on things that Ponce left hanging. Sigmund's plans to dismantle the Interplanetary Council and Interplanetary Court were now fully in place. With proper incentives offered, guarantees of support from several powerful families on four of the seven worlds had been secured. Shadows all over Ochen were deepening, coming alive, seeking to corrupt men's thoughts. Milo had even taken the initiative of contacting Heinrich, requesting that he work to increase the number of scroll worshipers on Glacieria, Corylus, and Arisima, something Ponce had been struggling with.

Sigmund especially appreciated Milo's finesse when, in perfect form, he saw to the quiet disposal of Lady Lilith's body. The annoyingly insane woman had waited for Sigmund on Nemora. Upon his return, she began a campaign of harping that drove Sigmund to distraction until he could no longer abide her presence and blasted her with dark fire. But Sigmund would have to train Milo in the fine art of creative play, the man had no imagination. Work was the only thing that seemed to give the man pleasure.

Sigmund looked forward to the arrival of his long-time colleague, Heinrich. That demon was a genius at damaging humans while keeping them alive and screaming. Sigmund looked over at Milo once again and ground his teeth. *Once Heinrich arrives we can begin the process of turning this excuse of a man into a rubiate. He did say he was eager to please our master and I am starved for good entertainment.*

With little thought, Sigmund snapped his fingers. A skinny, little, dark-haired boy wearing a silver slave collar, black leggings, and a sleeveless purple tunic scrambled to bow in front of him.

"Yes, M-m-master?" The boy stuttered. His voice high and quavering.

Reaching out and cupping the boy's chin roughly, Sigmund looked him over. Coronus had brought the boy to Sigmund a little over a week ago, thinking he would like him. He was pretty enough with long black hair. Coronus had even shown Sigmund's butler how to set a feather in a side braid. But he was not the slave Sigmund desired.

With a swift, brutal flick of his wrist, Sigmund sent the boy to the floor where he remained, cowering. Indeed, the boy was quite pretty. But his eyes were dark brown, and he had no fire.

Turning, Sigmund paced toward a black and gray damask couch with lion feet. "Bring me a glass of honeyed sherry, slave," he said over his shoulder.

The child scrambled to do his master's bidding, annoying Sigmund even more.

Sigmund had arrived in Inverness on the same day he left a message for the prince in Westvale Within hours he procured his new host body. Then, before leaving for his ancestral home in Bainard the next morning, he made arrangements for his new assistant to meet him there. Less than a week later, Milo arrived. He and Sigmund had been working ever since. Though he initially planned to stay on Nemora for no more than a month, he changed his mind. After so many years of preparation, his plans were all falling neatly into place and he decided to take some time to adjust to his new body. Although this host was physically attractive, it lacked the cultured appearance he so appreciated in his last body. This one was broader, more muscular, with flaxen colored hair and light blue eyes. Not his first choice, but a ready substitute for the time being.

Sigmund stood, facing the fire, brooding, when the slave boy approached him and carefully held out a cut crystal goblet of amber-hued sherry. Turning in frustration and boredom, Sigmund grabbed the boy by the throat and sent a shaft of fiery energy into the boy's chest just to hear him scream. The glass shattered on the floor, as the boy dropped to his knees crying out, sending sticky spatters of honeyed sherry flying around the room. Sigmund looked down on the child, his pale eyes burning with frigid fire. "Look what you've done now, you clumsy, worthless slave. Clean this mess and bring me a new glass."

The boy nodded and began picking up pieces of broken glass as tears dropped onto the tiled floor. Sigmund resisted the impulse to push the boy's cheek down onto the shards of broken glass. The boy would plead and cry in pain, ruby red blood would drip.

If only Ponce were here. Sigmund quivered as the sound of his assistant's pen scratching on paper reached his ears, irritating him. *Ponce would have joined me. Together we could have made the boy scream and bleed. And then he would have taken pleasure in tasting the blood and filling the boy with delicious darkness.*

Milo has been productive. Technically. But I can't stomach working with someone who isn't even a little bit interested in creative amusements. Perhaps I'll give him the boy to play with; that should inspire him. Coronus will understand. I'll ask him to find me another little boy. One with the right color eyes this time.

Sigmund cursed. There wasn't another one with the right

color eyes. Sigmund wanted the prince back. That beautiful boy with the hair like midnight and the jewel eyes. The rebellious slave who never fully lost his spirit. What pleasure Sigmund had taken in working with Ponce to break him. Yet, the slave had never fully broken. That unendurable princeling was the reason Sigmund's glorious plan failed and his beautiful body had been destroyed.

I'm finally close to realizing my long-awaited dream of taking control of all Ochen and yet I obsess over that insolent boy. Sigmund snarled. And it *had* become an obsession, a bleak, all encompassing, obsession. Sigmund had spilled blood daily while dreaming about those amethyst eyes shedding tears of pain and hate in silence. Of course, Sigmund was unable to physically touch the boy himself. But Ponce had been so adept at anticipating Sigmund's desires where the prince was concerned.

Ponce. When I locate that little traitor, I'm going to sear the skin off him one sliver at a time. He'll rue the day he turned his back on me.

The little slave approached Sigmund again, trembling. He held the glass of sherry in shaking hands. Sigmund was reaching toward it when a potent blast of power drove him back, away from the child and down to his knees. He sucked in a breath as spiraling pain tore through him.

The energy came from somewhere off-world. Sigmund could sense that it had circled between the worlds in expanding waves. And it was spiritual in nature, not physical. Suddenly the truth hit him. It was the prince. The little piece of garbage had found one of the scrolls Sigmund had been seeking for the last thousand years. Sigmund shuddered to think what his master's reaction to the blast would be.

Rising with a snarl, he shoved the slave boy away and stormed from the room. He ran from the house, needing room to think and move.

"No! No! No!" he screamed into the clear lavender blue sky above Nemora. "I'll kill him. I'll strangle the life from him and watch his eyes pop. I'll …" Sigmund roared.

Seizing control, he spoke in a more moderate tone, "I want him dead. That irritating little ex-prince must die before he gathers those poisonous scrolls. If only I could have found them and destroyed them before now. But my enemy cheats. Not only has he hidden each scroll, they are all protected. And even when I destroyed the one I located, it returned. That rebellious slave found it back at Coronus's. And now he has another. He's the key."

Sigmund looked out at nothing as thoughts circled and grew in his mind. *He's the key? The only way to destroy the scrolls is to incinerate all seven simultaneously with a blast of dark fire. This much I now know. Destroying them one at a time is useless. And as long as those accursed scrolls exist, I'm threatened by them. But what if ...* Sigmund paused, considering. *Yes, it might just work. Allow the boy to reclaim all seven scrolls, assure that he brings them to me, then take the loathsome things from him before he can unite them. Once I have all seven they can finally be destroyed. And if they're gone, I might even be able to possess the boy. Interesting.*

Sigmund turned and, squaring his broad shoulders, walked back toward his ancient home. "The boy is the key. I must speak with Heinrich about this. Yes, I must talk to Heinrich. He'll be here soon."

Despise the deceiving darkness that seeks to devour my people and open your ears to the words of the One. In the fullness of time, my chosen, my Light Bringer, will reclaim my Words and reveal the light of my truth, says the One. Though darkness seeks to extinguish his light, fear not. For when the cup of wrath overflows, my chosen will return. He will accomplish my will; my light will again illuminate the worlds of Ochen.

CHECK OUT MY WEBSITE

cswachter.com

for more information about the worlds of Ochen.

REVIEW?

Reviews help others make informed decisions about the books they choose to read.

If you enjoyed *The Light Arises* please consider leaving a review on Amazon and/or any site of your choosing.

THANK YOU!

THE SEVEN WORDS

The Sorcerer's Bane
The Light Arises
The Deceit of Darkness (August 2018)
The Light Unbound (November 2018)

75334266R00274

Made in the USA
Middletown, DE
04 June 2018